BROKEN
BEAUTY

KETLEY ALLISON

BROKEN BEAUTY PLAYLIST

The Way You Felt - Alec Benjamin

Traitor - Olivia Rodrigo

Rampampam - Minelli

MIDDLE OF THE NIGHT - Elley Duhé

Flowers - Lauren Spencer Smith

Birthday Cake - Dylan Conrique

Black Hole - Griff

Let Me Hurt - Emily Rowed

gfy (With Machine Gun Kelly) - blackbear, Machine Gun Kelly

Chaotic - Tate McRae

Listen to the rest of the playlist:

CHAPTER 1
CLOVER

In the dimly lit anatomical theater of Titan Falls's gothic university, I'm in the midst of a clandestine operation. My best friend, Ardyn, helps me, though her movements betray a struggle to keep herself composed.

As she carefully arranges the crystals within the protective salt circle, I watch her from the center, my gaze filled with a mix of curiosity and frustration. The atmosphere is charged, the weight of our unspoken secrets hanging heavy between us.

The theater is used by Titan Falls medical students to dissect donated corpses during the day, creepy and unnerving by itself. But at night, the renovated 17th century theater is haunting, terrifying, and full of the terrible acts committed centuries ago.

In other words, perfect.

A loud clatter sounds out. Ardyn loses her balance, and one of the larger crystals falls to the floor.

"Shit," she mutters.

I can't help but feel a rush of impatience. "Careful. Don't disrupt the delicate balance of energies we're trying to create."

Ardyn's eyes meet mine, a mix of exasperation and tolerance clear in her gaze.

"I didn't realize being a crystal guardian required such grace," she quips.

I raise an eyebrow.

"Well, grace comes naturally to some of us. It's an art form, really," I reply, a smirk tugging at the corners of my lips.

Ardyn rolls her eyes, but I can sense the undercurrent of tension between us. Our words carry more weight than jokes. We're both aware of the growing distance, the polar magnetic force pushing between us.

I reach for my tarot deck, shuffling the cards with deliberate intent. The soothing swish of the cards fills the air.

She notices the intensity of my stare and smiles.

"Planning to consult your spirits before lighting the candles, Clover?" she teases. "Isn't that against the witch code?"

I huff out a laugh, the sound tight. "The spirits have already been whispering their secrets to me." I nail her with a look. "I just need the right moment to unleash their voices."

Ardyn shifts uncomfortably, as if I actually have the power to dive into her head and pull out the skeletons hiding there.

She clears her throat. "Well, don't keep them waiting too long. You wouldn't want the spirits to think you're playing hard to get."

I lean back, holding the tarot deck lightly between my fingertips. "I can't light the candles until the chandeliers are turned off. Sarah Anderton wouldn't appreciate the two sources of light after she's been in the dark for so long."

"Uh-huh. Right."

I tense at Ardyn's placating tone—or pretend interest—it's hard to tell which it is, considering she's working hard to cover her nerves.

She's always been a terrible liar.

"Could you shut off the lights on your way out?" I ask, hoping my question will nudge her toward the exit.

"Are you sure you want to be alone?"

Ardyn pushes to her feet, taking in the auditorium's atmosphere with a sweeping gaze. The darkness surrounding us appears almost alive, contrasting sharply with the harsh light shining on an operating chair at center stage. Her attention travels to the walls, where old anatomical sketches hang in glass frames. There's an exit, a sort of portico, behind her.

Ardyn stares down that passage, then looks at me with wide eyes, her cardigan sleeves pulled tightly around her fingers as if for warmth or protection, like she can't believe I'd make her walk through it alone.

I refuse to feel any concern. I keep my expression neutral as I tuck my thick hair into a ponytail and reach into my satchel to grab the plain wax candles I brought for the ritual.

"I can't have you as a distraction when I try to summon her," I say calmly. "The last time you were around..."

"I know. I cut myself on broken glass, then hallucinated that a witch was behind me."

"She was there." I give a one-shouldered shrug. "But then you scared her away."

Ardyn's brows pull together at my matter-of-fact tone. She doesn't believe in the supernatural the way I do.

I hate creating distance between us, especially after reuniting with her after two years of no contact, but she should know better than to harbor another secret from me mere weeks after revealing she was seeing my brother behind my back.

My *brother*. Tempest Callahan. The guy who sends spiders scurrying with a curled lip of annoyance, whose whisper is more leveling than a shout, and who possesses such a polarizing personality he doesn't even have enough friends for me to count on one hand.

What my beautiful, sweet friend sees in him *should* make her believe in what she can't see because only paranormal forces at work could make them soulmates.

An ache forms between my brows. I rub the spot with my thumb. "It's almost sunrise. I have to finish this before the med students who don't sleep wander in here."

Looking at the dissection chair, Ardyn wrinkles her nose.

"Fine." She sighs. "Just promise me you won't offer up any of your blood this time."

"Can't. Not enough time for that."

My focus centers away from her and on the tasks below my hands.

I hear her murmured goodbye and have my lighter ready when she flicks off the lights and disappears.

With the small flame guiding me, I light the candles one by one, beginning with the smallest and working up to the largest flame. When an invisible wind blows across each candle's tiny flame in the cold theater, I lean back on my heels and chant an incantation to summon Sarah Anderton, a Titan Falls witch who died in the 1700s but still lingers in spirit form. Every time I've seen her thus far, it has been brief—quick glimpses of moving shadows or haunting grins. Her evil spirit is shy, never wants to come face-to-face, and it's never long enough to ask her what I really want—the name of her secret daughter and where she might be buried.

I'm determined to get my answer tonight.

The candles are bright enough to read by, and my thoughts quiet and undisturbed.

But no matter how many times I say her name or call out for her spirit, nothing but the drop in temperature to below freezing communicates her presence.

After twenty minutes and cramping thighs, I open my eyes and heave out a disappointed exhale.

"Fine, be that way," I murmur into the dark. "But I'm not giving up."

Working quickly, I snuff out the candles, wrap my crystals in cloth, and place them in my bag.

I say the words, "I open this circle," and break the salt border by brushing my feet through it, sending the debris under the first row of chairs so as not to draw suspicion.

I'm not supposed to be creeping through these spaces, considering I'm as far away from a med student as I could be, but it's in an original building from the late 1600s, with rooms Sarah might've walked through.

As I step through the portico of the medical building and outside, there's no sun in sight, just a dismal gray cast over everything. The decorative statues along the walkway seem lonelier than usual; their stonework faces contorted in sorrow. Even though I like wearing all-black clothing, I find myself wishing for something else—anything else—than this perpetual, boring misery I'm trudging through.

Sighing, I pull my leather jacket tighter to my chest and dart toward the arts building before the clouds come together and drop a storm on my head.

I'm so focused on the ground beneath my feet and watching for rain splatter that I don't notice the looming figure in front of me until my forehead collides with his chest—so solid it might have been stone—and sends me tumbling onto the ground.

"Ow!" I cover my forehead, the site of contact. "Did one of those gargoyles come to life and decide to take a walk?"

I say it mostly to myself but glance up under the shade of my hand.

A towering, muscular body blocks out the meager sunlight, with raven black hair slashed with silver threatening to burst into wild curls as the growing electricity in the air builds. His intense gaze traps me like a rabbit, his muscles tightening beneath his olive skin.

I gulp.

Not out of fear, but because of the place inside me the lightning has chosen to target.

I curl my knees closer to my chest, hoping he can't sense the sudden uncomfortable pulsing between my legs.

"Good morning, Professor Rossi," I manage to greet him, my voice tinged with a mixture of respect and something more.

His prominent Adam's apple bobs as he takes in my presence. Without offering his hand, he steps around me as if I were a mere obstacle in his path. My mouth hangs open in disbelief as I watch him continue on his way, a surge of both frustration and intrigue coursing into my chest.

"My humblest apologies for being in your path this morning, oh mighty one," I say under my breath.

To my surprise, Professor Rossi stops in his tracks, his body half turned toward me, and scowls.

"Consider yourself forgiven," he replies.

I roll my eyes, a mix of annoyance and undeniable attraction brewing within me.

"How gracious of you," I mutter.

As I rise to my feet, brushing off the dust from my jeans, I can't help but question why Professor Rossi still holds such an irresistible allure.

He's way older than me, in his 40s, and is basically an ogre in professor's clothing. He barks more than he talks, is my brother's boss, and happens to be the rudest grown man I've ever come across.

With a shake of my head, I ask myself, "Why the hell is he still so hot?"

The question hangs in the air, unanswered, as I watch him go.

CHAPTER 2
CLOVER

My morning classes are a slog to get through, and my afternoon ones are even worse. The way I ordered Ardyn to leave me alone gnaws at my conscience, and I can't seem to quell the itch of curiosity I've acquired since running into Professor Rossi.

After dinner for one in my dorm's dining hall, I escape from campus. There's not much to drive to when surrounded by the Appalachian Mountains, except for the little town of Titan Falls that rims the lake at the bottom of TFU's hill. I've made it a point to visit there often now that Ardyn's hands are full of my brother, gravitating toward the alchemy and Wiccan shop run by a wise, middle-aged woman who greets my penchant for collecting crystals with enthusiasm.

This time, though, I drive into town and pass the *Sarah's Apothecary* storefront, heading to the lakefront dive bar instead. Finding a parking spot isn't an issue. Titan Falls is a tourist town in the summer and a deserted wasteland in the winter, so I leave my bag in the passenger seat before stepping up to the door and swinging it open.

Most of the main strip is full of witch-themed shops, a quaint dungeon/horror wax museum, and bars and restaurants honoring the town's infamous witch settler, Sarah Anderton. Tourists and college kids love it, the most popular spot being Titan's Brew, a bar closest to the single road leading to the university.

This bar caters to the locals who shun campy Halloween decorations and prefer to drink their pilsner in cloudy glasses within the swaying spotlight of single hanging bulbs.

It's known as The Boiler—the name a small rebellion against the gift shop's year-round selling of plastic mini cauldrons. I found the bar during my solo treks into town when the itch I couldn't scratch writhed through my body, an unnamable sensation that made me feel trapped under my skin. It brings the unquenchable need to escape, break out, and be so totally different I'd be unrecognizable to my brother, parents, and handful of friends.

Sliding into my usual spot at the corner of the sticky bar, I scan the single room for the usual suspects—plaid shirts, trucker hats, and dirty jeans. Finding them grouped in the corner by the pool table, I lean in closer to observe their grim expressions and wildly gesturing hands.

"I swear it's true!" one with a tattered trucker hat says. "Some rich guy staying north of here went missing within ten minutes of telling his wife he was taking a piss outside. He never came back."

"Gotta be a bear," another responds.

"Nah." Plaid Shirt shakes his head. "They're hibernatin'. Pack of coyotes, maybe."

"Or a *human* did it. This guy's not the only one I've heard went—"

The one talking glances at me, frowns, and the four of them shuffle closer together, lowering their voices.

I lean back with a furrowed brow until my gaze snags on a hunched-over figure with finger-curling waves of dark hair speckled with gray at the temples at the other end of the bar.

My stomach clenches.

Professor Rossi lifts his focus from the bronze swirl of his drink and pins me with eyes of the same color.

I curl my fingers into my palms to staunch the nervous wave of *hello* that wants to come out of them. Professor Rossi made it clear earlier that greetings aren't his thing.

Maybe he's here and not at the regular TFU haunts because he wants the same thing I do—freedom from structure and expectation.

I receive his attention with a bold stare, studying the harsh lines around his mouth and eyes in a way I'd never dare under the lights of a lecture hall or passing him in the quad.

The professor doesn't blink. The bar moves around him— billiards balls clacking, jovial laughter, curls of cigarette smoke, and a lonesome country tune on the jukebox—while he stills the air that touches his body, maintaining our stare off until my ears buzz with embarrassment and I look away.

His lips twist, almost like he's disappointed before he lifts his phone from the bar and brings it to his ear, his voice low and words indecipherable as he talks into it and angles away from me.

Disappointment flutters in me, too. What was I thinking? Was I ready to seduce the university's surliest Zaddy professor in a dive bar? I have an itch, but not *that* big of one.

At least I don't think I do.

Movement—a swathe of sea green amid brackish shadows— shifts my attention.

A man ... well, a young guy, really, comes from behind Rossi, sleeves rolled up and showcasing undulating muscles under golden brown skin. His close-cropped hair, coupled with the lighting, looks like a shadow curled up on the top of his head.

If it weren't for the startling green of his eyes, almost like lightning flashed between us and turned them neon, I'd say he was borne from the glittering darkness at the bottom of the lake.

"What're you having."

The bartender—Jack—doesn't ask it. His handlebar mustache and bald head add to his indignant charm.

Blinking out of my study, I respond, "Single malt scotch, no ice."

I say it like I know what I'm talking about because all I can see is the brown liquor Rossi holds in his expansive, tanned hands.

Jack doesn't flinch, grabbing a nameless amber liquor from under the bar and pouring it into a short glass. If he recognizes me as one of his new regulars, he doesn't show it.

Jack slides the glass into my waiting hand, and I nod in thanks, dipping my finger into the liquid, then painting it around the rim before taking a tentative sip.

It burns. I cringe. Then it warms as it eases its path into my empty stomach.

This is what I came for, a smooth introduction into the night.

"How is it that you've made cheap whiskey appear so bloody delicious?"

I stiffen at the voice beside me.

It's the guy who appeared out of nowhere and made his way over without me noticing. He stands at a respectful distance, holding his beer and grinning with playful innocence.

He's close enough for me to catch a whiff of minty soap, representing a cool handsomeness completely at odds with the heat he exudes.

Dammit, *and* he has a gorgeous British accent.

"You don't belong here." I say it sharper than intended, but his presence sends me off-kilter and jointless, like my brain doesn't know how to direct my body anymore.

His smile widens, showcasing straight white teeth book-ended by dimples. "Neither do you, I'd say."

"I bet I've been here more than you have."

"Oh, a hardened regular, are you?" He gestures to the empty stool beside me. "May I?"

I rest my arm against the bar, squinting at him. "I'm not sure yet."

He chuckles, then offers his hand. "Xavier."

I fold my hand into his, pleased at how warm and dry it is. And at the *zing* that happens when his skin brushes mine.

I can't help but dart my gaze across the bar, wondering if Rossi noticed.

He's still on the phone, showing me his profile, but his eyes have turned to slits, and I see more dark irises focused in my direction than disinterested white in the parting of his lashes.

I inwardly grin. Maybe the ogre runs hot-blooded after all.

"And you are?" Xavier asks.

I refocus on the handsome stranger, offering a coy smile, and repeat, "I'm not sure yet."

"I can appreciate a lady of mystery." His tone goes low, buttery. "It's certainly a pleasant turn of events."

It takes a good hard squirm to get the throbbing at my center under control.

"What were you hoping for when you came into this place?" I arch a brow. "It's called The Boiler for a reason."

Xavier hums in agreement, those amazing green eyes of his roaming the bar but coming back to me within seconds. "I'm probably here for the same reasons you are."

"And that would be...?"

He doesn't blink. "An escape."

I clear my throat, refusing to let my surprise show. "That's too easy. This bar practically has a neon sign out front saying, *Lost Souls, Drink Here.*"

"True, but it says nothing about beautiful, haunted maidens with a tangle of black hair and the most metallic brown eyes I've ever seen taking a seat right across from me."

If any other man tried that line on me, I'd hand-chop them directly in the throat, but coming from this guy, with his golden smile and delicious accent, Xavier might as well be molding me with his long, firm fingers.

I tilt my head at him, reaching for more than my drink when I hold it to my lips and take a long swig.

Xavier watches as I swallow it all. "I feel like I should inform you, the barkeep didn't give you single malt. He reached for the cheapest brown grog he had—"

I risk one last glance at Rossi. He's watching.

That impatient itch inside me sweeps up into my throat and onto my tongue.

Xavier draws closer, his lips hovering close to my ear and providing a needed, temporary distraction.

"I have a confession to make," he murmurs, his breath tickling the side of my face.

"Oh?" I ask, my voice barely above a whisper as I continue to watch Rossi.

"I really want to fuck you."

My eyes snap to his.

CHAPTER 3
CLOVER

I haven't been stunned into silence that often. It's nice that, the one time I do, the man responsible happens to look like the type of clean-cut, highly sexy school quarterback you only see in the movies.

"Did I hear you correctly?" I ask.

My dumbfounded question brings a genuine smile to his lips. "I'm unable to resist beautiful, haunted maidens."

One side of my mouth quirks in acknowledgment. "You've come across a lot?"

"Only you."

Heart racing, anticipation seizing my throat, I slide off the stool, throwing a five-dollar bill on the counter. Jack grumbles, but I point a knowing finger at him. "Give me the good stuff next time."

"Show me your license and I will," he retorts.

I don't have a good comeback for that, but Xavier redirects my focus.

"My car's outside," I say, reaching for a different self. One who's seductive and confident.

The sides of my neck tingle with awareness of Rossi's study. I sneak another look. His expression is much too controlled to tell me what he's thinking, but I enjoy the way the muscles in his cheeks pop out whenever he closes his mouth. He cuts a glare my way.

Xavier replies, "I'm not taking you in the back seat of a car like a pubescent boy. Come with me."

Xavier says it with such confident authority that I follow his lead out of the bar.

He holds the door open. I duck under his arm, catching his fresh mint scent again. How a man can come out of a dive bar smelling like that and not stale beer and bleach is a talent. I find myself smiling again as he takes my hand in his and leads me down the rotting wooden staircase and into the skeletal trees surrounding the lake.

"Out here?" I ask, my breath coming out in clouds. "It'll be freezing."

So much for keeping with my whole seductress attempt. The farther we get from The Boiler, the more nervous I become.

"I'll keep you warm."

Xavier stops us at the edge of the tree line and the lake, just before the dirt ground becomes craggy with rocks and rushing water.

I can't help but cross my arms and look up directly into a full moon so bright it stifles the stars. The lake shines with its brilliance.

"Beautiful," Xavier murmurs.

I lower my gaze, watching his hands as he runs his fingers down my jacketed arms. I feel it as if he's touching my skin, and my lips part.

He tilts his head, moving into the crook of my neck. His hot exhales tickle my skin. "The moon has you in a perfect light."

"How did you know?" I whisper, then moan as his lips brush my jawline, tilting my chin up and exposing my throat.

"Know what?" Xavier asks, licking near my pounding pulse.

"That nature calms me. The moon speaks to me." My eyes flutter closed. "And she's telling me I'm safe with you."

Xavier moves into my vision, his eyes searching my face. He presses his thumb into my lips, smearing them as he says, "Your moon goddess is a fickle bitch. I'm not here to keep you safe. My job is to make you scream."

My heart slams against my ribs. Xavier folds one arm behind my back and puts his other around my neck before he slams his lips against mine.

I moan into his mouth, sucking his tongue into mine. My long, talon-shaped nails claw into his back as he throws me on the ground and climbs on top of me, keeping our lips sealed together.

Writhing under him, I try to feel as much of his hard, muscled body as I can. I find the hem of his shirt and pull.

"No." Xavier abruptly pulls his lips from mine.

"Sorry," I breathe, though my heart skips at the sudden hostility.

He seems to blink out of it and adds in a softer tone, "It's too cold to strip, though *fuck* me, I'd love to see you naked under my hands." Xavier takes one of my hands and presses it to the front of his jeans where a hard, rigid length curls my fingers. "Touch me here."

My mouth falls open at the sheer size of him. "Gladly."

Xavier's teeth flash white before he ducks his head and focuses on my chest, pulling on the deep V of my shirt until he exposes my bra. His hand curves under the cotton, cold now from the night, and I gasp as he brushes over my nipple, arching my back for more.

Xavier growls his approval, pushing my C-cup down until

he's exposed my whole breast, and replaces the cold with the wet heat of his tongue.

"Oh my god," I breathe, staring wide-eyed at the sky. I dig my fingers into the back of his head, pushing him into the soft swell. "Don't stop."

Sucking hard, Xavier tongues and bites my nipple until I'm wriggling beneath him. Instead of granting any relief, his other hand prods the front of my jeans until he's past my underwear and finds my damp center.

His finger curls into me. My ass lifts off the ground. I bite my lip and moan.

Xavier releases my nipple enough to mutter, "Keep making those sounds, and I'm going to come on you before I'm ever inside you."

The compliment brings a smile to my face, and I lift my head. "Then let me return the favor."

"Not yet. No way am I releasing you without tasting you first."

Xavier maneuvers off me, and the sudden release of weight makes me whimper in mourning.

He growls his approval, staying on his knees as he unbuttons his jeans and releases his perfect cock.

Long, hard, big. It spears out from him with the sole purpose of bringing me pleasure. My mouth waters at the sight.

It's been *so* long, and it's like the goddesses are gifting me with the best dick they could find to apologize for my dry spell.

I have to stop myself from reaching out for it with eager hands.

With a sly smile, Xavier sways out of reach. "I said I'm not done with you yet, my dark maiden." He nods toward my middle. "Unbutton your pants, then pull them and your panties to your knees."

The command in his tone turns my arms to jelly. I'm sure

that later, I'll be questioning my sexual response to dominant strangers, but for now, I'm trembling with want and do as he says.

Once finished, I look at him for further instruction, but Xavier's swung around into the dark. I have trouble finding him until his head resurfaces between my thighs.

I cry out in shock as he settles my calves over his shoulders, and his hands span my hips, essentially locking me into his face.

Xavier lowers his nose into my pussy and inhales, long and deep.

"Good god," he groans. "I'm going to eat you like a starving man."

The anticipatory tingles at his promise don't even reach my breasts before his tongue dives inside me, and he devours every drop that's formed since meeting him.

Squirming, I moan into the night, the opaque luster of the lake absorbing my sounds. Xavier joins in my pleasure, his voice adding to the silky texture of his tongue dipping inside me.

When the orgasm surfaces, my hold on reality shatters into a thousand tiny stars. I bite down on my lower lip, drawing blood and capturing the moan like I own it.

But I don't.

This man does.

As if reading my mind, he rears up and seals his lips to mine, subsisting on my audible orgasm like it gives him life.

I taste myself for the first time, and honestly, I can see where Xavier's addiction came from.

I'm fucking delicious.

Xavier lifts his head. I catch a fast, satisfied grin before he spreads his legs on either side of my hips and flips me over, exposing my ass to the chilly air.

"Fuck. Yes," he grunts, and his hand comes down in a jarring slap.

Grit and pebbles cling to my skin from all the grinding, adding to the sluice of pain his smack brings.

I don't hate it. My core rushes with warmth, re-lubricating all the slickness he'd licked away. My forehead digs into the rocky shore as I both cringe and groan.

"Like that, do you?" His cocksure tone flows against the gentle chill of the wind.

"Yes," I whisper, hoping the ground will absorb my shame.

"Good."

Another slap rings out in the same spot, the pain turning hot and pulsing.

Xavier lifts off, and I watch him sidelong as he straightens and pulls off his pants. The eerily bright moon gives me a glimpse of an angry scar running down his right thigh before he falls back on his knees and adjusts himself until he clamps his thighs on either side of mine.

With my ankles bound by my pants, there's not much I can do except rise onto my palms in an effort to meet him halfway.

Xavier pushes me between the shoulders, flattening my face into the dirt.

"Wrong way," he rasps.

I should be angry about the way Xavier manhandles me and probably scared at the rough treatment since I've never experienced it before, but I lie still, trembling with excitement at what will come next.

He cups my hips, lifting my ass into the air and spreading the cheeks wide.

A rush of heat spreads into my cheeks at the thought of him investigating my asshole. It's not daylight, sure, but the moon is preternaturally bright tonight.

Resting the side of my face on the ground, I stutter, "I've-I've never done that before."

"What? Ass play?" To add to his feigned question, he presses his thumb into my anus.

It's an uncomfortable, almost itchy feeling. I try to wriggle away.

He chuckles. "Relax, my dark maiden. As much as I'd love to feel your tight, virgin hole around my dick, I'll take your greedy pussy as a happy substitute."

I hear a sharp rip, then some eager grunts as he rolls on a condom. I know he's done when he smacks his dick against my ass cheeks one, two, three times.

"You're so fucking ripe for me," he says, the low whisper making my fingers and toes curl.

Xavier drags his dick from my lower back and between my cheeks until he finds my seam, then plunges in.

I yell at his sheer size invading my most sensitive place, so sudden and brutal.

Xavier doesn't relent, gripping my hips and sliding all the way out, then slamming into me again.

He hisses expletives between his teeth as he catches his rhythm, caught up in my wet heat—all for him.

"Touch yourself," he orders between a particularly unforgiving thrust.

My cheek scratches against the ground, sharp pieces of shell and rock warning of the impending ripping of skin, but I take the pain as part of the pleasure, allowing it to combine with the feeling of his fingers digging into my waist.

He's marking me.

I do as he says, sliding my arm underneath my torso, flipping my hand over, and finding my clit.

Xavier doesn't pause, not even when the sharp tip of my nails grazes his tender flesh.

"*Fuck*, that's good. Do it again," he says. "Claw me. Dig into your clit. Bring us into the best kind of sin, baby."

His accent makes his commands sound *so* much sexier than an American would be when saying it, and I'm eager to do as he pleases, especially now that the pain has expanded into a swell of promise.

I've never felt a penis sliding in and out of me, slick and soft as silk. My fingers start curiously, the underside of his shaft grazing against my nails.

His furtive thrusts communicate that he wants more, and when the idea comes to me, I'm not even shy about it.

I'm more turned on than I've ever been in my entire life.

Tonguing my top lip in anticipation, I curl two fingers inside myself to join in with his dick.

A string of curses leaves his mouth at the unexpected intrusion, my joyous surprise overlaying his.

I pull, stretching myself, then release, massaging my clit with my palm as I do.

"Oh my god," I moan.

"This is fucking sick. Fucking *divine*," he agrees before his palms slam down on either side of my head, and his quick, hard breaths tickle my neck.

"I'm coming," he rasps into my hair. "I'm fucking coming."

I mewl through my blossoming orgasm, my palm digging into my clit and my fingernails scratching the surface inside me against him.

The more I claw, the better it is, and when the burn coats my orgasm, I almost pass out.

Xavier comes with jagged breaths, his balls tightening against my pussy as he buries himself so deep inside me, I have no doubt that if he weren't wearing a condom, I'd be leaking his cum for days.

He collapses on me, my leather jacket squeaking with his sweat.

I need a few minutes to collect myself, but it turns out, Xavier doesn't. Rolling to the side, he sits up lithely, then rises, finding his pants and pulling them on.

He offers me another wink.

"It's been lovely," he says, then disappears the way we came.

Standing, I dust myself off as much as I can in the sudden silence, then tentatively make my way through the same winding path.

Xavier left without so much of a hand-up in getting me off the ground, but it was the only move I wanted.

The kind I *needed*.

CHAPTER 4
XAVIER

I was meant to wait out my time at The Boiler until my ride arrived, but my supposed ride is empty by the time I make it to the parking lot.

With a shrug, I pass the Mercedes G-wagon and go inside, the dampness on my inner thighs a pleasant interlude between fucking the mystery girl and meeting the driver.

A quick glance over my shoulder tells me the maiden has yet to make an appearance, but guilt doesn't follow.

She wanted a mindless fuck like I did? She got it. No need to stretch the awkwardness out.

And bloody hell, I'm still thinking of her, *feeling* her, and picturing myself wrapping her long, fragrant hair around my wrist and pulling her head back so I can suck on her plump red lips while she grinds her pussy against the rocky shore, and I stick myself between her ass cheeks.

My dick hardens, still sticky with her. I give an abrupt shake of my head, ridding myself of her after-image so I can step up to the door and enter the shithole that is my new life.

As expected, my ride, Riordan Hughes, is at the bar talking to an older Italian-looking man and drinking a pint.

The older man sees me, says something to my ride, then walks toward me.

I wing up a brow at his approach, but my curiosity is unfounded. He merely walks around me without another glance and exits the bar.

Too right, I think.

I'd love to walk around with a silent growl of a face and garner the kind of attention where people just give way to you, but my tongue likes to work overtime, hence my current predicament.

I claim the stool next to Rio, signaling the crotchety bartender for another.

"You're late."

Rio doesn't look up from the piss-colored swirl of his beer. His dark hair falls forward, casting a shadow over his eyes that adds to the quiet menace of his voice.

I've long since lost the shiver of dread which would normally follow a tone like that. "Wrong. I was early. Thought to take a walk around the area while I waited."

Rio cants his head at that. "Nothing to see past the main strip."

I respond with a secret smile and lift the pint Jack the barkeep has slid in my direction. *Stop thinking about her.* "I hear Titan Falls has quite the landscape to explore."

Rio stares at me curiously before shutting down again. "I was told you'd be less annoying."

"Mm," I agree. "Should've been beaten out of me by now, correct?"

I can't hide the edge to my voice, so I don't bother.

"Most wouldn't have come out of what you endured so..." Rio thinks for a moment. "Quippy."

"The worst of it happened years ago."

"Oh? Did therapy help?"

My vision narrows at his sarcasm. "And here I was told you weren't a man of many words."

Rio folds his arms. Such limbs aren't needed when one can amputate a person's soul with a single glare.

I'm unable to stop the answering swallow. "You're a part of them, aren't you?"

Rio hikes up his brows, playing dumb.

"Are they here? The Bianchis?"

"You tell me."

I take another long swig, in no mood for games. I lift my shirt, showing off the ugly scar across my abs. Then I hold up my right hand. "Doctors had to reattach my ring finger. It no longer bends all the way. See? Useless digit. You can't blame me for asking if you're one of them."

"You nearly lost your life because you ghosted a girl," Rio says.

I wave said useless digit in the air flippantly. "I tend to have ... insatiable qualities."

"On an enemy mafia princess of all people."

I palm my chest, widening my eyes innocently. "My savage heart doesn't discriminate against classes."

"Like I care who you prefer to screw." He jerks his chin to my damaged hand. "Consider yourself lucky all they took was your finger. Then gave it back."

My beer slams against the bar, losing the duel with Rio as images I've buried crawl to the surface with their putrid, zombie-like strength. "The Bianchis kidnapped me, tied me up in some godforsaken basement, and gave their rabid initiates *weapons* to maim me when I couldn't fight back, all so they could be "men of honor."

"*Uomo d'onore* is what it's called."

"Brilliant. You consider that to be equal to *breaking up* with someone?"

"You and I both know you went beyond a simple love note."

Rio smiles, and it's that famous one, the one lesser beings hear about underground. The one before he goes in for the kill. "She's his wife now. You know that? Marco Bianchi is having the time of his life in New York society with the girl who helped maim you."

"Shut up." My grip tightens around the pint. I picture the glass fracturing under my strength, spiderwebs of warning creeping out from my fingers.

Closing my eyes, I try to think of something else. Anything else.

The maiden's face comes to me like a savior.

I can breathe.

"Just remember, *you* sought them out again," Rio continues. "I could give a shit about your trauma. No favor goes unpaid."

"Understood. Now kindly shut the fuck up."

Rio returns to his drink. I take that as a sign the conversation's over and finish mine.

Setting his empty glass down, Rio stands. "To answer your question, no. The Bianchis aren't here. Not really. Just their scraps." He throws a few bills on the bar. "But we're something much worse now."

My interest is piqued, and my gut more than a mite curdled.

Rio's expression hardens when he notices mine. "Thank fuck it's not up to me to explain it to you."

We head out of the bar together, Rio taking long strides to his car until he comes to a sudden stop, staring at the empty parking space beside his.

I seem to remember a sleek vehicle in that spot before returning to The Boiler to meet him.

"Somebody you knew?" I ask, coming up to his side.

Rio doesn't answer, just looks off in the direction of the lake —too dark to be seen under the streetlights—then back at me. His eyes grow small.

I hold a fist to my mouth, pretending to clear a scratch in my throat and inch away.

"Did you come across a girl during your exploring?"

I shake my head as I round to the passenger side of his vehicle. "Just me and the bats."

It's unclear why I feel the need to lie to him about the girl until I rationalize that she's mine now. *My* maiden who splays herself beside moonlit pools of lake water. Not his, and he has no right to hear about her.

Rio makes what I'm coming to recognize as a perturbed sound in his throat before throwing open his door and muttering.

I catch some of his words while sliding into my seat. "I'm sorry, did you say this girl is a sorceress?"

Of which I entirely agree. Only an enchantress could have tits like hers.

He releases a rough exhale. "My buddy's sister. She likes to use New Age-y stuff for protection and wanders alone at night under the moon, oblivious to danger."

"Danger? Here? In the middle of nowhere? Apologies, but I moved here to escape certain nefarious problems, and I was assured this is the perfect spot for total exile."

Rio doesn't add anything more to the conversation but flinches when I use the word *exile*.

I don't push the issue since I'm 90 percent certain I just fucked this sister and confirmed his assessment of her. She allowed me to lead her into the woods and seduce her with no qualms. That's not someone who considers her environment before making important decisions.

Which makes me protective of her from here on out, even if I never see her again. I don't want this stick-up-his-ass bloke doubling down on his opinion about my dark maiden. Frankly, I'm not too stoked that he knows her.

"All right, Xavier Altese." Rio pulls onto the road. "Let me show you your new digs, far away from the life you knew." He pauses before pushing on the gas. "You realize you'll be a nobody here."

I meet his stare dead-on. "Exactly my intention."

CHAPTER 5
CLOVER

Rio's SUV, parked next to mine at The Boiler with the engine still ticking, means I have mere seconds to escape before he comes out and searches for me.

Out of the few of my brother's friends, he's the one who gives me the most leeway when it comes to my independence, but even Rio has his limits, and if he doesn't see me or isn't notified that my car is back at Camden House within the next twenty minutes, he'll alert my brother.

Nobody wants that.

I can only hope Xavier doesn't run into Rio because then I'll be fishing Xavier's pretty face out of the lake tomorrow morning, and I'm not altogether sure that's a metaphor.

He was *gorgeous*, though. Like movie-star good looking. Absolutely the hottest man I've had between my legs, and I'm surrounded by unnaturally good-looking men all the time.

Let's leave out the fact they're all associated with my brother in some way, and therefore off-limits.

Meanwhile, Tempest gives himself permission to hook up with my best and only friend in the world.

UGH, the hypocrisy.

But if anybody could potentially beat Xavier in a beauty competition, it would be Riordan Hughes.

I've watched him for years, sometimes across a room and other times under a table. He was a regular visitor to our Manhattan home. I think the first time I met him, I was five and he was nine.

After coming face-to-face with Rio, a lanky, quiet boy with eyes too big for his face and thick, curly brown hair that must've constantly tickled his ears, I didn't believe in cooties anymore.

My head clouds with thoughts of unrequited crushes and brief encounters with a sex god as I park in my dorm's student parking lot, walk through the quad, then merge with the other girls entering Camden House. There must've been a party at the boys' dorm, Meath House, because a lot of the girls stumble over the cobblestone path and cackle through tangled strands of hair.

I avoid the larger clusters by weaving between them and becoming invisible.

It fits. When they're not drunk and actually notice me, they consider me a devil-worshipping witch.

"*Awww*, if it isn't the witch coming back from her nightly jaunt at the cemetery."

Oh. I guess I have to scratch the whole *they don't notice me when they're hammered* idea.

Pausing on the curve of the stairs to the second floor, I glance down to where the voice traveled from.

Minnie Davenport is first up the stairs out of her quadrant of followers, all sporting balayage blond highlights that must keep the salon in town well into the red all year.

Her tanned arm snakes up the banister, and she arches a perfect brow, completely at odds with her smeared mascara, yet she still manages to be prettier than most. "Raise any dead bodies tonight?"

I study her disheveled appearance. She looks like a couple of guys roughed her up good and plenty.

The corners of my lips tick up. *I bet I was roughed up better.*

Minnie misinterprets my smile, her light-blue eyes growing small. "You're so fucking creepy. Get out of my way."

She stomps up to where I'm hovering, and predicting where she's going, I feint out of the way so she can't knock into my shoulder.

Without the expected contact, Minnie trips sideways, nearly toppling over the banister.

"Careful, Min," I say with a sweet smile. "I think the cheap tequila's getting to you."

"Bitch," she hisses. "I only drink top shelf."

I'm in the middle of scoffing at her retort when she takes advantage.

Her Valentinos kick out, catching the back of my calf, spikes and all, and sending me catapulting down the staircase.

Nobody bothers to catch me. Minnie's followers dart out of the way, and my cheek cracks against the tiles. I cry out, my hand flying to my face as I try to untangle my limbs.

All of them laugh.

"Too bad your little ghosty friends couldn't catch you and float you down to where you belong," Minnie calls, fluttering her manicured hands. "Stay out of my way next time, *Elphaba*."

I run my tongue along my top teeth, checking for anything missing. The side of my face sings with pain, but I refuse to show it. "Oh, you've seen *Wicked*? That's my favorite Broadway show. My brother takes me every year."

Mentioning Tempest usually gets them to back off. When he's around, everyone, including these bitches, are over-the-top nice to me, practically banging into each other to get his attention. It's to the point he has no idea how I'm treated when he's not in the vicinity, but that's how I prefer it.

"You're pathetic." Minnie laughs, then motions to her four minions to follow her up the stairs. They disappear around the curve, leaving me in a crumpled heap at the bottom.

Unfortunately, that's how Ardyn finds me.

"Clover!" She rushes up from behind, helping by lifting under my arms as I struggle to stand. "Are you okay? What happened?"

"Don't tell me you were at Meat House, too," I say, avoiding the question.

"God, no." Ardyn comes to my side, holding me at the waist. "Can you walk? Do you think you broke anything?"

"Just my pride." The forced laughter that follows is too hollow for my liking. I clear my throat to rid myself of it. "I hung out on Main Street with some of my study friends. Too many whiskey shots. I slipped on the stairs."

"You should've texted me," Ardyn replies. "I would've joined you."

"And brought my brother along, right?" At her answering silence, I chuckle darkly. "Yeah, total buzzkill. No, thank you."

"He's protective of you because he loves you. We both do."

We hobble up the stairs, Ardyn holding me tight. I work my jaw, relieved it doesn't feel broken. "So what were you two up to tonight?"

Ardyn's side stiffens against mine. "Just hung out at his place."

"Uh-huh." The dull ache I feel at her vague replies should be familiar by now, but each time it happens, I drift further away from my friend.

"It was just the two of us, which was nice for a change," Ardyn continues.

It's uncharacteristic of her to expand on her time with Tempest, so I listen with interest, so long as it doesn't get gross.

"Tempest's roommates weren't around for once. Professor

Morgan decided to grade papers in the library, and Rio had to go pick up a new student."

I purse my lips with interest, then wince at the movement. "Oh? Since when did Rio become part of the welcome committee at TFU?"

The idea of Rio, a man who prefers disabling glares over words, welcoming anyone into college brings an almost smile to my swelling face.

"Right?" Ardyn agrees. "I'd run in the other direction, asking for a cute nerd to guide me. But seriously, the new guy he picked up used to be famous. Tempest wasn't supposed to tell me, and I'm not supposed to tell you, but..."

"We're best friends," I murmur. "We tell each other everything."

Ardyn squeezes my side, quiet desolation flowing through her eyes before she blinks it away. "Exactly. He requested anonymity driving in, and the only one willing to make such an incognito trip was Rio. Have you become a fan of sports at all?"

Frowning, I shake my head. "You know I didn't watch many sports growing up."

"You'd have to live under a rock not to have heard of this guy, though."

I offer her a droll look as we reach our floor and limp down the hallway. "Yeah, that boulder is called Tempest."

Ardyn concedes my point, her expression softening. "It's been tough for you and me adjusting to this new normal. I'm sorry. But I'm hoping my relationship with your brother will help you, too. He might not be so suffocating now that he's turned it on me." She gives a smile that has me wrinkling my nose. "And I like it."

"*Ew.*" I push her away, a ghost of a grin pulling at my lips. "Keep that to yourself."

Ardyn laughs, and for the first time in a long while, we sound like the friends we were before.

As I unlock our door, she asks behind me. "Are you sure you haven't heard of Xavier Altese?"

My key scrapes against the lock, missing the keyhole.

"He played professional soccer in England—or football, as they say. He was the It Guy for a while before he got injured and went dark."

I respond with a one-shouldered shrug, fitting the key into the lock and pushing the door open. "His name doesn't sound familiar."

Ardyn sucks in a breath behind me. "Okay, well, we're looking him up as soon as we get inside. You won't *believe* how hot this guy is—don't ever tell Tempest I said that. Tempest is obviously the hottest man to ever grace the earth."

"You and I can agree to disagree on that, and fine, show him to me, but the last thing I want is to become part of the Camden cronies and start drooling over a guy I'll never have."

The lie feels good coming out of my mouth.

Even as Ardyn slides out her phone and pulls up search results for Xavier.

Kind of like I'm getting even.

CHAPTER 6

CLOVER

Hearty laughter, like a sunbeam through the mountain fog, grabs my attention as I cross the quad with Ardyn the following morning.

My subconscious recognizes him well before I turn in his direction while casually tripping over my own feet with Ardyn having to catch me.

"You okay?" she asks, steadying me by the elbow.

I clutch at her arm like a lifeline. *He's not supposed to be here. Students don't go to The Boiler.*

But it is. My fantastic one-night stand. My scratch to my itch.

Xavier stands in a large group at the center of the quad and near the stone fountain. A wave of envy rolls through me as I watch his relaxed shoulders, dimpled smile, and easy backslapping with other guys. One night was all it took for Xavier to fit in and make friends, both male and female.

His natural appeal should be at odds with the hybrid creatures the stonemasons carved into the center of the fountain, morbid and unconfined with their feathers, talons, and human faces clawing for the top of the spout. Instead, he melds into the sea of the curious—mostly female—all of whom are rapt while he talks.

I wish I'd told him my name.

"There he is," Ardyn says like we're both not already ogling. "Xavier Altese."

I clear my throat. "Oh, that's him?"

Ardyn cuts a curious stare my way. "That's all you have to say?"

I scoff. It comes out more like a choked snort, that dark maiden inside me snoozing for the long haul after her sexcapade last night. "It's not like a guy like that would be interested in me."

I pull Ardyn through the quad before she can argue. Xavier's proximity is like a bolt of electricity I must dodge.

We pass him, and his head moves like he feels the same edges of fire digging into his chest while we cross paths. Our eyes meet, and his lips quirk in greeting as he tips his chin in acknowledgment.

I lick my lips but can't summon a return smile before giving my attention to Ardyn by asking about yesterday's assignment.

She's stopped from replying when I feel a presence on my other side, tangible and effervescent, popping against my skin.

"Hello again. May I escort you to class?"

That buttery, smooth accent simply *drips* into my airspace.

I'm prevented from melting along with it when Ardyn stutters to a stop, head cocked in Xavier's direction.

I stop too, staring at him with my mouth open. At a time when I'd love for my rebellious itch/dark maiden to come forward, she remains annoyingly silent.

Xavier's lips tip up, his gaze sensual and amused before he turns to Ardyn. "Apologies, but I don't believe we've met."

He holds out his hand, which Ardyn takes.

"Ardyn Kaine. And you're Xavier Altese."

Xavier's chin dips in humble acknowledgment, though I notice the slant to his eyelids. This is a practiced motion for him.

"My reputation precedes me. And you?" Xavier refocuses his jewel-green gaze on mine. That flash of exhaustion I noticed in his posture is replaced by the subtle amusement.

And the knowledge that he's eye-fucking me right now with all our memories of last night.

I decide to play along because that means I know what to say. "Clover Callahan. Nice to meet you."

That delightful grin returns. "Pleasure."

He holds out both elbows for us to take. The cluster of women behind us flutter together and apart like small birds as they watch the attention they once had move to ... me.

"Please. Allow me," he says.

My hand slips through before I can think twice, the soft satin of his bomber jacket sending sparks of awareness through my skin and directly into my nervous system.

"I would, but my boyfriend would kill me for touching another man," Ardyn says, backing away from his proffered arm.

Xavier hikes a brow. "Truly?"

"Definitely," I agree. "He's a territorial asshole who's obsessed with her. And he's also my brother."

"I ... see."

Ardyn grins that secret one we used to share as kids when one of us got close to the boy we liked. "I'm obsessed with him, too. I'll go find him and give him a kiss before class. I'll see you there, Clo."

I don't argue as she leaves. Xavier's warm, his body hard and reassuring against mine. After what happened last night with Minnie, it's nice to have such kindness. It doesn't hurt that it comes from the hottest guy to step onto campus since, well, Rio.

I tip my head up to him. "I didn't expect to see you here."

His lips thin as he glances down, his brows lowering. Xavier thumbs my cheek. "What happened here?"

"I fell going up the stairs to my dorm too fast." I blurt it out, the lie slick on my tongue.

Deep lines of concern crease his handsome features. "I don't like to see you hurt."

"It's okay." I brush it off. "Thinking about you last night makes it hurt less."

There she is.

A thrill goes through me as his smile widens and his hand lingers on my cheek. "Me, too, dark maiden. Or should I say, Clover."

I give him a soft smile as he walks us forward, his arm clamped against mine. The ridges of his hard muscles can be felt through the silkiness of his bomber jacket. I shyly place my free hand on his forearm to get closer, both enjoying and ducking my head at the amount of attention he's getting as we walk through the quad and into the arts building.

I'm so unnoticed most days, or if I am, it's to be glanced at sideways, my outfit choices questionable, my passions weird, and my opposite traits to my smart, handsome, glorious brother remarked upon constantly.

It feels good.

I half-hope Minnie gets to see this, but it would be by luck. I memorized her schedule to avoid her. She doesn't have class in this building this morning, which I'm normally thankful for.

We stop at my classroom, where Xavier gives my arm one last squeeze before letting go. "Will I see you later?"

"Sure." I try to sound casual even though I'm fizzing with glee. This *never* happens to me.

Xavier nails me with that insane smile. "Then I'll find you."

I nod, then retreat into the classroom before I self-combust.

It's the moment he leaves my comfort zone that I realize I

should be suspicious that a guy like that only looks at me when there are at least fifty other prettier, more popular, more qualified girls for his caliber wandering around campus.

I immediately think, *Why me?*

Finding Ardyn, I drop my books on the communal table and find my seat beside her. The ten other students in the class join, all of us surrounding the rectangular table while we wait for the professor.

"Any update on the Anderton witches?" Ardyn asks as we pull out our progress reports.

I jolt at the direct question, but I appreciate her effort. My final essay, due at the end of the semester, centers around the history of Titan Falls and the two women who made it famous. Sarah Anderton, known initially as the town healer, achieved notoriety when it was unearthed that she assisted nobles in poisoning their enemies, including their husbands and wives. Once discovered, the nobles were so concerned Sarah would publicly name her clients that they branded her a witch. It's assumed they included her young, disfigured teenaged daughter in the torture and hanging, though the daughter's body was never found, and she isn't named in any records.

My chosen assignment is to solve the question that's continued to perplex the town and university for over 200 years: What really happened to Sarah's daughter, and why was her name deleted from all records?

I answer Ardyn, "I had no luck the other night in the operating theater."

"No?" Her tone rises like she's interested, but Ardyn can't match the obsession I've gained the more I look into the mystery. "Maybe you should try more traditional research, like the archives."

"I have to look deeper than public records. Channeling Sarah herself is the closest I can get. And I almost got her. The theater went cold like she was there."

"That place is always cold."

I pause. "I thought that was your first time there."

"Oh, it was." Her stare slides away from mine. "It just seems like the kind of place that would permanently chill the living. Because of the, you know..."

"Dead people?" I nod, somewhat satisfied by Ardyn's answer —or her learned ability to churn her mistakes into smooth butter, courtesy of Tempest.

I continue, "If Sarah was in there with me, she refused to say or do anything. Not even snuff out the candles and leave me in the pitch black for fun."

Our conversation is cut off when Professor Hunter Morgan strides through the door with a large coffee held in one tattooed hand and a file folder tucked under his other arm.

"Good morning, all," he says with a panty-melting grin.

Yes. Panty-melting.

Hunter Morgan is the youngest visiting professor at TFU. He's a young Brad Pitt, if Brad Pitt were covered from neck to fingertips in tattoos with cheekbones determined to escape the scruff around his jaw. They jut out, casting hollows on his cheeks and accenting his greenish-gray eyes.

Those same eyes lock onto mine. "I couldn't help but over-hear your attempt at a failed séance, Clover. Perhaps bring the acacia herb next time you try to communicate with the Anderton witch, used for psychic enhancement."

He says it offhand, but I notice what I always do when he discusses my topic.

It's only for a blink of a second where my mention of taking on the Anderton witches causes a rippling in his eyes. Professor Morgan's stare is unusually placid, sweeping his gaze across his students with a practiced ease, but I've come to believe that ripple, the shock of rabid excitement, is something he's willing to starve himself of in order to appear as normal as possible.

"I'll do that, thank you." I open my laptop and pretend to have a deep interest in the screen rather than keep his attention.

Morgan's focus gives me an eerie tingle I can't ignore.

"Any time." Professor Morgan smiles in response, yet his eyes stay on my face as if he can peel back the curtain of my polite smile and enjoys what he sees.

He breaks off right when it would be noticed by the rest of the class and sets his leather bag on the head of the table.

As soon as he does, I slouch forward, convinced my racing heart's making indents through my skin, and I need to hide it.

"The middle of the semester has arrived," Morgan announces, cupping his chair head's two spires for emphasis. "How are we all doing with our chosen subjects?"

Rebecca, the girl to his immediate left, jumps in with her update, and the professor listens while my mind stays focused on wondering what he was thinking when he looked at me. His interest isn't charming and sexy like Xavier or cool but intense like Rossi's. It's darker. Primal. And part of me unfurls and purrs every time he notices me.

An unexplained bout of panic coils in my chest when Rebecca finishes, and Morgan makes his way over.

"Ardyn?" the professor asks. "How about you?"

Ardyn folds her hands on her unopened laptop. "I'm fine."

Morgan doesn't flinch at her reply. Probably because he didn't care what she'd say anyway. Now he can ask about what he's really interested in. "Clover? Any updates on the Anderton witches?"

"I'm closer to the name of her daughter than I've ever been," I lie.

Morgan gives a placating smile. "You're going after a topic

many students have tried and failed to expose before you. Don't be upset if you can't uncover the truth."

I un-stick my tongue from the top of my mouth, refusing to look dumb in front of this man. "There's a reason her name's been erased, and I think it's because Sarah was trying to hide something."

"Is that so?" Morgan bites one corner of his lower lip in thought. On anyone else, it's an unintentionally sexy move. For him, I'm sure it's a planned attempt to bite down on his surprise. "You don't believe it was the nobles or judiciary that did it?"

"There's a chance the Anderton girl knew the names of the guilty nobles," I reason, but I shake my head, finding it easier to consult my notes than meet his assessing gaze. "Except there's no record of the daughter being questioned."

"That doesn't mean she wasn't." Morgan arches an empathetic brow.

"Records were easily forged back then, but with her connections, Sarah could just as easily have done it as well. Not every noble would've wanted her dead."

"So that's what you're going with?" Morgan wanders over, tapping the back of Ardyn's chair and making her thin her lips, then moving to pat my shoulder. "So Sarah struck her daughter's name from the history books herself. What an interesting theory."

Morgan doesn't linger, nor does he squeeze inappropriately before he moves on. But it's his touch. A mixture of panic and lightheadedness clouds my mind before I tell myself to act normal.

"Way to put all his focus on me," I whisper to Ardyn, leaning back in my seat so I can talk out of the side of my mouth.

"Your paper will be stellar regardless of his input." Ardyn

mutters her reply while glaring at Morgan's back. "You don't need his praise to know you have the best topic."

"What is it with him that makes you want to shove one of the swords on the wall between his shoulders?"

Ardyn shakes her head, but she won't glance my way. "Nothing I can put my finger on. His cocky attitude just turns me off."

My brows jump at her response, but I don't say anything more.

Class ends, and Morgan dismisses us. Ardyn stands, waving to me as she heads to her business class.

"Clover, could you hang back a sec?" Morgan's buttery voice rises over the general hubbub of the departing class.

"Sure." That creeping feeling returns, and I swallow it down, unable to think of a plausible reason to ignore him. I stand behind my chair and push it in, the scrape of its legs loud and awkward.

He waits until the last student exits and comes up beside me, so close I can smell the spice of his cologne.

It's pleasant—seductive—and I tell my traitorous hormones to cool it and grip the top of my chair like a crutch.

I don't look at Morgan, instead choosing to count the circular grains of wood on the table. A light tickle against my cheek turns into a buzz of electricity when my eyes flick up, and I realize it's his finger grazing my skin.

"What happened there?" Morgan asks.

Either surprise or instinct not to move under a scorpion's exploratory crawl prevents me from shrinking under his touch. "It's nothing. I fell down the stairs last night."

Morgan gently glides his index finger under the cut on my cheekbone. My lips part at the resulting shiver cascading down into the hollow of my throat. "Looks painful."

His eyelids lower, and his pupils grow large despite the overhead light. His lips part, showing off an inner shine on the soft pink skin.

I bite mine. Too late, I realize I've hindered my quickening exhales, the air hissing through my teeth.

That itch I have grows, demanding an audience. I tell it to knock it off. I can't be the person it wants me to be. This isn't a bar where everyone's a stranger. This is the professor of my favorite subject. He doesn't just know me. He *knows* me.

Morgan's seawater gaze dips, capturing my movement. His finger doesn't leave my face. "*Althaea officinalis.*"

My gaze shoots to his. This would be the time to joke that I don't need a Hogwarts tutorial, but I can never be funny around him. He always speaks so close to the truth of me.

"Marshmallow root extract," I say. "It'll help the wound heal and fight inflammation."

"Well done." The white of his teeth flashes in my periphery. "And let me guess. You were well aware of the acacia herb when I suggested it for your next séance and have already used it."

I control my smile. And my fear. I can never best Morgan with my knowledge, but I'm addicted to baiting him. Wondering when he'll move on from healing herbs to the shadier aspects of summoning and sacrifice.

"You bear the pain well," he murmurs. "Considering somehow, you *accidentally* fell headfirst."

He bends his finger, his nail scraping against my barely healed cut.

I suck in a breath at the graze of pain. My heart pounds inside my skull, yet I can't tear my eyes from his. I'm nothing but his know-it-all student. He couldn't possibly be *concerned* for me. "I tripped. It was a dumb drunk mistake."

Morgan laughs low in his throat. "The difference between a stumble and a push is more obvious than you think, Clover."

Deep, instinctual knowledge curdles to the surface of my

evolved mind, the certainty of meeting an ancient predator as tangible as the hot exhales on my lips.

It writhes within the blacks of his eyes, those onyx scales curving against its clear barrier, testing.

"Who made you 'trip'?" he asks lightly.

"It doesn't matter."

Morgan brings his face closer to mine. "Are you afraid of what I'll do?" he asks, his lips curving slightly.

"Afraid?" I repeat, the low tenor of my voice foreign on my tongue. "No."

I'm shocked at the truth of it despite the bravado leaving my voice.

My heart may be clawing to get out as he pushes into my comfort zone, but my core singes with a buildup of heat.

"What are you doing?" I whisper, picturing the tattooed runes between each of his finger joints transferring to my cheek, merging with my blood and telling me all his lurid secrets.

His tongue slides across his teeth as he considers the question. "I'll tell you when I figure that out."

I'd looked up those tattooed runes of his the minute I'd noticed them while Morgan quietly tapped on the table during a student's presentation. To many people, that tapping represents boredom or impatience. But the term actually comes from an ancient belief that the maneuver summons spirits of the dead. *Spirit rapping.*

That move, coupled with the runes on his hands ... I was enraptured with the visiting professor.

Read as normal, the symbols, through Wiccan divination, represent positive knowledge, power, and realization.

But from Morgan's vantage point, they'd be reversed, which comes with an entirely different meaning.

Failure. Greed. Destruction. Warning. Deception. Crisis.

Morgan notices where my attention lands—on his free hand, rapping against the table. His tattoos flow with his movement.

A cold wind whispers against my cheek when he drops his other hand from my face and steps away.

"My apologies," he says. "I should've asked first before touching you."

"Yes. You should've." I resume packing my things while my stomach whips around, wondering whether to throw up or *whoop* excitedly.

The professor doesn't pay attention to any girl on campus, and he just caressed me. An unbalanced mixture of excitement and dread pulls my heart and mind in different directions.

I risk a quick glance at him as I shoulder my bag. My breath hitches at the sight.

Morgan's biting down on his index finger, the same one that curiously prodded against my wound.

Is he tasting my blood?

Noticing where my focus is, Morgan lowers his hand and shoves it into his pocket. "I'm afraid living with your brother has made me overly familiar with you when I probably shouldn't be."

He offers an *aw shucks* smile that doesn't reach his eyes.

"Whatever he's told you, it's probably a lie," I respond, frustration at Tempest acting as a cooling balm against my whirlwind stomach. "I can handle a little flirtation without running away and hiding under his coattails."

His eyes widen. "Flirtation? Is that what you thought I was doing?"

Uncertainty locks my brows at the same time my heart plummets out of my skull and back into its cage. *Of course he wasn't flirting. He was checking that I hadn't fractured my face before tattling to my brother that someone tried to hurt me.*

Then Morgan smiles, and this time it sets his eyes alight. "I knew I liked you better than that storm cloud you have for a brother. I'm glad to see at least one of you is good at lying."

I return his grin, though I'm not quite sure what he means. I'm about to ask when a knock sounds at the door.

I jump back as if scalded by a strike of black magic. Morgan notices the movement with an amused tilt to his lips.

Morgan takes his time shifting his focus from me to the door. "Come in."

The door's pushed open by a tall, muscular, easygoing...

Morgan asks me, "Clover, have you met our newest transfer yet?"

CHAPTER 7
MORGAN

"I take it you two have met," I say.

Being an expert on body language in all its glorious anatomy, I read the rapture between the pretty boy hovering in the doorway and Clover, who seems to have transformed into a blushing bride right before me.

Sigh.

Just when I started appreciating her value, she gets tongue-tied over a Basic Bro.

I fold my arms across the top of the closest chair, addressing the two. "Then no introductions are necessary. Lovely."

When Clover doesn't move, I add, "No need to inflate his ego any more than it already is, Clover. Yes, he used to be famous, yes, he's attending our school, and no, he isn't as tall in real life."

Xavier snaps out of it and frowns at me before sauntering in and shutting the door behind him.

He doesn't stay on me for long. Who would, when a more lavish sight lingers to my right?

Clover is a difficult girl to forget once you've seen her. Those cloudless copper eyes, the jet-black hair falling to her elbows, and her snow-white skin. The coldest season has clearly marked her, but the sun has taken a bite too, dusting her with golden freckles.

Sad, that she has such a troll for a brother.

A tickle arises at the base of my throat the more I notice Xavier's body language toward Clover. Like I've swallowed a mosquito that somehow survived the scorching trip. Xavier's concern over the girl and his instant protectiveness makes me want to claw the bug out and fling its wet carcass at him.

I return to the task at hand. "Clover Callahan is my best student by far and will catch you up on the assignments you've missed."

"Clover." Xavier says her name like he's tasting her. I don't appreciate the playfulness in his tone when he says to her, "Beautiful name."

Clover fidgets with her bag's strap. With her pale skin, the uncomfortable flush to her cheeks is sweet and instant. "I don't know if I can. I have a lot on my plate this semester."

My balls tighten at the hesitation in her voice. My groin twitches.

Please, Professor, I don't know if I can fit all of you in my mouth...

Oh, one can dream. Clover's been a temptation of mine since the moment she stepped onto campus and I discovered she was Tempest's sister. I wanted her for that forbidden fact alone. But lately, something else draws me to her, like a true compatibility, for which I fear for her now.

No one should have anything in common with me.

"Really?" Strange disappointment crosses Xavier's face at Clover's denial.

Then he gives that annoying smile that likely disarms many women. "I wouldn't be a problem. I'm a fast learner."

"I ... I don't know."

It's unlike Clover to be so reluctant to delve into occult studies, even in her spare time. She does it anyway.

My gaze shifts between them, growing smaller the more I pinpoint their awkward movements, aversion to mutual eye contact, and in Clover's case, gnawing lips.

Xavier's mouth pulls tight. "Ah. I get it."

There's a cramped pause when Clover doesn't respond.

He continues, "No problem, Clover. Professor Morgan can find someone else."

"Wait." Clover notches her chin and hooks the straps over her shoulders so tight her fingers blanch. "I'll do it. I can help you."

I offer up an unconvinced, "Really?"

She nods. "Excuse my brain blip. I'm happy to go over the missed material with you, Xavier."

That infuriating grin of his returns at the thought of spending time with Clover. "Wonderful. Many thanks."

Alone.

Fuck.

I add, "As soon as you tell me what really happened to your face."

My request is more of a whiplash of the tongue. Both Xavier and Clover jerk at the sharp sound. It takes more effort than usual to regain control and push the memory of Clover's soft skin and her lowering eyelids, weighted with desire, as I thumbed the small, angry cut on her cheek.

And the soft, answering mewl that came from her lips.

Fuck. Fucking dammit. Get yourself under control. She's related to that poor excuse of a dickwad. She's your student. She's completely outside of your greater plans and would be horrified by what you do at night, never mind what you take pleasure in.

Yet none of that seems to matter as I watch Xavier inch his way toward her, that protective alpha-man concern over her well-being etched all over his pretty boy face.

Clover must recognize the looks of two stubborn men because she massages the back of her neck and sighs. "It's my business and neither of yours."

"So you didn't fall up the stairs," Xavier surmises.

My head snaps up. I bark out a single laugh. "You believed that? Wait. Of course you did."

Then two things hit me: one, I didn't know the boy had the capacity to possess such a flat, murderous tone; and two— "You've previously met?"

Clover shifts in the one section of carpet she's claimed in the classroom, wrapping her arms around herself and staring at the ground.

Xavier bites his lip and grins.

Outwardly, I glower. Internally, I envision all the ways I can legally roast Xavier on a spit and chew up, then spit out his eyes. "I see."

Clover's quick to defend, "It's not like that. We don't know each other well. I wasn't even aware he was, well—"

"The star of many Wattpad fanfics?" I finish for her.

Xavier scoffs, fisting his hands at his sides.

I smile. *Got him.* If possible, his ego's greater than mine.

Clover glances at him apologetically. "I don't keep up with soccer."

"No worries." Xavier's voice softens toward her. "I prefer it that way, actually."

"You're new here then, huh?" Clover smiles warmly at him, her earlier chilly introduction to him seemingly forgotten under the warm rays of his sheepish expression, like they're sharing a secret, like they're fucking *role-playing* with each other. "Welcome to Titan Falls. I'd be happy to help you out with not only Professor Morgan's class, but any other—"

A loud *slam* whips their heads toward me.

I curl my fingers against my stinging palms, glad my rage didn't leave a dent in the wood. That would be a problem to explain to the board—how an eighteenth-century antique was laid to waste by a jealous professor over a student relationship.

How *banal.* I order myself at once to forget about Clover and focus on more important matters.

Like getting Xavier out of this room so I can tear her clothes off and fuck her in a circle of skulls, salting her pussy and licking it up as she hisses with pain and pleasure—

"That's it. Out. Both of you." I spear my finger at the door.

Clover nods, then presses her lips together. "Sorry to keep you, Professor. We'll get out of your way."

"Yeah. *Thanks* for the welcome." Xavier barely suppresses a sneer in my direction.

"If I weren't ordered to supervise you, I'd kill you where you stand," I mutter.

"What's that?"

I lift my head, offering a beaming smile. "I said to take the gift Clover's offering. She's truly a bright student and can help you through any difficulties."

"That much is obvious." Xavier swings his praise Clover's way. The girl flutters a hand against her chest like she's actually taken with him.

My stare narrows. She's so much smarter than this failed athlete. It has to be an act.

"You'll need it," I say to Xavier's back as he escorts Clover into the hallway. "As I expect every assignment you missed to be completed by the end of this week."

"*What?*" Xavier sputters. "That's impossible. There are like..."

He looks at Clover for confirmation. "... eight essays you've required since the beginning of the semester."

I show my teeth with a wide grin. "Better get to it, then."

Grumbling, Xavier shuts the door behind them.

As soon as I hear the *click*, my face falls. I kick away my chair and pace, gluing my arms to my sides to prevent a temperous flare that would send precious artifacts on the shelves shattering to the ground.

I didn't sign up for this, to be a babysitting a talking head. I'm meant to be the heir to greatness, my uncle exiling me to this asinine town so I could study under the famed tutelage of Professor Miguel Rossi.

The Vulture.

I'm meant to learn business practices better taught in the isolated mountains and get my ... fetishes ... under control, *not* parry to the whims of a spoiled brat who probably waxes his pubic hair as a desperate cling to his previous successful endurance.

How *dare* Rossi order me to watch this boy? How the *fuck* did Tempest and Rio manage to dodge it? And why am I always made out as the outcast when I've proven more than once how vicious, skilled, and enthused I am every time we get a job?

Because they know. They know you want her. Dream about her. Wake up with Clover's name on your lips, wet with the fantasy of her pussy juices.

I haven't been able to forget about Clover since realizing how forbidden she is. Too many times this afternoon, I nearly lost control.

She's Tempest's sister, who he'll protect with his life. Rossi looks at Tempest as a son, making him an obvious ally in the *death to Morgan if he fucks my sister* department. And Rio, well, he's known Clover almost as long as Tempest and considers her a stepsister—that he'd like to fuck.

In my attempt to escape the past, I've gained too many personal problems in this isolated mountain town.

Whirling, I face the outside through stained glass, the bright colors masking the gray, leafless woods. I'm staring through an illusion. A hoax.

Sadly, the window doesn't survive my frustration.

CHAPTER 8
CLOVER

"Are you two fucking?"

Xavier's casual question brings me to a screeching halt in the deserted hallway. "Excuse me?"

"That professor in there." Xavier jerks his chin in the direction of the closed door behind us. Then his forehead smooths. "Oh. You're dating on the DL, and my presence in there freaked you out because you think I'll snitch."

I take a moment to process his words, tonguing my cheek.

Once I get over my initial shock and put my mental cards in a row, I ask slowly, "Snitch what, exactly?"

"Us." Xavier bites his lower lip as he smirks, the same smile that dampened my underwear in 0.2 seconds last night.

He adds, in a secretive tone meant only for us even though we're the only ones in the hallway, "Is that why you were originally so cold to me in there?"

I hold up a hand, blocking his too-handsome face from my view. It makes me think things I shouldn't. "Professor Morgan and I do *not* have a relationship, other than student and teacher. And I wasn't cold. Exactly."

He waggles one brow. "No?"

"It's ... complicated. I'm me. You're you."

"Doesn't sound too complicated." Xavier scrunches his brows.

I don't have much of an answer to that, considering I really don't want to confess that he's way out of my league.

So I revert to our initial topic. "Professor Morgan's ... odd. Super passionate about his subject, but he switches personalities so fast, sometimes it's hard to keep up. But what I got in there," I add when Xavier opens his mouth for another remark, "is that you need a tutor since you're new here, and being the top student in his class, he's asked me to help."

"I mean, yeah." Xavier leans against the wall, making himself comfortable as he folds his arms and smirks down at me. "All of the above, with one thing I must add."

I sigh. "Yes?"

"Can you conduct my lessons naked? You're fucking gorgeous. I've been dreaming about you since we parted under the moonlight."

My core absolutely gushes at his slick, accented words.

God, I'm so easy when it comes to him.

I mash the inside of my cheek between my teeth. "I did all that ... with you ... because I never thought I'd see you again. I thought you were a passing long-haul trucker. Or something."

He laughs, the sound as addictive as his accent. "You're something else. Do I look like a trucker to you? I don't even have a hat."

Okay. Yes. Terrible lie. But Xavier untethers me in ways I'm not used to, and wants me for reasons I don't understand, so I continue on blindly. "What I'm saying is, there's nothing between us, okay? I don't have time for a relationship—"

"Who said anything about a relationship? I want my maiden's pussy, is all."

Again, with the gushing. "I can't. Won't. I'll teach you because it'll put me in Morgan's good books—"

"I *knew* something was going on between you two."

"Would you listen? *No.* Morgan. Is. Not. Fucking. Me."

Someone clears his throat in our periphery.

Both our heads whip in the direction where Morgan stands, propping his door open with his arm.

My mouth parts to apologize, because regardless of what went on with us in his classroom, yelling at the new guy that I'm not fucking my professor for good grades isn't the smartest thing I've ever done, especially considering my reputation.

I'm halted by Morgan's expression under the gilded archway. Dark. Haunting.

Hungry.

Any apology dies in my throat. Fear and ... lust ... take its place.

Xavier comes to my rescue.

"Excuse us, sir, we were just leaving."

Then with a grin that can't be for me because of how arrogant, showy, and competitive it is, Xavier pulls me into an empty classroom and locks it against Morgan's growing hurricane of an expression.

CHAPTER 9
XAVIER

Clover blusters as I pull her into a dark classroom with the woody aroma of charcoal pencils, linseed oil, and clay.

Creatives often sleep in after all-night crafting sessions. I rely on the fact there are no art classes in the mornings (I tried to join one for a bird course, but they were all full) as I push Clover up against the far wall and cover her with my body.

"What are you doing?" she whispers beneath me.

"My dark maiden," I trail a finger down her wounded cheek. "Are you upset that I ripped you away from your professor?"

A streak of jealousy burns my throat at having to mention the prig's title.

Though, my intentions are on point. Two spots of outrage stain Clover's face. "I told you, Xavier, there's nothing—"

"Say it again."

"Say what?"

"My name." I lower my stare to her level. "Say it."

She hesitates. The whites of her eyes spark through the darkness.

With my chest pressed against her, I take both her hands in mine, lift them, and thread my fingers through hers against the wall. "Say my name."

I trail my lips over the cut on her cheek, kissing gently, treating her skin like it's precious.

"Xavier," she breathes.

I kiss the line of her jaw, and her breath hitches. "You're beautiful. Irresistible. I want you so badly, my dark maiden."

"But ... why?"

My head shoots up.

"Why?" she repeats when I meet her eyes. Her face is flushed from my kisses. "I'm not—I'm not anything special. Everyone here finds me weird. Too different—"

I silence her with a single shake of my head. "You don't ever have to be *enough* for someone, least of all me. You are an unexpected bright spot. Baffling, surreal, but if you'll let me, I'd love to keep feeling fantastic with you."

I bury myself in her hair, breathing deep. She smells wild, musky and floral and crisp, like she belongs in a mythical forest.

She *is* different. So refreshingly unique.

"Tell me what you want," I murmur.

"I..." She writhes beneath me, her hands locked in mine, but she's giving in. "What if someone comes in? What if Morgan breaks down the door?"

Her tone changes like she believes he'd do it.

"He won't," I assure her. "He has a reputation to uphold. Busting in and breaking school property isn't it. And I will swear up and down you and I were meeting privately so you could catch me up on all my missed schoolwork, nothing more."

I sense her smile at our continued shared secret.

"Now, back to what's important. What can I do to prove I want you, my maiden? Kiss you?"

She instinctively tilts her head to meet my lips, the warmth and sweetness of her trickling into my mouth and sensing my soul underneath all the bleak inside. Groaning, I sink deeper into the kiss, my tongue stroking hers, my hands squeezing hers, my body *needing* hers.

Gasping, I break off the kiss, forgetting myself for a moment. I can't fall into her like this.

I blink through my fugue. "How about I make a suggestion?"

"Okay," she agrees, eyelids heavy with want.

"I want to take you to the edge," I say.

"The ... what?"

I break the connection our joined hands have wrought over my spirit and move to the elastic hem of her tights and shimmy it down.

Clover tightens at the exposure, then relaxes as I massage her inner thighs.

"Look how you open up for me," I croon. "Are you just as wet for me, too?"

Her harsh breaths and lingering stare on mine tell me that indeed, she is.

I flick my finger over her swollen clit. On a mewl, she clamps her thighs together.

"We can't have that, love," I say, prying her thighs apart as I lower to my knees. "I want to suffocate in this cunt again, and you're not about to stop me."

"Jes—my *god*," she hisses when my lips clamp on her pussy.

Her fingers dig into my scalp, holding me steady.

The proximity to her hot, wet sex makes me want to devour her, but I force myself calm, my cock hard and *fucking* painful, but I remain gentle, kissing and sucking like I'm enjoying the last succulent peach of the season. Clover's so engorged against me that she has to shift and adjust against my ministrations, so sensitive it's almost agony.

"More," she begs above me. "Please, just..."

I place a sweet kiss on her clit and pull back.

Clover moans, pulling at my head, *this* close to hooking my ears and locking me onto her pussy. I chuckle.

"This is cruel," she whines. "Madness. And pure *mean*."

"You're not ready yet," I say simply, then lean forward to begin again.

I have no idea how much time goes by as I steadily eat her out, get her to the brink, then pull back after a light kiss on her mound, her clit, or a single, long, lick to signal the end.

Clover's body is a tightened spring that's been held to a flame. She wants to combust. She's desperate to explode. And she's begging in both the English language and one all her own as I bring her to the brink again, again, again.

When she literally tries to suffocate me with her cunt, I chuckle with my tongue inside her, then retreat enough to say, "Ride my tongue all you want, love. I'm not about to let you come until I decide it's time."

She chokes back a sob. "But I have class. You're going to make me late."

"Oh, my dark maiden, you've run out of reasons to beg, haven't you?" I say. "Because the number of flying fucks I give about you making class compared to playing with your pussy is little to none, I'm sorry to say. Now shush."

I spend the next thirty minutes destroying her.

Clover's dripping with sweat, her fair skin flushed red. She's discarded her jacket and now heedless of unintended company, she's lifted her shirt for relief, exposing her chest. I took advantage and pulled her bra cups down, tweaking her nipples as I leisurely lick and nibble.

My own pain and need, I've put in a separate compartment. This is about Clover and proving to her that she is more than enough to satisfy me.

On minute thirty, Clover doesn't have the energy to stand anymore. I'm impressed.

I help her to the ground so she splays out before me, her knees falling on either side.

I have her on the edge of insanity. Clover doesn't care how exposed her pussy is for me. I doubt she'd care if an entire classroom of art students flicked on the light and wandered in, so long as I got her off before their class started.

"Please," she cries out. "Please, Xavier. I can't ..."

The hair at her temples is slicked back with sweat. Her eyes roll in her head, unable to pinpoint.

When it verges on agony, when she's so engorged tears join in on the shine on her skin, I murmur, "Is it time, love?"

"Yes," she sobs. "*Yes!*"

Without any warning, my hands dig into her thighs, and I lift her hips off the floor, burying my mouth in her and sucking hard. My tongue is rough, my teeth exposed as they scrape against her clit, and I give in to the devouring I was desperate for the minute I saw her in the quad.

My dark maiden's found me in this Hell. She's meant to be in my life.

When she comes, her scream of relief joins her shuddering body. I keep my face on her, drinking every last drop of this delicious orgasm.

As her shudders abate into spasms, I reluctantly unlatch and crawl up beside her, taking her into my arms and holding her as she cries.

"I don't know why I'm so upset," she blubbers into my chest. "I just ... I just..."

"Just hold me," I finish for her, kissing her forehead. "You're all right. I've got you."

Clover clings to me, recovering from the edging as much as

she can, exhaustion hitting and her grip relaxing as we lie on the floor.

She's not the only one recovering. My cock has never experienced such sheer agony. I've never deprived myself of a good fucking and unzipping and plunging into Clover to bring her to climax after forty-five minutes of deprivation would have been the ultimate fuck.

I didn't do it. For the first time, I'm enjoying the pain and burning dissatisfaction in my groin as this lovely creature conks out in my arms from pleasure.

It's as if I had to prove to myself that I'm not the selfish prick that caused this rip in my universe.

I didn't bring this upon myself.

Not wholly.

Because why would I be given a girl like her if I did?

CHAPTER 10

RIO

I didn't notice Clover Callahan at first.

I initially saw her as a pale slip of skin, thinking she was blending into the furniture when in reality the white of her flesh acted as a beacon of obviousness.

She followed us around like an albino puppy, too freckled to be considered purebred, too sweet to be cast aside and kicked into dark corners.

I met Clover when she started using training bras, completely forgettable at eight years old, though we were fascinating to her.

She and her little sidekick, Ardyn Kaine, snuck around Callahan Manor at night, thinking they were so cloaked and cute as they eavesdropped on me and Tempest. We were like a fairy tale to them, the kings from strange realms who were experts in topics like sex, drugs, and general mayhem outside of the manor's fortress. The families my buddies and I grew up in might as well be fantasy royalty, since our childhoods were as different as the supernatural, save for one similarity: we were all forgotten sons.

When I was shipped off, I didn't give Clover a second thought, instead pitying Tempest for having such a defenseless baby sister he'd be forced to protect. She was an easy pawn used by their father, grounding Tempest when he'd otherwise rebel, cutting Tempest off at the knees when he'd tried to escape.

I considered myself lucky there was no one I loved to come home to, no innocent soul that I'd have to damage myself to defend.

Clover disappeared from my life at the same time Tempest did, when he was forced to join the Vultures at Titan Falls. I made it my business to locate him, joining Tempest in whatever trouble he'd gotten into. That's what you do for brothers.

Maturity does that sometimes—levels out or smashes your preconceptions when you realize some friends are more family to you than blood will ever be.

There I was, giving up my life for a friend—grounded and cut off at the knees.

Clover was never a passing thought during that time. I didn't ask about her, care about where she was, nor did I wonder if she'd avoided the kind of life sentence Tempest and I were in.

Of course she did. She's Tempest's baby sister. He'd never allow her to get dragged into the underworld.

Then she wandered into Titan Falls.

Her enrollment came as a surprise. Tempest doesn't talk about people important to him around the Vultures. His silence became so habitual, he stopped mentioning any potential weaknesses even when we were alone. When she arrived on campus, I endured the first quiver of emotion I'd felt in a very, very long time.

My heart somersaulted. I stopped breathing mid-inhale.

She wasn't the same gangly, Gollum-like creature I'd dismissed in her family home. She'd grown tall, filled out, turned her hair into onyx luster, enhanced her cheekbones, and pierced me with amaranthine eyes.

Clover was still as pale as marble, but now, her freckles marked her skin like her personal galaxy, the biggest star nestling bright between her breasts.

As soon as she strolled up to me and gave me a sassy, overly confident wink, I decided to name that star after myself.

My, how the sweet, forgettable sister has changed.

The energy around Tempest visibly shifted the minute his sister opened her mouth announcing her presence. It was clear he didn't sanction her move. Clover subverted him, going to their recluse father, and begging for an invitation to the exclusive university, no doubt assuring him that it'd be the best place for Tempest to keep tabs on her.

My upper lip twitched with amusement. *Does she still want to listen in on her brother's friends, imagining their tales as hers, wanting our lips to explore her skin instead of the random hookups we talked about?*

Thinking back on it now, it's funny I didn't contemplate how much danger she was putting herself in, bunking near *us*, the exiles, the unwanted, the most talented executioners the world doesn't know about, dragging around our chains and using them as garrotes instead of weights.

No doubt Tempest thought the opposite.

He keeps her as far from Anderton Cottage, our base of operations, but it's like asking a child not to open the cabinet of candy that's bolted with a flimsy lock and easily accessible with a stepladder. Clover's curious, and I've caught her more than once sneaking around our bushes or dawdling behind one of us in the campus quad, hoping to collect secrets like breadcrumbs.

The problem is, once I focused on her, I couldn't stop.

I have a problem, one gifted to me the minute I developed independent thought.

My childhood nanny became my first obsession. It never occurred to me that she was being paid to spend time with my four-year-old self. It was because she loved me. She couldn't wait to be around me—that was proven with her bright smile every time she walked through the door of my playroom. She did everything I wanted, from sitting on the floor with me, reading the books I wanted, and comforting me to sleep with my head nestled between her breasts, where she sprayed her perfume for the sole purpose of enticing me.

And she stayed. No matter my tempers, the nasty bruises my wayward mother left, the awkward breaks in my voice and sharp points of my growing limbs. No, she kept coming back because she *loved* me, couldn't be without me, nor I without her.

We slept together when I was sixteen, proving my theory that she shared my devotion.

Sadly, the guilt ate away at her, despite my assurances that we were meant to be. She quit as my nanny, which makes sense considering I only summered at home and spent the rest of my year at boarding school. I thought it was so we could be together in an official capacity, but then she stopped returning my calls and texts. She wouldn't answer the door when I found her address and ignored me when I waited for her at her favorite coffee shop. Her expression became rather distressed when I snuck through her window at night, but it was only to feel her arms around me. I insisted to the police I wasn't there to force myself on her—I would *never*, not to my soulmate—I was merely there to sleep beside her and remind her that we were only whole in each other's presence.

She tore my heart in two when she viciously screamed at me to get out of her life.

I did as she asked, since I'm not so pathetic as to hang around for crumbs of pity from a woman too stupid to see how good she had it.

Besides, a gorgeous teacher at my boarding school set her eyes on me. Then it was the girls' lacrosse coach who couldn't take her hands off my pecs. And a friend's older sister. An acquaintance's aunt. Then a few other soulmates who turned out to be poisonous brambles around my heart.

A few years of reluctant therapy diagnosed my certainty of true love as erotomania, or Fatal Attraction Syndrome. My family thought with the proper treatment, I'd be "cured," but they really should know, it's called an *eternal flame* for a reason.

I learned to better hide it and watch my lovelies via cameras or at a distance, so they don't get too excited that I've noticed them. Too often, I'm the one landing in hot water while they get to walk away pretending like we're strangers because they're too embarrassed to admit their everlasting love for a quiet guy like me. Some think I'm simple. Others, that I'm stunted in speech. Many believe I had my tongue cut out at a young age.

I'd given up hope that my wayward heart would at last find a home ... until Clover.

For years, I'd forgotten her. Now she's all I can think about.

Clover leaves Camden House at the usual time, dressed in tight black jeans and an oversized leather jacket. Her backpack's slung over one shoulder and she grasps a coffee cup in her other hand like it's a lifeline as she slogs into the quad.

She passes the fountain I'm standing behind without a second glance. Clover has no idea I'm here, watching out for her as she goes about her day like it's any other.

But it's not, is it?

Tempest keeps Clover under the radar as much as he can, but now that he's fallen in love with Ardyn, he's juggling two precious jewels while staying committed to our undercover operations. An impossible feat. Tempest won't admit it, but he needs help. He won't pass Clover over to anyone else willingly, so I'm taking it upon myself to ensure her safety and intercede with deadly precision if anyone related to the Vultures' business tries to come for her. I enjoy leaving her trinkets to let her know she'll always be safe. Maybe I should up them, make them more obvious, because so far, she hasn't said much about them.

I used to think being under the Vultures' employ was a prison sentence.

As I perch on the fountain's stone rim and sip my coffee, sweetened in the way Clover likes it, I'm reconsidering that notion.

A THIN COATING of frost sparkles on the few plants surviving the cold front before winter. My steps crunch through decay, slices of greenery clawing through the murky brown with the might of a stubborn summer.

Enjoying the natural quiet of mid-afternoon, I'm reluctant to head back to the cottage, but I'm called by necessity.

The mountains surround my rock-strewn glade as I meander. In the fading light that's neither sky blue nor dark night—more of a white fog of illumination through the trees, sunless and shadowless—the mountains surround me like a jawbone of flattened, elderly teeth, the trees from this distance resembling that morning fuzz before you remember to brush your mouth clean.

Too soon, Anderton Cottage comes into view, my current home, or, as I like to think of it, my place of entrapment. If I were a spirit, I'd be convinced the former resident witch contained me here for her own pleasure, watching my slow rot of boredom with entirely too much glee.

Nobody hears my approach when I open the front door, nor do they spot me as I stroll into the living room despite Miguel Rossi's impatient pacing in front of the old bookshelves, his hands shoved in his suit pockets.

Hunter Morgan, the other so-called professor, splays out on the one leather chair, his legs resting sideways in a V of contentment as he sips on a crystal glass of Tempest's favorite bourbon.

A brief assessment of those two allows me to read the room, but I glance at my sole friend regardless, noting his hunch on the couch, elbows resting on his knees and his down-turned mouth framed by clenched hands.

"Where've you been, buddy?"

Morgan's voice is the first—and last—I want to hear after leaving the peace of the woods.

He continues, "Out playing with sticks in our backyard? Or were you busy building some mud pies?"

I don't deign to give him a response, moving to stand behind the couch where Tempest sits instead.

Morgan's undeterred. "Silly me, you wouldn't do something so juvenile. You were out there digging up bodies, weren't you?"

"Somebody needs to make sure wild animals don't find the graves."

My lip curls after speaking. It's usually not so easy to goad me, especially from the likes of our resident psycho, but today isn't like usual days.

Morgan makes an intrigued sound in his throat, but thankfully finds his empty glass more interesting than continuing his one-sided observations.

"We have a leak," Rossi growls. He's moved on to folding his hands behind his back as forges a path through the wooden floorboards. "Rio. Inform them of the problem."

I answer as if the old man's flicked an ON switch in my chest. "There's a rumor going around town that people are disappearing."

Rossi pins the arrogant Morgan with a glare. "Care to explain, Hunter?"

"Don't look at me." Morgan straightens. "I haven't spoken to my uncle since my exile. It's not like I have anything to say to the man who sentenced me to this haunted forest in the middle of nowhere with only you three tree stumps for company."

Rossi doesn't believe it. "How else would a rumor like that get around? Three out of the four of us in this room are professionals. We've gone years without anyone noticing our executions. Especially the townsfolk."

"Not so," Morgan says. "You're forgetting Storm Cloud's girlfriend and his chatty little sister. They could've blown your cover."

Tempest's head snaps up. His eyes breathe green fire. "Go on. Say their names to me."

Wisely, Morgan moves past that particular argument. "And who the fuck knows what Tongueless over there is up to." He points at me. "He may not talk much, but I'm certain his intelligence is high enough to write or at the very least send carrier pigeons somewhere during his Boy Scout retreats into the forest."

I round the couch.

Tempest's hand shoots out, grabbing my forearm and stopping me mid-vault.

"Try again," he says to Morgan.

Despite nearly losing his head twice, Morgan flutters his lips in an exasperated exhale. "All I'm saying is, it's not me. You're all well aware how much fun I'm having with our targets. Hell, last time Rossi okayed my severing of limbs. It's been weeks since my last playdate. Why, oh *why*, would I prevent myself from hearing those delicious screams again?"

I'm forced to agree.

"Our cover isn't blown," Rossi says. "*Yet.* How else can we explain the rumors?" Rossi slows his pacing along with his tone. "The Vultures don't lose. We have one edict during our exile: dispose of the don's enemies. If we can't do that..." Rossi lifts his head, his brown eyes, harboring the wisdom of a wizened owl, landing on Tempest and me in turn. "Then we no longer serve a purpose."

The true meaning of his words is unspoken but weigh heavily on my mind. For months, Rossi, Tempest and I have been planning our escape from our servitude to the *Cosa Nostra*. The three of us were chained to this life for different reasons, yet our bonds remain the same. They don't break; they warp the longer we're forced into reluctant assassinations, melting and tightening until they cut through our bones.

Miguel Rossi, as the original Vulture and the most seasoned, came up with a traitorous plan once Tempest joined his fold and became a talented second. When it was clear I'd be a loyal third, Rossi let us in on his goal to ruin the mafia don, Marco Bianchi, then *take his place*.

The one issue we've run into is recent. None of us expected to babysit the don's nephew, Hunter Morgan, one Mr. Bianchi hopes can be groomed to be his underboss once Morgan gets his fetishes under control.

"... be easy."

I return to the conversation, realizing I'd missed enough that Morgan began rambling again.

"I'd be the first to figure out where these townies are getting tipped off," he continues, "but it seems as though I've been given the deplorable task of ensuring a B-list athlete's smooth transition into Titan Falls."

"Now you know how *we* feel," Tempest growls.

Morgan ignores him. "Why are we being so accommodating to the pretty boy Xavier? He has no connection to my family."

"It's none of your concern," Rossi snaps. His dark eyebrows eclipse his eyes in warning.

"Fine. I've shown Xavier around campus and given him enough homework to keep him in Meath House for days."

Morgan flaps his hand. "Anything else he needs; I've passed him off to Clover."

The air changes, electrifies, after her name is said out loud.

"You what?" Tempest's quiet question cuts through the silence.

"Don't you get all stabby with me," Morgan defends. "She's my best student, and that's saying something, because I don't show favoritism. I take my position at the university very seriously."

Rossi's frown lines deepen. My blood boils at Morgan's cavalier attitude toward Clover—like he has any idea what it's like to track her, scent her, and drag his lips across her recently used bedsheets.

Morgan continues talking to Tempest. "She and Pretty Boy have the same major, and I have it on good authority she's excelling in all her other subjects, including her electives. Even you must admit Clover's the best person to catch him up on the semester."

Tempest doesn't respond immediately. Rossi stays silent, awaiting Tempest's decision. I consider speaking first but hold my tongue—as much as I consider myself an expert on Clover Callahan, Tempest has the final say.

Though if it were up to me, I'd keep her far away from any relationship to the Vultures no matter how tenuous. She's too precious and irreplaceable to be risked like that.

Tempest gnaws on his inner cheek as he bores holes into the ground while he thinks. "I'll allow it for a few weeks. Xavier Altese is a favor, and as soon as he's assimilated at TFU, that favor expires." Tempest directs his next point to Rossi. "If at any point Clover doesn't want to waste her time with him, we don't push her."

Rossi nods, then grumbles, "Approved. The girl could use something to keep her busy on campus."

Tempest cocks his head in question.

Rossi, rarely finding a need to explain himself, moves on. "With Xavier taken care of, that gives us more room to investigate how this so-called 'danger' to the residents is being leaked. Our last target's disappearance was wrapped up tight, was it not?"

I nod. "His acquisition was silent and without witnesses. I brought him here with no tails or suspicion. Cleaned up the same."

Morgan reaches over to the side table where he's placed the decanter of bourbon and refills his glass. "My, so succinct. Can't we then send this hound dog to figure out where he went wrong?"

I bristle.

I'd throw a knife at him, but that would just give him more ammunition.

Tempest interjects, "He's right, Rio. You're the best we have, anyway, and you don't have the burden of representing yourself as something you're not during the day."

A fact to which I'm still sensitive about. Rossi, Morgan, and Tempest all have suitable roles on campus: two professors and a TA. With my constant travels to locate and acquire our targets, it was clear making me a student or professor was impossible. Instead, I'm delivery staff, relegated to food and item transport into and out of campus.

Or, as Morgan puts it, a glorified door bitch.

I'm awaiting the moment I can carve out his eyeball without repercussions, which will be about the time I cut ties with the Vultures. Then I can get my sweet revenge.

Hell, there's no use for Morgan now.

"Rio?" Rossi prompts.

"Yes. I'll do it." I push off the back of the couch, somewhat reluctant to leave.

I'd had a lot of free time lately and most of it was used watching Clover. With this new assignment, I won't have as much time with her as I'd like, leaving her open to idiots like Xavier Altese and Morgan.

"See that you keep us updated," Rossi says, then flicks his hand, dismissing the meeting.

Tempest and Morgan both rise.

"Rio," Tempest says, stopping me. "Be back by tomorrow night. There's this..." Tempest's rock-hard resolve softens into a cringe. "...party Ardyn wants to go to with Clover and I'd be more comfortable if we could flank them."

"You?" Morgan guffaws at Tempest. "And *you?*" He points at me. "At a party? Oh, those ladies will have a *fabulous* time with the likes of you gentlemen. Ardyn must really have a sugar-coated pussy if you're choosing to go to a freshmen party—"

Morgan ducks Tempest's swinging fist, darting for Tempest's legs at the same time.

Rossi, a man who reserves little patience for situations outside of direct orders, disappears without notice.

I endure Tempest and Morgan's scuffle with detached amusement. Not even Morgan can put out the fire that's ignited in my chest at the thought of spending the evening with Clover.

But Tempest and I have always operated best as a team.

Coming between them, I shove Morgan into the bookshelf on the way out, giving Tempest the opening he needs.

CHAPTER II
CLOVER

I thought Sarah Anderton would rise from her burned pyre in the woods before Ardyn would willingly go to a party.

"I'm trying something new," she says to me as she pulls at the hem of her dress in front of our floor-length mirror. She grimaces at her reflection. "Is this too short?"

I rise out of the supine position on my bed. It's been a few days, but my vagina is still very angry with me for allowing Xavier to do what he did.

I've never experienced such misery before pleasure. It was torturous, traumatizing, and the best goddamned orgasm I've ever had.

"Clo?"

I order myself out of my dirty thoughts and back to my friend.

Ardyn's slipped on a white, scalloped lace dress that from far away seems innocent, but upon close inspection reveals a ton of cleavage and leg. "Did my brother get you that?"

Her cheeks pink. She nods. "He likes me in white."

"I bet." If it were anyone else, I'd make a lewd gesture with my hands before smacking her on the rump and telling her to have a good time. "You look gorgeous, Ardy. He could get you a trash bag and you'd look good."

Ardyn stops messing with her dress and spins to me. "What about you? What are you wearing?"

"I'm not going."

"Yes, you are."

"Nope."

"Yes."

"Nay."

"Yay."

"Nuh-uh."

"Yuh-huh."

I clamp my mouth shut and cross my arms.

Ardyn mimics me, cocking one hip for emphasis.

I fall back on my bed, splaying my arms and asking the ceiling, "Why is it so important to you that I come?"

"Why are you suddenly against parties?" she counters. "What happened to the Clover that begged me to go to the freshman kick-off party a few months ago?"

"She's weighed down with class assignments." I roll onto my stomach, burying my face in my pillow so Ardyn doesn't read the lie coming out of my lips.

The truth is, high school was always difficult for me. I was labeled a witch the moment I offered a healing crystal to Sandra King when the most popular guy in school dumped her. After graduation and enrolling at TFU, I was hoping for a fresh start and way more acceptance for unconventional beliefs and wardrobes. That's what TV and college brochures lead me to believe.

But at the party Ardyn's referring to, I'd lost track of her and

Tempest for a while, running into Minnie and her asshole followers. They took one look at my heavy eyeliner, sexy pirate-witch wardrobe (I'll defend myself here and say it was a themed party celebrating the founders of Titan Falls), and my open fascination with the blood dripping from freshmen's hands as they cut their palms open to ring forth a prosperous semester and sneered.

I heard them talk about me the minute I jumped in line to participate in the ritual.

"It's always the weird losers that want to do this," Minnie said to one of her friends, not bothering to lower her voice. "Do they actually think calling on hanged witches will bring them good luck?" She snorts. "Fucking freshmen morons."

"What is she wearing? Does she think that's hot?" her friend asks.

I turned my head, catching Minnie's eye, though I didn't know her name at the time. She was dressed in a *Playboy* costume, pink satin bunny ears included.

I said to her, "I prefer my bunnies boiled instead of with lipstick on."

Her eyes widened a fraction before her brows furrowed, then she laughed. "Oh my god. Freak alert. Go cut yourself open and swim in a swamp for all I care."

I break eye contact to look at the front of the line where a masked man was handing out ritual knives, though everyone knew who was behind the mask—the gorgeous, young, unattainable Professor Morgan.

I noticed the girl next to him, then turned back to Minnie and added, "I don't need to use my crystals to know you'd throw one of your besties into the fire to be the girl cleaning his knives. Well, one in particular, but I don't think he'd reveal his sword to you no matter how many lip-plumping exercises you do."

This time, her eyes turn into perfect circles of shock. Two of her minions cover their mouths as they attempt to stifle a laugh-cough. Minnie's mouth thins and she steps up to me. "I didn't give a shit about you two minutes ago. Now? Now I want to make your time here pure torture."

"It's not my fault he doesn't love you back."

Minnie hisses. "You're so fucking dead, fresh-bitch. Watch your back." She poked me in the clavicle, her pointed, bubblegum pink nail almost breaking skin. "Because you just messed with the most influential girl on campus."

"I'm terrified," I deadpanned.

The girls behind her shake their heads in mourning as they watched the exchange, their attention on me.

Minnie turned on her heel, making sure to kick up dirt that sprayed my legs.

I wasn't afraid then. I'd dealt with my fair share of bullies and figured Minnie would get bored and move on. They usually do, especially when you fight back.

There was no way I could've realized how dedicated she would be in ensuring my lasting suffering no matter where I went, what corners I chose to hide in, or how strong my insults were.

She never relented.

I'm not proud of it, but I'd rather stay away than go another endless round with Minnie Davenport.

"Sorry Ardy, but I'm beat. Go on without me."

"Please, you have to come. I'll have a tough enough time with Tempest as my date. I've bought myself some leeway by getting him to bring Rio, but something tells me it will *not* be as fun with those two as it would be with you."

I hate myself, but my ears perk up at the second name. "Rio's coming?"

Ardyn shrugs, but not before I catch the concerned tilt in one corner of her mouth. "You're not still crushing on him, are you?"

Her words hit harsher than she probably intended. While I hardly think she has a right to an opinion about my feelings toward Rio when she decided to sleep with my brother, that's an argument we've had one too many times before. It takes my better self internally wrestling with my snarky one and winning that prevents me from voicing my feelings on the subject.

Rio is my brother's best friend and loyal sidekick, which means that whatever Tempest is into, he is too. I'd be more open to Ardyn's concern if she was willing to tell me what they're hiding, but she won't, therefore I can fantasize over him as much as I want.

Of all people, Ardyn would be the one to understand what it's like to pine for someone you can't have, to admire from feet away when it feels like miles, to want to touch someone who will probably never mark you in the same way.

"I lost my crush on Rio at about the time I grew boobs," I mumble, rolling onto my side until I give her my back.

"Clover, I—"

A firm knock sounds at our door, interrupting whatever Ardyn was going to say.

Ardyn whirls. "They're here."

"What? Now?" I bolt into a seated position. "But I'm not dressed!"

Ardyn pauses with her hand on the knob, regarding me over her shoulder. "Well, if you spent less time flinging yourself all over your bed hating parties and more time considering my proposal, maybe you'd look as hot as me right now."

I scowl at her through my bed hair.

She gives me a cheeky smile before throwing open the door.

Seconds separate the moment I notice Tempest in the doorway and Ardyn flinging herself into his arms.

He catches her, palming the back of her neck and murmuring into her hair, "Hi, princess."

I'll never admit it, but they do make a gorgeous couple.

"Bleh," I observe, then turn away, heading for the bathroom.

"Hi, Lucky."

That unassuming, sensuous voice slides through my ears like a silk ribbon, and he holds the ends.

My fingers clench on the doorframe, but I don't turn around. I can't—not if I want to hide the instant reaction Rio's personal nickname for me causes in my cheeks.

I say to the empty bathroom, "I haven't heard that name in years."

His voice comes directly behind me, stroking my nape like a feather. I turn enough to show my profile, the good side, responding, "I remember you cackling that name at me as you watched me trip over my own feet to catch up to you and fall face-first down the stairs."

Rio chuckles, so deep inside himself it's almost indiscernible. The rough-hewn sound makes me swallow.

I respond to his amusement. "You weren't too concerned back then. You walked off after Tempest yelled for our nanny."

I hear more than see him shuffle closer, then start when I feel his forefinger drag across the bridge of my nose.

He murmurs, "I think the bump there now is adorable."

This time, my swallow is audible.

I could turn and face him head-on, drowning in those shimmering chocolate pools, and truly call myself Lucky, but I cut the moment short by showing him my back and stepping into the bathroom.

"If he sees what you're doing," I say to Rio with the barest movement of my lips, "you're dead."

"A risk worth taking," Rio whispers behind me. Heat tickles

the side of my neck when he leans closer, adding in a whisper, "And I don't cackle."

I'm used to Rio's attention gliding over my head, all too eager to move on to something more interesting than his best friend's gangly, pimply little sister. These past few months have become strangely different, like he's testing the waters—specifically, my brother's.

I'm about to shut the bathroom door in his face, refusing to be yet another man's pawn to piss off Tempest, when cool air hits me between the shoulders as Rio retreats, whistling an inane tune as he ambles over to Tempest and Ardyn, Tempest asking, "How long are we supposed to stay at this party before we can escape and actually do something fun?"

Ardyn pulls away from Tempest long enough to respond, "Is it so wrong that I want to experience campus life?"

"Sure, but why pull us into it?" Tempest says.

Rio heads to my side of the room. Specifically, my bedside table, his eyes hooded, yet moving side-to-side as he visually explores my knick-knacks and reaches for my most phallic-looking crystal.

"Rio and I live in the outskirts of Titan Falls, are almost half a decade older than you, and hang out in an old cottage most kids here think is haunted. What part of that says *take us to a freshman party?*"

Ardyn shrugs with one shoulder, then tucks her hair behind her ears. I'm ten feet away, but even at ten miles, I can spot a calculated move.

My brother does, too. He glances at her sidelong, a ripple of suspicion passing over his face that makes me pause before retreating all the way into the bathroom.

"You don't want me to be hit on and dodge unwanted advances, do you?"

"I'll castrate them," Tempest snaps. "Slowly."

Appealing to my darling brother's jealous streak. Smart.

Tempest's relent comes with a warning. "We'll go like I promised, princess, but that doesn't change who we are. You know that, right?"

Ardyn smiles, but it wobbles at the edges. "Of course." She squeezes his bicep, her hand unable to wrap all the way around because it's so tense.

An unconvinced rumble comes from Tempest's throat. He doesn't push the issue and neither does Ardyn, who decides to stroke his cheek, then bop her nose with his, effectively disengaging his battle mode.

I wrinkle mine, sliding my gaze away to—

"Hey!" I rush to Rio's side, snatching my single-point crystal from his thief hands. "Don't touch that."

Rio's fingers slacken, and I get the sense he's allowing me to take the crystal rather than surprising him into giving it over.

Rio glances up at me, an undercurrent of amusement in his eye.

That current turns to flint. He spears to a stand, grabbing my chin along the way and jerking it toward him. With a stare that could shear through metal, he murmurs, "Who?"

Shit. In my desperation to protect what's mine, I exposed the injured side of my face. "No one. I fell."

Rio's eyes glitter dangerously, not believing one word coming out of my mouth.

His grip, firm and digging into my skin, heats my face, my blood pumping toward him rather than away. Without breaking our stare, he says with the strength of a gentle wind, "Incoming Tempest."

I have enough time to growl, "Dammit," before I sense the growing storm behind me.

Rio releases me at the same time Tempest charges into my

space. He pushes Rio aside and frames my face, his eyes narrowing with concern. "Who dies?"

He's somehow more succinct than Rio.

"What is with all the men in my life thinking I need defending?" I push out of his hold and settle my crystal back in its protective spot on my windowsill.

I straighten, but not before gently caressing where Rio's fingers seared into my cheek before I turn. "I got too drunk last night. Ask Ardyn. She can vouch for me."

Tempest whirls on his girlfriend. "You saw this?"

Ardyn parts her mouth, her expression torn between being honest to her boyfriend or protecting her best friend.

See? I want to say to her. *This is what happens when you mix pleasure with loyalty.*

The instant her gaze flicks to mine, I inject all the pleading my body can muster, begging her to side with me on this.

Tempest prefers to intimidate and threaten men, sure, but when it comes to me, he wouldn't be above ruining a woman's life—even if Minnie happens to deserve it.

I'm not my brother, though, and I don't enjoy siccing him on my problems.

Ardyn's gaze softens on mine. "I was there. Yes."

I pull my lips in, thankful for her choice. Clearly, there's more of our friendship left than I thought.

The sharp carving of Tempest's shoulders softens. "If Ardyn says it was an accident, I believe her."

"Gee, thanks," I say.

Rio's answering squint, directed at the three of us, tells me he's not as easily swayed.

"Have fun at the party," I say before Rio can mull over questions I'd rather not answer.

Rio's suspicion clears. He arches a brow in question. *You're not going?*

I shake my head. "I have too much work to do. I'll have a hot date with my shower, then I'm going to the library and meeting up with my study group."

"That's..." Rio's almond eyes lower. He finishes under his breath. "Disappointing."

I wave off the emptiness that follows after the intensity of his expression leaves me. "Maybe next time."

"Rio. Let's go," Tempest says.

Rio's gaze slides to the side, but he doesn't turn his head in Tempest's direction.

"If you change your mind," he says. "You have my number. I'll pick you up."

"Thanks, but I don't need male escorts around campus."

Tempest says, "Your crystals can't protect you from rowdy college boys."

"No, but this can." I grab my keychain from the tray near the door, where a mini can of bear spray is attached.

An invisible weight lowers Rio's brows as he studies it. He'd probably rather I carry a switchblade.

Reading his friend's silent communication, Tempest adds, "Might need more than that. If anything ever feels off to you or some guy gives you the creeps, call or text me."

"I'll also kick my phantom attacker in his ghost balls," I say to both of them. "Is that good enough for you?"

Rio gives one last glance at my keychain, mutters something, then swings around and stalks over to where Ardyn drags Tempest out the door.

Before disappearing into the hallway, Ardyn's face pleads with me in one last attempt. I shake my head, and her shoulders slump in defeat.

Tempest gives me a half-hearted wave, but his attention remains focused on Rio. "You think I don't protect my sister?" I hear him say as Rio shuts the door behind them. "I've built walls around her better than Fort Knox."

"Tell that to the cut on her face," Rio replies.

Ardyn's soothing tone follows, urging them not to kill each other. Their voices fade down the hall.

A clatter behind me makes me jump. One of the precisely placed crystals on the windowsill fell like a domino, taking down the three others.

CHAPTER 12
CLOVER

My steps echo into the chilled air despite the mild thumps of bass permeating through campus. Meath House is as far north from the library as possible, yet the boys dwelling there consider the entirety of TFU's airspace to be theirs.

The monolithic library comes into view like the castle in a fae fantasy story—or nightmare. With its sharp spires and dark-gray bricks, this is more the villain's headquarters than a hero's. I feel right at home. Most students prefer the cushy common rooms available on every floor in the dorms and academic buildings. Ardyn likes the warm fireplaces, soft couches, and unlimited coffee they provide, but there's something to be said about TFU's dark history and studying on its turf.

Too many have forgotten where this Ivy League college sprouted from and who had to die for it.

With that happy thought bubble above my head, I trek up the wide staircase and tip my imaginary hat at the two roaring stone goblins guarding the front entrance.

Once I've heaved open the double doors, electric wall sconces guide me through the turnstile after I press my student ID to the scanner.

The mixture of old and new is both convenient and saddening. Technology doesn't belong among the ceiling-high stacks, floorboards older than my greatest grandparents, and walls I wish could talk.

A brief scan between the rows of bookshelves shows that I have the library all to myself, save for the librarian I hear stacking shelves somewhere nearby. Her rolling cart is the only sound, other than the *thump* of my bag on one of the study tables and the scraping of my chair as I pull it back.

Throwing my hair up in a haphazard twist, I prepare to dig through the books I'd checked out yesterday. Their spines peek out of my bag—*History of Witchcraft, Colonization in the 1600s, Advanced Spellcasting and Curses.*

The last one is more of a personal preference.

Frowning, I pull out the books and stuff a hand in my bag, searching.

"Dammit, where is it?" I mumble as my nails collect nothing but the mysterious grit at the bottom of all purses.

I could've sworn I'd checked out the published trial transcripts of the Anderton witches.

My empty bag tells me otherwise.

Palming the table, I rise with a huff, confident I didn't leave it behind at the dorms since I tend to carry my Anderton research everywhere.

Of all places to realize I'm missing it, the library is the best one. Leaving my things scattered across the tabletop, I head to the archives section.

It's well in the back of the building and down a flight of crumbling stone steps, out of the way and almost forgotten by the students and faculty. Not many people are interested in dusty relics, most considering the Sarah Anderton/Titan Falls mystery solved. She was a witch. She killed people with home-made poisons.

But that's not the end. There's still the question of her nameless daughter.

The lights dim further as I turn into the final corridor and reach the archway to the stairs. The wall sconces lighting my way down flicker and sputter.

A couple of stairs down, a wall sconce sparks, then goes out.

I *yip* in surprise, glaring at the newly dark spot like the wires there specifically wanted to terrify me.

"I swear, Sarah, if this is you, I'm already working on the truth. You don't have to electrocute me to get my attention."

I wait a few seconds for a response, but nothing happens.

"All right, then."

Confident I've made my point, I continue into the occult stacks, one burned-out bulb doing very little to impede my progress. I'm so used to working after sunset I practically have night vision.

The basement is one enormous room with vaulted, cobwebbed ceilings and endless rows of shoulder-high book-shelves. Dusty, broken, scratched knickknacks clutter their top surfaces like old compasses, candelabras, and old busts missing noses and ears. I drag my finger across the spines of the closest stack, sneezing as I awaken sleeping debris, and follow alphabet-ically until I get to *witch trials*.

Bending low to reach the Ws, I peer closer, hoping to find the trials specific to Titan Falls.

"Who's there?"

The sudden, resonant voice makes me teeter on my haunches until I fall onto my ass.

"Hello?" comes the impatient follow-up. "Show yourself."

I don't move. The guy sounds pissed like I've interrupted his secret hookup in the archives.

Come to think of it, the forgotten section would be perfect for that sort of thing.

Quietly, I move to my hands and knees, intending to crawl out of there silent and unnoticed. I'm already known as the witch of TFU—the last thing I want is for some Meat House dude to find me as if I were peering through the gaps to watch him fornicate with some co-ed so he can tell all his bros how I like to watch peep shows at night.

"*Answer* me."

It's not a bark. It's a cavernous demand, causing my shoulder blades to scrunch together and dread to collect in my belly.

It also sets fire to my ass.

I slide across the dirty floor, approaching the end of the row and preparing to disappear behind a column when a hand clamps down on my ankle and drags me back.

I cry out, my squeaking sweaty palms creating white streaks across the dirty parquet floor as I'm yanked between the aisles, then flipped onto my back.

I lay there as stunned as a fish slapped out of the river by a bear. A figure looms over me. Two perfect rows of white teeth shine out of the darkness.

"Clover?"

I pull my expression out of a wince and take a closer look at the man looming over me.

"Professor Rossi?"

"Yes. Christ, I thought you were—" He stops himself, then straightens out of his threatening crouch over my body and flings out his hand like he expects me to cup his fingers and kiss his ring.

I just stare at it.

His eyes glint out of the shadows. "Are you going to allow me to help you up?"

"Nope." I pull into a sit, then rise. To give myself something to do other than shrivel under his unrelenting stare, I add, "You almost gave me a heart attack. What are you doing down here?"

"I could ask you the same thing. This area of the library is restricted to faculty only."

My brows pinch together. "No, it's not. I come here all the time."

Rossi sighs, the large span of his shoulders under his blazer sloping with the exhale. "I've harassed the board more times than I can count to increase security rounds or at the very least, put goddamn velvet ropes up."

My lips purse. "I've never seen anyone in this basement but me."

"You'd be wrong."

Rossi doesn't expand. From Tempest's limited discussions about his boss, I've gathered he's the type to make points, not arguments.

I don't fill the silence, either. Instead, I study the shape of him, sharp edges and jaded lines. The one softness about Rossi is his hair, dark waves reaching his shoulders with streaks of storm gray. Tonight, he has it up and away from his face in a loose bun at his nape. It exposes more skin than he normally shows during the day, and now his collared white shirt can't hide the fine, black spikes trailing up his neck, the top of a mystery tattoo that at least comes from his shoulders and back.

I cock my head in wonder. What would this man tattoo on himself? Skulls? A Do Not Disturb script? Fuck Off and Die with a smiley face emoji?

Rossi glances down at me, his impatience manifesting in the tightening of the skin around his eyes when I don't move out of his way.

"It is in your best interest to leave while I'm down here, Clover."

Even his use of my name sounds uppity and sarcastic. I cross my arms, unexpectedly miffed that all he sees when he looks at me is a young, naive student who requires lectures during his off hours.

"What makes your business more important than mine?" I retort. "I'm the student who needs passable grades to stay here and shares a room and can't find privacy anywhere. You're tenured and have a lecture hall, an office, a personal apartment..."

Rossi steps closer.

Hating myself for it, I drop my arms to my sides, spooked by his ghost-like ease into my comfort zone.

Rossi's obsidian gaze rakes across my face, his full lips twisted into a frown as he ... assesses me.

Breathing becomes difficult under such unexpected scrutiny. It's as if he's sizing me up, not as competition, but on what his chances are of snapping my neck, then disposing of me in one of the unexplored corners of this room and getting away with it.

I've only felt like this once before with another tattooed professor.

"Every location you've described," he intones, low and deceptively soothing, "does not consider what I like to do in my off hours."

I shiver. "So in your spare time, you enjoy collecting forgotten Titan Falls artifacts in spooky basements?"

"Maybe I do."

"But you're an economics professor."

"So you've stated."

Rossi's expression seems to heat the longer he remains in my personal space. He's bent low so we're almost nose to nose.

Unable to hold Rossi's low-lit gaze, I scrape my focus away from his dangerous features and down his sizeable, bone-crushing form.

A book at his side, clutched in his hand, catches my curiosity, the spine partially legible under his hand.

Ander—Rossi's thick palm obliterates the middle—*ials.*

That's more than enough for me to understand.

"I need that," I squeak out, pointing.

Rossi doesn't look down. "That's too bad."

"It's for an important assignment. What do *you* need that book for?"

"Not one ounce of me is interested in reasoning with you."

"Then why are you still here?"

A reluctant grunt leaves his throat.

I stand my ground. "There's only one copy of the Anderton Witch Trials."

Rossi doesn't counter. Or shift.

"Fine." I sigh, annoyed when it comes out tremulous. "Can I photocopy the pages I need?"

Rossi tilts his mouth into a terrifying grin. This man does not smile often. "No."

I shudder under his morbid amusement but not out of disgust. The tremor cups my breasts idly, curious and exploratory, before shooting into my core and lighting with his devil's fire.

It's an untimely, confusing reaction I avoid by saying, "It's a thesis I'm researching for Professor Morgan's class."

Rossi stiffens, the skin under his eyes hardening.

"Morgan." He practically spits the name. "I'm not surprised."

A tug occurs in my gut at his reaction, familiar and annoying. Tempest has mentioned his housemate and boss don't get along. Yet I wonder what two inked men, so handsome, single, and reluctant to exude any weakness of character could hate each other for. Or what more they could have in common.

I suddenly want it to be *me.*

I can't resist prodding further. "It's like everyone is uninterested in what happened to them—the Andertons. And it's so hard to stand out in Morgan's class when every occult topic is exciting and interesting, and he's probably heard it all. So I thought, not only will I document every aspect of the Anderton trial and persecution, I'm going to discover the Anderton daughter's name *and* why it was kept from all records."

One eyebrow shifts in intrigue. "And I assume you will also discover where this daughter was put to rest?"

I gaze up at him suspiciously, not enjoying his amusement. "Well. Yeah."

"That's very enterprising of you, Clover. Almost 250 years and no one has ever found her."

There it is again. The use of my name in a way that he knows me. *Predicts* me.

Rossi hasn't broken our eye contact once. My cheeks heat, and my thoughts spiral, but I refuse to be the first to retreat.

His lashes lower. The tenseness around his eyes fade while the intensity in his gaze quadruples. It's cold in the basement, yet all I can picture between us is the zipper of his pants straining, the metal groaning under the pressure of a giant, thick—

Air hisses through Rossi's mouth, and he shifts away like he can read my thoughts, but not before I notice him stroking his ring finger with his thumb, his nail digging into the tender skin.

The nervous habit is enough to snap me back to reality.

This is a professor. My brother's much *older* professor who he TAs for. Rossi is an expert in business and rides Ardyn's ass for her papers and is generally as much of a boring father figure as I can find at TFU. I am *not* attracted to this man.

Rossi seems to read the change in me. The boldness fades, and mild observation takes its place. "I wish you the best of luck in your endeavor. Perhaps your studies are better suited to the ground floor where most texts can be found."

I frown. "I've come to the basement a million times, and I haven't seen you once. I'm staying."

"I'm a professor. I retain privileges you can only dream of having on this campus." He draws closer. "I am your superior in every way. Obey me."

The way he says *obey*, I feel like I'm on my knees and opening my mouth like a good girl.

Saliva collects in my mouth so forcibly, I have to swallow. My brain follows suit, shoving an image of how big his cock must be to suit his massive body and how it would burst out like an anaconda.

I'd grab it.

Then I'd drag my teeth over it. And lick it. And suck it.

Hot blood shoots into my cheeks.

Oh God.

Rossi searches my face, his brows pulling lower the longer he assesses my reaction. His nostrils twitch like he's smelling my arousal.

His pupils dilate.

Without a word, I spin on my heel and sprint for the stairs.

"I'm coming back for that book!" I shout as I run, cringing when my declaration comes out more like a warble.

"You'd better not," comes his biting reply.

His warning sifts through the air, contorting into a dare before it reaches my ears.

And finishing as an invitation.

CHAPTER 13
MORGAN

With a flick of my finger, the towel around my waist puddles to the ground. The floor-length mirror outside my bathroom gives me a full view of my body. I inspect it carefully. No new freckles have invaded the small amount of un-inked skin that remains. Certainly no additional scars. I've covered almost every inch of my skin in tattoos. Old scars, moles, freckles—every flaw is needled over and replaced with impenetrable black.

Satisfied, I descend into a push-up, keeping eyes on my reflection as I begin a set of 100. Within seconds, the dampness from my shower morphs into a light sheen of sweat. My muscles burn, my lips curl back, and my eyes pierce into the mirror. To break eye contact is to fail. To utter one word is to give in.

Somewhere out of focus, my phone vibrates. I let it go to voicemail. At about push-up number fifty, it goes off again. And again.

Cursing, I frog-leap to my feet and stalk to the bedside table.

I swipe to connect the call and snarl, "What?" without glancing at the caller ID.

A beat of silence passes before a low, patient voice responds, "Some families might allow that level of attitude when answering the telephone, but I do not."

"Uncle." My shoulders go rigid, and I pace the small expanse of my room. "You caught me unaware."

"I expect you to answer my call with an immediate, respectful, 'how can I help you today, sir?' or we'll have to revisit how you enjoy doing your morning routine without fingernails."

If I were standing in front of him, not a single muscle within my control would twitch at his threat. But since I live well enough away from my uncle in Titan Falls—to the point that some might stupidly assume I've escaped him—I allow a wave of remembered pain to spasm through my body. One doesn't forget celebrating their fourteenth birthday after having all their fingernails pulled out, one by one, for daring to arrive at his house late after school.

"Yes, sir," I say now, my steps slowing until I'm standing in the center of my room and staring at the collection of bird skulls on my dresser, organized from smallest to largest.

My thumb involuntarily strokes the ridges of my pinky's fingernail. It never grew back the same. After the first nail was taken, he handed the pliers to me.

I hate excuses, but I also cannot stand my uncle's senseless demands.

So I add, "I didn't expect you to contact me so soon. I assumed my exile to Titan Falls included a complete cutoff from my friendly uncle."

"Don't get smart with me, boy," Uncle growls. "Your enduring proclivity to combine comedy with torture aside, I'll still cut your cock off and feed it to my dogs."

He means it.

"To what do I owe the pleasure then on this dreary morning, dear Uncle?"

"I'm hearing rumors. Receiving messages I dislike. All regarding my vultures in the mountains."

I shrug, though he can't see me. "I haven't seen or heard anything untoward."

"Are you certain? My messengers are normally accurate. More so than you've ever been."

Instead of listening to his guttural, sandpaper voice, I rewind the last conversation I had with Rossi, Tempest, and Rio. Rossi was worried about his bodies resurfacing. Rio insists he's covered his tracks, but with the town of Titan Falls worried about missing persons, there is way too much talk for my liking.

I assure Uncle, "We have everything under control. Every target you've sent to the Vultures has been disposed of. Is there another you'd like us to focus on? It's been a while."

The thought of enjoying another victim and painting the room with their blood sends a delightful leap in my gut.

"You think I give a shit about the men on my hit list?" Uncle spits.

I wrinkle my nose as if his spittle can hit me through the phone's earpiece.

"No, I want an update on the other task I sent you to Titan Falls for," he continues.

My shoulders fall. The only thing less interesting than a lack of human playthings is Uncle's pet project.

"You want to become a made man, don't you?" he pretends to ask.

We both know I'm not meant to answer in anything but the affirmative.

I spin to my closet—my morning workout is clearly over. "I have no updates, Uncle. Over 200 years have passed and there hasn't been any sign of Sarah Anderton's belongings."

"Glibness will only make you spend more time in exile." Uncle's voice tightens with temper. "The auction houses are certain she left behind her fortune and hid it somewhere in those mountains."

Uncle isn't speaking of the above-ground auction houses. He has a penchant for collecting antiques and other valuables, but only if they were stolen, killed for, or marked with the blood of war.

If I didn't hate him so much, I'd enjoy this hobby of his.

I remember my father taking me to many shadow market auctions as a child. He shared my uncle's—his brother's—passion for antiques and often engaged in competition with Uncle for coveted artifacts and paintings. In a strange twist of fate, my father was murdered at a black-market auction two years ago.

Thus, making me the sole heir to my uncle's empire.

It's due to that circumspect inheritance that I have the power to say to him, "Anyone who's befouled you ends up in these mountains. Why would an intelligent man like you send your slaves to the very place where highly valuable trinkets are hidden?"

Uncle goes silent, likely chewing over my insubordination and how to handle it hundreds of miles away. I admit, I'm braver at a distance but I've grown stronger, taller, and have a lot more experience than him in tolerating agony.

At last, Uncle says, "You will find the dead witch's fortune to add to my collection or my next hit will be you."

I've tried all I can think of to turn Uncle off me. Laughing as he cut into me. Twisting my lips into a maniacal grin when he held a saber to my belly button and offered to pull my intestines through it. My uncle is smarter than an overweight, sweaty pig who sits in his manor all day should be. He understood the way my brain worked almost immediately. How I'm able to turn pain into a humorous show ... and how invaluable I'd be as an assassin until the time came for me to preserve the Bianchi name.

"Does Miguel Rossi have any idea about the Anderton fortune?" my uncle asks.

I watch my brows shoot up in my reflection. Rossi hasn't so much as sneezed an interest in the Titan Falls witches. "Not to my knowledge."

"Keep a close watch on that man," Uncle grumbles. "He'll turn on me on a dime if given the chance."

"Well, you did murder his wife and child," I say while checking my cuticles for grit.

"Necessary punishment." Uncle harrumphs. "Make sure he doesn't find the treasure before you do, boy. You won't like it if he does."

"Rossi has his own matters to attend to."

Like cleaning up his messes.

Information is currency. I keep that to myself.

"Stay close to him," Uncle commands.

I tilt my head, my reflection following suit.

"It's no secret that Miguel has grown a soft spot for Tempest Callahan," Uncle continues. "I assumed Tempest was nothing but a debt to be paid by his father when he was sold to me, but as information filters in, I'm convinced Tempest was put into the Vultures for reasons other than his father paying off his loans."

I snort. "If you're asking me to become besties with that storm cloud, think again. He is not in the market for friendships, and I'd rather flay the skin off his bones than share a beer with the man."

"I'm not asking you to infiltrate the fatherly relationship Tempest has found in Miguel Rossi."

It can't be helped. Cold, numbing jealousy drips down my spine at those words, but I clench my back muscles, dissolving the feeling.

"Tell me more about the girl. His sister. Clover."

My chin jerks up. At first, my idea to center my occult class around a thesis where the students could do a bunch of Anderton research *for* me was a terrific idea. Two birds with one stone kind of thing.

Now...

Clover has a purity, an innocent curiosity I thought only existed in places like Disney World. But Clover takes that dream park and becomes the royalty of the upside-down version. The contrast between her bright inquisitiveness and the macabre subjects she enjoys brings on an addiction I'm having trouble handling. No one has ever come close to understanding what I like. The dark, the worship, the blood. And she's so sweet about it. So succulent.

Could it be possible this girl is like me? Was *made* for me?

"I'm told she has a deep interest in the Anderton witch mystery." My uncle jars me out of my thoughts. "Most especially the nameless daughter. And, with Tempest's family history, she may be smart enough to get closer to the treasure than our dear Rossi. Get in bed with the girl, Hunter. That shouldn't be so difficult for you. Just don't cut her up. Not until I say so."

The idea of cutting into Clover's warm, flushed skin repulses me. I refuse to mess with that kind of perfection. Poke at it, sure. Stroke it, lick it, suck her pink nipples and pink clit...

I grit my teeth. "Yes, sir." Then inject casual disregard into my voice in case my bloodhound of an uncle senses my off tone. "I could just drug her when and if she stumbles on this so-called treasure, or order Rio to grab her and force her into the back of his transport truck."

Neither suggestion appeals to me. An unconscious Clover wouldn't be nearly as fun to play with, and the idea of Rio touching her while she's hurt, staying with her for hours while he drives her to my uncle in Manhattan, makes my vision blotch into red.

"That is too much of a mess to clean up," Uncle replies. "Manipulation is so much better. Rossi is my most talented assassin. I don't want to alert him or give him time to intercede and take the valuables for his own. The Anderton fortune could provide him with wings, and I don't like my caged birds to fly. You are my fail-safe plan. I hope not to have to use it for many reasons. The top-most being, once Clover Callahan's usefulness runs out, I have better plans for that girl than *you*."

My lips are thin, but the intrigue behind my eyes is thick and hot. "What sort of plans?"

"A young Snow White like that will fetch me hundreds of thousands. So don't use her too hard."

Uncle's hacking, smoke-riddled laughter is the last thing I hear before he clicks off.

Slowly, I lower the phone from my ear. My eyes bore into their mirror image, my upper lip twitching into a sneer.

"You stupid son of a bitch," I whisper to my reflection.

A cloud of bone dust escapes as I crush one of the bird skulls in my hands.

If only my uncle's head were so easy to crack.

CHAPTER 14

CLOVER

With the library out of the question, I find myself at a loss for what to do. Technically, I could study on the upper levels, but I wouldn't be able to concentrate with the thought of Rossi underneath me. His intensity would thrum through the floorboards and into my body, fully distracting me from research.

Nope.

Shaking myself out of it, I propel myself forward and into the blustery weather. There's a reason I'm walking away from the solace of the library. Rossi is a diversion I don't need.

I'm faced with a crossroads once I exit to the pathway around the quad. To the left is the big party Ardyn, Tempest, and Rio are at. I can feel the thumping bass through the concrete sidewalk, a completely adverse sensation to the one Rossi's presence caused. To the right is my dorm, where I spend an abnormal amount of time and was hoping for a change of atmosphere.

The girl I wanted to be pushes against my subconscious. That girl was hoping to be free by the time college came around. Free from family, forgetting the past, and new to a future I could craft for myself.

Instead, I'm falling back into the cloistered, inexperienced girl who tried to act out in private school and break boundaries. Tempest always built them back up. It's out of love and concern, and I reasoned he wanted to protect me.

Now, though, I don't have that excuse. Tempest is literally at a party and invited me to come along. I'm the one who said no.

And why?

Because I'm afraid of Minnie? Because I've reverted to the girl who spoke the loudest and tried to be the funniest but ultimately had no voice?

Lips grim with determination, I turn toward the music.

Crossing the quad and into the open doors of what everybody calls Meat House, the party's on the ground floor common room, the largest on campus and more like a ballroom with multiple large arched windows on both sides. Multicolor lights flash, and a DJ booth is set up in one corner. Couches normally splayed out in the room have been repositioned into VIP areas on one side of the room. The rest of the space has been cleared for a dance floor and plenty of drink stations.

I don't need to look far to find Ardyn, Rio, and Tempest. They're in one of the VIP areas, Tempest's arms splayed out over the couch as he regards the entire environment with contempt. Rio's drinking clear liquid, cautious eyes roaming. It's with such alertness that I doubt he's drinking alcohol. I don't think I've ever seen him unhinged and vulnerable.

Ardyn's standing near the couch, dancing with a drink in the air. It had been so long since I've seen her so carefree and feeling safe enough to loosen up and dance to her favorite song.

Tempest has done that for her.

Any time a guy who's dumb enough to approach her gets a

murderous glare from behind her shimmying form, enough to send even the most stacked jock running.

I smile as I come up to them, oddly comforted by their predictable behavior and yeah, feeling safe, too.

"Clo!" Ardyn jumps up and down, grabbing my arms and dragging me into her solo dance number. "You came!"

"Couldn't resist." I laugh, accepting her drink while she pours a fresh one from the table in their section. She switches our drinks when she's done, then grabs my hand.

"We're going to the dance floor now," she calls to Tempest. "Look, I have a buddy."

Tempest begrudgingly tips his assent, but his inclusion of Rio tells me all I need to know. He'll be in the crowd, watching us.

Ardyn and I are both used to it. I squeeze her hand, enjoying the freedom to just dance and not think about our burdens and secrets. All we need to do is enjoy the music while under the watchful eyes of men who would destroy anyone who gave us shit.

I'm on my second vodka soda and into my umpteenth dance number with Ardyn when I feel pressure on my back. A familiar scent envelops me—sharp mint—and my body twists into his arms, fully aware of who it is before my mind catches up.

I tip my head up. "Xavier."

He can't hear me over the music, but he sees my mouth move and responds in kind as he wraps his arms around my waist, his hands spanning the small of my back.

He mouths, "Hi."

I move with him to the beat. I shouldn't be shocked at how smooth he dances, how confidently. He guides me with sure hands, his groin brushing against my belly as if in reminder of how successfully he can leave me panting before pushing away, spinning me, and grinding against my back.

Closing my eyes, I raise my hands over my head and sway

with him, his hands moving to my stomach and his body moving in tandem with mine.

I slit my eyes open enough to notice a black smudge in the dancing bodies surrounding us, the multicolor lights swinging over it and putting a pair of watchful black eyes in stark relief before spanning the crowd.

Rio.

He stands while everyone dances around him, his arms slack at his sides, his hands curled. Rio doesn't take his eyes off me as I dance with Xavier, but my moves start to include him, too.

They turn seductive, slow. Xavier senses the turn and follows suit, his hands gliding up my waist, then down. We spin until Xavier's back is to Rio, and I'm facing him.

I keep my eyes on Rio, playing with fire as I stroke Xavier's shoulders and flutter my fingers down his biceps, then hooking at his waist and pulling him so our middles grind.

Rio doesn't shift. He doesn't blink. Doesn't move. Just watches.

I'm dancing with Xavier, and I'm dancing for Rio.

My lips pull apart with sudden lust at the thought of two gorgeous, unattainable, amazing men appreciating my body.

I fall into the illusion, and when Xavier lowers his head to kiss me, I keep my eyes open and on Rio, yet give Xavier the attention he deserves, too. With my tongue.

Sensing the crowd shifting around us, I also take pleasure in Xavier Altese choosing me over all these girls who have spent hours getting ready and look unbelievably gorgeous, whereas I've just come from a library basement and probably smell like it, too.

He wants me, though. He's tasted me, had me, and with this kiss, wants me again.

A shadow falls upon us, larger and much more ominous than Rio.

Reluctantly, I break off the kiss.

And turn with no surprise to find my brother towering over us.

He points at Xavier. "Nope."

Before Xavier can respond, Tempest puts a possessive arm around my shoulders and points me to the exit. "Time to go, Clo."

"What? No!"

I try to shove out of his hold, but he holds firm.

"You had your fun. How about you go and get some sleep?"

"Tempest, you're not my warden."

I punch him in the kidney, which he doesn't even feel, but he releases me when we step out into the cold.

"I thought you didn't want to come," he says, crossing his arms.

"I changed my mind. People do that, I'm told."

He shakes his head. "It's hard enough keeping Ardyn in my sights. And the minute I do, you're over humping a—"

"I can hump whoever I want!" I say. "If I wanted to tear my clothes off, too, I should've been able to do that."

"God, Clo. Grow up."

My mouth falls open. "*You* grow up. You can't even bear the thought of me having fun, can you?"

He scoffs. "You are so off the mark. Just go, will you? Ardyn won't be far behind."

I could argue. Stand my ground like I've done a thousand times before and lost. But it's exhausting and often pointless. Now that Tempest scents blood, I can't lead him back to Xavier, who will absolutely search me out if I go back in there.

"Fine," I bite out. "But sending me home from one party isn't going to magically make me an indoor cat."

"I'll get Rio to walk you home."

"Yeah, do that."

I wait for Tempest to go back in before I take the stairs and walk the pathway to my dorm without waiting for a babysitter.

Tempest is so infuriating that I'm vibrating with outrage. His protection comes at a cost to him, and that's the only reason my ears aren't blowing steam. Whatever's going on, whatever he's into, makes him want to keep me under lock and key, but it gets in the way of *so* much. I can't even dance without his meddling.

Making unintelligible, pissed-off sounds, my mind works overtime, too high on adrenaline to even think of going home to sleep it off.

An idea floats into my head, dissipating almost as fast as it came.

Then it returns, with buoyancy this time.

Refusing to sink.

I couldn't. The last time I went there, I was literally chased out. But with everybody gone and a fresh argument with Tempest in my head...

I bite my lip. It doesn't take long to convince myself.

Spinning around, I take the path into the woods leading to Anderton Cottage.

THE 230-YEAR-OLD COTTAGE sits in an eerie hunch within a ring of dead trees. Smudged moonlight traces its uneven gingerbread shape through a cover of branches as I approach. My boots crunch against the path of decayed leaves until I reach the porch, where the creaking of aged wood takes over.

No light flickers within the windows to help my steps. The guys don't turn on the porch lights when they leave, a strange quirk the three of them share. It's like they don't want any attention on the house when they're gone. If I wasn't familiar with the route, I never would've found where they live, as deep and secluded as they are.

Knowing Tempest, it's exactly how he likes it. I can apply the same theory to Rio. But Professor Morgan is a different breed. I have no idea why he prefers shacking up with two younger post-grads instead of using Teacher's Row, closer to TFU's gates and where Rossi has a spacious, modern apartment.

I pull my brows in at the thought. Anderton Cottage is the perfect location for suspicious activity, a trait my brother has been known for all his life. Why I consider two professors to be involved as well is as confusing as it is inappropriate, but I can't shake it from my mind.

Rossi and Morgan are just so ... different from normal teachers.

And alluring.

Tempest gave me a spare key to the cottage for emergencies. He considers himself way more qualified than TFU security, and his reluctant passing of a spare key is solely what I'm relying upon when I slip it into the lock and enter the house that used to be occupied by the Anderton witches.

Honestly, Tempest's choice of residence is like Clover-nip. He shouldn't be shocked by my incessant presence, especially when he's not home. Without his brooding, grumpy shadow, I have more time to explore the nooks and crannies of the last place Sarah and her daughter were alive and free.

My curiosity stops in the main room with a fireplace and chimney in the center of the cabin. One side has the original flooring and wooden beams crisscrossing the ceiling. Velvet sofa chairs, a couch, and a wall of bookshelves add to the old-fashioned vibe. The other, renovated side houses the modernized kitchen and stairs leading up to the second floor—an add-on from fifty years ago and where everybody sleeps.

As I stand in the middle of the main room, close to the unlit fireplace, it's blackened maw seems to take shape in the darkness, mouthing *look*, like I should take advantage of the empty cottage while I can.

It's not often all the men are gone, so my fingers itch at the possibilities. Sarah might have stood right *here*, staring at the same brick-lined chimney extending through to the exposed ceiling beams. She could've grazed the same stone walls with her hand as she walked past, thinking of her next victim.

"I won't touch your things," I whisper to Sarah with assurance. "Just browsing."

The sound of my voice jolts me. It's a strange noise in such a blanketed environment. Foreign and unwelcome.

But I *must* use all possible resources to fulfill my vow of finding out the Anderton daughter's name. That's what will set me apart from all the other students. It's also what will give me Professor Morgan's admiration. Picturing his face, his perfectly symmetrical smile beaming down on me, gives me goose bumps and a loopy feeling in my stomach. It's a beautiful, unnerving, addictive motivation. I want Morgan to smile at me like that—and only me.

Forging on, I don't dare turn on lights, instead using my phone's flashlight. I've stood in this room a bunch of times, and it doesn't get boring. Each fleeting moment I get gives me time to spot another crack in the wall or a unique scar, flaws so timeless it has to be from long ago.

I give a testing jump, my black boots landing with a thick *plonk*.

Shoot. I was hoping for a hollower sound.

My past research in the archives unearthed a hidden basement where Sarah performed her rituals and human sacrifices. The university's official statement is that the basement was closed off and filled in, and they have the amended blueprints to prove it.

A part of me will never believe it, considering people love the morbid and are happy to revisit ancient history. Yet the faculty insists the basement doesn't exist anymore, Tempest included.

I pull my lips into a thin, impatient line. My scientific jump seems to confirm it, too. Oh well. Had to try.

I told myself I was here to study, and the couch is the perfect spot, but I round the back of it with my head tilted up, my flashlight running along the book casings against the wall.

A *hush* of sound strokes the back of my neck.

My soul leaps out of my body at the unexpected brush of electricity against my skin, my arm jolting and losing my grip on the phone.

It clatters to the ground at the same time I whip around, only to have a hand shoot around my throat.

CHAPTER 15
MORGAN

*S*hit.

    Fuck.

    Satan's ass.

The second I realize who I have by the throat, I fumble, but not enough to set my unintended victim free.

I've shoved her back against the bookcase, my knee between her legs to lock her in place. Both my hands are busy—one wrapped around her exquisite neck, the other brandishing a sharp blade near her jaw.

She whimpers, and it nearly undoes me.

I can't hurt her. Not Clover, my strong leaf that grows beautifully among weeds.

"Is it me..." I murmur into the darkness, "...or do you keep popping up in places you shouldn't?"

She doesn't reply.

I realize I'm squeezing her trachea too hard and release pressure enough for her wheezes to turn into words.

"I'm—Tempest—lives here. I should—be able to come over."

I hum with suspicion and keep her where she is. Clover's scent wafts into my nostrils, old paper, fresh earth, and incense.

A bead of blood forms at the tip of my blade.

Utterly irresistible.

"That may be true," I reply, sending my thoughts forward instead of into delectable sin. "When your brother's here, but you and I both know he's with Ardyn at whatever festive costume party the boys' dorms have thought up."

Clover writhes underneath my grip, attempting to get free. I tighten my hold.

Did I just feel a surge of heat against my knee? The idea of her pussy getting hot for me in this position leaks into my nerves and blazes a trail up to my groin.

I groan. Quietly.

Clover stops moving. I hope it's because she's feeling my growing erection against her thigh.

"You know I'm not a threat," she says. "Let me go."

"Not until you explain why you broke into my home."

"I just—"

"Spoke a lie. You're fully aware no one's home, yet you invited yourself in."

"Not true. *You're* home."

There she is. My mouth quirks.

"Why do you smell like blood?" she asks.

I stiffen and look down at my shirt. Frown.

It's the opening she needs.

Clover rams her free knee into my crotch, and I go down with a grunt but with the wherewithal to take her with me.

She lands on top of my chest, the air compressing out of her in a fragrant, bubblegum wave. I use her temporary shock to my advantage and wrap my arms around her torso, immobilizing her against my chest.

"Should've known the scent of blood wouldn't intimidate you," I observe, "I'd venture to say you like it as much as I do."

Clover tips her head to meet my gaze, her lips lined with tension. "I'm not scared of it, but I certainly don't go looking for it."

"Oh no? Are you not in Anderton Cottage to get a taste of witch's blood?"

Clover pulls her lips in, caught.

I chuckle, the rumbles transferring into Clover and making her breasts press into me.

My arms turn solid around her, keeping her glued to my body and picturing her rosebud nipples hardening through her shirt.

Clover's glittering eyes widen. She stills, as if sensing the slightest wriggle will turn my hardening cock into solid concrete.

I jerk my chin up and snap my teeth, taking a bite of the tiny piece of air between us.

Clover startles, her lashes fluttering as her eyes lower to my teeth ... my lips.

The astonishing urge to take her plush mouth into my own washes over me, yet I lay still underneath her. Daring. Wondering. *Wanting.*

Her lips part, slivers of teeth cutting through the pink.

Clover's phone lays somewhere beside us, disregarded yet essential in its flashlight caressing the planes of her face, the slope of her nose, and the look of lust tightening her features.

My cock grows painful.

I twitch underneath her lithe body, the friction rubbing against her soft belly.

I can't help it. My head falls back with a groan.

Her sweetened breath flutters against my mouth. Clover shifts, and I wince.

"Unless you want me to—"

I can't finish the sentence. Clover's tracing the row of buttons on my shirt, her fingers moving lower, exploring the dried blood on my shirt, lingering in the wet.

"Whose blood is this?" she asks.

"Why don't you taste it and find out?"

Her eyes shoot back to mine.

"Some cults believe consuming human blood gifts them with sexual energy," I purr.

"Or healing," Clover answers without hesitation. "Or intelligence."

"Such a smart, good girl."

The fact that I approve of her studies as I lay beneath her causes an entirely new layer of want to curdle inside me. I don't seduce, lust after, or fuck my students, even while forced into a professor role.

But this one. This girl.

Don't use her too hard.

My uncle's voice perverts my thoughts. It ruins any chance I might have taken at this moment.

As much as it pains me, I shove her off. Though surprised, Clover deftly recovers, showcasing her grace as she gets to her feet.

I sit up, readying to stand until I notice how the whites of her eyes glow as she looks down at me.

She whispers, "Being here in this cottage, alone with you, is doing something to me."

I arch a brow but indulge in a closer study of her.

"Do you feel her?" Clover asks.

"Who?"

Though I know.

"Sarah," Clover answers. "She would appreciate a blood offering."

I get to my knees, becoming level with the hem of her leggings. While staring up at her, I take a sniff.

Clover's eyes widen. She doesn't step back.

"Do you also appreciate a good blood ritual, Clover?" I smile with closed lips. "It certainly smells like you do."

"If..." Clover has to clear the thick desire coating in her throat before continuing. "If it means I could learn her daughter's name, I would."

"You'd do anything to learn it, hmm?"

I don't move from my delectable position.

With her arms slack at her sides, her hips moving minutely forward, Clover softly asks, "You're not a real professor, are you?"

I angle my head. "If I say no, can I smell your pussy again?"

Clover sucks in a breath, and Satan have me, I can't resist her any longer.

I bury my nose between her legs, clutching her ass to bring her closer, and *fuck*, she smells sweet and divine, a potent mixture that spears into my dick.

Clover mewls, her fingers digging into my hair. At first, she pulls at the strands, but as I bare my teeth and take a few testing nips, her shock turns into moans.

Wasting no time, I hook the elastic hem and peel down her leggings, exposing her milky thighs and a hot-pink thong I make quick work of.

Clover gasps, her hands remaining on my head when I push on her hips and get her to lean against the bookshelf.

Her shaved pussy glistens in the single flashlight that illuminates us. Saliva collects in my mouth at the sight, and my breaths grow heavy with effort.

This is no regular girl, and I don't consider Clover to be a single roll in my silk sheets.

No, she deserves better.

She deserves *me*.

I splay my hands against my shirt, collecting what wet blood remains. Then I smear it across her stomach and pay special attention to her inner thighs.

A cry escapes her throat, high with intrigue and absent of disgust—just how I predicted it would be.

My bright, twisted leaf.

Fervor overtakes me at the sight of her painted with my victim's blood. Growling, I dart forward and lick under her belly button, gliding my tongue across her exquisitely soft skin until I collect it all and swallow.

Her nails cut into my scalp. Clover tosses her head back and moans, her dark hair escaping from her loose bun and tumbling down her shoulders.

Fuck, she's a sight.

I move to her thighs before I explode from the beauty of my blood goddess, stroking the sensitive skin with my tongue, lapping up the red and leaving only pure white behind.

And then.

Then.

I get to imbibe in liquid gold.

Clover chokes on a moan when I dig my tongue into her pussy and suck at her clit like I could milk it. The sensation overtakes her, and she buckles, held up by my palms against her ass.

She tastes like she smells, with a slight metallic aftertaste. It's a cocktail I'll be chasing for the rest of my life.

I devour it, get drunk off it, and sacrifice myself to any god she wants as I bury my face in her.

I feel the tremble before she does, the rush of orgasm gushing into my mouth when Clover cries out her release, her body sagging against my face.

I could stay here. I really could. Suffocate me now because I'll gladly return to hell with her taste on my tongue.

Clover's fingers slacken, and her hands fall from my head until they dangle at her sides, satiated.

Reluctantly, I pry my lips off her soft, wet pussy with a *pop*. Getting high off her beauty and body is a weakness, one I hoped not to indulge in while my uncle has her in his sights.

Damn you, Clover.

Certainly, my professorship is now in doubt.

Clover's hooded eyes watch me as I unfurl my legs in and rise to my forelegs like a spider. "Whose blood was that?"

"Be honest, Miss Callahan, does it matter that much to you at this moment?"

"You put it on me. Licked it off my skin. You..."

"Sucked you off senselessly? I absolutely did. You've never come that hard before, have you, little leaf?" I grin. "You and I both know it's because of this." I gesture to the stains on my shirt.

She cocks her head. "And you."

I raise my brows.

My shocked expression brings a genuine curve to her lips. "I've never been taken like that by a professor before. Sorry, a *visiting* professor."

Oh, so she jests now.

"Will this affect our relationship now?" I tease, though a part of me worries endlessly. "Do you need to drop my class?"

"*No.*"

Relief washes over me at her adamance. She's not ashamed.

She's exactly who I thought she was.

Clover peels herself off the bookshelf, bending down and shimmying back into her leggings. My little leaf's still breathless when she asks, "You're not going to explain how it got there? Or why?"

I mirror her curious expression. "I wouldn't be a believable occult professor if I didn't dabble in the practices myself, now, would I? And you *are* still my student."

"Of course," she demurs.

Damn, how badly I want to pounce on her again.

Clover asks, "Did you use anything relating to the Andertons in the blood ritual?"

Ah. There's my answer as to why she went straight to the blood in my shirt and not to the question of why a professor just ate his student's pussy and risked his career. My clover leaf is *obsessed.*

Something I know much too much about.

"Now, I wouldn't be a respected occult professor if I gave you any clues to your thesis, would I?"

Clover's mouth twists, and sadly, she turns away. "You're right. I'm sorry I entered your home without permission, but I'm even more sorry I gave in to your tongue and couldn't find any Anderton relics."

My chest rumbles with dangerous amusement. "Don't test me, little leaf, or I might have to make you regret it."

I sense rather than see the shivers spread over her at my threat.

I lead her to the door, my gaze ensnared by the perfect apples of her rump as she walks ahead of me. No one will ever make black jeans look good ever again. "Perhaps if you asked your brother to explore the cottage, he may be more forgiving."

She snorts. Adorably. "I'm more likely to get him to agree to perform a root canal on me than get him to give me free rein on this place."

My lips pull down, and I cock my head in silent agreement. I've seen Tempest do that very thing on a Bianchi debtor.

"Well, it's been nice having you, Miss Callahan."

We both smile at our inside joke.

I swing the front door open. Clover stares outside with abject disappointment.

"It's too chilly to go tramping about the woods looking for my ritual circle," I add.

Her lips flutter with a sigh. "I hate that you're both the best and worst professor I've ever had."

My eyes crinkle with genuine amusement. *And I hate that I can't fuck you senseless right now.* "Good night, Miss Callahan."

She glances over her shoulder and squints at me, her lips motionless. Clover is not about to give me the same platitude. Instead, I watch the calculation behind her gaze, searching for answers to what happened between us. I'd lay them all out for her if I had them—I would absolutely join her in her adventure, use the Anderton's very bones as a dildo, and commit Clover to me in ways only her nightmares could dream up. That's how fucked over for her I am.

No one's allowed me to paint blood on them before, then have a casual conversation afterward. She's an enigma. A forbidden, curious, valuable treasure.

Clover doesn't know it yet, but she's forged a forever bond with me for that reason alone.

And I'll protect it at all costs.

But my family name, my purpose and presence on campus, is for one reason only. Ensure the Vultures continue their commitment to my uncle and use Clover as leverage if necessary. Or ... make him think I am.

I watch my little leaf disappear into the night, dismissing the thought of escorting her back to the dorms.

Truthfully, the only predator with a likelihood of snatching her is me.

I shut the door as she traverses the pathway that will return her to campus before the idea of stalking her through the woods becomes too exciting to resist.

Movement near the staircase catches my eye when I turn back into the hallway. I slow my steps, peering closer.

I cross my arms and sigh. "Enjoy the show, Tongueless?"

A sliver of moonlight catches Rio's profile before he silently slips back into the darkness, then pads up the steps to the bedrooms like the ghost he is.

My heart dropped at the sight of him. I was sure he'd report my interaction with Clover to Tempest—until I saw the movement of his hands against his pants as he tucked himself back in and zipped up.

Shaking my head, I move to the bookcase and straighten every item that my scuffle with Clover caused, pausing long enough to stroke the spines that touched her ass. I swear I can feel her wetness against the old leather.

Inhaling deep through my nose, I catch her lingering scent, my hand stroking near my shaft.

I will, without a doubt, be relentlessly jerking off tonight.

CHAPTER 16
CLOVER

At the entrance to the woods outside the cottage, I notice a pale glimmer on the dirt path, too shiny to be natural.

Curious, I move closer, conscious of Morgan at my back, then forget all about him when I bend down and clutch one of my crystals.

My mind works as I straighten from my shocked crouch. This wasn't here when I walked the path up to the door. I would've noticed its pale white sparkle among the dirt.

How did this get here? Who did this? Minnie wouldn't—way too much effort on her part and not nearly the pay-off she'd want. I think back, figuring out who the last person toying with my crystals was...

Rio.

His name swims through my mind like an ancient sea serpent.

I could've sworn all my crystals were accounted for before I left. Does that mean he broke into my room and took one? For what reason?

But more importantly, he was here. Did he see? Does he know what Morgan and I did?

I return to Camden House unbalanced and confused. With two after-hours confrontations with my professors under my belt tonight and a bewildering, silent message from Rio, I should feel improper, not turned on. The intimacy I experienced with Professor Morgan compared to Professor Rossi was so different yet so visceral. Morgan satisfied my dark itch in the way it always wants—with the forbidden risk and taboo.

If Rossi also chose to make one move toward me tonight, I would've bared my teeth and met him halfway, grinding against him and begging him to satisfy my itch in a different manner. One he's uniquely triggered under my skin.

This isn't me. I'm more interested in the twisted history of Titan Falls than banging my teachers, but holy hell, I'm in need of them.

Them.

The notion of wanting two men at once is both foreign and addictive. I want these two older, experienced, hot-as-fuck men.

And adding Xavier to it, with his famous good looks, charm, and svelte athletic body ...

Oh my god, I would be in heaven.

I never want to choose between them. So far, they've satisfied such different parts of me that I almost feel whole.

Almost.

There's still Rio and all his mixed signals.

I rub my temples as I approach my building in hopes of ridding myself of these budding addictions.

Instead, I decide on a desperate hunt for my vibrator and then locking myself in the bathroom for the rest of the night.

My key card *blips* against the side entrance, and I let myself into the dim interior at the base of the staircase. After a few seconds of listening, I'm confident the dorm's deserted, everyone still partying at Meat House. I figure I'll have the room to myself with Ardyn choosing to sleep over at Tempest's.

Where Morgan and Rio live, too.

A sliver of annoyance embeds itself in my gut. While I'm constantly kicked out of Anderton Cottage, Ardyn's welcomed. Probably because she has no interest in the witches and won't rifle through all the guys' shit, but still.

My boots thump up the stairs, traversing past the spot where Minnie shoved me into a near-concussion. A small, dried patch of my blood stains the concrete where I landed. The sight of it makes me shiver. My core pulses with the memory of Morgan's tongue and what he painted on my skin...

With him so vivid in my mind, you'd think I would've missed the small package sitting outside my door. Based on the mood I'm in, I'm surprised I didn't kick it out of the way because of my sole focus on finding my vibrator.

My better instincts push my intense want to the side and tell me to pick up the plain-wrapped box, inspecting it closely.

Testing it, I tip it to one side, then the other. It's heavy, with not a lot of space left in the box.

Humming with intrigue, I unlock, then shoulder my door open and close it before turning on the lights.

It's wrapped in twine, and I undo the knot with a tug. The paper peels apart easily, and I lift open the cardboard lid, uncovering a simple white card on top.

For Lucky, it says, **in her quest to find answers. I believe in you.**

He signs his name with a flourish, but I can recognize it anywhere. I've seen it enough. Rio.

I stroke his penmanship. Does this mean the crystal on the forest floor is a good thing? A clue to his feelings?

I pull out the book with a gasp.

The old, embossed writing on the leather is faded and barely legible. As soon as I register what it is, I drop it on my bed in a panic, then go in search for my winter gloves.

I can't find any in the mess that is my room, but I eventually discover a pair that Hermione has decided to sit on at the foot of Ardyn's bed.

Nudging her fluffy white butt aside and avoiding two threatening swipes, I scoot Hermione onto Ardyn's pillow, side-eyeing me the entire time I dismantle her hard-won nest.

With cat hair clinging to the black cotton, I pull them on, rationalizing that pet hair is less damaging than skin oil when handling old books.

And this book is *old*. Like hundreds of years with faded ink made of soot and paper created from cotton and linen fibers.

Leaving the book on the bed, I carefully lift the cover and parse through the pages, Hermione watching me with cool observation from her perch.

"Oh my god," I whisper, my heart pounding over my words. "This is it, Hermy. This is what I could be looking for."

Ardyn's cat is neither for nor against my revelation.

But Rio, bless that handsome, silent man, dropped Sarah Anderton's grimoire right at my feet.

CHAPTER 17
RIO

L urking has its advantages. Most important is the ability to discover people's secrets lying around—even if those people are long dead.

With stealth I've accustomed myself to, I beat Clover to the dorms and drop the Anderton relic off at Clover's door after painstakingly wrapping it with materials I found around my room.

I'd planned to return to the cottage and get a good night's sleep directly after but couldn't stop playing what Clover's reaction would be once she came across my gift. If she was so desperate for clues to the Andertons that she was willing to climb on top of Hunter Morgan of all assholes, then I had to leap at the chance to impress her before he got her all to himself.

While I wanted to be the one to paint joy over her features and press desire into her skin, the sight of him stroking her hot spots and eliciting sweet moans sent me to the brink. I couldn't stop myself from stroking my length while I watched, picturing her lips around my cock while Morgan tongued her from behind.

My imagination may have run away from me, but the reality

of Clover half-naked in my home singes my mind. I can't get rid
of it. I don't want to.

I want *more*.

A tree grows directly outside Clover's window, elongated and
twisted from centuries of time. I climb it smoothly, as familiar
with its knots and limbs as I would be if ever given the opportunity to explore Clover. Perching on a thick branch and under the
cover of its thinned, gnarled children, I peek through the wood
and into Clover's window, the curtains conveniently parted;
otherwise, I would've jimmied the window and done it myself.

The lights flicker on, putting her in stark relief as she inspects
my trinket. Her thin, perfect fingers stroke the box like a lover.
My dick lengthens at the sight. I bring a hand to it, both pushing
it into submission and relishing the blood flow that the sight of
Clover brings. Only she can make my cock this hard this
suddenly, and I've never touched her.

She opens it. I hold my breath. My grip spasms against my
balls. Clover pulls out my note, penned for anyone who might
come across the present but written only for her, my lucky
clover.

I trace her features as if I were standing directly in front of
her, stroking the curve of her lips as they tilt up, brushing against
the skin under her eyes as they crinkle with an emotion I've only
seen on other people. Sweetness. Warmth.

Every one of her freckles cresting across her nose makes their
way into my memories as I soak in her wonder at receiving such
an important gift. From me. I'll replay this in my mind on a loop
for the rest of my life, especially when she presses the note to her
chest, then gently puts it aside.

The minute Clover pulls out Sarah's spell book, and with a
flawless gasp, drops it onto her bed and retreats like it's on fire, I
pull back, scale through the branches and leap off the trunk.

I don't care what she does with the Anderton book. I only

wanted to witness her reaction to my gesture, and it went beautifully.

Every time she goes to that book, she'll think of me, perhaps as much as I've been picturing her.

I hope when she lays in her bed sheets tonight, she'll sense my presence there mere hours ago and how I jerked off in her scent.

Of course, I cleaned up after myself. I wanted my essence there, my spirit to mix with hers. Maybe, when her eyes drift shut, she'll scent me before she dreams of me.

With a pair of her underwear tucked safely in my pocket, I know I'll be doing the same.

My phone vibrates in my pocket as soon as my feet hit the packed earth. I pull it out with a frown.

Tempest: Get back to the cottage. Now.

THIN GRAY WISPS of clouds scud across the sky, obliterating any light through the skeletal forest canopy. It's a path I've walked countless times, the blackness merely acting like a comforting blanket during my stroll.

Unlocking the front door to Anderton Cottage, I expect to see the Vultures convalescing in the main room near the crackling fireplace, arguing politely but decapitating each other with their imaginations.

We weren't brought together because we got along.

The entryway is unlit and so is the fireplace, the wingback chairs and couch empty.

There's only one other place they could be.

I swing to the right and stop at the wall covered with bookshelves.

Clover's spirit appears in front of me, her body writhing, her image blue-white smoke against the shape of Morgan, bowing to her at his knees.

I keep my focus on the memory of her face. Clover's lips splitting open with an orgasmic cry, my cock twitching at her every spasm.

Blinking out of it, I force the remembrance to disappear and return to the task at hand.

A map of the original Titan Falls settlement is on the wall beside the bookshelves. I swing it open.

It took Morgan multiple attempts before he figured out there was an electronic keypad behind the map to unlock the trapdoor. I revealed it on the first try.

In less than five seconds, a section of the bookcase unlatches, and I pull it open and slip through, shutting it behind me.

A single bulb illuminates my descent, the mutterings of my brethren hitting my ears soon after.

All my previous steps are expected. What hitches my stride is when I make it to the concealed room and notice who sits within the circle of Vultures.

Sitting is such a kind term. More like strapped in.

I angle my head. "Why do we have Xavier Altese tied up in our basement?"

Tempest whips around at my voice. "Good. You're here."

I take my place beside him, folding my arms and studying the desperate eyes of Xavier over his gag while the tendons in his arms pop from pulling against his restraints.

They've zip-tied his ankles to each front chair leg. His clothes are on, a dirty white tank and black slacks. His feet are filthy and bare, like they dragged him through the woods in this state.

I say through the side of my mouth for Tempest's ears only, "I thought I was responsible for retrieval."

"This is a special case," Tempest replies, then tips his chin in the direction across Xavier's head where Rossi fumes nearby.

Rossi nods his head in greeting to me. "A local man was reported missing a few days ago. He was found a few hours ago. Dismembered."

I raise a brow in question. I assumed Xavier was down here because he danced with Clover. Any other boy would be. With Rossi's statement, however, perhaps it's just a side benefit that neither Tempest nor I will argue with.

"We don't know who did it," Rossi continues, "only that it occurred the moment we allowed this boy on campus. A boy connected to our world and who is more than willing to screw us over."

Xavier shakes his head in a panic, denying Rossi's statement.

To my left, Morgan remains stoic, but I catch the twitch at the corner of his mouth after Rossi finishes.

My eyes narrow. Morgan's changed his shirt, no longer bloodied from the supposed black magic ceremonial shit he'd seduced Clover with. The image of her on top of him, then him between her legs, ripples into my vision, but I shake it off. My territorial nature is best redirected at the moment.

I take precious seconds to study the collar of Morgan's clean shirt where I noticed most of the blood on his old one. More of a spray pattern of a live victim than the throat-slashing sacrifice of a dead animal if you ask me.

Nobody asks.

"Tempest," Rossi commands, "go into the chest and find your favorite weapon."

Xavier wheezes, his admittedly startling green eyes blood-shot and bulging.

Tempest nods and strides to the old apothecary chest, one of the last remnants of Sarah Anderton's brutal work in this base-ment and also where I found her grimoire.

He pulls open a small drawer and pulls out his garrote, a specialty of his.

Chair legs scrape audibly across the floor as poor Xavier, noticing what's in Tempest's hand, tries to hop away.

Morgan grins. "Oh, goody. A struggle."

Tempest positions himself behind Xavier.

"He should say his piece," I cut in before Tempest can raise his weapon.

Tempest glances at me with caution. Once Rossi initiates a command, we're not supposed to question it.

"We've allowed targets in the past to say a few words," I say. "Why not this one?"

"What's with the sudden, full-on sentences, Tongueless?"

I ignore Morgan.

"Rio does have a point," Tempest muses between snapping the garrote taut between his hands. He stares at the top of Xavier's head with a mixture of bloodlust and disappointment. "And Morgan, you do love it when they beg."

"Can't argue with that," Morgan says, yet his expression seems oddly against allowing Xavier to talk.

I angle my head again, chewing on the inside of my cheek while I regard him.

What's he hiding?

Rossi rolls back his broad shoulders. "Xavier can have the floor for a moment. I'm interested in his motives to kill a local. Did you truly believe killing a farmer would bring enough scrutiny to expose us?"

I have to agree. What talents can a twenty-year-old lamed soccer player bring to the mafia? Is he really so brilliant as to fuel the town's rumors about people going missing?

Movement from Rossi distracts me. In a blur of motion, he pulls out a switch blade and swings it in a vicious arc, embedding it under the kneecap of Xavier's bad knee.

Xavier's cry is more of a muffled attempt to vomit. His head falls back, and he gurgles to the ceiling, tears leaking from his eyes and pooling in his ears.

Rossi pulls the blade out, Xavier stiffening, then heaving from the unexpected removal.

"That is so you know we're serious," Rossi says mildly while wiping his knife with a handkerchief.

I step forward and pull the gag from Xavier's mouth. While he spits out pieces of black fabric from the dirty rag splitting his jaw apart, I ask, "Why did the Bianchis want to bring you here?"

Xavier's throat bobs, a sheen of sweat coating his upper lip. His head droops. "I-I was dumb. Made a mistake. Fell out of love with the wrong girl and tried to break up with her. She—her family was the O'Malleys."

A family the Bianchis have generations of beef with. But I knew all this. He told me when I picked him up at The Boiler.

This is more so the others can hear.

"I didn't, well, I kind of knew who she was, but I was making loads of money, in all the gossip rags, famous in all the right ways, and I thought I was untouchable."

"She's the daughter of Magnus O'Malley, you moron," Morgan says, shaking his head with an eye roll. "You couldn't have chosen, oh, a distant cousin or adopted niece? It had to be the clan chief's daughter?"

"Like I said, I was arrogant. And I paid for it with a permanent injury and the inability to play football for the rest of my life."

"That's not enough of a reason," Tempest says behind him. "How did the Bianchis get you from the O'Malleys? Why were you sent to us?"

"They—he, Magnus, sold me, as some sort of offering. I was useless goods without my knee. I begged him, *begged* him, to use me for other means, like throwing games and making him money, but in his words, breaking his daughter's heart meant breaking my legs."

"He allowed you to keep your life. That's a positive," Morgan adds merrily. "My uncle wouldn't be so gracious."

Xavier continues, "The ... what's his name, Marco Bianchi, your uncle, sent me here. To become one of you. A Vulture. He wants me to work for you guys. That's it, I promise. I didn't go looking for targets or debtors or whatever the fuck you call them, and I certainly didn't kill anybody to bring you under suspicion. I can't—the thought of—" Xavier gags, either from the lasting pain of getting his kneecap dislocated again or the thought of taking a life. Probably both.

Rossi clucks his tongue. "The men Bianchi's sending me just get weaker and more pathetic."

Morgan frowns. "Hey. I was the last guy sent here before Sports Balls."

"I know," Rossi answers dryly.

"I torture with the best of them!" Morgan defends. "You want a trophy head? A finger necklace? I'm your guy."

Morgan continues to argue, and Tempest twirls his garrote impatiently between his fingers. I use the distraction to observe Xavier, noting every twitch, every wheeze, and his defeated slump. The boy just had a knife twisted through scar tissue of the knee, one of the most painful experiences you can give a person, yet he's not begging for his life.

The answer strikes me immediately. Xavier accepts his fate because he truly does not want to be here and would rather die than become a Vulture who kills in excess and without mercy.

"I believe him."

My quiet words break through the other men's words.

Tempest sighs and reluctantly pockets his weapon. "I do, too."

"What?" Morgan asks. "But we haven't even taken any

fingernails or broken any toes. Fucking kindergarten is what this is. Rossi?" Morgan splays out his hands to our leader. "Are you going to allow this to stand? This boy went rogue, which is strictly forbidden. He deserves to die slowly, painfully, and preferably in my salt circle so I can take his heart."

If possible, Xavier's eyes widen farther. "No. Please. You don't have to do this. I won't say anything, all right? I'll be so invisible you'll barely notice me. You don't even have to train me. Just let me pretend to be a normal student, graduate, and then—"

"What? Go back across the pond for a happily ever after?" Rossi gives a fatherly, doting grin, but it's terrifying on a face like his. "Come now, boy, you understand we can't do that. What we must do is make you a Vulture, in the same way Tempest, Rio, and yes, Morgan was, too, although they came from vastly darker backgrounds than you."

"You mean, you're really not killing him?" Morgan pouts. "We can't even have one thumb as a warning token?"

"What's more important is the discovery of who murdered a farmer. If Xavier knows nothing, then we have to expand our interrogations. Perhaps to a family we're at war with."

"That leaves a lot of families to go through," Morgan points out. "My uncle doesn't enjoy making friends."

Rossi exhales through his nose in thought. "This isn't ideal."

"No," Tempest agrees. He shares a long look with his boss, a silent communication I read as *we have to find the individual responsible so we can figure out who wants us dead.*

"Where did you get that blood on your shirt?" I ask Morgan.

Morgan startles, recovering enough to glance over at me innocently. "Hmm?"

"The blood I noticed earlier on your white work shirt. After your scuffle with Clover upstairs."

Tempest goes rigid. "Excuse me?"

Xavier's chin snaps up with a surprising amount of energy at the mention of Clover's name.

I smile at Morgan, closed-mouthed and without using the rest of my face. "Care to explain?"

Morgan laughs, forceful and loud, as he raises his hands in surrender. "There's nothing to expand on, my friends. I discovered Clover in our house that she was expressly forbidden to enter—"

Tempest growls, "My sister will be the death of me, not some mafia rival."

"And I told her she should leave before any of you came home. So she did. Right, Rio? You witnessed her leave unharmed and untouched."

Morgan's testing me.

What Morgan doesn't yet understand is, I meet little fires with bombs.

"Was this before or after you pushed her against the wall or fought with her until she landed on top of you?" I ask.

After a moment of appalled silence where Tempest processes the information, he takes a threatening step forward. Morgan raises his chin toward him on a dare, allowing Tempest to think the worst.

What a stupid thing to do.

Even Rossi's features darken, his stare intent on Morgan. "You'd better explain yourself before I replace Xavier with your insipid form. I don't care whose blood you carry in your veins."

Morgan looses a breath in a tight-lipped huff. "It was dark, I didn't know who she was at first. I think we can all agree the girl loves to dress in black and skulk around old buildings without any fear of getting caught or hurt. So yes, I did restrain her—*temporarily*," Morgan enunciates the last word before Tempest can take another step toward him, fists clenched.

"Then we talked," Morgan continues. "Briefly. Politely. I was ever the gentleman."

He sends me a warning look in case I want to interject, like I didn't notice the animalistic sounds he made while he sucked her pussy dry.

Frankly, I'm enjoying his discomfort too much. But I'll keep what I witnessed to myself, until a more opportune time arises.

I say, "I can vouch that Clover left without any injuries, so your interaction with her doesn't explain the visible blood on your clothes."

Morgan glares at me. "*Why* have you picked tonight of all nights to discover that your mouth works?"

Because I'm still on the high of two delicious yet very different tasting Clover sightings in one night. Of gifting her a token only I could bestow on her. Of seeing her smile, a delighted curve of her lips meant just for me.

I stay silent.

Morgan puffs out an impatient breath. "I was coming from the woods when I ran into Clover. Doing my usual nightly ritual, thanking Satan for my life, all the sorts of things you three are vastly uninterested in, and it involved some animal blood. That's all."

"It smelled human," I say.

"The fuck?" Morgan squints at me. "How does one smell the difference between animal blood and human blood? Have you become Mowgli all of a sudden? Who am I kidding?" Morgan laughs. "Of course you have. You spend more nights out in the forest than you do in your own bed. You probably fuck wolves in your spare time—"

"Which gives Rio a lot more credibility than you," Tempest warns. "If he smells the metallic tang of a person rather than the fetid stench of an animal carcass, I'm taking his word for it."

My mouth softens at my best friend vouching for me. Indeed,

there is a distinct difference between a dead animal and a live, pleading person.

The latter being Morgan's preference.

"Goddammit, it was you," Rossi realizes. He storms past a wisely silent Xavier and catches Morgan by the throat, tossing him against the wall like shipwrecked debris.

Morgan lands with an audible thump but doesn't stop laughing as he struggles back into a stand. "You know, I came back to this ridiculous cottage thinking you'd be *proud* that I found the source of the rumors and slayed him. It's not my fault you Vultures wandered around with your heads cut off, unable to stop the townsfolk from speculating over your kills. Such amateurs, making it look like wild animal attacks." Morgan glares my way. "But then Rossi comes back with this toothpick of an athlete under his arm, demanding answers on why a local farmhand was killed. That looks to me that I made the wrong move." Morgan brushes off his pants as he regards us one by one. "Why would that be? *Why* would my brothers not want me to nip that gossip in the bud, hmm? A local murder will certainly redirect the police from looking further into the increased bear attacks around here. Besides"—Morgan flaps his hand dismissively—"I left enough evidence to solidly frame his eldest son."

Shit. I doubt it occurred to Rossi that Morgan would take it upon himself to help us put a stop to the growing interest in our covered-up kills. Up until this point, Morgan's made it clear he doesn't care for his uncle's instructions and would much rather wait for the victims to be located and trussed up for him so he can play with his devil's toys.

It's a total surprise that he'd take the initiative—and suspicious as fuck.

Tempest feels the same. "Why are you suddenly intent on living up to your Vulture role?"

Morgan shrugs, but I catch the bleakness in his eyes. "If I'm to live out the rest of my days here as a glorified professor, I might as well impress my uncle and give myself a little freedom."

"And get closer to us." I tap my chin in thought. "Why be a participating brother?"

Is it to stay close to Clover? I almost ask before stopping myself.

Morgan shrugs again. "Family protects family. That motto is practically carved into my skin by my uncle's favorite knife. I would never have hurt Clover, Storm Cloud," Morgan unexpectedly beseeches. I stiffen as if he read my thoughts. "Believe me on that. She's ... special."

No one has time to reflect on the odd cadence to his tone because Rossi immediately accuses, "You were about to let Xavier take the fall."

"Yes, well, obviously," Morgan says. "He's a limp noodle."

Xavier finds enough strength to sneer at him.

"Why not tell us outright?" Tempest asks.

"Because I *love* this," Morgan says brightly. "The game, the intrigue, the fucking panic in your faces when you realized you were intercepted. Let that be your lesson: I'm smarter than I look."

"Fine," Rossi grunts.

He stuffs his hands in his pockets, glancing back and forth between Xavier and Morgan as if deciding what to do with his new, reluctant initiates. Tempest and I have been loyal to him for years. These two, though? Fuck knows.

"As your reward," Rossi continues, directing his words at Morgan. "You can be responsible for training Xavier and making him live up to our standards."

"*What?*" Both Xavier and Morgan protest.

"Anyone but him," Xavier begs. "I'll take..." He glances at

Tempest warily, then slides over to me. "Him. Rio. You can train me."

"I'm afraid Rio is often off-site, gathering intel and bodies for us," Rossi says. "And Tempest is much too valuable an asset to waste his time with a newborn."

"What am I, then?" Morgan asks.

"An annoyance," Rossi snaps. "But a necessary one. You've proven yourself useful today, I suppose, if the framing of the son pans out. I'd like you to continue to be useful and work with Xavier. Bring him to a passable skill level."

"I don't want..." Xavier sighs and trails off, earning him more respect from me by continuing not to beg for his life. "All right, then. Please untie me."

"Aw." Morgan pats Xavier's head as he passes by. "He said please."

I do the honors, pulling out the blade in my ankle-holster and unsnapping the zip ties holding Xavier down.

He immediately tries to stand and just as quickly starts to pass out. I catch him mid-fall, shaking him awake, then throwing his arm around my shoulder and trudging upstairs with the poor boy.

No one agrees to this life, but at least Tempest and I witnessed it since childbirth. This kid? He has no idea of the purgatory he's agreed to, just to preserve his feeble life.

I'm the first to push through the bookcase and return to the main room of the cottage where I'm not surprised to find Ardyn anxiously sitting.

Her head shoots up at my footsteps. She pushes off the chair, aiming for Xavier.

"Is he okay?" she asks, then says more to herself, "If he's still alive, then that means he's innocent. Good. I'm such an idiot for letting him dance with Clover..."

I let Xavier slide onto the couch in a shaking heap, leaving the mess for Ardyn to clean up. She endured the worst and still came out kind. Ardyn will know what to do to return him to sanity.

"Can I make you some soup?" she soothes while rubbing his arm. "Tea? Super-strong painkillers?"

Tempest shadows me temporarily before moving to his love, staring at her with a fondness he reserves for no one else but his sister.

It pains me that he's allowed Ardyn full entry into our sinful life but clings to the veil protecting his sister. What Ardyn did to gain such access into Tempest's true self, I wish I knew.

All I understand is, Tempest can never find out just how badly I want Clover to accept me the way Ardyn has rallied around him.

CHAPTER 18
CLOVER

S arah Anderton's grimoire smells foul.

My nose is in a permanent wrinkle as I carefully turn its pages, unsure if the spillage of her apothecary poisons or ancient blood stains are the cause of the decaying, sour scent that wafts into my face every time I think I've gotten used to it.

Hermione is long gone, choosing the smells behind the toilet rather than subjugating herself to the further insult of my refusal to put this thing away.

Sarah's writing has me spellbound, my eyes hungrily devouring her potion recipes, spell casting rituals, and curses. It's fascinating, really, how advanced in science she was compared to the limited knowledge of those in the 1700s. She knew the exact mixing of chemicals that peers in my chemistry class still can't manage to complete without smoking out the room.

The scraping of a branch across the window snags my attention. I raise my head, blinking out of the grimoire's fugue, and notice the time. It's well after midnight. I have an early study session with Xavier tomorrow, a time I reluctantly agreed to because it was the only opening I had in my schedule.

I just hope I can keep my hands off him and memories of our explosive sex on a hard lockdown while I try to impart knowledge on the guy. I mean, it's not his fault that both he and academics talk turn me on. I'm an adult; I can be a professional tutor. Not that I've ever tutored a gorgeous ex-athlete before.

Especially after having both his and our professor's tongue between my legs.

Suddenly hot, I rise from my kneel at the side of the bed, carefully lifting and placing the grimoire in a spare leather satchel tucked under the mattress. Hopefully, it's enough to contain the yuck smell, or I can sleep through it nose blind. There's no way I'm letting it out of my sight, so I better get used to it.

Another scrape sounds against my window. I whip my head toward it, focusing harder.

A shadow, darker than the night, takes form. Small, like a raccoon or an extra-portly squirrel. It's hard to tell with the reflection of my dorm room's light.

Galvanized now, I flick the switch so the night outside can absorb my room, too.

The shadow grows eyes.

A sound like an *eek* leaves my lips. I scuttle back, nailing my rump on the corner of my desk chair.

The eyes don't follow. In fact, they stare straight ahead, vacant.

My forehead tightens as I tiptoe forward, unable to resist a closer look now that it doesn't seem to be alive and ready to claw at my face.

I push the window open with a *shush* of sound, the frigid air goose-pimpling my skin as soon as I do.

Once the barrier of the window's gone, I can see the thing in detail.

Jesus.

Not an overfed squirrel. Not a raccoon.

A porcelain doll.

One who looks just like me, with glass eyes and copper irises, cascading black hair, and wearing a pristine ivory dress like those in the Victorian era or the pilgrim era.

She sits prettily on the sill, and as I bend down, I notice the smattering of freckles on her nose, some on her arms and legs. The bigger ones are in the exact spots I have them on my skin.

My stomach goes cold.

I notice an envelope nestled against her lace corset. Tentatively I take it from her and open it.

I'm always watching you.

I rub my lips together to stop their trembling. My focus darts outside, scanning with sharp awareness.

Someone had to climb this tree to put this doll here. They would've seen me stooped over the grimoire in the middle of the room, so consumed by Sarah's writings that I wouldn't notice a doll—a creepy porcelain avatar of me—being settled against my window as a treat for later.

And that's how I think of it: this person thought it was a gift, a compliment, a sweet gesture.

"Rio," I whisper, lifting the doll carefully.

Squinting, I scan her empty eyes. She smells old and musty, yet her clothes aren't yellowed with age. Her hair is perfectly combed, like someone's been grooming it and making her perfect before they gave it away.

The freckles look new, the ink stark against the pale face. Drawn on.

Rio's aware of what I like. The creepier, the better. And what's more unsettling than haunting porcelain dolls?

Nestling her against my side, I shut the window against the wintry chill and place her on my dresser below my mirror.

"I wish you would just tell me how you feel," I whisper to her, then tidy up the rest of my mess and get ready for the night.

After I've showered and changed, I tuck myself into bed. Hermione braves another venture, notices the new decoration, and curves her back and hisses at it before she curls up against my face, as if to protect me from the doll getting a good look at me while I'm vulnerable and can't defend myself while I sleep.

CHAPTER 19

CLOVER

My dreams consist of a porcelain doll come to life and leading me to a meadow with a sky painted in ash-ink calligraphy and a complete view of the most poisonous flowers and mushrooms to fell the strongest of men.

A crack of sunlight drifts across my eyes, waking me better than my alarm. I rub my eyes against the brightness and gently nudge Hermione out of the way to get ready to meet Xavier. Before I leave, I make sure to slide the grimoire out from my bed, cover it in one of my scarves, and tuck it into my backpack. I wave farewell to my new friend before leaving.

Xavier's found a table inside the library by the time I swipe through the turnstile and enter the ground floor's study section. He lifts his head from the textbook he was reading, sees me, and offers a half-hearted wave.

My stomach flutters when we make eye contact, but not in a good way. Xavier's eyelids are lowered with heavy bags under them, his lips downturned. When he waves, his hand barely lifts from the table.

"Hey," I greet, sliding in across from him.

He nods, then rubs a hand down his face.

"Are you okay?" I ask.

"Yeah, fine." He doesn't make eye contact. "Long night, is all."

I busy myself by plopping my bag in the vacant chair next to me and pulling out our assignments. It's then I notice the crutches leaning against the end of the table.

My eyes slide back to him. "Do you want to talk about it?"

Xavier notices where my attention is split. "Not even slightly."

I've had enough experiences with my brother to understand when to back off. It doesn't stop my mind from whirring and wondering what happened. Did he trip on the many uneven pathways at this campus? Get too drunk at the Meat House party last night and fall? Or is it something more malevolent, like meeting the male version of Minnie?

I dismiss that last one. Guys like Xavier don't have to deal with bullies or people who have a problem with oddballs and weirdos. Xavier is as handsome and sought after as they come. The only enemies gods have are other gods.

As if to prove my point, a trio of guys wander by searching for a free table. They notice Xavier and slap him on the shoulder in greeting as they pass. The table across from us filled with sophomore girls keep sneaking glances at him and whispering to each other beneath their hands. Even the librarian does a double take when she spots him as she pushes the return trolly past.

"Good god, what is that smell?"

My hand pauses inside my bag at Xavier's vocal disgust. "Um..."

"It's like someone brought their vomit from last night with them to eat for breakfast," he says while gagging on air.

I subtly zip my bag shut and shove it onto the ground. "Yeah, who knows what people drag into the library with them on Saturday mornings."

"Oh, good." Xavier sniffs again. "It seems to have dissipated."

"Should we get started?" I ask brightly.

"Let's."

His enthusiasm matches that of mine when facing a chemistry test.

I fold my arms across the table, leaning closer. "Have you figured out a topic for your occult studies essay yet?"

"Not really. Haven't had the time."

I furrow my brow. Then I think, *screw it*. "Do I have to remind you that you asked me to be here? You charmed your way into getting my help, yet you're sitting across from me like you'd rather be anywhere else." I slide my books closer to me and stack them. "Frankly, so would I. This is a waste of my time."

Xavier jerks upright. "No-no, Clover, wait."

He folds his hand over mine, stopping me from pulling my books to my chest and standing. His warm, dry touch reinvigorates the *zing* of our first meeting. "It isn't you, promise. There's ... fuck, I can't exactly explain it, but I'm going through a lot right now. What has kept me going, though, the *only* thing I've been looking forward to, is meeting you. Being here with you. So please, don't go." He smiles with true sincerity. "I promise I'll try to get past your utter beauty and listen to what that lush mouth of yours has to say on the dark arts."

It has the intended affect. The tension around my eyes dissolves. "You're too smooth for your own good. And you can't possibly be that interested in the occult sciences and parapsychology."

"When it comes from you, I'm all but addicted."

His corny lines should have me cringing, but with that accent of his, I practically puddle to his feet.

I cover it up by saying, "All right, Romeo. Let's get down to a topic that interests you so you can impress one person you need to—Professor Morgan."

Xavier visibly stiffens. He falls back into his seat, clearing his throat. "Yeah. Right."

Strange reaction aside, Xavier seems to be ready to learn, so I launch into the part of the syllabus he missed, catching him up on Morgan's class discussions.

He listens intently, but I start to note the flinch every time I mention the professor's name.

I want to ask Xavier about it, but whenever I try, he gets bolder with his flattery or asks me to clarify something. I can't argue with either.

"I'm *so* sorry to interrupt, but this is the only table with seats left," an overly sultry voice says behind me.

Xavier pauses in his follow-up question and stares over my head, his expression bland despite my knowing *exactly* who's standing behind me.

The gorgeous, voluptuous, blond Minnie Davenport.

Any red-blooded man would fall over himself to get her to sit next to him, but all Xavier does is hike a brow, then direct his gaze at me.

He says, "Clover, do you mind?"

Yes, 1000 percent yes.

But a quick glance around proves that Minnie's right—there aren't any study tables left. "She can sit."

"Gosh, thank you for your generosity, Clover," Minnie simpers. I catch the subtle, hard edge to her voice as she rounds the table.

"I don't think we've officially met," she says to Xavier with her carefully crafted *come fuck me* voice. "I'm Minnie."

She tries to perch next to Xavier before Xavier sticks out his hand to stop her.

"Sorry, darling," he says to her, "but Clover and I are in the middle of important coursework, and if you'll be sitting with us, I'd like her closer to me so we can chat without disturbing you."

A flush of warmth hits my cheeks, heating further when Xavier's green eyes snag mine with the type of gaze that includes me and no one else. "Care to join me, Clover?"

I lick my lips to cover my smile at the way my name sounds coming from his mouth—*Clo-vah.*

I stand, aware of Minnie's death-eating glare the entire time I shift my things over to Xavier.

"There you go, Min," Xavier says. "You can take Clover's old spot."

Minnie forces a smile. "Great idea."

I make myself comfortable beside Xavier while the smell he brought with him to the forest floor encompasses me, bringing with it the memory of him sucking on my nipples in the cold.

My breaths stutter. I cover it by laying out my notes and pointing at the pertinent ones Xavier should copy down.

With a knowing grin, Xavier cants his head to the side and squeezes my thigh before writing what I tell him.

"I like a woman who knows how to boss me around," he jokes.

Minnie makes a sound of disgust across from us. Before I can respond, she checks her phone, then whirls around in her seat, gesturing for her two friends to join us.

"Fuck," I whisper, slumping in my seat.

Kirsty and Lauren eye our table as they approach, their expressions flitting between revulsion to calculation to flirtation when they realize Minnie's not sitting with me—she's sitting with Xavier.

"All right, love?" Xavier murmurs into my ear.

I shiver at his warm breath tickling my nape and straighten. "Nothing I haven't dealt with before. Let's keep going."

Minnie's friends take their seats beside her. They communicate with Minnie silently with their *Mean Girl* eyes before Lauren glances over at me and says, "That's quite the shiner you have there. I hope you didn't break your face too hard."

My jaw hardens. "It takes more than knock-off Valentino shoes to throw me off my game."

All three of them sneer, but not so much that Xavier would catch it and think less of them. No, they're too good at subterfuge to come across as so blatantly basic.

I inch closer to him and lower my voice so he has to lean into me, putting us in our own private bubble that Minnie's jealousy practically begs to pierce.

I'm enjoying annoying her way too much.

Minnie's momentarily distracted from us when there's a beep at the library's turnstiles and a man steps in, the type of man who sucks all the energy from the room and brings it upon himself as a spotlight.

An audible hush spreads through the library as heads pop up from their textbooks and everybody looks to where Professor Morgan navigates the tables with a self-deprecating grin.

My lips pull to one side as I watch him, intent on dismantling his facade and find the true man who's arrogantly basking in the attention.

Morgan knows he's hot. He's accepted that many of the women in this room have named their vibrators after him.

I can't say I'm turned off by his hidden, cocky attitude. I'm drawn to it, even when Xavier is idly tracing figure 8s on my thigh. Morgan was so professional, so calm, so utterly twisted when stroking his hands down my bare hips.

I'm so busy observing Morgan that I fail to notice how Xavier's teasing fingers have stopped until Morgan's practically on top of us.

My leg hits Xavier's, and it's like hitting a stack of cinder blocks. I glance over at him in confusion.

"Miss Callahan," Morgan says smoothly, "Mr. Altese, working hard on your final essays, I hope?"

We're saved from having to respond when Minnie pipes up. "Professor Morgan, hi! I can't wait to participate in your class next semester. I hear your class is amazing."

I suppress an eye roll. She's after me constantly for my love of witches and the underworld, yet get a hot guy to talk about it and she's all ears. Leave it to Minnie not to sense one iota of danger in this man when he practically screams it at me.

"I'll be glad to have you," Morgan answers smoothly, then swings his gaze back to me. "Can I help answer any questions?"

The mirth behind his eyes is heavy with meaning. Morgan stares at me like he's remembering how I taste, and that makes me think about how his tongue felt during my blinding orgasm.

I shift and cross my legs. "Not so far."

Xavier's so taut, he's vibrating.

The two men exude powerful, opposite sensations so tangible that one side of me is ice and the other fire.

The blue of Morgan's eyes darkens as he assesses Xavier. He blinks, then recovers with a wide smile. To anyone else, it'd seem genuine and innocent. To me, it looks like he's hungry.

My insides twist, and I'm horrified to realize it's not in alarm. It's in *heat.*

"Very well." Morgan taps his knuckles lightly on the table before retreating. "I'll be nearby grading sophomore papers. Feel free to seek me out if there's a need."

I nod, pulling my lips in as he walks away. I'm conscious of Minnie's study on the side of my face, her expression akin to *what could these guys possibly be interested in?*

Ignoring it, I focus on Xavier. When I look at his face, I realize maybe I was better off figuring out Minnie's mood.

Xavier stares at Morgan's back with such abject hate that it spreads tangibly between us, like ink dropped in water. I haven't known Xavier very long, but this is an emotion I never thought would mar his features, as chiseled and sun soaked as he is.

Hate doesn't belong on a man this beautiful.

My heart lurches. I lay a hand on his forearm, squeezing to get his attention. "Xavier?"

He sucks in a breath like he'd forgotten to take in oxygen. He glances down at me, his expression softening as fast as a switch being flicked. He lays his hand on my thigh again, this time leaving it there. "Where were we?"

"Right at the—" I cut off when I feel his hand travel up my leg, his fingers tickling my inner thigh.

I bite my lip at the sensation, glancing at Xavier's face to decipher his intentions. I'm appalled to realize he's staring at Morgan while he traces over my leggings. Morgan's found a seat at the other end, easily kicking out the students and snagging the table for himself. His head is bent, deeply focused on his papers, but every now and then, he looks up, his eyes glazing over Xavier and landing on me until I furtively look away.

Xavier's fingers don't relent.

I breathe through my nose while I figure out whether to stop this. But it's Minnie's snide mocking and her obvious remarks to her friends about me that cement my answer.

Xavier won't be the only person to get something out of this.

I lean back and spread my legs, allowing him better access.

His lips part in shock, but he scrawls on his notepad like he's actually writing sensible things while his other hand draws circles against my sex.

I hiss in a breath. Never have I wished for crotchless leggings until this moment.

I reach under the table and take his hand, guiding it under the hem of my pants and pushing it down my stomach until his fingers reach my bare folds. I have to resist letting my head fall back as he parts them and curls one finger inside me.

Writhing in my seat, I lift my hips a desperate few inches. Xavier's attention stays on his notes but his teeth flash with a satisfied grin as he flicks my clit and tugs on it, shooting electricity down my thighs and through my belly.

I lean forward, putting an elbow on the table and covering my mouth to stifle the moans.

Minnie glances over, but at my benign smile, she narrows her eyes, then goes back to her studies.

I look at Xavier and giggle softly until I register the intensity in which he's tracing my face with his eyes.

I lose a breath. Blood flows into my cheeks.

He breaks our heated connection to write something down, then slides it over to me.

I want to see you come while following library rules: Quiet, please.

I open my mouth wide to inhale enough oxygen. His relentless hand strokes down my slit and back up, circling my clit with his thumb in the same way his tongue did, but this time choosing to be slow, drawing out my pleasure but refusing the climax.

"Xavier..." I whisper brokenly.

He brings a finger to his lips, partially obscuring his smile. *Shhh...*

Minnie is so close that if I slide down my chair, our knees will knock together. I resist the urge to melt and clutch at the edges of my chair instead, air hissing through my teeth.

"You good over there?" Minnie asks, sounding like she could give two fucks.

"Fine," I reply tersely. My arms turn into lightning rods on either side of me. "Totally—good."

Xavier cups his chin in his free hand and studies his textbook, brows raised innocently as he works feverishly to bring me to a climax.

"F..." I have to stop myself from screaming.

The burn becomes a blossoming, then turns into heaven as it surges from Xavier's fingers and through my body.

I whimper, clutching his wrist to keep him there and prevent me from floating away.

Once I've caught my breath, Xavier gives me one last stroke before removing his hand. He leans back in his seat and I'm not even mad at the arrogant grin pulling at his mouth.

I open mine to whisper that one day I'll return the favor until I notice where his attention's gone.

He lifts his hand—the one that was inside me—and brings his fingers to his mouth, sucking them in to the bottom knuckle, then pulling them out casually.

All while his eyes are on Morgan.

While I'm processing what he's doing and *why*, my attention flits to Morgan, whose expression mirrors Xavier's: Categorical hatred.

Morgan's eyelids are at half mast, and he's staring at Xavier like he wants to kill him.

That doesn't make sense. What does Morgan care that Xavier just fingered me, other than it breaks school rules? Rules Morgan couldn't give a shit about?

"It makes no sense," I hear Minnie whisper to Kirsty and Lauren. "She's a fucking *freak*."

Suddenly, the air becomes thin. I don't enjoy being a pawn in anyone's game, yet it feels like I'm participating in a play where I don't know my lines.

The grimoire seems to pulse at my feet, urging me to take it and flee.

"I have to go," I say to no one, scraping my chair back and collecting my books.

It startles Xavier enough to say, "Really? But we were just getting started."

"Minnie can help you catch up in your other classes," I say. Minnie brightens at the mention of her name to Xavier. "I just realized how busy I am."

"Busy?" Xavier echoes, his angular cheeks making him seem more contrite than he actually is. *Damn that perfect bone structure.* "Are you sure? I'm happy to move this somewhere else..."

The suggestion is clear. But his little stare off with Morgan has left a peculiar taste in my mouth—not altogether bad, but definitely foreign. I shouldn't *enjoy* that Morgan probably knew what we were up to and watched the whole thing. Should I?

I definitely shouldn't imagine Morgan coming over and making out with me while Xavier finishes me off with his fingers.

With teacher-student group sex warring for my attention in my head, I get the hell out of the library, leaving a stunned Xavier and a furious Morgan behind, hoping that the stone walls are enough to put between them and me.

CHAPTER 20

CLOVER

I climb the staircase to my dorm room, becoming increasingly aware of the stillness around me. This usually brings me a sense of peace, but I'm overwhelmed with feelings of loneliness and desperation today.

Lonely for friendship and desperate to be wanted.

That melancholy trails me all the way to my door, my lips pursed, yet I'm not motivated to fix it. I kind of like the dark cloud hovering above me lately. It makes me believe I have secrets, like Tempest and Ardyn and all the rest. Even Xavier, who wants to explore my body yet cuts me off from discovering anything about him. Same with Rio.

Rio, who feeds my obsession.

Prickles of delight war with the invisible pall around my body as I pull out my keys and—

Hit the side of my doorframe. Rough and hard.

"What is it with you, huh?" a wet, fierce voice spits into my ear. "Why do hot guys adore you while everyone else is creeped out by you?"

At the second question, I understand who it is.

I respond, with my cheek squished up against the wood. "I assume those are rhetorical questions."

Minnie pushes off me with disgust. I have enough time to straighten from the door when Kirsty or Lauren or both grab me by the upper arms.

"Invite us in, would you?" Minnie smiles in my periphery, cat-like but not at all Hermione-like.

I don't struggle. Yet. "I'd rather not."

"Too bad."

With my arms locked behind me, Minnie yanks the keys out of my grip. "I was only asking because, unlike you, I grew up with etiquette."

My skin prickles with annoyance. "I left '*all these hot guys*' in the library. With *you*. Why bother tailing me when you could've used that beautiful etiquette of yours on them?"

Minnie's eyes narrow. "Because they seem to prefer dirty, outcast skanks over perfectly groomed women like me, and I want to know why."

"Well, I don't have the answers to their lack of attraction to you in my underwear drawer, so maybe don't look there."

"Careful." Minnie steps closer. Her voice is a low purr. "I may want to smash that face of yours more than I already have."

I smirk dangerously. "Careful, your etiquette is shining through."

Minnie whirls away and yanks open my bedroom door, forcing it open. Lauren and Kirsty shove me forward despite my feet dragging in protest.

"What do you want with me?" I demand of Minnie's back as she examines the room with contemptuous scrutiny. "Why give me all this attention? I'm happy to live in the shadows away from the three of you. I don't want anything to do with you."

"See, that's what gets me." Minnie spins around, her icy glare slicing into my flesh. "This act of yours is so revolting, yet it

draws a motherfucking harem of men. It shouldn't be possible—
you're a pathetic tease of a human being—but it works. And I'm
gonna figure out your secret."

I snort. "What harem? No guy wants—"

"Xavier Altese. Professor Morgan." Minnie ticks off her
fingers. "Fucking Professor *Rossi*, old enough to be your dad yet
looks at you like he wants to strip your clothes off. And Riordan
Hughes."

I bark out a laugh. "You're delusional. None of them have any
interest in getting to know me."

Xavier might like the sound of my orgasms, but I've yet to
see him want to dig into my mind. Morgan only wants me
because I'm forbidden, and he likes to see how far he can push
Tempest's little sister. Rossi is nothing but a fantasy, and Rio
...

Rio's been untouchable since we were children.

I add, "If anything, the only one who truly wants to understand me is you, and as far as I know, you're not into girls."

"Not swampy witch ones, anyway," Minnie agrees.

Her mouth sags with unenthusiasm. I relax in her friends'
hold. Maybe, if I bore her long enough, she'll want to leave and
go chase down one of the guys she mentioned.

A sinister thought hits me—I'd love to see one of them deal
with her.

I'm shocked to realize how much I want Minnie to discover
their hidden danger the hard way. I can't possibly be the only
one who senses it in them. And ... I wouldn't mind if her lesson
included violence.

This isn't you. Stop thinking this way.

Yet I can't stop. It's like Morgan inserted his poisoned tongue
inside me, and over time, my blood will turn black.

Minnie turns. "This is your side of the room, huh? "

Her gaze slides across my moon-phase comforter, the posters

of rune keys, the reed diffusers and line of crystals. She halts, her hateful eyes coming to rest on the porcelain doll on my dresser.

"What the ... *fuck* is *that*? Is that *you*?" Minnie's lips split open with heinous laughter. "Oh my god, did you have a crusty doll made in your likeness? Holy fuck, you are beyond gross. Guys, do you think it's haunted?" Minnie bends until she's eye to eye with it. "Do you think it sees me?"

"I hope it comes alive and takes your eyes for its own," I spit.

She grabs the Clover doll, holding it up. She dangles limply with no defenses. "Looks expensive."

"It means"—*everything*—"nothing. It was a cheap tourist piece the lady who owns the apothecary downtown gave me."

Minnie gives me the side-eye. She smirks, then throws it onto the ground with a sickening crash, shards of the doll's face flying everywhere and scraping over my skin as they land.

My body shakes, but I will myself to stay silent and stoic. Lauren chuckles behind me.

"Oh wow, Min, she's livid," Lauren sneers. "If I bend her over, she'll snap like a twig."

Minnie's grin widens into a devilish smile as she reaches for one of my crystals that I have collected for over ten years; some more rare than others, but all holding immense sentimental value.

When she hurls it against the wall above my bed, I buckle.

"Stop!" Though my body reverberates with shame, I plead softly, "Please."

Minnie's friends force me to stand and hold me still despite my desperate struggles, thrashing around my head and trying to use my teeth while they laugh hysterically at how helpless I am.

Minnie cackles amidst her noise of destruction, joyfully shattering each one of my crystals one after another.

The emotional pain becomes unbearable. I break down into tears.

Lauren and Kirsty hold me tighter and ask her gleefully, "What next?"

Minnie's predatory focus drops to my bedside drawer. "What do you have hidden in there, Clover? Something good, I'm sure. Something that'll make me very happy."

I pull against my human restraints but refuse to say anything that would spur her on.

Minnie snatches open the drawer, rummaging through my tarot cards and bottles of essential oils.

"Guys"—Minnie grins—"she really is a witch! What kind of spell are you casting on us without us knowing? Is that why you're so irresistible to all these boys?" She lifts each card up and rips it in half.

My heart shreds with them, and an animalistic scream tears out of my throat. I've done nothing to deserve this. I can't take it anymore.

Lifting my heel, I hammer it into the shin of Minnie's friend. She yelps in agony, both of their grips loosening. I shove against the other one—Lauren—but she recovers by looping an arm around my neck and dragging me back against her.

"Go get her bag!" Minnie bellows, standing safely away from any danger. She points at Kirsty who's jumping up and down, shaking off the pain in her leg. "I think she broke my bone!"

"You'll be fine," Minnie grits out. "Just get her bag. I bet she has more fucked-up witch shit in there, and I want it."

I pull against the forearm across my neck, scratching and baring my teeth. Lauren falters but pulls me harder against her chest. "Hurry, this trash panda might just break free."

Kirsty limps toward me, pulling back a few times when I snarl and snap at her.

I hate being small and defenseless. *Hate* it.

With two against one, Kirsty manages to get the bag off my

shoulder. She tosses it to Minnie, who searches it with feverish intent.

I watch uselessly, my vision fading when Lauren presses down on my trachea. *No, no, no.*

"What's this?"

Minnie pulls out the grimoire, wrapped carefully in my vintage Alexander McQueen skull scarf.

And like the idiot she is, she unwraps it.

"*Ugh!*" she says when the smell hits her. "What in the septic tank *hell* is this?"

Her gaze snaps up to mine. "You really are a Satan worshipper, aren't you? To be carrying around something so fucking repulsive."

Minnie's talking to me, but I don't hear her. It occurs to me that Sarah's grimoire smells so bad because she was probably trying to repel ignorant sphincters like Minnie Davenport.

"If you hate it so much, put it down," I grit against the pressure on my throat.

"I'll do better than that," she says, then turns and shoves open the window between Ardyn's and my beds.

Before I can protest, she flings it out the window. I hear the *thud* against the ground, and my eyes shutter in defeat.

"Um," Kirsty says worryingly beside me, "I think you're about to make her pass out, Lo."

"Really?" Lauren responds.

Their voices start fading in and out.

"Doesn't matter," Minnie says. "We're done here. Clover can't do anymore of her devil worship or cursing shit. We've made sure of that."

Lauren releases me. I drop to my knees at the sudden fresh air.

"Aren't so lucky now, are you?" Minnie laughs as she strolls past. "Maybe next time we cross paths, you'll know your place.

This campus may have had its fair share of witches, but they were tortured and hanged. Let that be a lesson to you."

At her friends' ushering, Minnie walks out of the room, slamming the door behind her and laughing down the hall.

With my head hanging low, I sit among the rubble of my beliefs, the talismans that gave me purpose and strength. I pick up two ripped halves of my tarot cards, one the Fool and the other the Magician.

And I wish Minnie a lifetime of pain.

There's a brush of softness against my arm. I lower my gaze, my heart swelling at the sight of Hermione, unhurt and shockingly affectionate.

I lift her to my chest and bury my face in her pure white fur.

"You hid behind the toilet again, didn't you?" I ask against her warm, purring body. "Good girl. Because they would've hurt you. With how feral they were..."

No. I won't think of it.

"I'll be okay," I assure Hermione before releasing her, though my voice is thick with the opposite of okay.

Wiping my eyes with the back of my sleeve, I struggle to my feet. When I'm sure Minnie's no longer in the hallway, I slink out and into the stairwell and down, in hopes of finding the grimoire so Sarah can help me curse Minnie, Lauren, and Kirsty into fucking oblivion.

CHAPTER 21

RIO

I join Ardyn and Tempest on their walk back to campus.

Tempest doesn't mind. I'm always by his side, anyway. He doesn't have to know my true motive: to get one last glimpse of Clover before I turn in for the night. I wouldn't even be able to admit the reasons to him if I wanted to—why her quiet expression and soulful eyes comfort me, how her presence makes me feel more human than weaponized beast.

The lovebirds talk idly as we stroll, the conversation carefully directed away from the violence of our current issue. Morgan's trying to be helpful to the Vultures, a fucking apocalypse of a problem if I've ever seen one. His little Dudley Do-Right adventure could ruin our comfortable abode at the isolated university.

Hopefully, commanding Morgan to train Xavier will be enough of a distraction for him not to fuck any more of our shit up.

Camden House looms in front of us, Ardyn and Tempest walking ahead of me with their joined hands swinging.

If I could smile, it would play at my lips as I observe my best friend act like a lovestruck teen in the midst of so much political tension.

As soon as my thoughts move toward the hope that I could have that one day, I shove them to the vault at the back of my mind and spin the lock. There isn't time for such fantasies.

We move through the foyer after Ardyn uses her key card to let us in. We take the elevator and arrive on Clover's floor without any other resident joining us. It's late—well past three o'clock in the morning, and the girls in this dorm are likely hungover from the night before, turning in and shutting off their lights with the goal of gathering enough energy to go hard another day.

To have that kind of life, full of studies and parties and light drug experimentation ... I'll never know what that's like. I haven't been trained for anything other than inflicting abuse and fear.

Then again, so has Tempest, yet he's found his light in the perpetual darkness.

No. Hope is for the weak.

Ardyn's the first to step through her door, and if it weren't for Tempest's and my above-average reflexes, we would've rammed into her back at her sudden halt.

"Clover? What's wrong? What happened?"

The fear in Ardyn's voice has my head snapping up. I'm propelling myself in front of both Ardyn and Tempest before I can rationalize otherwise.

A heart-wrenching image of Clover on the floor, surrounded by the debris of her precious relics with a despondent curtain of hair cloaking her features comes into view.

She doesn't glance up at Ardyn's question. She turns a yellowed, putrid page of the grimoire instead, awakening more spores and sending them into our nostrils.

Tempest and I don't react—we've smelled worse. Ardyn wrinkles her nose but has enough experience not to comment. Not when Clover's surrounded by such personal destruction.

Ardyn's shoes crunch against shattered crystal as she walks toward her.

I glance down at the sound, and notice, with bone-chilling clarity, the faceless trinket I gave her, cutting shards framing what used to be beautiful eyes in the perfect color.

"Clover?" Ardyn asks softly.

It takes effort to redirect my attention from the destruction, my chest tight and throat hot.

"Can you look at me?" Ardyn asks. "Did you do this?"

There's no need to ask that kind of follow-up. A brief once-over and I can note that Clover, while always in some kind of black clothing, wears it tonight not out of preference, but in mourning. The curve to her back shows her pain. The trembling of her fingers as she turns another page showcases her fury. And her refusal to meet the eyes of the people she loves most tells me she's grasping at the last of her strength because it's likely full of tears.

My hand twitches at my side, desperate to comfort my broken girl.

And a fire alights in my heart on who I'll have to kill now.

"Clover."

Tempest's voice seems to register with Clover. She jerks at the tone. Her voice follows, a wisp of what it once was. "You should leave me alone."

"Why?" Ardyn asks, then bends to Clover's level, resting on her heels. "We want to help. Talk to us."

"I don't want to explain," Clover says, her expression hidden by her dark locks. "I'm busy trying to find a curse of hellfire against my greatest enemy."

Ardyn rocks back. Tempest's brows jump in surprise. I'm not at all unsettled by the vengeful bent to Clover's motives. It's so much better than defeat.

"And ... who might that be?" Ardyn asks carefully.

At last, Clover looks up, her hair parted by the movement, and her eyes bright metal fire. "Minnie Davenport."

"She did this?" Tempest scans the debris around his sister. "Why the fuck?"

"Because she's a psychopath who blames all her failures on me," Clover says. "So I've decided to give her a *reason* to blame me. I'm going to kill her. Truly kill her with the worst curse Sarah Anderton can cook up."

Ardyn inches closer. "Maybe we should take a beat. Rest a little. I can help you clean up."

"I didn't think you were coming back tonight." Clover loses the inflection in her voice when she says it. My ears prick with warning.

Ardyn gestures behind her to Tempest. "We decided I'm spending too much time at the cottage. I want to spend more time with you."

"Oh, you mean the Anderton Cottage you practically live in, but I'm forbidden from trespassing into?"

"Clo," Tempest warns.

"What? It's the truth, isn't it? You're so big on protecting me, yet you glue Ardyn to your side and leave me alone to fend for myself. You make me vulnerable in a place where bitchy cupcakes can break into my home and destroy my things."

Tempest doesn't rise to the bait. Or so I think.

"Is that not what you wanted?" he asks. "You beg me for freedom, but the instant I cut you any slack and you realize the world isn't as welcoming as you assumed it would be, you cast the blame my way."

"I didn't do anything to deserve this."

"No. You didn't. But you deliberately push boundaries, with me and anyone else who crosses your path. You worship crystals and hold séances in old classrooms and use toy cards to cast unrealistic spells, and then you wonder why you're targeted."

"Tempest." Ardyn stands and puts a calming hand on his arm. "Stop. She doesn't deserve this, either."

"The girls who live here," Tempest continues, heedless of Ardyn's caution, "are not like Ardyn. They don't understand you or our family or where we come from. They don't want to. These girls want the same things they've grown up with—parties and sex and high-salary cushy jobs their parents are bound to find them. *You* are not them. And I love you for it, I do, but you need to stop living in this parallel world where you get to function within them but remain unscathed by their disdain."

I frown at Tempest, understanding the point of his speech but unhappy with how he wants to change his sister. Clover is perfect as she is. She's unexpected and intriguing and filled with eccentric delights. Why would he want to stifle that, even if it is for her protection?

"Thanks for the wake-up call, big brother, but you can kindly fuck off now."

Tempest's lips thin with annoyance.

"Maybe you should go," Ardyn says to him. "I'll stay."

"I'd rather everyone leave," Clover says. She remains in her crouch on the floor, her fingers resting on the open pages of the grimoire.

"Clo, I don't agree with him," Ardyn says. Tempest casts his frown on her, but Ardyn's impervious to it. "I love you for who you are. Minnie and her minions deserve the hell you want to rain down on them. I can help you. I *want* to help."

"It's too late for that," Clover answers quietly. "This is my fight, and I want to win it. You should go with Tempest and keep discussing whatever you're keeping from me that's making you keep your distance from me."

Ardyn's mouth slants with hurt. "That's not fair. Tempest and I, we don't—we haven't—"

I use enough precious seconds to pull my eyes away from Clover and watch Ardyn with sympathy. She could never lie to Clover, so why try to start now?

"Please go," Clover says. "I'll talk to you in the morning, when I've had time to cool off."

I smile. *What a lie.* Clover will bubble like a boiling cauldron all night.

"Clover ... please," Ardyn tries again.

"*Go.* I can't properly curse someone with you helicoptering around me making sure I don't set fire to your side of the room." She includes Tempest. "Or watch how *abnormal* I am and try to convince me my life would be better if I became a basic bitch."

Tempest is exasperated enough with his sister to gently guide Ardyn away. After furtive glances over her shoulder, Ardyn follows him out the door.

I follow, but Tempest stops my progress with a hand to my chest, exactly as I thought he would.

"You know what to do," he says under his breath, his eyes on mine.

"Of course."

Even my cold-blooded friend can feel the heavy weight of guilt.

Ardyn seems to relax at this development, content for the time-being that Clover won't be alone tonight, despite her best intentions.

After brief goodbyes, Ardyn and Tempest leave the way they came. I head to the staircase, readying my body for a long night in the crook of a tree branch until Clover's door, still ajar, stops my retreat.

I stare at it for a while.

Then come to a decision.

I push the door open.

CHAPTER 22

CLOVER

Containing my anger while preserving the pages of Sarah's grimoire is close to impossible. It's not like the book has a table of contents, so I flip each page using gloves and tweezers in anticipation of coming across the perfect poison for making a girl's hair fall out or how to give her painful diarrhea for a week. I'm also not above drugging her to the point that she acts like she's drunk off her face in class and gets kicked out of the university for running through campus naked.

Before Tempest, Ardyn, and Rio interrupted me, my finger had paused on a potion Sarah called *Shadow Elixir:*

ITEMS TO BE COLLECTED:

1. Moonlit Orchid petals: these rare and delicate flowers bloom only under the light of a full moon. For rare moments of power.

2. Belladonna Extract: dark and potent energy.

3. Essence of Nightshade: manipulation.

4. *Wormwood Infusion: illusion and confusion.*
5. *Baneberry Essence: punishment and consequence.*
6. *Shadow Moss Powder: secrecy and stealth.*

CAREFULLY COMBINE *and distill under a new moon, a time associated with new beginnings and transformation. The potion should be infused with the caster's intentions for revenge, channeling her anger and determination into the brew.*

When administered to the target, the effects of the elixir are specific to the nature of violence endured. It could bring vivid nightmares that reflect the torment inflicted, causing the recipient to experience the pain they have caused. Alternatively, it might invoke a temporary loss of power or influence, exposing their true nature to those around them.

MY BROWS FLICK UP. This could not be more perfect for Minnie.

Finding the ingredients, however...

Some will be at the university's greenhouse, for sure. TFU botanists enjoy researching and testing deadly plants and those that when ingested, can affect the human brain.

But shadow moss powder? What *is* that?

I cast my gaze around the ruin of my room. I could've used my crystals to help meditate on it.

Tempest, Rio, and Ardyn don't know how it is to rely on crystals and tarots like best friends. They were my constants throughout the uncertainty of my life, shields that kept me safe and gave me the right advice while my brother mysteriously disappeared during high school and came back a hardened, tortured man. My talismans soothed where my parents wouldn't. They surrounded me when I was left alone by my family for weeks on end until my father deemed me invisible enough and with little chance of being weaponized by his enemies to leave Manhattan. Or maybe he'd paid off his debts and was at the point when his loan sharks no longer wanted to deal with his emptied-out home and stripped businesses. Either way, he released me to university without the usual bonds keeping me in place.

And I took my precious collection with me.

Ardyn might have an idea of what it's like to be devoid of friendships, but when she was having a hard time, I don't think she used objects as a replacement for human affection.

None of them understand what it's like to witness the only protectors that *you* got to choose laid to waste at your feet because of pointless bullying. All those years of solace, every night when I meditated my fears and frustrations into those crystals—gone.

My new edition, a doll I didn't know well but infused with all that Rio can't say to me, destroyed.

I'm left with a skeleton of myself.

Ardyn and Tempest leave the room, finally accepting they can't logic me out of revenge. I watch Rio follow them out through my lashes, returning to the grimoire before he looks behind him and catches me staring.

Grimly, I bookmark the elixir with a torn piece of a tarot card, then turn another page in case something better, *harsher* comes up.

I flip to the back in hopes Sarah might've gotten more vengeful as time wore on, and the thickness of one of the pages catches my eye. Curious, I run my finger along the inner edge, finding a seam.

My breaths quicken.

I lay the book flat, bending closer and angling the tweezers with surgical precision so that I can pry whatever is hidden out when I lift the seam.

It takes a few seconds of wrangling, but I pull a thick shape out of the makeshift envelope ever so delicately. Inspecting it under the light, I notice the complicated folds keeping it together in an octagon. With the greatest care I can muster while adrenaline surges under my skin, I pry open the folds to reveal a stack of A5-sized papers, each one so thin, they crackle dangerously in my grip. With shaking hands, I lay the small pile on top of the grimoire.

I carefully turn over the first page, and colorful imagery catches my eye. Most of the pages are browned with age, Sarah's black-ink cursive faded into a rusty hue. But this...

Intricately drawn crystals or jewels, illustrated with almost 3D-like splendor, are inked onto the rough pages with a lined ledger beside them containing names, dates, and locations. The first is a blue-black, pear-shaped gem framed in yellow gold. Written next to it is **Sapphire Pendant, Duke of Soverington, paid in part.**

The next illustration draws my eye. It's a horse pendant, but nothing about its replication on paper is cheap. It's surrounded in pearls and rubies, sketched in extravagant detail. **Spanish Horse Pendant, Rubies, Diamonds, Pearls, Earl of Newhope, 1 of 2 items due, disclosure necessary.**

Even a woman's ring, etched with an elaborate *house* on top, so detailed it would be like wearing a dollhouse on your finger. **Manor Ring, Turquoise, Pearl, Emerald, Citrine, Diamond, Marquis Benedict, paid in full.**

There are more—at least ten pages worth, containing crosses, a Sphinx, white coral carved human profiles, sea creatures and dragons, jewelry from all over the world—documented with names and descriptions.

I'm so engrossed in what I've found that I don't notice movement in front of me until it's too late.

A pair of polished black shoes enter my tunnel vision and as soon as the intruder registers in my mind, I shove the drawings between the pages of the grimoire and close the book, scooting backward on a quick inhale.

My gaze shoots up into dark, hooded eyes. Rio's apathetic expression bears down, heavy on my shoulders but light and tingly in my lower belly. I didn't hear him come in and didn't register him until he was on top of me—deliberately. Rio doesn't know how to be loud.

With the same silent movements, he sits cross-legged across from me, his expression placid despite the open stinking heap of the grimoire between us.

Rio's not about to break the silence, so I do.

"Why did you come back? I thought I told you guys I'd be fine."

I tell myself to break eye contact after asking the question. His gaze holds me still, the fathomless depths sending me into a black hole I'm afraid I won't want to climb out of.

His full pink lips, the only slash of color on his pale face, move enough to answer, "Tell me what happened."

I shake off his eerie hold. "It's nothing that would interest you. It—"

"Anyone who hurts you will hold my interest."

My gaze flicks back to his. I swallow, choking a little on my saliva when I realize he's deadly serious.

"I wouldn't be so sure," I say under his intense scrutiny. "It's girls who also live in this dorm. They've decided, I guess, that because I'm not conforming to their giggly, pink standards, everything I love must be destroyed."

"Their names?"

This time, I choke on a stupefied laugh. "Your tone suggests you're going to hunt them down."

Rio angles his head side to side in a *maybe I will, maybe I won't* type gesture. "What did these girls do, exactly?" He adds before I can open my mouth, "Don't brush me off again."

I bristle at his quiet warning. "What part of *I can deal with this* don't you understand? My brother and best friend can't help me, and neither can you. I need to handle this alone."

"Why?"

By all accounts, Rio's casually sitting on the floor, his hands relaxed on his knees as he regards me curiously. It's only because I grew up watching him that I sense the alarming undercurrent to his questioning.

He and Tempest were always slinking around the manor, and not just to avoid the dorky little sister. The art of stealth was ingrained in them somehow and a secret they keep close.

I lift my chin. "For the same reasons you and Tempest like to deal with problems in your own way."

The skin under his eye twitches subtly. After a beat, he responds, "I very much doubt that."

"Well, then, maybe I believe I can handle this without annoying, overly forceful brotherly intervention—or my brother's scary loyal sidekick," I add.

Rio leans forward, his nose inches from mine. He's so close I can smell his breath of cinnamon and smoke. I tense at the proximity, the rigid line of my back sending heated signals under my skin.

He says, "First, you arrive with an inexplicable bruise on your cheek."

Rio lifts his hand, trailing a finger down one side of my face. I hiss in a breath but not because it hurts. Rio isn't one for soft touches, yet this is the second time he's risked contact in less than two days.

His exploratory glide down my cheek sends my blood blooming under the pad of his fingers.

"Then," he continues, "I walk in to find you standing among the debris of your beloved trinkets, your room ransacked."

The breath accompanying Rio's words sets fire to my lips, swelling and numbing them at the same time. I'm frozen within his wall of flames with nowhere to run.

Rio pulls back, the cold air of the room amplifying the sensation across my mouth.

"I don't take that kind of treatment toward you lightly," he says.

And there it is. Tempest's guard dog, baring his teeth because he was told to obey at all costs, including keeping watch over his sister, too innocent to leave the shelter of an older brother.

"You don't have to worry about getting in Tempest's bad books," I say. "I'll tell him you investigated my problem and found my use of an old grimoire to get back at the Minnie Mouse Club both immature and a typical Clover response."

I turn back to the grimoire. The room grows so quiet, my page flips are grating against my ears. I'm almost convinced Rio left in the same noiseless way he came when he says, "Is that how you think I see you? Immature and ... typical?"

I shrug, unable to meet his eye.

"That is so far off my perception of you..." Rio cuts himself off, drawing my gaze up. His expression is pinched like he can't believe I consider him to be doing nothing but dutifully carrying out Tempest's wishes.

Rio lowers his hand, pressing his index finger on the open page of Sarah's grimoire. "I gave this to you."

I can't argue with that, so I nod.

"And I'm aware of what it contains. Animal and human sacrifices. Poisonings. The art of undetectable murder. And I gave that to you," he repeats.

"I doubt you did it with the thought that I'd actually want to carry one of them out." I lift the book to our eye level, then lightly set it back down. "Adorable, gloomy Clover, who prefers voodoo dolls to Barbies and spell books to textbooks, won't this be a cute addition to her spooky collection."

Rio exhales sharply. If I didn't know any better, I'd say it was a laugh. "I consider you more than capable of trying out Sarah Anderton's methods. You just don't yet have the skill level needed to fully execute your plans."

I pull my brows in, regarding him.

He lays a hand on mine, where it rests on the grimoire. I may be wearing gloves, but his dry warmth seeps through into the marrow of my bones.

"Do you want to kill them?" he asks softly. "These girls?"

"I..." The fact that Rio so seriously asks that question should give me pause. The fact that I'm *hesitating* should cause me great concern. I'm caught in Rio's silky, sinuous web, and this time, I don't want to shake myself out of it and drop to the ground. "Well, no. Not actually. I do want to make them miserable, though. Especially Minnie."

For the barest of seconds, Rio's expression shifts to disappointment. And for some reason, that disappoints *me*.

It propels me to add, "Like really fucking miserable. I wouldn't mind if I get all of them kicked out of Titan Falls, too. Destroy their reputations. Make the entire campus ashamed of them—"

He covers my mouth with his hand yet regards me over it with bemused affection. I stiffen at the sudden, heated contact, then tell myself not to *melt*.

"Point taken." Rio's chest vibrates with a subtle chuckle. "I can help you with all of that."

My lips move under his skin, the rough friction against his palm sending a delightful shudder down my spine.

Rio takes his time lowering his hand from my mouth.

Without the distraction of his skin on mine, I ask him, "Why would you want to waste your time on some triggered freshman's revenge plan?"

Rio lifts one shoulder. "Because it's you."

I'm not sure what to do with that statement other than evaporate into delight the instant I'm alone again. "Thank you."

Rio breaks the moment of connection by scanning the writing below my fingers, his stare narrowing with displeasure. "This is what you are planning?"

Glancing down, I realize the grimoire's fallen open to the page I'd bookmarked—the shadow curse.

Rio spins the book to face him. In his velvety, barely detectable tone, he recites the ingredients and instructions on how to make Minnie suffer from nonstop hallucinations.

I suck in a breath at how easily the words fall from his mouth. His tongue softly caresses each syllable, striking them with meaning. In most circumstances, I'd be embarrassed and therefore highly defensive of someone picking apart my interest in witches in the occult because most people don't understand—and don't want to. But Rio...

"Tempest can't keep you cloaked and isolate you anymore," Rio says once he's finished. "You're out on campus, meeting people and being yourself in public, inviting intrigue. You need to be able to defend yourself from those who don't understand where you're coming from."

Rio's voice strains against his vocal cords by the end of his speech. He doesn't use it often enough.

I'm not usually the recipient of such roughened emotion, and I want to fold my arms over myself, almost in protection from him *seeing* me. The real, vulnerable one I try very hard to keep hidden.

I say the one thing that comes to mind. "No one has ever accepted me this way."

"You're not strange for enjoying the darker aspects of humanity," Rio says softly. "If anything, that makes us have a lot more in common."

Before I lose my nerve, I use the opening. "Will you tell me what happened with you and Tempest all those years ago? What made you change?"

His features shift into obtuse confusion. "Change?"

I smile sardonically. "I've been around you most of my life, Rio. I can tell the difference between the fourteen-year-old jerk who put dog shit under my pillow and the quiet, defensive stance you have now. And your eyes…" I risk lifting my hand and lightly touching his temple.

Rio, a man who never so much as displays a tic, flinches at the contact.

Embarrassed, I pull away.

In an imperceptible move, Rio catches my wrist between us. He says, his gaze level on mine, "You don't think that was just puberty doing what it's done for centuries?"

His hand circles my wrist firmly, almost painfully as his stare dives into my soul and pulls out the pieces most interesting to him.

"No," I murmur. "I don't think growing into an adult can give you the type of silent scars you carry now."

The skin under Rio's eyes pulls taut. He squeezes my wrist once, then releases me.

Pushing his hands against his thighs, he rises. "These girls, how many were against you?"

I try not to appear too confused by the rapid change in topic or the cold wind of his absence as he shifts. "Three."

"Did they restrain you?"

He asks it with a light cadence, but the tendons popping from his neck give his contained temper away.

"Two did. The other..." I clear the emotion from my throat and stand. "Minnie was the one with the freedom to break my things."

Rio gives a somber nod. "Do you think they'll try it again?"

I hug my stomach, scanning the debris on the floor in a place I considered my haven. Minnie ruined that. I'd like to think I'm strong and can handle myself when it comes to her, but the idea of being held down again and violated sends shivers down my bare arms.

I don't notice Rio's come up behind me until I feel his touch along my shoulders, the lightest trail of his fingers over my clavicle.

The shiver I'd harbored morphs into sweet tingles. I close my eyes against the sensation. The tenseness in my jaw fades.

"I want to teach you," Rio says near my ear.

My eyelids flutter open, and my lips part. "Hmm?"

"Self-defense," he clarifies, the movement of his mouth playing with the small hairs at my temple. "So next time, they won't stand a chance. Not three against one and certainly not one-on-one."

I nod before thinking clearly, Rio's presence a dangerous, soothing balm. I picture his energy swirling around us before entangling my arms and pressing close.

Stroking, soothing ... claiming.

"Meet me at the northern base of the woods Thursday night," he says, continuing to play music against my shoulders and down my arms. Goose bumps follow where his fingers lead.

"Okay."

The word is out of my mouth before I can stop it from turning into a moan. My eyes shut again. My heart races.

A soft click, the shut of a door, makes me open my eyes. I look back and forth, wiping my sweaty palms against my pants while my stomach drops with disappointment.

Rio left without a sound, leaving me a shuddering, hot, aching mess.

CHAPTER 23

MORGAN

I sit adjacent to the low, flickering fireplace in the den, my eyes fixed on the doorway as Rio enters Anderton Cottage. I lift my whiskey to my lips, the air crackling with ash and tension.

Rio, the silent and lethal abductor hidden within the gothic university's shadows. Me, the sadistic professor, a wolf in sheep's clothing. We share a common goal, a burning desire, yet our methods and intentions could not be more different.

"Well, well, well, if it isn't the little boy back from his tree house," I drawl. "What secrets have you uncovered about our lovely Clover this time?"

Rio's gaze meets mine, his eyes narrowed with a mixture of suspicion and curiosity. He knows I'm unpredictable and prone to violent outbursts, but he's yet to discover the depths of my craving for Clover. He might have seen me with her once and dismissed it as a moment of bloodlust. I'm known for those. He might've been turned on by it. He might dream of himself in my position.

Either way, what's concerning is how much I'm thinking about her despite satisfying my curiosity.

Damn. There's the problem. I'm not satisfied. I want more of her.

"I've unearthed something troubling," Rio finally responds. "A girl named Minnie and her two friends destroyed something precious to Clover. She's hurting."

Only Rio can give me information so sobering and so enraging at the same time. Unburdened wrath courses through me, mirrored by the protective fire in Rio's gaze.

A shared emotion emerges between us, unspoken but palpable.

Despite our differences, Rio and I both hold something for Clover. It's not respect demanded from her being a Callahan, Tempest's sister, no. It's the shared understanding of the darkness that must lurk within her for her to accept us so guilelessly.

But is it our job to dig it out of her?

Well, it's certainly becoming *mine*.

"Minnie Davenport, huh?" I mutter, pretending disinterest by swirling my drink. "Looks like someone needs a lesson in manners, and I'm just the professor to teach her."

Rio's eyes sharpen, a glimmer of amusement hidden within his wariness.

"Save your theatrics," Rio retorts, his voice irritatingly flat. "We need to focus on protecting Clover, not indulging our personal vendettas."

I raise an eyebrow, the challenge evident in my gaze. "Who said anything about it being personal? The banter, the clash of wits —it adds a certain zest to our secret endeavors, don't you think?"

Rio's lips quirk, a fleeting smile breaking through his stoic facade. "Our priority should be safeguarding Clover, not engaging in pointless conversation."

I chuckle. "Ah, Rio, banter reveals our true selves. It exposes the vulnerabilities we hide. No one is ever *really* joking, even when they say they are."

Rio's eyes narrow, a flicker of irritation crossing his features. "Your true self may be best kept hidden, Morgan. Don't assume I'm eager to reveal mine."

I lean back with an impish curve to my lips. "Mark my words, even your guarded facade will crumble one day."

And it might be for the same woman I've lately had to stabilize mine against.

A hint of begrudging respect seeps into my expression. "It seems we're on the same page for once. We can make sure Minnie understands the consequences of her actions."

The slightest, most baby-sized intrigue flickers in his expression. I consider that a win. We share a common understanding, a silent pact to protect Clover at all costs. The enemy of our enemy has united us in a delicate alliance.

"Tell me, Rio," I begin while a plan forms in the lizard part of my brain. "Do you ever speak voluntarily, or is it only when forced?"

Rio glances at me, his eyes narrowing. "Silence is a virtue, Morgan. Something you should try."

"So what's your favorite pastime when you're not lurking in the shadows? Don't you have any hobbies? Homemade kombucha? Making TikToks? Perhaps a secret talent for interpretive dance?"

Rio's lips twitch. "You have a gift for annoying people, Morgan. I'll give you that."

I chuckle, relishing the momentary break in the wall he's built around himself.

I pull on my coat, my expression a mix of feigned innocence and wicked delight. "Life is all about embracing the chaos, dancing with danger, and watching it all burn. Let's do just that."

A flicker of uncertainty crosses Rio's face, a glimmer of doubt in his unwavering loyalty. He knows that the line between damnation and redemption is thin, and I straddle that line with delight.

"Don't underestimate the mercilessness within me," I say, my voice a low, dangerous murmur. "For I am the storm, the madhouse, and the whispered nightmare in the darkest corners of her mind."

Rio's eyes narrow, his stance firm. He's the picture of stoic determination, the embodiment of silence. But I can see the flicker of doubt in his eyes. Doubt that he can protect Clover from the venom that courses through my veins.

But he also knows that he, too, stands on the precipice, torn between protecting Clover and the tantalizing pull of their connection.

"Do you want to talk about what you saw the other night?" I goad.

He doesn't respond. At last, Rio chooses to lose his tongue again.

A smirk tugs at the corner of my lips as I turn away from his resolute form, a torrent of outrage brewing beneath the surface of my casual smile. This is my game, my quest for vengeance for touching my lucky charm, and Minnie will feel the weight of her transgressions.

"Come, doggy," I say, opening the door.

My coattails billow with the sudden wind as I step through, and I don't have to look back to know he follows.

As we make our way to Minnie's dormitory, the internal war I'm battling with my monster is exposed, my face displaying more than my carefully crafted professorial charm. My presence is enough to send chills down the spines of those who dawdle on the path this early in the morning as they scuttle out of my way. Add my independent shadow to it, lurking behind my deadly form, and we simply *exude* terror. It's mostly athletes hurrying to the training center with puffy eyes and fistfuls of energy bars giving us a wide berth, no witnesses I'm concerned with.

It's easy to slip into Camden House, the girls' dormitory. We Vultures have lots of little access points on campus, gifted to us by our pompous overlord Rossi as a way to slip in and out of the shadows unnoticed while we complete our tasks.

Once we're outside Minnie's door, my body thrums unbearably with anticipation.

"Are you ready?" I ask Rio. "I'm not one to hold back."

Rio studies the wood, his brown eyes morphing to black. His assent.

It's said that four in the morning is when people are at their most vulnerable, a good amount of the population ignorant and asleep in their beds. Completely exposed to predators like me.

Including *her*.

I stare down the hallway at Clover's closed door, murmuring, "Don't worry, little leaf. I'll teach our dear Minnie a lesson she won't soon forget."

I push open the door, our malice shrouded in black.

I CARVE specific words into Minnie's skin while she sleeps from Rio's injection of a strong concoction of drugs I brew myself. The girl didn't even jerk at the feel of a needle in her neck while she snored in her bed.

Must've been some party.

Rio always keeps a few spares in the hidden pockets of his coat. One never knows when one needs to incapacitate another.

Minnie and her roommate may be chemically slumbering in

peace (screams would draw too much attention, so the room-mate had to visit Drugland, too), I want her to feel the same pain that Clover felt when she wakes, and *I* want to be the one to inflict it on her.

I grin as I work, humming a tuneless melody while Rio watches placidly from the corner.

This is my art, and I am its master.

Once finished, I step back to admire my work. The words are etched deeply into Minnie's skin, ensuring a scar, and blood seeps out of the wound, staining the sheets.

I lick my lips at the rush of excitement the vision brings.

Rio comes up beside me, assessing Minnie's still form. "Something's missing."

"Are you criticizing my art piece?"

He gives a single shake of his head.

Rio stands for a moment, still as a statue. Then he creeps forward.

I smile when I see him pluck from Minnie's nightstand a small, ornately carved wooden jewelry box.

Carefully opening the box, he lifts out its contents. He holds one item reverently, admiring the weight and the feel of it. A single, large diamond heart pendant on a gold chain. Then he presses it to the bleeding wound on Minnie's back, pushing it into the skin until it's forced to collect her blood under its prongs.

I take a deep breath, relishing how the metal must warm against his hands and sink into Minnie's inner flesh.

"*Never* touch what's mine," he rasps to Minnie's slumbering face.

Rio moves on to the roommate, pocketing the blood-soaked jewelry and pulling out his switchblade.

I purse my lips in interest as he works, choosing the tops of her hands instead of the wide expanse of skin I preferred.

"Why the hands?" I ask, truly curious.

Rio doesn't look up. "They touched her."

"Mm." I nod, folding my arms.

From my vantage point, I see he's carved an eye on each hand. Not nearly as detailed or intricate as mine, but it gets the point across.

Rio straightens.

As he walks toward me, I say with a sinister smile, "Eye for an eye."

"Feather for feather," he agrees in a rare show of brotherhood.

Then after putting our playthings back where they belong, we exit the same way we came, leaving nothing in our wake.

CHAPTER 24

ROSSI

My men are distracted tonight in a way I don't care for. Morgan, Tempest, and Rio lounge in my office, splayed against whatever comfortable flat surface they can find. Two of them wear pensive frowns and stare at the wooden flooring like it contains the answers to their confinement at TFU. Morgan, however, wears an expression that makes him appear oddly pleased with himself.

"Is anyone going to tell me why you're all moodier than usual?" I drawl from my desk, leaning against my leather chair.

Not one shifts their attention, not even to glance at me through their brows.

"All right then, shall I guess?" I twist a Montblanc pen between my fingers, feigning thought. "I'd hope none of your current distractions are due to a woman. We don't have time for unrequited love."

All three gazes shoot toward me.

Dammit.

I'd prepared myself for the fuckeries that exist when taking charge of a handful of boys in their twenties—not that I was given a choice in the matter. But I'd hoped, with their peculiar histories, girls would be far from their minds.

"We're in the midst of a delicate, *dangerous* situation with our outfit," I warn, "so if I'm right, I would hope you'd either fuck these ladies out of your systems or forget them entirely."

Tempest is the first to speak. "I swore to you that Ardyn would not become a problem, and I meant it. She accepts our situation as much as she can, and I've kept her away from our targets."

My lips crimp with disapproval. I've developed an unavoidable fondness for Tempest, and as is his nature, he's taken advantage of it. He shouldn't have any relationships outside of the Vultures. None of us should. Yet he's managed to take advantage of our convenient isolation, too.

Morgan slants his gaze at Tempest. "It doesn't have to be a girlfriend to give you female problems."

Tempest turns to him. "What's that supposed to mean?"

Morgan responds with a lopsided smile. "I'm sure Rio's told you of our recent late-night visitor at the cottage."

I scan the three of them in less than five seconds, assessing Tempest's slitted eyes, Rio's unimpressed sneer toward Morgan, and of course, Morgan's self-satisfied puffery.

When they don't offer up any more information, I growl, "What visitor?"

Morgan answers. "Clover Callahan can't stay away from our private areas."

The mention of Clover piques my interest and smooths my brows. My late-night run-in with her floats into my mind's eye, the bluish black of her hair under the dim illumination of the library's basement and the mischievous sparkle to her eye. She had a familiar tenseness to her mouth as she sparred with me and attempted to see the forgotten section in a way no other student wants to—as a treasure trove.

It wasn't fear that tightened her rosebud lips. It was stubborn curiosity, and it sent such a wrenching chill through my gut I nearly broke in half at the sight.

Not her, too.

Being inexplicably drawn to a student half my age is worse than ordering these boys, my men, to keep their cocks zipped up. To find familiarity with Clover is a fate worse than death. No matter how beautiful or wonderfully clever she is, Clover must never come that close to me again.

Tempest's shoulders morph into a straight, concrete line. "What have I told you about my sister's name coming out of your mouth?"

"Yes, but I'm explaining her constant trespasses into unsafe areas—*our* territory—to our boss," Morgan simpers. "Even you can't punish me for that."

"Morgan's correct," I snap. "That ..." *lovely creature* "...sister of yours keeps popping up in places she shouldn't."

Morgan shrugs as if he hadn't just cranked open a can of worms. "She's obsessed with answering the Titan Falls mystery of the Anderton witches."

"I'm well aware," I say dryly.

All too aware. History has done a wonderful job of erasing the pilgrimage of Anderton Cottage, hundreds of settlers looking for the jewels she hid away, paid by nobles who wanted certain people dead.

I say, "I've found Clover prowling around the library's basement looking for clues like some sort of dark arts detective."

"None of that puts her closer to discovering our truth," Tempest defends. "The Andertons have nothing to do with the Vultures or the Bianchis."

I quell my thoughts so none of them show on my face. I've yet to explain to Tempest and Rio that the key to our escape is to find that pile of jewels if it exists. It would be worth billions in the black market. *Billions*. Enough for the boys to get out of this life.

"We're using many of the Anderton's secret hideaways," Morgan says. "Three hundred years later, hidden basements and underground passageways are still very much well-traveled, and we've yet to come across anything of interest."

I raise a hand to Morgan. The last thing I want is to get him curious about the Andertons. He is Bianchi's bird and therefore my enemy. "If Clover won't stop sniffing around, what can we do to appease her?"

"I've tried."

Rio's low tone draws all of our attention.

I prompt, "And? What have you tried?"

"I gave her Sarah Anderton's grimoire. Her diary and spell book."

The breath freezes in my lungs. Morgan's head whips toward Rio, his eyes narrowing like a cat's.

That grimoire has value—way too much value to be lifted from the spot it was buried in and given to a freshman girl with no idea what she's stumbled upon.

And it's my damn fault for not informing Rio of my plans sooner.

Tempest leans against his thighs with his forearms, cocking his brow with interest. "Why would you do that?"

"You told me to keep an eye on her," Rio reasons calmly. "I thought it would distract her enough to keep her in her room."

"More importantly, *where* did you find it?" Morgan asks.

He leans closer to Rio, a tell that he's very interested in the answer.

"There is a back panel to the apothecary cabinet in our dungeon. Morgan was doing his ... administrations ... to our last target, and I was bored."

Rio shrugs like he hasn't just given away the most important discovery of the Anderton witches in centuries.

I do my best to control my temper.

Rio continues, "I leaned against the side of the cabinet, and when my shoulder hit, there was a hollow sound. I took a closer look. There's a tiny, needle-thin latch along the seams. I picked it."

Morgan curses and paces away. "And I missed it."

"Too busy drawing carvings in your victim's back," Rio says.

Morgan stills, slanting Rio a look. Then he blinks, seems to recover, and snarls at him instead.

What the hell was that about?

I run my hand down my face, muttering through my fingers, "Next time I'm at the cottage, show me where you found it."

Rio nods his assent.

Tempest takes that moment to stand. "That grimoire is the reason my sister was attacked."

My gaze darts to Tempest. Vengeance coils where numbness once lay in my gut. "Clover was attacked? When?"

Morgan stops in his tracks and crosses his arms, deep frown lines bracketing his mouth. I've watched this man enough to recognize when he's putting on an act.

Then it hits me. These boys aren't distracted by girls, plural. They're being pulled toward *one*.

The same damn one I think about, too.

"It was a bunch of students who jumped her in her room. Schoolgirls," Tempest says. "But they did some damage to some favorite items of hers and probably ruined this grimoire, too."

Harm coming to that grimoire would mean a literal end to my plans of getting Rio and Tempest out. But for reasons unknown to me, Clover's well-being is important as well.

"But she's unharmed?" I aim for the question to be idle, even with the subtle grit of concern running through my voice.

Rio answers. "Physically."

The idea of Clover coming to harm on my campus, my grounds, doesn't sit well, but I can't allow it to cloud my judgment.

"Clover's bullies should not be a concern of ours," I lie. "Not unless it brings her closer to discovering us and what we do here. Tempest, I was under the impression she was so removed from your family's crimes as a child that the thought of stumbling onto her brother's involvement with the mafia would appall her."

"That's true," Tempest says. "And why Ardyn's keeping the secret, too. Neither of us wants to lose Clover's trust."

It strains my voice not to roar, *"Then why is she so drawn to us?"*

"She loves the dark. The occult is anything but dangerous," Morgan answers, undeterred by my death tone. "Macabre, sure, but it's also layered with history and healing. A lot of tribes who still practice it don't have fatal societal issues like cancer, depression, or a whole host of mental and pharmacological issues. Frankly, I'm shocked more people aren't into it."

I stare at him with *what the fuck* eyes.

Tempest pinches the ridge of his nose. Rio shakes his head with exasperation.

Morgan is the bane of my existence, yet right now, I need him most. "So what do you suggest we do to keep her away from discovering—" I almost finish with *from the Anderton jewels* but catch my tongue before I clue Morgan into my true interest.

The thought of Clover discovering it and publishing it in a public essay, sending droves of media to our little slice of exile, makes my veins pulse in my forehead.

Tempest's lips turn down as he regards Morgan. "This is your fault."

"Mine?" Morgan points at his chest. "If history is anything to go by, I solve problems."

"If it weren't for your stupid final essay topic, my sister wouldn't be tramping all over our cottage looking for Anderton artifacts."

Morgan cants his head in an *I'm not so sure* motion. "I'm held to a strict syllabus standard by the faculty. A thesis centering around the Andertons is hardly unique to her. Plenty before her have tried and failed."

"Yes, but it's Clover," Rio interjects.

No one asks him to expand. We're all aware of her Callahan tenacity.

"Of all the girls on campus," Tempest says, "she *cannot* discover us."

"Then keep her fucking busy," Morgan says, his shoulders lifting then falling. "Bullies can be dealt with. But her inquisitive mind is another thing entirely unless you make her so busy that she can barely do her research and pass my course."

I'm massaging my jaw as he says this, my daylong stubble scratched and sharp against my fingers. And it comes to me. "Enroll her in my business class, Tempest."

Usually calm and collected in situations of shocking horror, Tempest's eyes widen slightly at the mention of messing with Clover's schedule. "Our advanced economics course that my sister will have no interest in participating in?"

"Yes, that." I splay my hands on the desk, settling the matter. "Better for me to keep an eye on her."

I say this with intent. Anything she discovers, I'll make sure I find out first. Somehow, I'll have to get that grimoire from her, too.

Morgan's eyelids lower, none too pleased with my idea. Not that I give a damn.

"Good ole Tongueless can always offer her more Anderton

gifts," Morgan says. "How about Sarah Anderton's skull from my office? Do you think she'd like that offered on her doormat, too?"

Rio's hands ball into fists at his sides. "I was—"

"Following the orders of your master. Yes, we know." Morgan rolls his eyes, his gaze casting away the moment Tempest holds up a finger to Rio, halting the lethal assault Rio's desperate to counter with.

In another life, I'd hail the unfettered loyalty between those too. Right now, it could be my undoing.

Morgan continues, "Honestly, what does a freshman with a witch fetish have to do with us? Our attention is better suited to my uncle's next targets. Rossi, you got the message that my uncle has two more to be dealt with, didn't you?"

"Yes," I reluctantly admit through my teeth. "I was about to send Rio out to attempt to acquire them. They're two financiers who can't survive much longer in the wilderness, even with professional gear. They must be getting lazy and leaving tracks by now." I say to Rio, "You have forty-eight hours to bring them to us."

Rio's mouth pulls to the side, and while subtle, his eyes move frantically in their sockets as he calculates something in secret. "I'll have them here in less than that."

Morgan snorts. "Such a fucking overachiever."

"Good." I wave a hand. "Meeting adjourned."

The men head to the door.

"And Tempest?" I say, holding him back. "I meant what I said. Put Clover in my class."

Tempest dares to respond, "Your class is full."

"Then drop the student with the lowest grade and slide her in." I swivel to my computer. "You swore you had your sister under control. Prove it."

There is no movement at my back until I hear a quiet, venomous tone. "Yes, sir."

"And the next time you're in that dorm room, get the grimoire and bring it to me. I'm interested in taking a look."

Tempest knows not to ask why, though I'll have to confess to him sooner rather than later. How would my clever, all-too-realist protégé react when he discovers his mentor wants to uncover an ancient treasure buried on university grounds?

Not happily.

I've found solace in academia. I'm good at it. It helps me keep my lethal tendencies at bay. But it's also provided me with unexpected knowledge.

Titan Falls's history never appealed to me other than the irony of my exile into a dead, vengeful witch's town. Learning about her was unavoidable, but with a brain like mine, I absorbed the information, nevertheless.

Until mention of her fortune wormed into my ears.

Lost to this day, rarely spoken of in public records likely so the nobles who paid her could save face—and their necks. A stash of gemstones, gold, and rare pearls Sarah hid away before her arrest and execution, burrowed so deep somewhere not one surviving noble could find them or any generations thereafter.

Such a tale of fantasy. Yet it took on earworm properties that I can't get rid of the potential.

These boys of mine can still be saved. They can leave this world of violence, heedless punishment, and a wooded prison.

Tempest can have the kind of love that was taken from me. Rio, the same chance.

As for me, discovering Sarah's trove must not blur the lines between my past and present self. I must keep my darker impulses under control. Unlimited cash could give me the weaponry to unleash unlimited ruthlessness to those who've harmed me and mine.

Sadly, I believe Clover's mind, untouched by cruelty and so optimistic, could help me stay grounded. She brushes against this world, dips her toe in it, yet possesses a full heart that still has the capacity to love.

Tempest clicks my office door shut soon after my command to put Clover under my wing. I push away from the desk, the muscles in my face twisting into cords of tension.

Forcing Clover into my classroom to keep her from snooping is a legitimate excuse, but I will never admit to anyone, especially her brother, that I will quite enjoy relaxing under the shade of her beauty at regular, consistent intervals every week.

Her innocent, sweet face calms me and reminds me of better days.

I rub my temples, closing my eyes, the vision of Clover's dimpled smile rippling through the black spots.

Look, but don't touch.

CHAPTER 25

CLOVER

I rush through my classes, sprinting between buildings and throwing an arm across my eyes to prevent most winter flurries from numbing my vision into blindness.

I come to a fast halt at the entrance to Camden House.

A small moving truck blocks the staircase into the building with two uniformed men carrying boxes down the steps and into the back of the truck.

Not every student can handle the high expectations and course load of TFU, even if rich parents bought their spot.

I resume walking, shocked no one's dropped out sooner.

My steps slow when I notice Kirsty dawdling by the entrance gnawing on her thumbnail as she watches the men work. Both hands are wrapped in white bandages spotted with red.

After what she did to me, I couldn't give a flying fuck why she's there, but her injury gives me pause. A mover accidentally steps on the toe of her shoe, and he barrels forward with a stack of boxes.

She recoils and screams as if he tried to shoot her, Kirsty's mouth gaping open and her tongue so far back in her throat as she screams, I swear she swallowed it.

"Oh my god," I whisper in horror, frozen mid-stride.

The man drops the boxes and shouts, arms out to appease her as Kirsty screams and screams and screams.

Lauren bolts out of the dorm, running to her friend and throwing her into a bear hug, saying calming things into her ear.

Kirsty closes her mouth, her red-rimmed eyes skating everywhere until they land on me.

"*You!*" She breaks out of Lauren's hold. "*You did this to us!*"

I fall back with wide eyes. "Did what?"

Lauren grabs Kirsty's arm and yanks her back. "You can't. Don't even look at her."

"Minnie's mutilated because of you!" Kirsty screeches, then lifts both her hands. "What the *fuck* did you do to my hands? Why? Whhhhhyyyyy?"

Her wail is so wrenching that black-feathered birds escape from the trees above us and caw into the sky.

I gaze at the moving truck, dumbfounded. "I have no idea what you're talking about."

"You dumb cunt," Kirsty snarls through fresh tear tracks. "That was so fucked up, what you did."

"Kirsty." Lauren jerks her friend toward her until Kirsty's looking at her. "Stop. Talking. To her."

I dodge out of the way of the movers still working, my stomach doing loops in sickening swirls. "What happened to Minnie?"

Lauren twists to me before Kirsty can open her mouth. "Minnie's not coming back to campus. Kirsty's leaving too. We have nothing more to say to you. In fact, you don't exist to us anymore. Stay the fuck away from us."

Lauren's words are harsh, but her lips tremble with fear.

I wrench my brows together. "Lauren, what—?"

"Leave!"

I jump back, blinking rapidly. I manage to collect myself and stride into Camden House, but my legs shake, and I have trouble walking up the steps.

The fabric of my coat is too cold as I come to my door.

A flash of gold draws my attention, dangling prettily from the knob.

Lifting it, a heart-shaped diamond glitters from the overhead hallway lights.

It's truly beautiful, and I hold it in cupped hands, a soft smile curving on my lips.

Rio.

He's replaced fragility with an unbreakable gem. Only he could find the heart of me and want me to carry a jewel forged without scratches.

I put it on, the necklace cool against my heated neck and chest, then tuck it into my shirt so it can warm with the rest of me.

I turn the key into my dorm room. The humiliation of Minnie's attack still stains my cheeks, but now they're reddened with confusion and anger.

Minnie and Kirsty are gone, just like that?

No confrontation, no revenge, no closure?

I'd worked so hard to find the ingredients to the shadow elixir. I even found the damned shadow moss. I'd spent all night boiling the mixture under the new moon and woke up early so I could grab two iced coffees, one drugged and one sweetened with sugar. Pulling an all-nighter meant I needed copious amounts of caffeine.

My plan was to switch Minnie's coffee out at the library today while she was making heart eyes at Xavier.

When I didn't see her in any classes or studying today, I

didn't think much of it. Same with yesterday when I couldn't find her.

It wasn't a big deal. The girl parties a lot. But now, with all her belongings being moved out and still no sign of her...

What the hell happened?

I find Ardyn lounging on her side of the room when I step into our room. "Oh. I didn't expect you to be here."

Ardyn lowers her textbook and smiles. "I live here."

"That's up for debate." I say it with a grin to remove the sting. "Did you see what's going on out front?"

"Yeah, Minnie's moving out." Ardyn pulls her lips in and stares at our closed door with concern. "Weird, right?"

"So weird," I agree.

"Maybe it's for the best." Ardyn sits up from her pillows and crosses her legs. Her face tightens with deeper worry. "I'm sorry I wasn't here when Minnie cornered you."

"You couldn't have known." I walk over to my closet, choosing black leggings and a black cashmere sweater to go under my leather jacket tonight. My eyes stray to my mini fridge, where an iced coffee sits with masking tape warning DON'T DRINK in case I blindly reach for it one groggy morning. "Plus, I guess it's over now."

"Lauren's still here."

A hanger screeches on the metal rod as I shove shirts to the side. "Well, according to her, she's not going to bother me anymore. All my research on curses, dark arts, and other deals with the devil to ruin their lives is worthless now."

"That easily? Whoa, what happened with the three of them?"

"That's what I'd like to know. You have an in. Why don't you ask my brother because he sure as hell won't tell me anything."

"Clo..."

Years ago, Ardyn and I always hid inside my house together,

eavesdropping on the boys and wondering what they were up to that made them so secretive and guarded.

Now she's in that secret club.

I want to confess it all to her now that I've agreed to let Rio teach me combat moves tonight (which I am still going to because *Rio*), and I'm having public sex with Xavier and flirting shamelessly with danger with Professor Morgan, every single one of those men a devil in disguise, including Tempest.

I've spent all my life avoiding the worst in people and sinking into fantastical worlds and sorcery. That doesn't mean I'm blind to the strange holes in my brother's history or the way he turned from sarcastic goof to a tight-lipped prowler seemingly overnight.

There was always something rotten with the Callahans, and I'm sure Ardyn's discovered it. The fact Tempest chose to share it with her instead of me is a cut that burns deep.

"Where are you off to?" Ardyn asks.

"Study group." I search around the foot of my bed for my black combat boots.

"That's too bad."

Ardyn's sincere disappointment draws my head up. Her tone makes me miss our old days.

"How about we meet for lunch tomorrow?" I say. "It's been a while since we've caught up."

Ardyn brightens. "I'd love that."

I crouch on the side of my bed, tie my laces, then grab my bag and head to the door.

Before I turn the knob, I say to Ardyn, "I'll meet you by the fountain at—*shit*, Tempest!"

My brother's bulk takes over the doorway.

"Really, I should be used to your lurking rock formation," I say while clutching the lapels of my jacket and getting my breathing under control, "but I'll admit it. I'm not."

"Sorry."

"You don't mean it."

"No. I don't."

Tempest's attention strays above my head, scanning the room behind me. He finds Ardyn and softens. But then, as if it physically pains him, he pulls his focus from her and glances around the room as he pushes past me with a light squeeze to my shoulder.

"Something we can help you with?" I ask.

He pauses in the middle, directly between our beds. "I'm making sure there's no permanent damage after what happened last night."

"Other than to my ego? No, I cleaned it all up."

My heart lurches at the re-envisioning of my treasures shattered across the floors.

"That's good." Tempest turns toward me. "Are you all right?"

I shrug, my tote bag's strap heavy on one shoulder. "I've been better, but I'm trying to get over it with dark fantasies and twisted revenge plans, though now that's been foiled."

Tempest responds with a wince, which isn't like him.

Ardyn lifts from her perch, coming to Tempest's side and rubbing his arm. "You look like you need a break from campus. Want to grab dinner in town?"

He instinctively leans toward her, and I soften toward my friend. Whatever's going on between us, she has true love and concern for my brother, a feat not many people other than me can manage.

"Yeah, sure," he says, but his eyes lose focus. "I'm wondering, though, what are you going to do about that smell?"

Tempest looks at me.

"Don't look at me," I defend. "I showered recently."

Tempest is unamused. "I meant the book you were poring over last night. The secret to all your dark arts or whatever."

He says it with such an unnecessary blasé attitude that I zoom in on him. "What do you care if it smells up the room? You don't live here."

"Ardyn does," Tempest says, "and I doubt she wants to live with that scent in her clothing."

Ardyn jolts like she told him no such thing. However, she remains silent, her lips thinning.

"Ardy? This true?" I ask.

Ardyn shares a long look with Tempest and sighs. "To be honest, I'm not here enough to judge. If you want to keep the book here while you research, I won't complain."

"Fine, then it's affecting me," Tempest argues.

My brows wrench up, and I splay my hands. "*How* are you affected, dear brother?"

"The scent catches on Ardyn's clothing, and she brings it to my house. It's disgusting."

Tempest folds his arms over his chest, and he looks like a cross, overgrown toddler with no argument to stand on.

"Oh my god." I point a finger at him. "You are so prissy and immature. Wash Ardyn's clothes then with your personal laundry machine while the rest of us share nineties relics in the basement."

"Okay, cease-fire." Ardyn holds up her hands between us. "This argument is literally pointless."

"Agreed." I lift my chin. "But to appease the Sir Sensitive Nose over there, I'm not leaving the book in this room."

Tempest arches a brow. "You're not?"

I shake my head and gesture to my bag. "When I'm not carrying it and risking becoming a social pariah by wafting it around campus, I'll stash it somewhere safe."

"Where?"

I frown at Tempest. "Why do you care? It's not your class, so I don't have to answer to you."

Surprisingly, Tempest responds to me with a long-suffering sigh. "Speaking of which..."

My voice lowers with suspicion. "What?"

"You're enrolled in my economics course."

"*What*?" Both Ardyn and I ask at the same time.

"My class?" Ardyn clarifies. "Like, the super-hard one that is impossible to get into without Professor Rossi's approval?"

Rossi.

During all the annoying hullabaloo with my brother, I forget Rossi is in charge of the class he TAs. He'd be very sexy to witness lecturing, all powerful and knowing, an arrogant expert in his field as he walks behind me and trails a finger across my shoulders...

No. I shake myself out of *that*. "I have zero interest in business topics."

"Yes, but you can study them just fine," Tempest says. "You aced all your classes in high school, took advanced-level courses, and graduated with a 5.0. And my class will look great on your transcript."

I think fast because he isn't wrong. "Isn't there a conflict of interest with you being my TA?"

"I wouldn't be your TA. Rossi has another one for his other classes who he can use."

I frown. "Besides the fact that this makes no sense for me to do in the middle of the semester, *why* would I want to drop one of my carefully selected courses and take up yours?"

"Because your family wants you to."

Ardyn sobers at the finality of Tempest's tone. My feathers only ruffle further.

"Don't bring our parents into this like you give a shit about what they say," I say.

"This isn't about me. It's about you and your future, something that our parents and I have in common. You're our lucky star, Clover. I'm only asking you to do what's best for you."

"Except you're not asking."

Tempest rolls his lips. "No. I'm not."

I shake my head and puff out an exhale. "College was meant to get me *out* of the Callahan clutches and decide my own way. Dad agreed, so long as you were around. What changed? Why is a collar being put back on me?"

I don't mean for my voice to break, but it cracks through the air, the emotion too sudden and large to contain.

Tempest's wince is more noticeable this time. "I'm sorry, Clo. I really am. But what's done is done."

I ball my hands into fists. "This isn't fair. They promised. *You* promised to give me independence!"

"And you have it, just with one change in subject," Tempest reasons.

"I have way too much on my plate as it is. How am I supposed to do this research paper for Professor Morgan when I'll have to catch up on Professor Rossi's syllabus?"

"I can help you," Ardyn says. "He's tough but not unreasonable. You can read all my notes and use my textbooks until you get your own."

A part of me wishes Ardyn would stand up for me. The other, more reasonable side understands how reluctant she is to get between her best friend and boyfriend. I wouldn't want to get between the Callahans, either.

Tempest holds out his hand. "Give me the grimoire, and I'll pass it along to Morgan with your apologies. Business is more important than witch history, anyway."

I clutch my tote tighter. "It's not more important to *me*."

Tempest's attention darts to my bag, then away, but I catch the flash of interest in his eyes before he returns to my face.

"Enough of this," I say, so angry that my face is pulsing. "I have somewhere to be."

"My instructions still stand," Tempest says to my back. "If you want to stay at TFU, you have to switch to Rossi's class."

"Yes, *sir*," I hiss, then whirl to the door. "But I refuse to drop my occult class."

I hear Ardyn whisper, *"I'm so sorry, Clo,"* as I leave the room.

When I turn for the stairs, a hearty whistle hits my ears in total conflict with my whirling thoughts. Looking over my shoulder, I notice Professor Morgan strolling out of the elevator with his hands in his coat pockets.

"Professor Morgan?" I ask.

His eyes snag on mine, and he stops mid-tune, his lips pursed.

I cock my head. "What are you doing here?"

"Well, this is pure kismet. I was just about to knock on your door." Morgan stalls outside Minnie and Kirsty's room a few doors down. "Oh my, what happened here?"

Their door was left open by the movers. I was too stunned to get a good look, but I did see a whole lot of empty room when I blew past.

At the sound of our voices, a large form barrels out of my room.

I cast my eyes to the ceiling. Tempest. Of course.

He comes to a stop in front of me, blocking my sight.

"To clarify my sister's question," Tempest growls, "why the *fuck* are you about to knock on her door?"

I walk around Tempest, giving him a good shove as I move in front and stand my ground. He barely shifts at the contact.

Morgan smiles. As usual, the gleam of his teeth doesn't reach his eyes. "I was merely checking on an intrepid student, Tempest."

Tempest snaps, "Do you usually make house calls to freshman girls?"

I whip my head around to glare at him. "Don't talk about me like I'm a child. While this might sound crazy to you, I can have a conversation with my professor outside of class without risking my so-called virginity." I shrink my gaze at him. "Which I'm *not*."

Tempest's upper lip curls like my not being a virgin physically pains him. Ardyn picks that moment to step out of the room, and with an understanding nod at me and an amused smile, she sidles up to Tempest. "Come on. Let's grab that dinner."

I'm about to thank her for her timely pest control services when she adds, "I'm sure Professor Morgan will be happy to join us back to Anderton Cottage."

"I have no idea why neither of you want me to talk to a professor about an important final essay in my favorite subject," I say, keeping the thought of another chance at Morgan's tongue to myself. "Other than to force me into business studies."

Morgan's brows smooth. "Ah. No wonder we're all prickly at the moment."

He directs his next question at me. "Does that mean you'll be dropping my class, Miss Callahan? I hear you discovered an amazing artifact of the Andertons. Something the university will be more than interested in acquiring and displaying to their donations committee, I'm sure."

Tempest mutters behind me, "Such a role-playing cocksucker..."

I study my brother with suspicion. He's defensive and threatening most days, but his animosity toward Morgan is a bit much, even for him.

Morgan continues, "I'd love to look at this grimoire. Do you have it handy?"

"Sure."

Tempest hisses behind me. Ardyn bites her lower lip, her fingers digging into his arm to keep him in place.

"What?" I ask them defensively. "Professor Morgan has a vested interest in the Andertons. Why wouldn't I give him a look?"

Morgan grins with a closed mouth. I recoil from the sheer predatory satisfaction of it, though I'm also a little turned on by the arrogant tilt to his lips.

"Wonderful," he says. He simpers the word, and it's directed at Tempest.

"*After* I've done my research," I add.

Morgan's attention snaps back to me. He frowns.

"I don't want you going through the grimoire and finding something I might've overlooked in my essay," I say to him. "You could lower my grade because of it."

Morgan presses a hand to his chest. "I would never."

"Oh," Tempest snorts. "You would."

Morgan ignores him. "If you could just give me a peek. Right now, even, I'd love to see what's been so successfully hidden for so long..."

Tired of the conversation and navigating my brother's temper, I move to walk around Morgan and risk taking the elevator, where I'll be forced to wait directly in front of Minnie's empty room.

But it's better than standing in the middle of a pissing contest.

Morgan halts my retreat with a deft step into my path, our chests knocking together. I gasp at the contact, tilting my chin up to face him with surprise.

His grin is so much sexier up close, framed with stubble and sun-lined skin. I hold my eyes with his, and Morgan's hand brushes against my hip, so light and subtle there's no way Tempest could catch the bold move.

But I do. My mouth parts at the *zing* it brings out in my stomach. The corners of Morgan's lips twitch at the sight, his eyes growing hooded.

"If you really want to piss your brother off, give me the grimoire," he murmurs so only I can hear.

His fingers play with the hem of my sweater, but there's something sinister in his features when he asks. Almost like ... malice.

I whisper in return, "Tempest doesn't care about the Andertons. Giving you the book will only satisfy his alpha dog need to drag me out of your class, and that's the last thing I want."

Morgan's sea-glass eyes develop an intriguing sheen. The malice I thought I saw is long gone, replaced with softened concern. "Oh? You want to stay with me?"

"Back. *Off*," Tempest warns.

Rather than shudder and rub against Morgan like I would *love* to do, I force my gaze off Morgan's and over his shoulder.

Escaping his hold allows me to catch my breath.

"This has been great," I say, pushing off Morgan's chest. *Holy crap, he's ridiculously sculpted under that button-down.* "But I have to go."

"Clover." Morgan's eyes harden.

I wave whatever his request is away. "I'll come in during your office hours tomorrow and bring the book for you to preview. I know I have to give it to the university at some point, but you understand my absolute need to go through it first, right? It could answer everything."

Morgan's voice goes down a decibel when he answers. "Indeed, it could."

I still have to get through Tempest and Ardyn to make it to the stairwell. Surprisingly, Tempest steps aside while Ardyn brings me in for a hug.

"Be careful walking around campus at night," Tempest says to me. Ardyn squeezes her agreement against my shoulders.

"It's a study group," I say with a sigh, separating from my friend. "Not a murder club. I'll see everyone later."

All three of their eyes trail goose bumps along my back as I step into the stairwell and leave them behind.

RIO ISN'T WAITING for me when I reach the edge of the woods near the university. The trees are so tall they block out even the mountains from view as I walk down the path, crunching frozen twigs and crinkled leaves beneath my feet.

Minnie's gone. Vanished with an NDA. Technically there's no need to learn self-defense with Rio.

But it's Rio.

And I never want to be that vulnerable again.

Besides, Minnie's not the only girl disdainful of my activities. She was just the loudest.

Not to mention what they say about cockroaches. There's always another one to take its place.

After a few minutes, I drop my bag to the ground and tuck my hands into my jacket pockets. I chose to dress lightly against the cold winter night, expecting that training with Rio would have kept me sweating until midnight. But the longer I'm forced to wait, the more I understand how silent and eerie an old forest can be after its daylight animals go to sleep.

A distant hoot of an owl echoes through the woods. The spires of the university send golden light through its many windows and sharp-tipped towers, illuminating an archaic scene of ancient trees overgrowing stone buildings in a way modern cities never experience.

As more time ticks by, I slow my pace and take in the view. I wonder if Sarah and her daughter ever had a sight like this. Did they hide among these trees, watching people come to shore, figuring out who would approach them for their next victim?

My mind sparks with an idea. I could speed up time by diving into researching the Anderton grimoire rather than waste it wondering why Rio didn't show up. My heart still feels heavy with disappointment, but at least it'll keep me distracted from realizing that Rio wanting to be alone with me is only a fantasy.

I crouch down to search through my bag when a hand clamps against my hair and pulls.

CHAPTER 26
CLOVER

I'm thrown off my feet by my hair, then caught by a hand hooking under my jaw, my hands shooting up and clawing against the assault.

Choking, eyes bulging, I kick out but only meet air.

I scratch against solid forearms and a deadly grip. My nails peel back from my fingers, some breaking off and sending burning pain into my hands, but none of that compares to not being able to breathe.

The person whips me around and slams me against a tree trunk. Their hands slide off my neck and grip my shoulders, pressing them against the rough bark.

I have to blink the tears out of my vision to get a good look, my chest heaving and my voice making garbled sounds I never knew could come from a person.

When his eyes steady, the brown in them shifting to liquid black in the night, I realize who it is.

"Rio," I gasp.

It takes a few seconds to sort through the shock, but anger doesn't have any trouble flaring to the surface.

"You *asshole!*" I shout.

Or try to. My voice is scratched and raw. I slap at him and even shift my leg so I can knee him in the crotch.

He catches both moves in the palm of his hand, smooth and unruffled, his expression carefully blank.

Rio grabs both my wrists. He shifts until our noses are almost touching. "Now I see how you were so easily overpowered by unskilled students."

"Thanks for the pointers," I bite out.

"You were distracted," he continues levelly. "Completely unaware of your environment even though you're standing at the entrance to a wild forest. Your back was to the shadows while you focused on a clearing where you could easily see any attacker approach. It gave me my opening. All I had to do was crouch..." He loosens his grip, pressing against the bark on either side of my face. "And wait for my opportunity."

My heaves subside. My heart rate doubles at his proximity. "That's exactly why I agreed to let you teach me."

"I am teaching you."

"Attacking is not a lesson."

Rio angles his head in thought. "It should be."

I've learned, through decades of experience, that dealing with Rio is rather like dealing with an exotic pet no one has any business owning. You have to approach it carefully and always be watchful of its next move. "Okay, so how should I have escaped your surprise strangling?"

A shaft of moonlight catches the approving curve of his lips. "Let me show you."

Reluctant to relive what was a terrifying experience seconds ago, but reminding myself of the whole exotic pet thing, I step away from the tree and around its thick, gnarled roots poking out from the ground and give Rio my back.

So he can strangle me again.

What a fun dream date.

Sure enough, his cold fingers slide around my throat. I shudder, both eager to feel him again and fully aware that he could end my life with an idle squeeze.

But my heart rate settles. My shoulders come down from my ears.

"I trust you," I whisper.

Rio's fingers still. His breath falls short. Then he murmurs, "Never trust anyone, Lucky. Not even me."

I want to twist and ask him why since he's been my brother's best friend for years and even lived with us for a time. If there's anyone I should trust to keep me safe other than Tempest, it's—

"Option one." Rio tightens his grip on my neck. Not as brutally as the first time, but he definitely means business.

I swallow, the tendons in my neck rippling under his firm forearm.

"Go for my eyes. Scratching at my arms is useless. Reach behind and gouge me with your thumbs."

My lips curl in disgust.

"You won't hesitate to burst eyeballs when your life is being squeezed out of you," Rio adds, reading my thoughts.

"No, I guess not."

"Option two. You can stomp on my instep," he continues, his voice close to my ear. "Your first instinct was to kick out. That was your first lethal mistake."

"First?"

"Of many."

I frown but stay quiet.

"Do it," Rio demands. "Stomp on my foot."

I hesitate. "I did this. To Kirsty."

Rio stills as if impressed. "Good. But she has the wingspan of a squirrel. Go on. You won't hurt me," he says in a rare moment of amusement.

That almost sounds like a challenge. Firmly into it now, I lift my leg and shove my heel into the top of his boot.

Rio lets out a grunt. It's muffled inside his closed mouth.

"Nice," he grits out. "And surprisingly accurate."

"I'm small but mighty," I say. "And a great student."

His chest bumps against my back. Even though we're both clothed, the sensation of his warmth moves through my leather-clad body and into my blood. I shut my eyes on an exhale, wishing he'd wrap his arms around my waist and not my neck.

"Moving on." Rio's voice takes on a rough, strained tone, and he retreats. "I lifted you off your feet in an instant. You're small and light and might not have the opportunity to reach my instep. Your next option, when my arm comes around your throat, is to turtle your neck down and your shoulders up so you have space to breathe and prevents me pressing into your trachea. Do it."

I follow his instructions.

"Good," he says. "Then instead of scratching pointlessly at my skin, hook your hands into the bend at my elbow and pull down. It'll force me to bend forward and will give you another chance to stomp on my foot. It's painful for your attacker, but I may not yet release you. Therefore, shift a little so you can use your elbow to anvil-punch me in the groin. Elbows are the strongest weapon women have on their—*don't*—" He catches my fist before I hit him in his sensitive bits. "—experiment with that part."

I snort. "Just checking your reflexes."

He unwinds his arm from my neck and steps back enough for me to turn and face him.

His eyes dip to the V of my chest where my jacket is open.

"You're wearing it," he says.

I look down. The diamond is the sole glimmer in the darkness. "Yes. You gave it to me to wear, I assume."

He doesn't respond, but his silence is answer enough.

I reach up to hold the jewel in my hand, twirling it on its chain.

"Thank you," I whisper.

His lashes lower as he tears his attention from the diamond and returns my stare. "You are more welcome than you know."

The glitter of the diamond turns into a flash of light between us, one I can't escape from. One I don't want to.

I don't want the tutorial to end.

"What about if two people are restraining me?" I let go of the necklace. "Like ... last time."

Rio's gaze darkens into two opaque holes, blacker than an endless night.

"Where did they hold you?"

"By my wrists and arms." I rub my arms at the memory, the bruises invisible but sore.

"Then I'll show you how to break their wrists."

My chin jerks back, though I shouldn't be surprised. Everything Rio says, he means.

He steps closer the moment a chilling wind wafts his scent in my direction. It's not his normal one. I've been around Rio long enough to memorize the woodsy, soapy deliciousness on his skin.

This time, it's sharp. Coppery. Yet ... familiar.

"They grabbed you like this?"

His grip on my wrist distracts me from attempting to think about where I know that scent from. "Yes."

"Twist your hand so you can grab onto my wrist in turn. Yes, like that. Now, using your hips and keeping your elbow close to your body—don't move it, this is where your strength comes— and twist. She'll be forced to follow you to prevent her tendons from snapping. And then, kick. Don't give her enough time to use her free hand to punch you. Then turn to the next assailant and do the same. One at a time."

I'm listening to Rio's words, filing them away like a good, smart student, but I can't help but also follow his eyes, staring at his face in wonder at his feral beauty. The moon slashes his cheekbones white and shadows the crevices between his teeth to look like fangs. Yet he's beautiful, and closer to me than he's ever dared to come before.

"This is the first time you haven't been afraid to touch me," I blurt out.

Rio goes rigid. His hand doesn't leave my skin.

"I know my brother's ordered you to stay away from me."

Rio releases a soft scoff. "He orders anyone with a dick not to come within ten feet of you."

"Yes, but why you? You're the safest out of all the men I've met—"

"I'm not safe."

"Why do you listen to him? He's not your master or owner just as he isn't *mine*. Why the *hell* do we listen to him?"

Rio's thumb strokes the inside of my wrist, halting my next complaints in my throat. "It's not as simple as following orders. I respect him. He's my family, and so are you. I can't jeopardize that as much as I'd..."

At the break in his tone, I lift my chin, tipping my face close to his. I whisper, "As much as you'd what?"

"I would do anything for Tempest. And anything for you. In turn, he would do anything for me. It comes down to loyalty, a bond. I don't want to ruin that."

I dare to ask, "Then why are you still touching me? Meeting with me in secret?"

"I'm teaching you how to defend yourself. Tempest would approve."

"Then why didn't you tell him? Why don't you tell him what you've been leaving me?"

At the lowering of his eyes, I know I'm right.

"I'm having trouble staying away from you," Rio confesses.

My eyes flare.

"I watch you, Lucky. I can't stop tracing your movements, wondering what you're doing, who you're with. You take up so much of my thoughts that I almost didn't come to meet you tonight. I knew it'd be dangerous. If you felt the same, I knew we'd forge a perilous connection."

"I feel the same." It comes out in a rush of breath. "Rio, I feel the same—"

He holds a finger to my lips, shushing me yet not moving away. "Don't say it again. Please."

His other hand still holds my wrist. With a burst of rebellion, of fire and deep heat, I pull the very move he taught me.

Rio's forced to twist into the move. I use his imbalance and surge forward, pressing my lips to his.

Heat surges from his lips and into my body. This is what I'd dreamed would happen tonight, our freezing bodies morphing into blue fire the instant we connected.

Rio's arms wrap around me, pulling me into him with bone-crushing strength. His mouth sucks me in, his tongue warm velvet against his hardened, icepick body.

We stumble over tree roots until my back crashes against the trunk, our mouths hungry, starving, clashing and striking against each other like a match. His hands move, furiously tracing my body, climbing over my breasts, framing my face. He groans, the sound of a pained animal escaping his throat, yet he doesn't stop.

Thank God he isn't pulling away.

I don't think I could survive the rejection after tasting him, that metallic tang surrounding us like a savage blanket.

In one lithe movement, his hand dips down, and he lifts one of my legs, exposing my center. His finger follows the seam of my leggings, the one sewn directly in the center of my folds.

I moan into his mouth.

Rio lifts his lips from mine, releasing a shuddering breath. "I'm going to hell for this."

I bury my fingers in his hair. "Allow me to hold you all the way down."

I pull his mouth back to mine.

Rio groans into my mouth, sliding his lips away and kissing my cheek, then leaving a trail down my neck, sucking and biting. My head falls back, allowing him access to one of the most vulnerable parts of my body, the very spot he squeezed, then defended, and now strokes.

His erection presses into me through his denim, hard and rigid. I'm desperate to strip him, to pull him out and bury him inside me, but he's so tentative, so tortured, that I don't think pushing him further would cement our chemistry.

Because we've already exploded.

Rio parts my jacket and lifts my sweater. He pulls down both cups of my bra, exposing my nipples to the frigid air.

I gasp at the sudden change from comforting warmth to cold, my nipples peaking instantly. He lowers his head and sucks on one while twisting and massaging the other.

I moan into the sky, the forest canopy catching my pleasure and keeping it close by.

Rio moves to give my other nipple his tongue-centered attention. Without warning, his free hand finds the hem of my leggings and dips inside. I surge at the contact of a cold thumb against my clit, then shudder in absolute ecstasy as he circles it.

"Fuck," he breathes out against my breast. "You're irresistible. You've always been my obsession. And smelling you now, coating my fingers with you, you've made yourself mine forever."

His vow doesn't scare me. If anything, it ties a rope around my soul, one attached to him.

I wriggle against his fingers, silently begging for more. He pinches my clit, sending sparks into my belly and breasts, then slides through my slickness until he finds my entrance, prodding gently, then pulling away.

He does it again. And again.

"Please," I beg out loud. "Please, I want more, Rio."

Rio raises his head, fusing his lips back to mine as he shoves a finger all the way to the knuckle inside me.

I push down on his hand, desperate to fill the ache he's caused and riding his finger for all it's worth.

He pushes another finger in, then another, until all four fill me, and his thumb plays my clit like his own unique instrument.

"Is this enough for you?" he asks harshly against my mouth.

"No," I moan. "I need your dick. I want your dick inside me, Rio."

I gyrate against his fingers. He circles and thrusts, following my lead.

"Come," he commands. "Come on my fingers, Lucky. Let me see your face."

"Oh fuck," I say when he pushes in hard.

The sensation becomes too much. I crash and burst inside, my thighs quaking around him. My orgasm pulses against his relentless fingers. I dig my nails into his shoulders, crying out against his neck as he holds me for the entire ride, breathing roughly into my ear.

The tingles subside, leaving behind a satisfying ache. While my limbs tremble, I can't seem to let go of him. I don't know if I ever want to.

Rio's palm slams into the tree right beside my face. Head bowed, he straightens, gently extricating my arms from around his neck.

It's at that moment I believe it's over, whatever it is we had.

But he doesn't retreat. Rio looks deep into my eyes instead, his expression tense but unreadable.

Breathing heavily, he says, "We shouldn't have done that."

"No," I agree, "but I don't regret it."

One side of his mouth lifts in a small smile. "Even now, you're irresistible."

Bolstered by his words, I reach for his zipper. "Let me return the favor."

In a move invisible to my naked eye, Rio slides out of reach.

My hands hang in midair, my mouth hanging open in a surprised *O* of hurt.

Frost crunches under his boots as he slows his movements, his arms slackening at his sides. "We can't. I can't go any further with you."

"But why?" In my mind, what we've already done is punishable by death in Tempest's view. Why stop now?

Rio's lips twitch. "I was weak tonight. You deserve better than this. Better than me."

I resist the natural eye roll that wants to occur at those words. "I'm old enough to choose what I want, Rio, and I choose you."

He shakes his head. "This is a mistake. I was supposed to help you, not seduce you."

"I'm pretty sure we seduced each other."

"This was a bad idea. Someone else should teach you self-defense. Maybe your brother will finally realize you're better off learning the skill of a chokehold than wandering around campus at night with nothing but bear spray in your bag."

I frown. "Bear spray works wonders."

Rio arches a brow.

"Or so I'm told," I mutter, considering I've never had to thwart an attack before until Minnie made me all too aware of how weak I could be.

And if I'm to be honest, how weak I made myself, too, considering I've always followed Tempest's rules and assumed I could reach into my bag at a moment's notice.

Rio walks backward, about to assume his habitual melting into the shadows before he disappears.

My chin jerks up in a panic. "I don't want to stop."

Rio pauses.

"The lessons," I clarify, although I'd be more than happy to continue our pleasure sessions, too, but I don't want to scare my tortured panther off.

"Please," I say. "You call yourself the weak one, but of course you aren't. You could probably take a bear in the woods *without* bear spray. But me? You said it yourself. I'm vulnerable. I couldn't fight off three overprivileged trust fund babies who wouldn't know a self-defense class if it went on sale at Lululemon. So please, don't stop teaching me."

He answers softly, "You can enroll in one of the university programs."

"You and I both know you can teach me better. And faster."

Emboldened by his lack of answer, I add, "I don't know exactly what you and my brother are involved in, but I know it's risky, and you've acquired the kind of skill to combat it. I'm not saying I want to be the next Black Widow, but I *do* want to scare the shit out of Minnie's friends if and when they come after me again."

I also want more chances to be alone with you. That part, I keep to myself.

Typical Rio, he knifes straight through the heart of my argument. "Why not Minnie?"

"She left." I shrug as if it doesn't matter despite her departure nagging at me. *This is all because of you!* Kirsty keeps screaming in my head. "Movers were outside our building. Lauren said she wasn't coming back."

Rio frowns a full upside-down crescent. His brows crash together in thought, and his gaze slides to the side. "Is that so?"

"It doesn't mean I'm safe," I say. "The girls here, the people here ... it's why I go to The Boiler. I feel safer at a dive bar than on campus. How sad is that? I want to feel confident again, Rio." I notch my chin. "I want to stand my ground."

A jaw muscle tics on one side of his face—the sole tell that he's mulling my argument over.

Rio's stare rakes me from head to toe, a burning intensity belying the frosted woods we're standing in. My insides surge with warmth, and as if pulled by a string, I take a step toward him.

He gives a minuscule shake of his head. "I'll think about it."

Rio disappears into the woods, denying any further argument.

CHAPTER 27

CLOVER

When I return to my room, every crystal I have lost has been replaced on my windowsill. A scan of my nightstand shows a new set of tarot cards and incense sticks.

A single-note placard sits on top of a cinnamon-scented candle, containing a flourished signature. **Rio**.

I smile.

Fantasies of him gave me the best night's sleep of my life, especially when Xavier was added into the mix. One pleasuring my pussy while the other teased my lips with his cock.

I've never had group sex dreams before. I've always assumed it was an activity reserved for porn videos or drunken college parties. But here I am on a random Thursday night, dreaming of Rio and Xavier arguing over who could eat me out first.

Then Morgan comes into the fray, calling dibs and burying his head between my legs.

My eyes languidly crack open in the morning. I stretch like a cat beside Hermione, naked except for the diamond between my breasts, enjoying the pulled muscles in my thighs from wrapping around Rio last night. If it weren't for those twinges of overexertion, I would've thought my night with him in the woods was a dream, too.

I have to scoot Hermione's butt out of the way to roll to my side and check the time. Eight o'clock.

"Crap!"

I shoot up in bed and throw the covers off. Those gorgeous dreams of mine have made me late for my first and favorite class.

Ardyn's side of the room is empty, so I can run around without worries of being modest or waking her up. As for my downstairs neighbor, they'll just have to deal with the pounding of feet this morning.

I fling on loose ripped jeans and an oversized red shirt, throwing on my jacket and grabbing my bag during my panicked sprint to the door. Time is slipping away, and I can't afford to be late for class again. But just as I reach the door, a knock resonates through the room, freezing me in my tracks.

Curiosity tingling on who it could be—Rio, Morgan, Xavier, *Tempest*—I turn the knob and swing open the door.

Xavier stands before me in designer jeans and a black tee stretching over his chest with a mischievous glint in his eyes.

My heart skips a beat.

Xavier grins, his gaze sweeping over my disheveled appearance. "Late for class? Lucky for you, we're in the same one this morning, and I can walk you."

I lean against the doorframe, raising an eyebrow. "How did you know I'd still be here?"

He chuckles. "I've been keeping an eye on the most captivating girl on campus. You tend to leave a lasting impression."

A mix of flattery and embarrassment washes over me. "I suppose you're here to rescue me from the clutches of tardiness?"

He takes a step closer, his presence filling the air with an undeniable magnetism. "I thought I'd offer my services as your personal escort. Consider it my good deed for the day."

I pretend to ponder his offer, feigning nonchalance. "Hmm, this isn't the first time you've committed a good deed. I can't have the hottest guy in school walking me to class and causing a ruckus. People might get jealous. Again."

An impish smirk dances on his lips. "Jealousy can be quite entertaining."

Heat rises in my cheeks, his words sparking a mixture of excitement and nervousness. I think of what we did in the library with Morgan looking on. Instinct tells me I'm right, that Xavier was trying to make him jealous. The fact that these gorgeous men would fight over *me* of all people...

I bite my lip, unable to suppress a grin. "You win. Let's go."

It isn't until I'm downstairs and outside that I realize the grimoire is in my bag. I can't return it to my room since that space has been thoroughly violated and can't be trusted anymore. I can't bring it to class due to its smell.

I stall in the pathway with Xavier for a few precious seconds.

"Everything all right?" he asks.

I nod, an idea forming. "Would you mind picking us up a couple of coffees and meeting me there? I have to go grab something."

"Can I help?"

Xavier's presence in the girls' dorm has garnered attention. Those in the lounge and exiting the building swing their attention in his direction, making them walk a lot slower.

I can't have him anywhere near me if I'm going to hide the grimoire. He's a hot boy beacon.

"It's girl stuff. I'll see you there, okay?"

"With coffee." Xavier's lips tilt up. "Black with two sugars, correct?"

I squeeze his hand in thanks. I'm not used to such acts of

service, like walks to class and coffee orders and limitless pleasure, especially from a man of his caliber. It's both disarming and
amazing.

He brushes my cheek with the backs of his knuckles before he
leaves. When he turns, I swing in the other direction,
commanding my legs to move fast.

I'll be even later to Morgan's class, a transgression I'm
hoping a cute smile from me will fix as soon as I slide in and take
my seat.

Morgan will either want to humiliate me in front of the
class or be charmed by my ability to smile at a snake so
sweetly.

As if conjured by my thoughts, my phone chimes with a text
from Ardyn.

Where are you? Morgan's glaring at your empty seat.

I text while making a brisk walk to the library. **Running late.
Can you tell him I have period cramps or something?** An
effective tactic against men, even in the 21st century. Although
with Morgan, you never know. **Anything to make him not want
to question it.**

Ardyn texts back with an eye-roll emoji. I'll take that as a yes,
she will.

The campus is almost deserted during my walk. Most
students are in class or hunkered down in a warm room. The
mountain air is fresh and pure but also known to freeze your
lungs solid in the winter.

My fast pace brings me to the library's doors in less than ten
minutes. I swing open the solid wood on a groan.

The long tables are sparsely populated once I swipe in and
trek between the aisles. Nobody looks up from their studies as I
pass.

I head to the back of the stacks, and with Professor Rossi's
Faculty Only warning in my mind, I glance left and right before

ducking under the velvet rope and descending the stairs into the basement.

After the bright winter sunlight, the basement takes on a darker hue as my eyes adjust. It takes careful steps to navigate through the dusty shelves until I remember Rossi is in class and therefore not posted here, ready to scare the bejesus out of me and drag me out by the arm.

I turn my phone's flashlight on, thoughts of Rossi teaching class reminding me that I'm due at his lecture after Morgan's.

My lips twist with an unexcited grimace.

Somehow, I'll have to wiggle my way out of my family's new demand. I'm tired of being their puppet.

I shove that reminder to the back of my mind because right now I have to find a nice spot for my stinky book. Here, the scent shouldn't reach too many nostrils, what with all the other old, dusty, forgotten relics in this room.

I don't have much time, so I choose one of the last rows of forgotten books and carefully nestle Sarah's grimoire between two other leather-bound tomes. I steal a few of their cobwebs to drape over and kick up a thick coating of dust from the floor to make it appear as if it's always been there. Then I carefully memorize where I've put it so I can come back for the grimoire later. I have big plans to thoroughly go through it tonight and research some of the jewelry from that handmade account ledger I found now that my potion is a no-go. A profit sheet I'm thinking that laid out her blood payments from the nobles.

Satisfied with the grimoire's disguise, I head out of the library and to class—one I'm thirty minutes late for.

With a wince, I crack open the door to Morgan's room, sliding inside just in time to hear him say, "I've expedited the due date on your final essay."

Every face whips toward him in horror, including mine.

Ardyn is the first to speak. "Excuse me, Professor?"

Morgan lays his palms at the head of the table as I walk around and find my seat. Xavier's head lifts as I round the table, offering me a smile when he nudges my coffee across the table and toward my seat. I return it with a little too much enthusiasm because Morgan's preternatural eyes find mine as I lower into my spot, narrowing with displeasure and dampening any lasting tingly effect I had before coming under his scope.

"Miss Callahan, what a relief modern medicine is. I'm so glad you're feeling well enough to attend the last twenty minutes of this class."

My cheeks flush, but I keep my gaze steady on his. "Sorry I'm late."

He straightens, including the room. "Don't let it happen again."

Morgan resumes his lecture, and I take a grateful sip of the hot coffee. My attention flicks to the table at the sight of a folded piece of paper under the cup.

Brows tight with intrigue, I move until I can read it under the table.

I dreamed about your gorgeous ass walking away from me in the coffee line. Shall we try that next?

My heart stops at the sight of Xavier's loopy scrawl. One line of suggestive innuendo and promises of fun later, and I'm blushing like I've never slept with him before.

Xavier's so sweet, genial, and thoughtful, yet he can write this dirty tease like we're in high school and don't own phones.

I can't help but admit that I like our continued role-play.

Smiling, I refold the note and start to tuck it in my bag, but I'm too late. Morgan's gaze burns a hole into me from across the room. He's been watching me, even as he lectured, and now his eyes are narrowed with suspicion.

Morgan strides across the room, and in one swift move, he

yanks the note from my hands. Heat rushes to my neck as everyone stares in shock.

"Miss Callahan," he says with an edge of malice. "I believe this belongs to me now. What do you think? Would you like to read it out loud so everyone can hear? Or shall we keep this little love exchange between us?"

His mouth says one thing, but his eyes say another, blazing in retributory promise.

Promise that he could do these things to me given the chance.

Warning that he'd take it so much further.

Or am I imagining it?

My heart thumps in my chest, and I swallow.

"I think this is between us," I say.

Morgan looks me up and down. He pauses before a slow smile stretches across his face. "Very well then, Miss Callahan. Let's keep it between *us*."

Xavier releases an audible exhale, massaging his temples like he wished his fingers would just pierce through his brain and end his misery already. "Professor, perhaps we should continue class?"

Xavier sends me an apologetic look, like maybe he's gotten so immersed in our pretend life that he's forgotten who we are in reality.

My brows furrow, noting the shadows under his eyes and the sallow tinge to his skin I didn't notice under natural light. Enrolling halfway through a semester can't be easy, but Xavier's emotional heaviness is at odds with an increased course load.

Morgan breaks his trance and turns back to the lecture board, but not before giving me one last look that seems to carry all the secrets of our shared moment together.

Morgan folds his arms and scans every occupant of the table.

And like a pack of turtles, each student shrinks into their shoulders when he lands on them.

"Magical beliefs and practices have a dark and tragic history. Need I remind you all of the witch burnings in the sixteen hundreds? You should give it the respect it deserves, or at the very least, put some effort into the syllabus I gave you."

"But, Professor," one girl squeaks, raising her hand with hesitation. "What about those of us who *do* take this class seriously?"

I give an imperceptible glare in her direction. This morning aside, I love this class.

Morgan seems to read my mind. "You are learning this subject as a collective. Therefore, you go up and down together. I suggest you all start taking this class seriously before I decide to give you an early final exam, too."

"You can't do that!" a male student says, appalled.

"I certainly can." Morgan smiles. "And before any of you decide to complain to the chancellor, bear in mind that I have more influence with him than you do."

There's a gleam to Morgan's eye that I can't place after his statement, a kind of arrogance mixed with hidden knowledge. I've learned not to read into Morgan's expressions too much, lest it give me more information into his mental state than I'll ever want, but I can never stifle my curiosity. Not when it comes to hidden mysteries.

Morgan completes his sweep of the room by stopping on me. He says, "Class is dismissed."

Books slam shut, chairs scrape back, and moody grumblings of my classmates signal Morgan's dismissal. I rise with the rest of them, packing up my things, when Xavier catches my eye.

"Why did I come here again?" he asks with a wry twist to his lips. "Sorry to put you under the scope like that."

I notice Morgan stiffen in my periphery as he's stacking his textbooks and putting them in his leather satchel.

Xavier squeezes my shoulder. "I guess I'll see you on the other side, then, eh?"

I find myself saying to Xavier while keeping my gaze on Morgan, "I have a few hours this afternoon if you need more help catching up."

Visions of my sex dream interpose with Xavier's note. I can't resist giving him more opportunities to stroke me under tables.

"I wish I could today." The earnest sparkle in his eyes shows he means it. "But I'm meeting Morgan during every spare hour that I have."

"Really? Why?"

Xavier's neck goes stiff at my question. I quickly realize my mistake. "That was nosy of me. Sorry."

"It's fine, really." Xavier lifts his backpack strap onto one shoulder. "I'm, uh, hoping to get his leniency on this essay thing by doing some volunteer research work for him."

I pause in pushing in my chair. "He had spots open for that?"

Xavier's mouth works. He glances at Ardyn briefly, then snaps his gaze away.

I frown, watching the exchange.

He says, "Ah—not publicly, no. He offered it to me since I was late enrolling, to give me some extra credit."

I open my mouth to ask more questions like, *Why didn't I know about this? I totally would've done occult research for the school,* but Ardyn lays a hand on my arm, pulling me toward the door.

"Come on. We're gonna be late for Rossi's class."

Right. That.

My lips turn down, but I say to Xavier, "Good luck. Text me if you need my help with anything."

Xavier's handsome face softens. "Thanks, Clover. I mean it, and I truly wish I could."

I'm not sure what that means, but I respond with an "Anytime," before turning to walk with Ardyn out of the classroom, my stomach twisting unnaturally.

My instincts tell me to be on the lookout, but I'm not sure what for. My mind has always worked overtime, but with all this mysterious manly behavior around me, it's difficult to parse through and find the answer to all their secretive weirdness.

"Clover."

Both Ardyn and I grind to a halt.

I'm used to having my name barked out and usually have a witty remark to whomever I've annoyed, but when it comes so sharply out of Morgan's mouth, I'm both hesitant and intrigued.

To date, I've been nothing but his teacher's pet. Did my being late to class really piss him off that much?

"Stay behind, will you?" he asks, throwing his blazer on as he strolls toward us.

"I can't. I have class in the business building in five minutes."

His eyes flare like I've struck a match directly between them, and he's none too happy with the proximity. "Yes, with Rossi. I remember."

"How do you...?" I begin, but recall the hallway incident with my brother, of which Morgan was a reluctant witness.

God, Tempest is so embarrassing.

I say, "Never mind. We could talk during my free time this afternoon if it's urgent. I have a ton of work to do, as you know."

The skin under Morgan's eye twitches. "Now is as good a time as any. I'll send Rossi a note that you'll be late because of me."

"Rossi doesn't allow excuses," Ardyn pipes in. She squeezes my arm, pulling hard. "Like Clover said, maybe later."

Morgan's eyes shrink. "Thank you, Ardyn, but I believe I'm the professor here, and I'm telling you Rossi won't mind."

"And I believe Clover has enough on her plate, including

taking on the most advanced business course of freshman year. You had your time with her, and now she has to go."

I watch their sparring like a tennis match.

There it is again. That weird stomach-lurching thing happening inside me.

"And I believe Clover's standing right here," I say, coming between them. I direct my next words to Ardyn, "If Morgan needs to talk to me, it's fine. I'm not looking forward to Rossi's class, and to be honest, I'm searching for any way out of it. This seems like a good one."

Ardyn's expression fills with concern. "Clover..."

"I'm not telling you to choose sides," I assure, though I wish she'd side with my brother less and me more. "This class means a lot to me." *More than a business class I'm being threatened into taking.* "If Professor Morgan has concerns, I want to hear them. And if he says Rossi will understand, then he will."

Ardyn sighs. She gives me one last loaded stare before glaring at Morgan, where they seem to communicate silent insults until she relents. She can't argue if a professor wants to talk to a student privately about an assignment.

Because that's all this is. *Isn't it?*

"Fine. I'll give you my notes," she says.

I nod, then wait until she leaves the classroom and shuts the door before turning to Morgan.

Morgan pulls out one of the chairs at the class table. He sticks out his hand with a flourish and a wicked grin.

"Sit down, Clover."

CHAPTER 28

MORGAN

I t's difficult to keep the desperation off my face when Clover sits in front of me. For a moment, I'm hovering over her, her perfect neck within reach of my twitchy fingers. I don't want to kill her. I *do* want to press my thumbs into her trachea, controlling her breaths until she begs hoarsely for me to do more.

My eyelids flutter at the vision. I swallow. Clench and unclench my fingers. Then take my seat at the head of the table so we're diagonal to each other, a safe enough distance so long as I don't leap for her.

Clover glances around the room, refusing to meet my eye. It's as if she's reading my twisted, dirty thoughts and wants to avoid them at all costs.

I smile.

The flush to her cheeks tells me she's remembering our time together.

But the lined bookshelves hold her interest for only so long. "You wanted to ask me something?"

"Yes." I lean back into my seat, appearing as if I have all the time in the world while my heart pounds. *I want to tell you about my gift to you. What I did for you.*

"How are you coming along with your essay?"

Her stare lands on mine with a cute line between her brows. "I didn't choose an easy topic, but I like it that way."

"You've never made use of my office hours. I thought it best to pull you aside and make sure your research is going well. Finding the name of the Anderton daughter is next to impossible. Many before you have tried and failed along with their grade."

Clover nods, her lips pressed tightly together. "I'm not afraid of a challenge."

Which is why I'm so utterly addicted to you.

Clover is proving herself a serious distraction. It's enough to force myself to complete the task at hand—find the fortune my uncle is due.

"You've made a discovery none of your previous peers were able to," I say, "Sarah's grimoire."

Her eyes return to mine.

I keep my curiosity under control. "Have you found anything interesting?"

"Actually, yes."

My heart is near to deafening. "Oh?"

"There were small pages buried into a hidden seam at the back of the book. But they weren't just laid flat into a pile." She raises her hands to aid her description. "They were folded in an origami shape almost. It was so strange. Did you ever play that game as a child where you folded a piece of paper a bunch of times and wrote between each fold to predict someone's future?"

Clover's words hit my ears as loud as ring in a bell tower. Their meaning is so resounding my pulse becomes nothing but the heartbeat of a fly.

"A letterlock," I answer.

Her chin jerks up. "A what?"

"It's an art of communication dating back to the Romans and Greeks. It was a way to send correspondence where one could tell if the letter had been intercepted." For a moment, I forget who I'm talking to and *why* I need her to confide in me, so interested am I in her discovery. "A person would write their letter, then fold it into specific patterns where, if opened and tripped, they could tell if an unintended party had read it."

Clover leans forward, her lips slackened with curiosity. She's so close I can see the white shine on her inner lower lip, not to mention the ample cleavage jutting out of the deep V of her top and the pendant dangling between.

It was Rio's idea to snatch the necklace, but I consider myself part-owner of the gift.

I want to ask her if she wore red deliberately. I can't resist the color, and I most definitely am doing everything I can to resist the girl currently wearing it like a glorious second skin.

"Tripping something means there's a trap involved," she says. "What did they do to booby trap their letter?"

I blink. Recalibrate. "That's where the lock comes in. Usually in the form of a piece of paper—we're not talking advanced technology here, although back then it certainly was. If you weren't familiar with the folding techniques, you would either tear or expose the small section of paper hidden within the folds. The sender and intended receiver would know to look for it."

Clover falls back into her chair, her expression slack with shocked intrigue. "So Sarah had these pages in a letterlock because she wanted to send it to someone."

"Possibly." Now it's my turn to lean forward. I find my nose going first, attempting to follow her musky incense perfume.

I force myself back on task. "What was written on the pages?"

Clover hesitates.

Impatience gets the best of me. I drum my fingers on the corner of the table.

At last, she admits, "It wasn't what was written so much as what was drawn."

My fingers stop tapping.

"Someone drew jewelry in detail. I've never seen anything like it. Like sculptures surrounded by rare gemstones, all on necklaces and rings."

My breaths turn shallow. "Jewelry at that time is legendary in its detail. Pieces so valuable you can find them in museums."

"Yes."

My cock twitches at the flush in her cheeks and swell of heat into her plump lips. *I must tell her. I must. She'll be delighted that I danced with the dark for her.*

"Are you wondering why she hid those pages away?" I prompt, my voice gritty with the torture of not tasting, not touching, not *being* with her.

Clover shakes her head. "I think this jewelry is what she received in payment for assassinating whoever contracted with her."

My answering smile is slow and filled with satisfaction. "Good girl."

Clover's head comes up sharply at my praise. I internally chastise myself for allowing my lust and approval of her intelligence to intermix so blatantly.

Luckily, she's too focused on her findings to dwell on it. "I wonder who she was sending such detailed drawings to, and why."

I lift a brow, ceding her point. "From what we know, Sarah was an incredibly private person. So much so—"

"That she kept the name of her daughter a secret," Clover finishes, then straightens, her ass nearly leaving her seat. "Do you think her *daughter* drew those pictures?"

I answer with a one-shouldered shrug, though internally my thoughts race with how quick Clover is and that it's possible—no, *probable*—that she could actually locate this fucking treasure.

Clover spins as if to leave, and my heart leaps into my throat. *No. She can't leave. She CAN'T.*

I'll die if I don't taste her again. I'll die if I don't come inside her. I'll die if I don't make her beg for all of me, including my black soul.

I'll die.

"Clover, may I be frank with you?"

She nods, biting her lip. She's nervous about what I have to say.

"I've noticed that you've been the target of bullying lately."

Her cheeks flush pink, and she folds her arms across her chest. "What does that have to do with my essay?"

I take a deep breath. *I have to tell her. What's the point if she doesn't know how far I'll go for her?*

"I know who's been bullying you."

Clover's eyes widen. "You do?"

I nod, my heart rate quickening. "I don't tell many people, but I have a special gift that allows me to deal with bullies in a unique way."

"What kind of gift?" she asks, her voice barely above a whisper.

I rise, then lean in closer, my lips almost grazing her ear. "I can carve messages into their skin, reminding them who they really are."

Her breath hitches in her throat, and I can feel her pulse racing beneath my fingers. "That's ... that's not normal."

"I know," I reply, resting a hip against the table. "But it's effective."

She shivers, but she's not running.

I knew it. My sweet, little leaf likes to flutter in dark winds.

"*Revenge*," I say.

She shakes her head in confusion, her eyes never leaving mine.

"Minnie has that on her body now."

Clover's lovely complexion pales to that of a ghost.

"And I wrote it in reverse," I add, "So every time she looks at it in the mirror, it will be a legible, constant, inerasable reminder."

I smile.

Clover recoils. Her eyes drop to my hands where my runes are strategically placed.

Little leaf. She knows so much of me already.

"W-Why are you telling me this?"

"Because I want to protect you," I confess. "And I want you to know that I'm on your side."

I wonder if her heart races with a strange excitement. If she loves how my deranged mind could turn her pain into something so deliciously monstrous.

"Who *are* you?"

Clover's question is barely above a whisper. Her eyes gleam with unshed tears.

I push to my feet, lifting my hand to stroke her hair behind her ear. Clover flinches.

"You wanted revenge, didn't you?" I reason. "You wanted her to suffer like you did."

She shoves me away, hard enough that I stumble back into the table.

"You don't know what I want," she says tremulously, but the words are hollow.

"Tell me, little leaf." I push off the wood, invading her space. "Tell me what you planned to do to her before I took care of the problem for you."

"*For* me?" Her expression twists. "You did this because you liked it."

"True. But." I end the word with a hard *T.* "I'm not you, a girl who plays in daylight but dabbles after dark. I *live* there. What did you want to do to her?"

Her gaze slides away. She blinks, her forehead rippled in confusion and fear.

"Hmm?" I press, cocking my head so close, oh so close, to her face.

Clover can't hide the spark of desire in her eyes the moment I said the word *revenge*, the same desire that burns within me.

I know I'm not the only one who craves the twisted when I'm wronged.

I want to give her the world, to give her everything she desires.

"I ... I had an elixir."

"An *elixir*?" I repeat with glee.

"I was going to put it in her coffee. It was supposed to make her hallucinate, a karma sort of thing where she'd have night-mares about the same thing done to me being done to her."

I raise my brows, delighted. "You're making me feel I inter-vened too soon."

"I didn't want this. I didn't want her..."

"Hurt? Yes, you did, you devious girl."

"No. *No.*"

"Then show me," I say, my voice low and dangerous. "Show me what you want from me instead."

She hesitates, her eyes locked onto mine.

I'm around the table in a heartbeat. I have my hands at her waist. She's suspended in the air until I slam her against the wall and press my hard-on into her stomach.

My voice is dark and rough. "Or is it me that has to show you what you want? Is that it?"

She writhes in my hold. My hands tighten on her waist. "Do let me know if you're going to knee me in the balls this time."

The reminder, the *remembrance* of what we did the last time we were in this sick embrace, flashes over her face.

She's panting, a flush to the high points of her cheeks. Her nipples are hard and prominent against her thin red top.

That blasted diamond of Rio's fucking *shines* against her skin.

It doesn't take much to pull the neck of her shirt aside, pop her breast out of her lace bra, and suck the peak into my mouth.

She throws her head back and moans. "What makes you think I'd be interested in another round? With someone as unhinged as you?"

I nip her breast and slip my hand between her legs.

She hisses and grinds against my palm.

My voice is a growl. "Don't be coy with me, Clover. You're wet."

"You know nothing of me, and I certainly know nothing of you."

I glare at her with her nipple in my mouth.

I unlatch long enough to scold, "This is what you need. You don't want a

Prince Charming; you want a monster."

Her breath hitches in her throat, and I can feel her body trembling beneath my touch.

"You want someone to ravish you, satisfy your every craving. Someone to make you feel pleasure in the morbid."

The tension between us is palpable. I lift my head closer to hers, our lips just barely touching. "I can be that for you, Clover. Let me be your monster."

Her eyes are wide and pleading. She takes a deep breath, tries to say something, and then stops herself.

Something inside me shatters, like the bars of the prison I've been living in have finally been pried open.

I cover her lips with my own, inhaling her whimper. My hands travel over her body, exploring every curve. My tongue delves into her mouth, tasting her sweetness, a nectar I can't create on my own.

And oh, her innocent scent...

I rip my mouth from hers. Clover squeals when I flip her around, shoving her into the edge of the table and bending her forward.

With one hand, I keep her down. I hook the other around her waist and unbutton her jeans, baggy enough that they slide down her legs like silk.

A neon green thong flashes into my vision before I tear the floss-sized string and pocket the fabric that's been nestled in her slit, damp with want for me.

Her perfect, round ass is exposed. I spread it, taking a peek at what awaits.

Fuck. Even her asshole is wet.

"You've been soaked since the moment I spoke of what I did to your enemy, haven't you, little leaf?" I croon approvingly, then smack one cheek.

The slap rings out, but not as loud as her surprised scream.

"Professor," she begs.

My cock was hard and uncomfortable before. Now, it's unbearable. It stops me from making her beg for longer. I stick my finger inside her, curling it for maximum ache and pleasure.

Clover presses her ass into me, a delectable moan escaping from her mouth.

I would love to draw this out, stretch her to her limits, but I'm so far past patience that it's laughable I haven't driven into her yet.

I pull my finger out, sliding it along her slit and swirling my glistening finger around her puckered asshole.

Then in.

She stiffens, clenching tight around my finger.

"Does that hurt?" I ask softly. "Or does it burn so good?"

Clover gasps. Her fingers turn white where they're clutching the table's edge. "So—"

I don't give her time to answer. A wild growl escapes. I pull out my cock and bury myself in her cunt.

Clover's upper body sags. She bends to her forearms, her hair falling from her back and pooling onto the table's surface. She makes a hedonistic sound between a croon and a cry. I tilt my head back as it meets my ears and have to prevent myself from howling at the feel of her, the *sound* of her while I've buried my cock in her, the sheer smell she exudes, a pheromone resulting from *me*.

I pull my finger out of her ass and insert two thumbs, stretching her while I pull my dick out and slam it back in.

Her nails scrape across the wood.

"I'll never let you go," I grit out between thrusts. "This monster doesn't have his leash anymore."

Clover moans, arching her back to take in more of me. I'd sink my balls into her if I could. My dick is covered in her juices, she's so slick and so tight. I clench with the oncoming storm but control it, enjoying the pain that holding myself back brings.

Clover lifts her head and turns to look over her shoulder at me. Her body trembles under my hands as I span her ass and pull her hole wider with my thumbs.

There's a wild look in her eye, similar to mine but without the bleak history.

I feel like I'm in a fever dream, sweaty and sex fueled. Half of me is in this room. The other half is gone, finding its nest of vipers and drawing upon their venom.

I pop a thumb out of her hole and grab her hair, yanking her head back and exposing her neck.

Between bestial grunts in tune with my onslaught, my fingers untangle from her hair and go for her throat.

Squeezing.

Dominating.

Killing.

"Pr—Professor," she wheezes, her head thrown back.

My fingers dig into the soft points of her neck. I'm too far gone to hear her or frankly care.

Her chokes and gasps spur me on, my lips peeling back from my teeth and saliva pooling on my lower lip.

I feel the quivering of her pussy, the greedy nature of it as it squeezes my cock until she gets what she wants.

I can't contain the guttural sound roaring from my chest when I spill into her and she bucks underneath me, both from orgasm and lack of air.

My vision glazes over. My free palm slams down on one side of her so I don't fall on top of her.

Clover rears up, knocking me into an unsteady stand, and then her finger goes for my fucking eye.

"The fuck—"

I bat her hand away and retreat, my hand slipping from her throat.

Clover bows forward and gasps, massaging her neck. "You ... squeezed ... too long ..."

"Oops." I twist my expression into one of chagrin. "I'm afraid that's a habit of mine."

She looks at me through sex-tangled hair, her cheeks flushed and dewy. All chagrin leaves my face.

"You're amazing," I murmur. "Everything I pictured."

Clarity ripples through her formerly lust-filled eyes. She bends to pull her pants up.

Sadly, sense seems to be returning. I much preferred her bowed under my hands.

She collects her bag, picking up her phone and waking the screen.

Clover sees the time and groans. "I'm late for Rossi."

"Yet you came just in time for me." I wink.

She darts a look my way—*shame? regret? intrigue?*—then shoulders her bag, readying to leave.

I don't care if a woman I've ravished wants to run away from me after. I have that effect.

Yet Clover is not a woman of my past. She's shiny, new, innocent, and has just sold her soul to me by giving me the greatest gift, a marriage of the wicked with pleasure.

My uncle can go die for all I care. He didn't warn me how utterly disarming Clover Callahan could be with that delightful pussy of hers.

It's only fair I give her a gift in return. I can be magnanimous when I want to be.

"The drawings you found, the jewelry Sarah was paid in. It's still around."

That gets her attention.

"No one has ever found it," I continue. "It was searched for by those same nobles who tortured and killed her. She never breathed a word of where she hid them. As far as the records show, her daughter didn't confess, either."

Clover hovers near the door. If I jerked forward and snapped my teeth, I could catch her lips, draw her blood, drink her in.

Her eyes lose their shame and flash with wonder.

"If that's the case," she says slowly, "We're talking millions of dollars hidden away on this campus."

"More than that," I say. "We're into priceless territory."

Her attention lowers, pausing on my lips. Her curiosity is magnetic, her excitement over the same things I love a drug. I dare to inch forward.

Clover doesn't draw away.

Her gaze darts up, holding my stare. I note the multicolor flecks in her eyes as scattered and beautiful as the freckles along her nose. She is a contradiction of galaxies, dazzling and immense, endless to the eye.

Then she flinches against whatever thoughts she's battling and whirls to the door.

I let her escape, idly stroking the ridge of my cock against the zipper of my pants.

CHAPTER 29

CLOVER

M y effort to appear nonplussed in front of Morgan disappears as soon as I close the classroom door.

I slump against the wall.

What have I done?

This isn't me. I don't sleep with multiple guys at once, and I 100 percent don't fuck professors.

Yet I just did.

The most perverted of them all.

Morgan's obsession with me has reached new heights, and his possessiveness is starting to become too much for me to handle. I need to get out of there, away from the lecture hall and away from him, but my legs are too rubbery to move.

My mind races as I try to come up with a plan. I can't go to the authorities; there's no concrete evidence that Morgan has done anything wrong.

And I just slept with him.

I know I have to confront Morgan. I need to tell him we can't do this, that what we have contains such *wrongness* and depravity. It's a risky move to deny him, but I don't see any other way of saving my morals.

What he did to Minnie was inexcusable. Unforgivable.

And what I did with him? Also inexcusable and unforgivable.

But he saw me. No, *her*. The one buried inside me, that insatiable itch, and made it fucking *sentient*.

She liked what he did. Loved how he defended her with violence. And that revenge I sought, that vindication, was done.

Was I any worse, wanting to drug her and make her act against her will?

Am *I* a monster for wanting to play with him?

I can't forget Xavier and Rio. Jesus, I'm collecting them like Sarah collected jewels. Each man brings something different and I'm not sure if I want one without the others.

Morgan, with his enigmatic allure, awakens a primal fascination within me. He has hidden desires, fueling a dangerous attraction that defies reason.

Xavier, with his charismatic charm and seductive words, can make me forget the world and lose myself in moments of pure bliss.

And God, Rio, with his unwavering devotion and protective nature, strikes a chord of comfort and safety within me. I'm finding solace in his watchful presence, not fear.

Each of these men possesses a unique quality that captivates me and balances their personalities out. Their individual intrigue combines to form a tapestry of emotions and experiences I find impossible to resist. It is the sum of their complexities, the allure of their contrasting personas, that leads me down a dangerous path.

With a long-suffering sigh, I make a U-turn and head to the business and technology building. The wind kicks at my heels, blowing my long hair into my face, but I'm not even annoyed. I'm too busy turning over my lack of shame when Morgan bent me over the classroom table and fucked me—a table I'll never look at the same way again.

I'll never look at *myself* the same way again.

I made the right decision to end the conversation after we finished. But then Morgan, demon that he is, gave me crucial details into Sarah Anderton's history. I do have to apologize to my vagina, though, since it's now aching with emptiness and begging for a sexy, tattooed, slightly unhinged professor to keep introducing it to new fetishes.

And to make matters worse, I now have to enter Professor Rossi's classroom flushed, excited, and sick to my stomach.

For the second time this morning, I attempt to slip in unnoticed.

"If it isn't our newest member, Clover Callahan, showing us all respect by wandering into class late and unexcused."

Rossi doesn't raise his voice. He doesn't have to. The gravel tone sinks into my ears and shames me more than pointing a finger and yelling ever could.

I move farther into the classroom, searching for an empty seat. "I'm sorry, Professor Morgan needed to talk to me for a moment after class."

"Morgan?" Rossi asks.

His piercing stare breaks from mine and moves to one corner of the room, where Tempest stands at his post, glowering at me.

They share an impenetrable look before Rossi returns his attention to me. "That is what office hours are for, Miss Callahan. I expect you to give me the same respect as you do Professor Morgan."

My mind candidly travels to the moment I "respectfully" allowed Morgan to finger my asshole and transposes Rossi in his place instead.

No. Not another one.

Does Sarah have me under a spell? Is this her answer to all

those times I've tried to summon her and show me she's annoyed?

Right now, Rossi's annoyed, piercing authority is turning me on. I clear my throat to rid myself of the feeling and move closer to Ardyn, who thankfully saved me a seat beside her.

She gives me a funny look as I plop into the chair but doesn't comment on the obvious, hot blush to my cheeks or unkempt hair.

I say to Rossi demurely, "It won't happen again."

His dark stare smolders as he regards me. "I've sacrificed enough to get you into this class at your brother's behest. Don't disappoint me again."

"No, sir."

The blacks of his eyes ripple with a ring of fire at my use of *sir.*

Maybe I've gone too far, but his towering form and arrogant air practically demand the title. It fell out of my mouth as naturally as talking with Ardyn and as soon as I do it, I want to do it again.

The urge must be written all over my face because the fire in Professor Rossi's gaze sputters out and he moves on from me as if scalded by his own heat.

"As I was saying, the metrics of..." he continues, addressing the class.

Everyone is dutifully typing on their laptops or scribbling notes around the table, some lounging in wingback chairs and seats in the corners. It's very much a scholarly vibe, if one appreciates lots of mahogany, maroon carpeting, and leather chairs intermixed with floor-to-ceiling bookshelves and a working fireplace.

With the fourteen of us packed in here, the room takes on a cozy meeting space. I use Professor Rossi's speech as a chance to take out my laptop and follow what everyone else is doing. A quick check of my student email shows Ardyn's sent me her notes up until this point, and I gratefully pull them up and copy them into a new document.

Tempest keeps to his corner. I prefer he stay there, refusing to acknowledge him until forced. It's no secret I don't want to be in this class, but it's also a well-known fact that I prefer to excel in everything I do, even subjects I have no interest in.

Rossi's voice melts into my ears, soothing and addictive. He paces around the room, rarely using his hands as he speaks except for when he has to scrape back his silky black hair, salted at the temples. His tanned skin pulls tightly over his sharp bone structure, his salt-and-pepper stubble darkening at his jawline and adding to the perfect craftmanship of his face.

His charismatic handsomeness holds me for only so long before my mind drifts back to the Andertons and the priceless jewels Sarah Anderton wanted to hide from the people determined to kill her and annihilate her bloodline. She may have been a killer herself, but she dealt with some very bad people who knew her secret.

I straighten in my seat, biting my lip as I open my browser on my computer. I can't stop thinking of how Sarah folded up her ledger and hid it in her grimoire for someone to find.

Not someone—a letterlock is done with intention, to be opened by a specific recipient. Sarah put it in her grimoire for that person only, and it would've had to be a person in great trust.

Her daughter. It has to be.

My first search is to learn more about letterlocking methods. As Rossi drones on about practices I'm wholly uninterested in (no matter how beautiful and mesmerizing his voice is) I read about the unique folding methods used to "lock" a letter with pieces of paper, triggered to rip or disappear if opened by the wrong person.

I'm left wondering what else was invented in those times to secretly communicate with one another.

I open a new tab and search that exact question. One of the first things that comes up is *uses of invisible ink.*

Intrigued, I click on the link.

Items like vinegar, saliva, lemon juice, and ... *ew*, urine, could be used to write hidden messages to someone.

I peer closer at the screen, Rossi's voice a sweet melody to my ears despite the dry subject he's focused on.

The way invisible ink is revealed piques my interest, and I use my cursor to highlight the passage: **these messages can be revealed through the use of heat, such as fire. Dragging the flame over the page will force the organic ink to brown faster than the rest of the paper fibers, as they have a lower burn temperature.**

I tongue the side of my cheek. Is it possible Sarah did more than locking her letters? Sure, these locks proved someone not meant to read the message intercepted it, but they still *read* it. What Sarah was doing for nobles couldn't be so easily discovered. She was exposed over a decade after she committed her first assassination. That's a long time to operate under the radar and took a lot of talent to conceal.

If she was leaving messages to, she wouldn't stop at one firewall of security. She'd have layers.

At least, I would.

The lid of my laptop flies toward my fingers. I yank them back with a yelp before it's slammed on top of them.

"Miss *Callahan.*"

Rossi's growl flutters the hairs on top of my head.

With my fingers still hovering in the air, I look up.

"Care to share with the class what you've found more interesting than one of the most competitive placements in the university? That is, *my* class, where I take the time and effort to teach intellectuals who are on my same wavelength, of which you clearly are *not?*"

I bristle but don't comment. The body language of every other student here—hunched, avoiding eye contact, some even *trembling*—communicates it isn't smart to goad Rossi on his territory.

Rossi's lush black lashes twitch. "Do you have anything to say for yourself?"

Well, I'm not about to tell him I was researching a secret stash of Anderton treasure possibly hidden beneath his feet. That would probably make him breathe fire at me.

He's standing much too close. I'd made the mistake of tying my hair up after leaving Morgan since it was so tangled and damp, but now I've exposed the back of my neck.

It prickles with awareness, electric heat exuding from Rossi's body as if he were standing behind me naked.

I try to make my voice sound bored when I reply, "If you're referring to your question about identifying competitive risk, then no, I haven't found anything more interesting than that."

"You're lying," he says quietly. "You haven't listened to a word I've said."

I spin to face him, resting my arm on the top of the chair. "Corporations base their success on consumer ratings. If a similar product comes on the market or a cheaper one, their product or development could become less appealing. Therefore, companies are primed to respond to competition through price, distribution, or research and development strategies."

Rossi's resting asshole face would never emit positive emotions like amazement, astonishment, or happiness.

But I note the slightest tic in his cheek at my answer.

He bites out, "If I catch you browsing anything but my impressive faculty biography again, you will receive an instant failing grade, which, no matter how much you try, the university will *not* remove from your transcript." Then he thankfully backs away.

"Yes, sir."

His shoulders stiffen. Rossi's look crashes down on me as if he'd love to teach me a private lesson where his punishment would know no bounds.

I'm somewhat shocked to realize I want him to.

As he moves down the table, the electricity between us diminishes, though Rossi's scent remains. Pine and wood-smoke cologne coils through my senses.

Rossi's gaze drifts to my closed laptop. It rests there for a moment, his thumb pushing on his ring finger before he moves his attention to Tempest across the room. They share a prolonged, wordless communication before Rossi folds his hands behind his back and resumes his lecture.

My brother shares a special relationship with the professor. I'm not suspicious over their mutual disdain for my attitude. What does bother me is the amount of odd, closed-mouthed conversations I've witnessed over the past few days between Tempest, Ardyn, Rio, and now Rossi. It makes me feel like I've been deliberately left out of something.

But I've observed Professor Rossi enough to know he makes good on his threats, so when I open my laptop, I make sure it's to a blank document and exit my browser.

Resigning myself to another thirty minutes of this, I turn my fingers to autopilot and dutifully type notes while Rossi discusses key topics for the upcoming exam.

I jolt when I feel an unwanted presence near my ear but don't give my brother any attention as he hisses near my shoulder, "Whatever you were searching for on your computer, *stop*. Rossi saw it. Your future is more important than whatever bullshit you're baiting the professor with."

I whisper, "Is this how you talk to all your students?"

"Stop being so immature. You're in this class because you have the intelligence to ace it. Either suck it up and do the work or drop out and prove to me you're the defenseless baby girl I locked in our manor and crawl back home."

I whip toward him, my eyes hot with fury.

Tempest doesn't blink. "All you're doing by rebelling against my wishes is showing me you're exactly who I think you are."

My hands ball into fists. Tears prick into the corners of my eyes.

Tempest straightens and walks away, his steps smooth and unhurried.

CHAPTER 30
XAVIER

I've trained with the best athletes, attended preseason conditioning, and challenged my speed and agility more times than I can count. My body used to know no limits, and I always pushed it to its max. I was never crippled by it. I'd mastered mind over matter a long time ago.

Until tonight.

A hand shoves my shoulder, forcing me closer to the man on his knees, his hands bound behind him and his filthy work tie dangling like a broken noose as he hangs his head.

"Go on," Hunter Morgan purrs behind me. "Slit his throat."

My fingers spasm around the knife Morgan forced upon me moments ago. "I—can't."

"It's the role of a Vulture. You must."

"I don't want to be—"

"You've been given no choice in the matter. Either you do this or you become *that*."

Morgan moves to my side, pointing at the man slumped in front of us.

Rio found him yesterday, depositing him in the concealed

basement of Anderton Cottage before wandering off to wherever he gets to go after finding mafia targets to kidnap and bringing them to the assassins.

I want his job. It seems all he has to do is stick a syringe in an unsuspecting businessman's neck and drive them to a cabin in the woods. The horror show only begins once he leaves.

I side-eye Morgan.

And they've left me with the serial-killing psychopath.

"Rossi specifically asked me to train you," Morgan says, shoving his hands in his pants' pockets and rocking back on his heels. So casual. Lovely. "So here I am, giving you the most basic of fundamentals. I'm not even asking you to chop off a digit. Just stab him in the heart if the throat is too much." He checks his watch. "I have somewhere to be."

Morgan's voice takes on a meaningful tone, like he can't wait to get to his next appointment. I've only heard that tone when he's reminiscing on his kills. It sends a shudder down my back.

With whip-like speed, Morgan grabs my wrist and forces it up until the knife flashes in the single overhead light. "It's either this or I make you participate in my special form of torture, which I warn you, involves animal skeleton masks, cloaks, and carving out the heart while it's still beating."

The man on his knees bleats at Morgan's words.

My eyes stretch so wide when I regard Morgan, I have trouble keeping them in their sockets.

Morgan grins. "So what'll it be, Sports Balls? Either way, we're not leaving this basement until this starved, dehydrated, weak man is dead."

He allows his head to loll toward Mr. Edwards—*yes*, I've made the mistake of giving him a name, like a poor lame dog I've found on the road and can't muster the nerve to end his misery —and drawls, "it's honestly pathetic, how easy it is. My first kill? I had to chase the guy through the streets of Harlem until he disappeared into a sewer grate like a fucking Ninja Turtle. You do *not* want to know what the lower levels of New York City are like, let me tell you. His stench should be barely detectable by now, though..."

I let Morgan drone on in hopes that his ego will replace his need to witness me kill someone.

Unfortunately, it doesn't work.

"*Do it*, Sports Balls," he barks.

"What'd he do?" I ask in a panic. "What was so horrible he's here at our feet needing to be executed?"

Morgan's brows furrow. "Do you really want to know?"

"Yes."

Morgan shrugs. "He diddles little children. That make you feel better?"

"You're lying."

"Of *course* I'm lying. It doesn't matter if he's Jesus resurrected, you are to kill him because it's an order. It's best you learn that before my uncle gets it in his head to start giving you physical reminders of where you stand."

Morgan's jaw juts out. I'd call it petulant if I didn't notice the darkness creeping out from his pupils as he says it.

This man acts so cavalier, but perhaps he's endured more torture than I've given him credit for. It appears we all have, us Vultures.

Except I'm not a Vulture yet.

Reluctantly, I limp forward.

"Yes," Morgan encourages with impatience. "Expediency, please."

In a desperate move, my mind flashes back to what brought me here, falling in love with a freckled, posey-cheeked girl who came to every one of my matches and was delighted when I packed picnics for us instead of treating her to five-star restaurants and luxury hotels. Money fell on my shoulders like rain.

Admiration rolled over me like waves. I was, I thought, untouchable, and my ego grew.

It expanded like a balloon, unable to contain anything but
hot air. That included Meghan O'Malley, too sweet for my fame,
too adoring and clingy for my newfound pro-athlete nature.
During the entire four months we dated, I never caught a whiff
of who her family was. Since we saw each other under the radar
(I didn't want the paps to find out I had a girlfriend, as that
would deplete the obsessive fangirls waiting for me at the gates
every night), her heritage was never revealed to me.

When I dumped her unceremoniously via text, *that's* when I
realized my greatest mistake.

If I tell you I learned my lesson, would you believe I
deserve a better situation than the Vultures? Could you rally
behind me, watch me kick Morgan in the nuts, and help me
escape?

"I don't have all day, man. You're keeping me from a hot
date."

I turn my head toward Morgan. "*You?* A date?"

"Well, she doesn't know it as such, but we have a deep
connection. So chasmic, in fact, that we share a secret only she
and I know."

"How romantic."

He smacks me in the back of the head with the side of his
own blade. "Sarcasm has no place here."

My expression twists, since Morgan is nothing but sarcastic,
but leave it at that.

"All right." Morgan sighs with defeat.

I perk up, thinking maybe he'll just do it himself and I can get
out of here. Maybe I can find Clover and pretend I need more
tutoring. She's a wonderful, unsuspecting break in the clouds
within my shitstorm of a life, her vibrant spirit only positive
thing to come out of my prison sentence. I picture her smile, the

light dusting of freckles across her skin, and her melted caramel eyes.

She is my peaceful river. My cooling balm. The slick warmth I can find ecstasy with.

"Whatever you're picturing," Morgan muses beside me, "keep it there while you watch me work."

My attention flicks to him.

Morgan busies himself in the complicated, old-looking cabinet on the side wall. Mr. Edwards hasn't moved a muscle since we descended into the basement, and he doesn't care to look at what Morgan's doing now.

I do.

Morgan rifles through the lower drawers. My blood runs cold as he pulls out exactly what he promised—black cloaks, animal skulls, a fucking *saber,* and a bag of salt.

"I tried to be nice to you, Sports Balls," Morgan says while remaining bent over. "That says a lot. But it appears your cock is as lame as your leg, so we'll have to do this the hard way."

"I..." I look down at the knife hanging limply in my hand. "There's no need to use props. This is a human being, not theater."

"Oh, but that's where you're wrong." Morgan straightens, his hands on his hips. "This is what makes it *fun.*"

Morgan shifts and a rusted, macabre gleam hits his eyes.

Christ, he's serious.

Bile swells in my throat.

I can't do this.

Morgan returns to the cabinets, jars clinking. Mr. Edwards whimpers, catching my attention.

To my surprise, he's raised his head, and he's looking straight at me.

Bloodshot eyes bore into mine. They dart to Morgan, then back to me, pleading.

I shake my head at the implication, my lips wrenching to the side.

Mr. Edwards nods furtively. *Do it. I've accepted my fate. Do it before he tortures me.*

Acid burns my tongue. My teeth feel sharp—too animalistic for my mouth. I don't want to do this.

Mr. Edwards nods again. He shuffles toward me on his knees, a muffled keening coming from behind his gag.

"What's our dude saying?" Morgan asks, his back turned.

"Nothing. Begging for his life."

"Mm," comes Morgan's bored response.

I stare between Morgan's shoulders, suddenly overcome with purpose.

My grip tightens on the knife.

Now is my chance to stab him, release Mr. Edwards, and drag us both up the stairs while Morgan bleeds out on his beloved sacrificial floor.

Morgan slows his movements. He doesn't turn around.

"What are you doing, Sports Balls?" he asks, his tone high with amusement.

I lick my lips. Hop between the balls of my feet like I'm waiting for the football to be kicked in my direction. I can't feel the pain zinging up my bad leg.

Mind over matter.

"Sports Balls?" Morgan asks again. He holds a jar of something in one hand, but otherwise, he hasn't spun to face me yet.

This is my chance. I won't get it again.

With my heart pounding in my ears, I lift the blade and vault forward.

I don't expect the knife to slide in so easily. Nor can I register the clank of metal against bone as my victim writhes against the intrusion. Not right away.

I force the vision of Clover forward as I push the knife deeper. My moonlight goddess, splayed among winter grass, the sparkling lake reflecting against her pale skin as she parts her legs for me. In her, I can forget who I've become. With her, I can be the man I should've embraced instead of the one I'm a slave to.

She smiles in my thoughts, holding her arms out to me. Clover whispers how wet she is while strands of her dark hair brush my bare back as she straddles me and embeds herself on my cock.

I'm not holding the knife anymore. I'm holding her.

A wrenching cry leaves my throat, foreign and brutal. The resulting scar on my vocal cords will last forever.

Mr. Edwards falls back. I release the knife as his lifeless body smacks against the floor at an odd, dead angle, his legs bent beneath him.

Heaving, I push against my thighs and come to an unsteady stand.

"My, my," Morgan purrs nearby. "I didn't think you had it in you."

Neither did I.

I can't say it out loud.

Morgan's hand comes down and squeezes my shoulder. I want to vomit.

"Well, Sports Balls. I think I have enough time to share a cele-bratory beer with you upstairs before I go."

I sit across from Morgan in the living room, the fireplace crackling between us.

Morgan reclines in the wingback chair with a frosted bottle of lager in his hand and a self-satisfied smile.

He uncapped one for me as well. It sits in my hand, numbing my palm.

I stare at the dancing flames. "What will happen to the body?"

Morgan waves his hand dismissively. "Tongueless will dispose of it."

Ah. I guess Rio's job isn't so easy after all.

Morgan allows his head to fall back against the leather as if he's just finished a particularly good massage. "I don't know about you, but taking a life is almost as good as sex, don't you think?"

I slowly move to stare at him, unable to contain the derision from my mouth. This is nothing like sex. Making love to Clover and hearing her delirious sounds as I tongued her pussy and branded her taste like a tattoo in my throat could never be seen as depraved and callous. Clover is black light, illuminating my darkness with neon brightness.

"Oh," he says.

I was so immersed in my thoughts I didn't notice Morgan lower his head, nor did I register his careful study of my features.

He grins, his eyes sparkling with mischief. "You're thinking of sex right now, aren't you?" Morgan leans forward with his elbows on his thighs. "Go on, tell me, who's the lucky lady who managed to catch your eye during all this, as you call it, *violent theater.*"

I clamp my mouth shut.

"Oh dear, I've hit a nerve. Do I have to torture it out of you?"

Sadly, I believe he'd do it.

"I couldn't tell you even if I wanted to."

Morgan arches a brow in question.

"Look," I say, mirroring his posture. "I'm here because I have to be. We're not friends. I won't even flatter you with a 'coworker' title. You are my prison guard. And I don't have to confess shite to you."

"Actually, you do. What the Vultures get up to is of great interest to the higher-ups. You wouldn't want me to inform our boss of your unsanctioned canoodling, would you?"

"Even if I gave you a name, what would stop you from doing that anyway?"

Morgan gives a one-shouldered shrug, leans back into his seat, and crosses one leg over the other. "I enjoy knowing information our bosses don't. I'm an heir if you didn't already know. What's the point of taking on a leadership role if I don't keep an arsenal of my own?"

I snort, at last lifting the lager to my mouth. The cool, carbonated liquid soothes my overworked throat, even if bland and American. "My love life is hardly a weapon."

"Oh, *love*, is it? Much better, since it worked out so well for you the first time."

I glare at him over the bottle.

He uncrosses his legs, slamming his foot to the ground. "*Clover.*"

It takes every ounce of breath to keep my expression blank. "Who?"

"Don't you play games with me." Morgan's tone takes on deathly caution. "I know it was you who wrote that note to her."

The thick emotion in Morgan's voice entices me to put up a higher, skyscraper level guard. He reaches into his pocket and pulls out the receipt to the cafe which I wrote on the back off, the paper crumpled, and the ink smeared.

"You kept it?" I ask with sick astonishment.

I'd expect his mirth at the thought of my attempt to court Tempest's sister, a girl more off-limits than the Virgin Mary herself. Indeed, I braced for it.

Instead, Morgan surprises me with a face mottled with rage

and a murderous glint to his eye that doesn't usually appear even when he's literally ending lives.

And there, between the clogged spaces of his words, I see my opening.

Morgan *cares* for Clover.

Rather than jealousy seeping into my gut, I grin.

"What would you do if I told you I've fucked her, Morgan?"

His beer shatters to the ground. Morgan's fingers dig into the arms of his chair, the leather groaning under the pressure. "You *lie*."

Jesus Christ, I'm baiting a fucking shark.

But I think of my moonlit goddess and forge on.

"The first night I came to Titan Falls, I met a mysterious, raven-haired girl at a local bar. Perhaps you know it, The Boiler? And here's the kicker—*she* came on to *me*. And we fucked at the clearing by the lake. Out in the open, she spread her legs for me, and I made her moan so loud, we woke the birds in the trees."

I send an internal, sincere apology to Clover for speaking of her this way, though I believe she'd understand if she knew the serpent I was attempting to trap and rid the world of.

Morgan's nostrils flare. His painstakingly controlled features morph and twist into the reptile he's so adept at hiding.

Morgan doesn't give me any time to celebrate his exposure.

"You touched her. You put your rot on that perfect skin. You *ruined* her, and for what, you senseless *prick*?" Spittle flies from his lips.

I can feel the blood leaving my face. I shift uncomfortably. Too often, my words get away from me, and as I stare down a demon from hell, this is one of those moments.

I say in defense, "Clover accepts me for who I am. She gave me a reason to find kindness in this pointless existence."

Resolving myself, I jut out my chin as if readying for a blow.

"So much so, that I'm willing to face Tempest if that's how you want to resolve this."

Morgan's chest seethes with furious breaths. "How brave. How sacrificial. I don't have to offer you up to that Storm Cloud in order to watch you suffer. Clover Callahan will never belong to you. You can lust after her all you want, claim her body if that's your endgame. Because I, *I*"—Morgan slams a palm to his chest and stands—"have her mind. Her *soul*. She loves what I love. She covets the history I do. She will follow me to the ends of the earth if I keep satisfying her. You may suck on her breasts and stroke her cunt, but I can sink into her mind, body, and soul because she and I are bonded as one."

Morgan fires words at me as if with a gun, scattershot bursting across my chest and blowing me into unrecognizable pieces of flesh. If it's possible, this hurts more than killing a man senselessly in the basement, for Morgan threatens to take away the very essence that's keeping me grounded in this hell-forsaken world.

"So we both want her," I grit out. *We're both obsessed with her.*

"No," Morgan corrects with a hiss. "We both *have* her. I'm just better at nurturing her and keeping her whole."

With a disgusted curl to his lip, Morgan swipes the beer bottle from my hand and throws it into the fire, where the flames spit with anger and spark with shattered rage before the heat dies down.

By the time my attention leaves the fireplace, Morgan's disappeared from view.

Throwing my hands onto my head, I curse into the air.

Morgan is twisted. Evil. Mad and deplorable. But he's right about one thing.

I still have so much to learn.

CHAPTER 31

CLOVER

I palm the door to our room shut, then whirl to face Ardyn. She stands in the center, arms folded.

"What's going on?" I ask.

I hold up my hand before she can make something up. "Be real with me, Ardyn. Ever since you've started dating my brother, we've grown further and further apart—and it's not because of jealousy. I love that you're happy and that he's like a relaxed porcupine around you. Something else is going on. You've pushed away from me, Ardyn, and I want to know *why*."

Ardyn's eyes fill before she blinks it away. "I went through a lot four years ago. I know you did, too. You and I didn't see each other for *four years*. A lot can happen during that time. Maybe—maybe I'm not over it."

"Don't do that," I choke out. "Don't try to deflect by using our gap in friendship. All it does is show your desperation not to let me in on what you and Tempest know."

"That's not fair. I'm trying to say that you and I have already been through so much. Why pile on more? Why can't you just be satisfied pulling all-nighters studying, going to parties on week-ends, meeting other average people, and living a non-dramatic life? Why can't you—"

"*Because I miss you!*" I cry.

Ardyn jerks back.

"And because I'm not normal, no matter how hard you and Tempest try to make me be." My voice lowers to a hoarse rasp. "Don't you think after all the years I spent at private school in the city, every tutor that was background checked and hired, every nanny that was deemed grandmotherly enough to babysit, that I would've chosen a normal life by now?" I shake my head while Ardyn looks on. "I didn't because it's not *in* me, just like it wasn't for Tempest, either. We may have decided on our own paths, but I clung to a world outside my own—one of healing, crystals, a pre-written future, because I wasn't satisfied with what was laid out for me. You of all people have to understand that."

Ardyn's face falls. She nods. "I always thought our friendship was special."

"It truly is. But whatever's holding you back is creating another chasm between us. One I thought we fixed when we came to Titan Falls together."

"I'm here for you, Clover." Ardyn reaches out desperately. "I am. I just..."

"What? Want to protect me? Keep me from danger?" I scoff. "Too many people have underestimated me. Please don't be one of them."

Ardyn drops her hands to her sides, clenching her fists and turning away. Her lips curl into a frustrated snarl as if she's fighting an invisible gag.

I push against those restraints. "We've come too far and been through too much to have secrets between us. Don't let my brother convince you that I'm this innocent maiden who'll faint as soon as she realizes the clouds in the sky aren't made of cotton candy."

Ardyn rubs her lips together so hard, her teeth whiten the skin under her mouth. "There isn't much I can say."

"You heard what Tempest said to me in class today," I say. "He's a broody asshole, that's true, but he's never been so mean to me before. Not like that. And he's never forced me into a situation I didn't want to be in, not until this week when he told me I had no choice but to enroll in Rossi's class. You were there, Ardyn—you heard him. He *threatened* me. What made him do that? Is he under pressure? Is there an outside threat making him want to isolate me again?"

Ardyn's shoulders fall. She closes her eyes.

Watching my friend gives me pause. For the first time, I'm seeing the situation differently.

"It must be killing you," I say softly. "Being put in the middle."

Ardyn nods, her lashes sparkling with tears. "I'm either distanced from you or pulling away from Tempest, trying to make both of you happy. I hate this as much as you do."

"Hate *what*? Explain to me what this is, Ardyn."

Ardyn's expression wrenches open. "What I've been exposed to. I don't want to have this inside me. Carrying it around is ... it's almost like a poison. I love your brother so much I'd rather die without him and I'll take him for all his faults. But this..." She shakes her head. "I can't burden you with this."

I blow out a breath. This is the closest I've come to Ardyn admitting *anything*. I feel like if I make the slightest twitch, I'll send her scurrying, and I'll never find out what goes on in the cottage in the woods.

"I'm sorry if I've pushed you to your limit," I say. "But I feel the pressure, too. I always have as the daughter of a man who did better dealing with criminals than with legitimate businesses, and now as a sister who believes her brother's gotten involved in the same thing. I hate that this is taking up all the energy you have." I step forward.

Her eyes flare. She hugs her stomach before she turns away. "I can't."

Ardyn slumps against the side of her bed. She covers her face with her hands. "Everything I've done," she says through her fingers, "is to stop you from traveling on the same road I did to get Tempest to confess. You *don't* want to know, Clover."

I sit on my bed, taking a position directly across from her. "I want to make that decision for myself."

Ardyn doesn't lift her head from her hands. Seeing her bowed over, defeated and conflicted, makes me relent. Slightly.

"Is my brother involved in dangerous, life-threatening activity?"

She sighs. "Yes."

"Is Rio a part of it?"

Her gaze slides away, and she nods.

I think of the other man residing in Anderton Cottage with them. Professor Morgan and what he did to Minnie.

"And Professor Morgan? Is he involved in this activity, too?"

Ardyn licks her lips and nods.

Her confirmation sends a jolt through my body. Wow. I'm way more behind in discovering my brother's secret than I thought I was.

"God, this is making my throat so dry." Ardyn pushes to her feet. "Do you have anything to drink? I haven't stocked my fridge in forever."

"Yeah, go ahead." I wave a hand in the direction of my fridge, just as emotionally fried as she is. "I think I have some—"

Panic grips my heart. I'd forgotten about the spiked coffee I prepared with the shadow elixir intended for Minnie until this moment.

Springing from the bed, I shoot my hand out. "Ardyn, wait."

Ardyn's already bent over, rooting through my mini fridge. "Why does this say, 'don't drink'?"

My stomach sinks when she straightens with the iced coffee in her hand.

"It's, um..." I start.

I can't tell her what's in it. That would mean admitting what I wanted to do to Minnie. Ardyn, a quick thinker like me, would immediately connect confession to Minnie's sudden departure. And then I'd have to explain I never drugged Minnie, all while thoughts of what Morgan did to her flit through my head and *how* he managed to silence her after. She could be dead. Maybe she never left, and it was all a terrible plot...

It's too much to explain. Too much guilt for me to handle on top of the strange exhilaration I felt with the man who cut into Minnie.

"It's mine. I want to drink it," I blurt.

"Okay," Ardyn says slowly, holding it out to me. "You didn't have to call dibs. I wouldn't take anything of yours without asking."

"Of course, yeah. I know that." Nerves bundle in my throat. "It's—it's old. Probably super gunky. Just toss it."

Ardyn shrugs, not suspicious at all despite my dance in front of her like I have to pee. Another layer of guilt coats my skin as I watch her head to the trash can by my desk.

I don't think I'm a good person anymore.

All these lies. All these men. And a witch who won't talk to me but also won't set me free.

My eyes land on the liquid, glistening in the plastic cup from the ceiling lights.

A seed of doubt sprouts within my mind.

Sarah wrote that the shadow elixir was about showing the recipient her true self, in whatever form that may be. For Minnie,

I wanted it to show her how vile she is, how pointlessly cruel, and have her experience what I've endured from her.

What if the shadow elixir could offer *me* answers? What if, through its hallucinogenic properties, I could unlock these hidden truths about myself that I can't solve while awake?

Like my insatiable quest to push boundaries, my draw to multiple men, and why I can't ignore the mysteries Sarah left behind.

"Wait."

Ardyn stops and turns.

"I've changed my mind," I say. "I want it."

Ardyn angles the full drink in her hand and stares at it in confusion. "I thought you said it was old."

"A caffeine addict has no boundaries."

Before I can change my mind or Ardyn has a chance to drink from the straw, I grab it, pop the lid, and take a big gulp.

The cold liquid slides like silk along my tongue. I'm surprised it tastes exactly like black coffee. No extra bitterness, no sweetness, no suspicious flavor at all.

Wow. I really could've gotten Minnie with this. If Morgan hadn't—

Ardyn frowns as she watches me. "You're holding it in your mouth like you're afraid of it."

"Mm-mm," I deny. It coats my throat when I swallow. Maybe it's slightly thicker than normal.

I don't mention that I'm a little afraid of taking another sip. As I'm pondering it, an idea takes hold.

I hold out my hand to Ardyn. "Come with me."

"I'm still thirsty, Clo."

"We'll stop at the canteen downstairs. But then you're coming with me to the library."

"Can I ask why?"

"I'll tell you on the way."

CHAPTER 32

CLOVER

I didn't realize how much I missed the feeling of my best friend walking beside me until I'm heading across campus with Ardyn.

I sneak a peek at her as we pass under a streetlight while she sips on her soda, the golden cone illuminating the can's shine before her form darkens under the night sky again.

So far, I'm feeling nothing. Maybe I didn't drink enough? I take another hesitant sip, this time through the straw.

Ardyn doesn't ask where I'm taking her, another trait that I missed. Perhaps the crystals and candles I'd grabbed and placed in my bag clued her in.

Ardyn and I did everything together when both of us were cloistered in the Upper East Side by overprotective parents. Hers were for more traumatic reasons, but I've always been drawn to tortured souls with scattered pasts, even when I was too young to recognize it.

We come up to TFU's library, its gothic spires staking the night sky like ancient arrows aimed for the stars. The first floor is open twenty-four hours a day for the early birds and night owls who can't properly study in their dorms or common rooms, but in the middle of the semester, it's largely deserted when Ardyn and I walk in.

One or two souls have headphones on, bent under their desk lamps as they pore over their texts and take notes. We pass by them without garnering any interest. I don't see the night librarian anywhere, either. Luck is on my side.

I grab Ardyn's hand and pull her between the stacks until we reach a dead end.

Ardyn can't contain her curiosity any longer. "What are we doing here?"

I hold a finger to my lips, certain the librarian is about to pop her returns cart around the corner any second.

Ardyn doesn't fight my urging into the corner, where I turn the iron doorknob and pull us into the stairwell.

"Do I want to know where this goes?" Ardyn whispers as I shut the heavy wooden door behind us.

Her face comes out from the dark when I turn on my flashlight app.

Leading the way down the stairs, I respond, "Do you want the actual version or the Titan Falls brochure version of the answer?"

"Give it to me straight."

"The library was built on the remains of the old church that was here in Sarah's day. In this basement, they tortured heretics and accused witches, including Sarah."

"Awesome. Great. Okay."

My phone offers a path over the rest of the stairs and into a widening chamber with old, crumbling support beams and low-level bookshelves. I take a minute to appreciate all the items brought down here to be forgotten since they had no place in the sunlight that beams through the stained-glass windows upstairs during the day. Relics like old busts of nameless men, rusted-over candlesticks and broken sconces lie on top of the bookcases, cobwebs curving over them like ripped, discarded lace.

Ardyn casts her gaze around dubiously. "Do you think there are rats down here?"

"Probably."

Her lips flat line as she follows me through the aisles and toward a sidewall.

Our arc of light disappears when I bend down and focus it on the bottom shelf where I hid the grimoire. To my great relief, it's still there, the cobwebs I draped over it undisturbed.

When I rise with it, Ardyn nods her head. "Great hiding place."

"If only the treasure were so easy to locate," I say while laying Sarah's grimoire on top of the bookcase.

"I'm sorry—treasure?"

I nod without taking my eyes off the book. "I've found out the jewels Sarah was paid in were never recovered. She hid them somewhere in Titan Falls. Her grimoire could be the answer. Look."

Ardyn sidles close as I open the book to the section I need. I don't have gloves this time or tweezers, but I'm extra careful as I handle the pages.

"Here." I hand Ardyn my phone so she can hover the light over the grimoire.

Finding the clandestine seam on the last page, I delicately pry it open and pull out the flattened pages of the jewelry ledger.

"Whoa," she breathes next to my shoulder. "Look at the detail."

"Priceless," I agree. "Can you imagine if I find these in real life?"

Ardyn chuckles, slightly indulging, but I ignore it.

"And what would you do with it?" she jokes. "Take over the world?"

"Give it to my brother," I say, studying the detail of the jewels. "If you say he's in trouble, I want to help him. Them."

Morgan. Rio.

Ardyn goes still. "You'd do that?"

"If this exists? Yes. Sarah wanted to save her daughter with it. She'd understand wanting to save family."

Ardyn's steady light showcases the paper replicas of the jewelry handed to Sarah in exchange for murder. I drag my finger down the edges of the page, the writing turning squiggly.

I blink. Lean forward. *Not yet, shadow elixir.*

"They're gorgeous, aren't they?" I say. "Imagine if I found them. Straight As across every subject."

Wait. We've already had this conversation. I grin. Ardyn's my friend for a reason.

"Are you okay?" Ardyn's concerned face comes into my vision. She's slightly Picasso, but I can see her.

"Let's hurry this up," I say. "I need to set up for a séance."

The crystals clank as I dig them out, not as careful as I usually am. I unroll them out of the protective suede cloth and place them strategically on the ground.

"You replaced all your crystals," Ardyn says. "That's great."

"Rio gave them to me."

Whoops. Did not mean to blurt that out. Nor do I expect the *whoosh* of tingles and swelling as soon as I mention his name.

Uncomfortably so. Every time my thighs rub up against my core, I shudder.

"Candles?" I ask Ardyn with a shaky voice.

"Here. You sure you're all right?"

I line the thick white candles north, south, east, and west around me.

"Yeah." I release a long exhale. "Salt. Need salt."

Ardyn, a perfect apprentice, hands me my salt container.

I pour, my circle not as circular. But it'll do. I close it with me inside.

I lower into a sit, crossing my legs. Without needing to ask, Ardyn reaches over the circle with the grimoire, her nose scrunched, but she manages not to gag.

Settling it on my lap, I ensure the drawings are stacked on top.

"Light."

Ardyn complies, turning off the phone's flashlight.

I close my eyes on a sigh, laying my fingers gently on the papers.

My skin is set on fire.

My spine shoots straight. I gasp, my mouth falling open.

"Sarah," I whisper. "If you're here..."

The backs of my eyelids aren't black as night. Like an ink drop, a deep purple spreads, turning indigo edged with blood red.

My nipples itch, then tingle. My core follows, and I moan.

There's a shuffle close by—Ardyn's shoes—probably in concern. She's seen me enough times not to break my focus, but this is different. She knows it, and I know it.

Shadow elixir.

As if summoned by the name, four faces take shape from the colored ink. Xavier, Morgan, Rio ... Rossi.

One by one, they reach for me, their mouths moving, but I can't make out what they say.

"W ... watch her?" I ask them, scrunching my eyes farther as if that would give the vision more clarity. "Is that what you're saying?"

The first one, Xavier, shakes his head with sad, sad eyes.

"Culture?" I try again.

I hear Ardyn's gasp. "Clover—"

"*Shh.*"

Bad Ardyn. She should know better.

The elixir makes me sway back and forth, and a smile forms on my lips.

And by the magic of the potion, the inky concoction makes my four men lose their clothing.

"Oh, wow," I breathe, my smile stretching. "I know you two are big, but *you two...*" I point where Rio and Rossi stand in my vision. "What a nice surprise."

Rossi's image ripples, neon light bordering his flowing hair. He smiles at me in return.

Smiles.

It's such an easy one that crinkles his eyes. He has dimples. Who knew? Warmth exudes from his expression, such *love*, and I find myself choking on tears.

Baritone laughter circles my ears. It's coming from Rossi as he bends down and catches someone, a little girl, in his arms, then lifts her into the air. Her carefree, tinkling laughter follows. Such sounds should fill my chest with hope and light and air. Instead, a drowning sorrow rots my heart until it's hard and black.

I sob.

"Oh. Oh my god. He had a daughter."

"*Clover.*" Ardyn's tone becomes more urgent. "Wake up."

In a burst of bright, flames ignite the child first, then Rossi.

"No! Rossi!" I cry.

Rio looks at me with anguish, and his form follows, his gorgeous face melting and falling into the black in droplets.

Morgan gives me a thumbs-up. He casts his gaze upward and spreads his arms as he's consumed.

Xavier tries to run from it.

I hold out my arms. "Here! I'm here! Come to me!"

He looks at me over his shoulder, terrified and shaking his

head and saying, "Not you. I can't let this have you," before he ignites.

I heave out a cry, hunching over. Why would Sarah do this? Why would she show me such love and then such hate?

Hands clamp around my shoulders and shake me.

"Clover! Clo! Wake up!"

I don't. I can't leave them.

If they suffer, you must suffer too, a voice that isn't mine says in my head.

"CLOVER."

Cold fingers clutch at my cheeks, rocking my head back and forth.

I wrench my eyes open, blinking, stretched wide, blinking.

Ardyn's ghostly face comes close to mine. "Jesus, what *was* that? Are you okay? Tell me you're okay!"

My brain's flipped upside down. My body fills with nothing, an ache, an emptiness, a terrible longing to be satiated.

"I'm fine." I don't sound like myself.

"This wasn't like any other time," Ardyn says, crouched in front of me. I don't even mind that she broke the circle.

She adds, "There was—you sounded—"

"I know what I have to do."

Ardyn pushes her brows together. Her eyes follow my hands when I reach for the stack of old papers.

"I have to burn it."

She wavers on her heels. "Clover, no."

I fish into my jacket pocket and pull out a lighter. "With this."

The whites of Ardyn's eyes shine with the candles' small flames. "You're not serious. You could destroy it. This paper is so old it could go up in flames in less than a second." Ardyn gestures to the dusty, decrepit, forgotten basement. "Not to mention us with it."

"If I'm wrong," I continue, my voice tight. I wriggle on the floor in hopes of quelling the prickles shooting from my pussy.

It wants. *She wants.*

"I want you to bear witness," I grit out.

For a moment, the only sounds coming from Ardyn are her breaths. Then she says, "This is your adventure."

Holding my breath, I lift one of the petal-thin pages. With my right hand, I flick the lighter, its flame flickering anxiously as I move it closer to the paper.

I cautiously, *carefully*, glide the little flame across the page, my hand shaking dangerously. And outlined in neon pink.

"Do you want me to do it?" Ardyn asks.

"It has to be me."

On the first pass, nothing comes to light. Air hisses between my front teeth, but I try again. And again.

"Maybe if I move lower," I mutter.

My shift makes my lower half pulse with warning. All I want to do is take one of these thick candles and plunge it into myself, giving myself the orgasm I'm desperately craving.

Ardyn watches, riveted, as I draw the flame toward the middle of the page between the drawing of a sapphire necklace and a manor ring.

"Wait." Ardyn grips my wrist, pausing my movement. "Do you see that?"

"No." Frustration laces my voice, and I allow the flame to sputter out. "There's nothing."

Just the four men I dream about, care about, and *need*, dying before my eyes.

Ardyn nudges me, then reaches toward one of the dust-coated items covering the top surface of the long bookcase.

Ardyn's found a magnifying glass, cracked at the edges and cloudy, but better than nothing.

We turn back to the page I'm still holding in the air. I relight the flame, and both of us gasp.

"Did that brown dot grow?" I breathe. "Please tell me it did."

"It did!"

I center the magnifying glass over the stain, and *yes*, it's turned into a loop.

"Holy shit," Ardyn exclaims. She glances at me with an expression that slightly believes in ghosts, now. "How did you know there was hidden writing?"

"Invisible ink," I mumble and don't expand.

My body's so overheated my eyes hurt. *It wants, it wants, it WANTS.*

I mouth along as it is revealed.

we are at war, my flower, may ye find spiritual peace where our stone is circled by summer.

A strand of my dark hair falls into my vision and nearly into the lighter. I realize how close I've bent to the page and straighten while tucking my hair behind my ear, nearly falling backward.

Ardyn steadies me.

"What do you think it means?" Ardyn asks.

I gnaw on my lip. I wish it were someone else biting me, making me beg, before stretching me *fulllll.*

It takes effort to reason, "Sarah wouldn't make things easy. I'm sure this was meant for her daughter, though. 'My flower,' that has to be—"

A husky, masculine voice rebounds the walls, cutting off my sentence and reaching our ears at a pissed-off velocity.

At the sound, my pussy simply *celebrates.*

"I thought I made it damn clear you are not to be caught in the library's basement again?"

CHAPTER 33

ROSSI

T he girls, lying in the center of a fucking witchy circle, whip their heads in my direction, just in time for Clover's hand to go up in flames.

They scream, leaping up and hopping back. Ardyn drops the flashlight, and Clover frantically shakes her arm to douse the flames, scattering embers.

I bolt forward, unscrewing my thermos of coffee and tossing the lukewarm contents over Clover's arm in a long arc of liquid over two aisles.

Fire effectively snuffed, Clover freezes with her arm in the air, gawking at me. "Wow. Direct hit."

I'm too furious and pumped full of adrenaline to respond. Rounding the last of the aisles, I storm toward her, grip her wrist, and yank up her sleeve.

"Are you hurt?"

I twist her arm side to side, looking for angry scorch marks on her porcelain skin.

She winces at my rough treatment. I don't give a damn. She could've hurt herself. Clover could have permanently scarred her innocence, and so stupidly. "What were you doing, thinking you could—"

Once I register what's lying open on the floor between them, I do a double take.

"Is that...?"

Clover turns to liquid in my grip. "Yup."

I blink at her. Drop her arm despite her pulse quickening under my thumb. It feels like a little bluebird's heartbeat—one I'd love to cage beneath my palm. "That is a priceless, irreplaceable Titan Falls piece of property that *you shouldn't fucking be setting on fire.*"

"Oh, is that all?" Clover giggles, then by God, spreads her hand and drags it down my chest.

She does *this* after I used a tone on her I usually reserve for my Vultures.

Ardyn moves, coming from behind and settling into a defensive stance next to Clover. I almost chuckle—if it weren't for her stare. Too familiar for my liking.

She says, "We were just leaving."

"What's wrong with her?" I ask, swatting away Clover's hand, though it felt like she'd dragged a straight line of fire to my crotch.

"She does this. Tries to summon Sarah Anderton. I'll take her up to the dorms."

"Not until you give me that grimoire." I block any forward momentum they were planning.

"It's your fault."

My stare, always so rock steady, seizes against Clover's. "Excuse me?"

"You heard me." She juts out her chin. "If I weren't feeling so guilty over my attraction to you, I wouldn't have taken a potion and come here sniffing around for the Anderton treasure."

So much of that sentence hits me between the eyes.

She wants me.

She knows about the jewels.

She's staring at me like I'm about to push her to my knees and make her groan against my dick.

Oh, fuck me, I want to do just that. And I haven't wanted for a very long time.

"Clover!" Ardyn whispers harshly. "Potion? *What?*" Her forehead smooths. "The *coffee?*"

Clover holds up a finger. "From Sarah's grimoire. Meant for Minnie."

"No one speaks to me that way," I rasp. "Not even freshmen idiots who drug themselves and make themselves a séance in a basement."

"Idiot?" Clover's laughter reverberates around the room like a church bell. "Far from it. You wouldn't have let me in your class if I was, Mr. Hoity Toity Stick So Far Up His Ass He Can Lick It. What do you have going for you besides a sizeable dic—"

I see red. I fucking see red.

"I will gladly force you on your knees and hold you by the back of the neck until that silver tongue of yours dampens my shoes."

Clover's stare widens. Her mouth snaps shut.

Ardyn sighs. "She's not herself. And she didn't drink all of this ... potion. Just a sip."

The flush creeping up Clover's neck and the answering heat in her eyes tell me a different story. My jaw slackens behind my closed lips at the sight. I'm desperate to know if the rubescent color reaches the white globes of her breasts.

"Professor Rossi?"

Ardyn's voice is oddly calm despite the echoes of my very *real* threat to Tempest's insufferable sister with a death-wish. Not to mention the forbidden fantasy playing out in my mind's eye.

It's a reminder to exhale the hot air building in my chest and resume the mask of a stern professor, not a lethal assassin who wants to celebrate his kills by coming home to a woman like Clover.

With a strained voice, I ask, "What caught fire?"

The two of them share a look.

Clover is the first to break off and return to me. "We were looking for a quiet place to study."

I arch a brow.

Ardyn rubs her eyes. "He knows what we were doing here, Clo. You told him. Let's just go."

Clover bites her bottom lip. A thrill goes through me as I watch her leave puncture marks on the blush rose of her lips. The sensation settles at the bottom of my stomach—too near my groin.

I snap. I *do not* have time for daydreams of Clover. "Will you force me to take this to the chancellor and have this incident permanently written on your transcript?"

"What? No! I was trying to reveal invisible ink, okay?" Clover sputters.

I groan. This is my damn fault, trying to reason with her.

"All right." I hold up a hand to stop Clover from saying more and slide my gaze to Ardyn. "Tempest is looking for you. You should go find him."

Ardyn's thick brows cast shadows over her eyes. "Sure. Clover and I will be on our way."

She grabs Clover's arm, but my voice stops her from pulling Clover away. "No. Just you."

Ardyn's forehead smooths with stubbornness. "I'm not leaving Clover down here on her own in this state."

"If anybody will know what she took and how to cure it..." I eye Clover. "It's me."

Ardyn squints at me, her lips curled with distrust and suspicion. But this is the one time I'm thankful for her knowledge of my true self and my vast experience tending to my men, both before and after my exile. The warring families can be rather creative with their attempted kills.

"It's fine," Clover says, cutting off further protest from Ardyn. "You can go."

"This is not okay," Ardyn says. "I don't want you cornered in a musty, unmonitored basement with him."

"I'm her professor, Ardyn, just as I am yours." I lace my voice with warning not to raise Clover's suspicions.

Ardyn's lips peel back like she wants to curse me out until Clover lays a hand on her shoulder.

"I can handle it, Ardyn. Besides, Hermione needs her dinner, and we all know Tempest will tear the campus apart if he can't find you."

"He's certainly not looking here," I add, crossing my arms.

Ardyn hesitates, her gaze darting between us.

I give her a nod of confident assurance. "I'll figure out what she took, then make sure it's not poisonous and that she sobers up."

At last, Ardyn gives a reluctant nod, though her shoulders stay rigid. "If you're not out of here in an hour, I'm coming to find you."

"Deal," Clover says.

Ardyn leaves us, her footsteps heavily annoyed as she ascends. I wait until I hear the top-level door open and shut before I turn to Clover.

"Show me the potion you found," I say.

Eyes burning with irritation at being caught out, Clover says, "Only if you tell me why you rub your ring finger when you're nervous or angry?"

My hand freezes midway between grabbing her arm and pulling her to the mess she made behind her.

"I see you do it all the time," she continues. "I bet you don't even realize it."

I swear my heart stalls in its beats.

"Are you married?" she asks.

It takes me a minute to respond. I'd banished that habit a decade ago, careful never to give anyone, not even my Vultures, that part of my history. How is it I'm doing it again? And around Clover?

"Not anymore," I say roughly.

Something close to relief washes across her face. I notice, pulling my brows in at the sight.

"What happened?"

The question brings to life a beautiful woman with dark curls and the little girl beside her, a mirror image of her mother.

A slash of pain cracks through the image. My stomach clenches and roils.

I funnel that wrenching grief into Clover's audacity. "*Don't.* What was in the potion?"

Clover jolts at the fierceness of my tone. "Elixir. It's all natural ingredients. Flowers, Belladonna, wormwood, some mushroom called shadow moss that I had to grind up into powder—"

"*Belladonna?* That's poison." For reasons unknown to me, fear shoots into my heart at the thought of Clover dying.

And it's not solely because I see her brother as a son. I certainly don't see her as a daughter.

Anything but.

"It was only a smidge," Clover explains. "Enough to make me hallucinate. Same with the shrooms. What Sarah did *not* tell me was how horny I'd be. God, Professor, I'm aching to be filled, and it can't be just anyone. It has to be you. Or Rio, or Morgan, or Xavier. You're all so different and so *perfect.*" She groans.

The girl actually ruts the air as she says our names, and *dammit*, my mind can't handle what she's throwing at me.

How she named all of the Vultures, save her brother.

For the life of me, I'm not riveted because of the danger of exposure that presents. All I can think of is that she wants us. *Us.*

Including me. All my flaws, my haunting past, and my violent present. This girl, she's the embodiment of a hopeful future. She could see beyond my frightening exterior, could offer me the acceptance and compassion I thought I could never deserve.

And I can't—*I can't*—do that to her.

"You'll be all right, not that I see you're too worried." I stab the air above the grimoire, desperate to get her mind off sex. With me. "Do you realize how valuable a book like that is to a town like this?"

Clover blinks at the change in topic. She recovers except for her hand that travels dangerously to the button of her pants. "Of course I do. I was only trying—"

"To be an amateur." I force myself to keep my eyes on her face. "To disrespect history. To put your Gen Z fingers all over the tomb of a tortured and persecuted woman and post it to social media."

"*Hey.*" Her voice ratchets up. "I do not take insults well, especially when it comes to defacing the property of witches and their rituals. I am the *most* kind when it comes to handling these relics. I won't even touch that book with my hands if I can help it! Also, it stinks. Really bad. It's so gross I can only look at it in isolated areas. And I have to open it because it's crucial to my grade in Professor Morgan's class." Clover comes up to me and prods a finger into my chest. Touching me distracts her, but she blinks, keeping her finger between my pecs. "You do not have the monopoly on stressing the fuck out of students, you know."

I stare down at her finger. If she were anyone else, I would've snapped her wrist in half and broken both her legs until she was begging and pleading for me to end her misery at my feet.

She raises her head. Clover's eyes are shattered crystals in daylight or in shadow. And in a dank basement smelling of dust and ash.

I still in her gaze. She whimpers. "I need you. This horrible itch won't go away. It's torture."

Clover is so close, if she thrust her hips an inch, she'd feel how hard her proximity has made me.

I rasp, "What did you destroy?"

We're so close to jumping each other, I'm surprised to see her part her lips in answer. "A page, separated from the book. An accident. I was being careful until you..."

I lower my chin to be closer to her. "Until I what?"

"You distracted me." Her breath stutters out. "Please distract me. Stretch me. Bury yourself inside me."

"What did you destroy?" I repeat with a strained voice.

I can't resist her much longer, but the jewels, the potential escape from this servitude, it's important. It's necessary.

She says, "It was one of a few pages of drawings. Pictures of jewelry that Sarah Anderton was paid in."

I hiss in a breath. "You found her ledger?"

One shoulder jerks in a shrug. The tip of her left eyebrow twitches.

Goddammit, she will be the end of me.

"The jewels were never recovered after Sarah was killed," she says.

My heart claws at my chest. I force myself to laugh. *She actually did it. The girl discovered a clue.*

I don't like myself for this, but I sneer, "Don't tell me you're searching for a mythical treasure chest of gemstones?"

She glares up at me.

Damn. The girl is beautiful, especially in furious relief.

"I wouldn't expect a tweed-wearing spreadsheet to understand."

I can't resist. "Oh, you find me boring, then?"

She rolls her lips together. "Apparently not, since I'm dying to tear that tweed off your body."

Thrill-seeking behavior has always been foreign to me. That is, until Clover's standing within inches of my body, and I'm overcome with a toe-curling need to grab those long locks of hers, tangle it at her nape, and pull her head back so I can devour her.

My tone is rough. I battle with the mental conflict of prompting her versus walking away. "Clover?"

"Yes?" Her eyes hang onto mine, beguiling and needy.

"I need you to back away."

"I can't," she says.

"You must."

"It's not up to me."

"Then who?"

"My witchy bitch."

"Your..."

Clover nods. "She likes it when I'm naughty. And tonight, she won't relent. She feels you."

"Jesus," I hiss, the tip of my hard cock popping out from the top of my pants. "You're talking about your pussy."

Her gaze darts to my lips when I say the word, and she licks hers.

Our faces move together in tandem. Pulled by a magnetic force neither of us questions.

Clover's breath changes, erratic and short. Her cheeks color. I must have night vision to notice it, or the lust as sharpened my horizon to such an extent that I could find her in this low-lit basement in a second if she chose to run.

God help her if she tries to escape.

Internal conflict wars inside my head, my fingers shaking as I lift them from my sides and rest on her shoulders. Lightly, like I'm about to play the piano.

She sucks in a breath. Her eyes stay on mine.

With a bare touch, I trace her exposed clavicle. At the dip in the middle, I glide my index finger down, stopping at the deep V of her shirt.

Clover's chest lifts, those pert breasts of hers molding into her ruby shirt. They're a perfect palmful, and I can't breathe at the thought of holding them against my palms.

With both hands, I pull at the V of her shirt, widening it, stretching it until it exposes her bra. I tuck the material under her breasts, fire lighting the backs of my eyes as I take her in.

She says in a cracked whisper, "Professor..."

I find I can't lift my gaze to hers. I'm too enthralled with her perfection. It's without thought, abstaining from consequences, that I pull her cups down to join her shirt collar, exposing her entirely.

Her rosebud nipples peak at the whisper of air over her soft skin. Clover's head falls back and her eyes flutter closed, my hands hovering so close, but I cannot...

Look, but don't touch.

Heart hammering in my chest, I allow the pads of my fingers to move along the sides of her breasts, the heat of them sinking through my skin and branding itself there as a unique, lust-soaked warmth that I'm certain I'll be addicted to forever more.

"Professor Rossi ... please..."

Clover could be asking me not to stop. She could be begging me to leave her be. I don't know because I'm deaf to outside noise. Blood rushes to my head like I've taken a drug. My cock strains at my pants' zipper, the metal teeth digging through my briefs and reminding me to wet it. To put myself in *her*.

I cannot.

CHAPTER 34

RIO

Crouched in a neglected corner near the library's basement stairs, neither Clover nor Rossi notices my presence.

I can't blame Rossi for falling under Clover's spell, elixir infused or not. I have the same obsessive need to bury myself in her—as if that could staunch the addiction.

Loyalty blurs whenever I think of Clover. It dilutes when I consider what Tempest was able to do with Ardyn with only minor consequences.

And most worrisome, losing Tempest versus hearing Clover cry out my name starts to be less of a danger to my well-being and more of an option.

The one place I've found pleasure is ... her.

Clover's a marble carving in the middle of the room, her arms out in supplication and her head tilted up as if she were mesmerized by the starry sky three floors above.

Rossi registers my movement, his eyes darting toward me. He watches me in silence as I come forward.

His eyes hood with relief when I stand beside him, like he's desperate not to destroy her and was coming so close. He lowers his hands from her chest.

I gaze ferociously at her breasts.

My head lowers. My hands cup her hips as I pull her closer.

And I put my mouth on the mole between her breasts— *mine*.

She gasps at the sudden contact, her hips molding into my hands like I was the artist who created her.

Clover's heated skin presses closer, burying my breath between her plush breasts. I groan, happily succumbing to her suffocation.

She stiffens. Her hands dig into my biceps, and I know she's lowered her head and discovered who's in charge of her tasting.

"Rio?" she whispers hoarsely.

I pause my tongue-swirling long enough to glance at her through my lashes.

"Where is—?" She glances to the side with wide eyes.

"I'm here," Rossi says, his voice a rumble. "Don't stop sucking on her breasts until I tell you to, Rio."

I cock a brow at that but have no qualms resuming my sampling.

Clover shudders. She takes in the sight of both of us and smiles. "This ... this is what I want. What I've dreamed of."

Rossi rumbles, "Rio. Nip at that sensitive skin. Show her how dangerous we can be."

I hold his stare when I peel my top lip back and bite.

Clover hisses an inhale, and her pain mixed with pleasure buzzes in my ears.

Her grip slackens on my arms until they slide off, and she arches back, allowing me full access.

"Play with her now," Rossi rasps.

I hum my approval, using one hand to tweak and play with

her nipple and the other to hook the hem of her leggings and yank.

I slide my gaze to Rossi, who is standing to the side and fisting the base of his dick. He's unbuttoned his pants, his large appendage spearing forward.

My mouth tenses with surprise, but the coil of need in my groin doesn't mind. Let him watch. Let him get off on this gorgeous creature while I give her what she's begging for, and he tells me what to do. He does so in all other aspects of my life—at least in this case, I'll enjoy the fuck out of it.

"Pull her pants down. Expose her for me."

Red circles bloom in Clover's cheeks. She watches me drag the black fabric down her thighs. My mouth pops off her breast long enough to tangle the pants at her ankles.

"Her coat. Her shirt. All of it."

Straightening, I do the same to her jacket, leaving the leather bunched at her wrists and locking her arms behind her back.

"You want this?" I ask in a low voice.

Her irises are the sole burst of shine in the room. "Yes. God, yes."

I don't smile. I give her a measuring look, one of true consequences and the inability to alter the past once we commit to this. "This potion. Has it denied you of all reason?"

She doesn't hesitate. "The opposite. It's given me the truth."

The honesty in her eyes as she says it is undeniable.

"It *hurts*, Rio. I'm swollen. I ache so much it's like this potion has sent a rush of blood to everything sensitive down there. I'm cramping, it hurts so bad."

Gorgeous tears shine in her eyes, flickering orange and white in the small dancing flames.

I hook her under her jaw with my thumb and forefinger, sending her flat against the wall.

My porcelain doll. She doesn't break our stare.

"I won't be gentle," I warn.

She speaks through my hold, her lips stiff, her teeth bared. "I don't want you to be."

I haven't allowed myself to fully appreciate what I've torn away from her until now.

"Her throat, Rio. Put pressure on it. Redirect some of that pain of hers," Rossi commands hoarsely.

Taking an arm's length step back while keeping hold of Clover's throat, I assess her heaving chest, slick with my saliva, her breasts pushed up from her shirt and bra I've yet to unhook.

Her thong pools at her ankles just like her leggings. I'm not sure when she shimmied out of it with her hands locked behind her, but I definitely don't mind it.

Last time, I didn't get to appreciate the view of her pussy. Exploring her with my fingers was glorious, but the sight of her is pure ecstasy.

Pressing forward, I mold my body into hers, making sure her shaved pussy feels every inch and ridge of my dick through my pants.

"Tease her." Sharp, pumping movements come from where Rossi stands. "We don't give in so easily, no matter how much she begs."

Clover whimpers, whines, and writhes against my body. "Please. It *hurts*, Rio. I thought you didn't like me hurt..."

I don't move my hand from her throat, torn between taking her hurt away and obeying my leader. It's ingrained in me, this obedience.

But Clover's invaded my reason.

I lower my head and trace my lips along her jawline.

Her pulse batters against my thumb. Tiny squeaks escape with her breath—part fear, part agony, part desire. I nestle my lips under her earlobe and flick my tongue against her sensitive spot.

Clover's nails dig into my shoulders. She arches her hips against mine, rubbing, searching for a sensation on her clit against all my denim.

"*Mark her,*" Rossi's feral command intones.

Yanking Clover's chin to the side, I clamp my teeth against her smooth flesh.

Clover yelps, her grinds becoming fervent, but I have such weight against her all she can do is wriggle under my teeth.

Rossi grunts with approval, his voice tight with restraint.

Relenting to Clover's cries, I release her, kissing the indented flesh and collecting small droplets of her blood along the way.

A metal tang invades my tastebuds. It mixes with her unique scent, consuming me from the inside out.

Possessive, obsessive rumbling comes from deep within my chest. *She is mine, and I am hers.* I move down her chest, cupping those precious globes, a part of me mourning for the scarring I'm about to give, but it is nothing compared to the roar of dominance flowing through my bloodstream.

"Not until I tell you to, Rio," Rossi barks.

I pause, my tongue inches from her nipples.

Counting the seconds, I strain against my clothes, close to tearing them off and leaping on her, protecting her, damn what Rossi wants, until at last, he allows, "Now."

I bite the top of her breast. Clover moans between her teeth, arching and retreating, bucking beneath my shadow. I do it again, aiming for a trail from one breast to the other, droplets of blood glowing black in the meager light.

A choked sob comes from above, and I look up. "Do you still want this?"

Her lashes glisten the same as her blood. I straighten, brows tight.

"No, it's not that," she says, her expressive face wrenched

with prolonged anguish. Then she looks at Rossi. "Come here. Please, please, come here, too."

Large, hard dick in hand, Rossi shakes his head, his face pinched. "Rio. You know what she's begging for. Give it to her."

"You deserve to be worshipped," I finish for her softly. "In all ways possible, including with damn desires. Because I am sin, Lucky, just as you are light. My vow to you is this, pain rising to ecstasy." Angling my head, I continue, "I answer to Rossi. I don't know how to be any different, so if this isn't what you pictured when you touched herself thinking about me, then..."

She hesitates. My hand remains curved around her throat. I can feel every space between her erratic pulse, a physical manifestation of her conflict against the peril we represent.

Clover says, "You ruined me the moment you came into my life. Now I can't think of anything else."

I allow my mask to fall and my beast to show at the moment Rossi demands, "Show her what you are, Riordan."

Before Clover can change her mind, I thumb her chin and yank her mouth open. I purse my lips and suck, collecting her leftover blood and swirling a concoction of her essence and mine, then spit in her mouth.

Clover's head jerks back, clunking against the wall with a dull thud. The whites of her eyes grow.

I force her jaw shut before she can force it out.

"Swallow," Rossi orders.

She shakes her head beneath my grip. My thumb and forefinger dig into her cheeks, dimples of my own making.

"I taste you and you taste me, that is the deal," I say. "I want to be in your mouth when I do this." I stroke a finger up her slit where I saw the arousal glistening before claiming her.

Her resulting cry is muffled against her locked lips but sounds as painful as if she were screaming at the top of her lungs.

Clover can't take much more, not in the heightened sexual condition she's in. Whatever concoction she's brewed, it's given her the female version of blue balls.

I say, "I want to be in your throat when I do this."

With fingers wet with her juice, I unbutton my jeans and pull my dick out over the hem of my briefs, angling it until the tip prods against her pussy.

I nearly lose my balance when her thirsty pussy collects my pre-cum with a single swipe.

With a rebellious glint in her eye, Clover's throat bobs as she swallows.

"Are you close, Miss Callahan?" Rossi asks in a strained voice.

He's paused in his pumping, his hand clenched around his dick as if to stop the forceful explosion that's desperate to come out.

She nods, her cheeks glowing in the candlelight with sweat.

I push my dick in up to the tip. With her legs locked together by her pants knotted at the ankles, she's as tight as a virgin, and *fuck*, do I ever want to be the villain to defile her.

"Then do the same as your oath to me, Rio," Ross purrs, releasing his dick. "And bow to her."

Getting onto my knees in front of Clover is the type of knighting I wish I could have the honor of participating in every damn night. The close scent of her pussy rockets through me, my muscled thighs trembling with the urge to pounce, the scales under my skin desperate to show themselves.

Stroking the inside of her leg, I'm thrown off balance by the sheer silk of her skin against my calloused palms. Clover's softer than a new leaf, more tender than a sparrow's belly, and as vulnerable to me as I am to her.

"*Bite,*" Rossi says.

I open my mouth and snap.

Clover jolts, but I keep her still by clamping my hands on her ass cheeks and sucking a milky section of her thigh into my mouth. I suck hard, forcing blood to the surface and to weep through the small holes I've put there. She'll be bruised and sore tomorrow, close to the color of my soul, actually.

"Rio," she cries. "Please. Rossi, don't do this to me anymore. I need, I *need*—"

"*Bite.*"

I move up her thigh and give her another sharp bite.

Clover wrenches against my hands, but after a collective breath, she pushes against my mouth.

I glance up between the apex of her thighs. "Are you desperate for me, Lucky?"

Her breasts move with shallow breaths. "I want ... I want your mouth on me."

"Not until Rossi allows."

Her wide eyes try to focus on Rossi. She's in a fugue state. Not one where she doesn't know what's going on around her, but one in which her sole focus is to *fuck*.

"Rossi," she moans.

He gives a slow, torturous headshake, denying her.

"Miguel," she sobs. "Please..."

Rossi's form takes on a razor-sharp, straight edge. He pins her, though he doesn't move. Impales her without so much as a strike.

I take advantage of his frozen shock, asking my Lucky gently, "Where?"

Clover's eyes turn to frustrated slits. "You know where."

"I want you to say it," I croon. "Dirty your mouth some more for us, Lucky."

She breathes above me, her sweet breath curling against the top of my head. I wait, though I'm close to roaring my frustration.

"My—" She clears her throat. "My *pussy*."

"Good, *good* girl," I praise before I take her pussy in my mouth and drive my tongue inside, staring at Rossi while I do it.

I'll take his punishment for not waiting for his permission. Gladly.

Clover's head thuds against the wall. She moans above me and curves into my face until my nose is buried inside her, too.

I don't mind it. This is an excellent way to die.

Nipping along her labia, I dare another sharp bite against her clit. Not enough to draw blood. I just want to hear her cry of pain before she exhales in pleasure again. It's like a white noise I'll play every night now, especially when I'm watching her from afar.

Her taste conquers my mouth, salty sweet and purely her. I lap it up, my chest tight with lack of oxygen, though my heart doesn't care.

Ferocious, territorial need drives through me, and I unlatch from her pussy, clutch her ankles, and pull until her ass smacks against the floor.

Clover yells in shock, but I'm beyond reason. I'm deaf to Rossi if he's even recovered enough to roar his disapproval.

This is exactly what I worried about if I ever got the chance to have her. Brutish possession. No use being conflicted over it now.

I yank again until she's splayed on the floor, her dark hair curled around her head like a devil's halo, and I spread her open by pinning her knees, her ankles still cinched together.

Candlelight doesn't do her glistening pussy justice.

"Rossi," she mewls, stretching a hand out to him. She somehow got her hands free, my flexible, breakable doll. "Fucking. Come. Here."

Unlike her metallic glow, Rossi's eyes are dark and inscrutable in shadow.

I lift my head and nod at him to come over. What the enchantress wants, she gets.

And Rossi *wants*.

My gaze flicks to his cock, so thick with need it has to be killing him. He's swollen, leaking pre-cum all over his hands. His balls are stretched and weighing down.

Clover gets up on her elbows. "Rossi. I need you, too."

He groans, curses, and his expression wrenches into one of pain and desire. But he moves, limps really, toward her.

Clover lifts up and leans forward, her mouth opening for his cock. When he comes close enough, she sucks one of his balls in her mouth.

Rossi buckles, shouts, his fingers whipping into her hair and redirecting her lips to his cock. "Suck me. Oh, Jesus fuck, *suck* me."

Clover opens wide. Rossi's hips nearly hit her face when he drives into her mouth. She gags, her eyes watering, but her hands fly to his ass, keeping him where she wants him.

"You're so wet for us, it's collecting on the floor," I rasp before sucking in my cheeks and spitting on her pussy.

Her hips lift from the floor in shock, but her plump lips are too busy with Rossi's dick to allow her voice to escape. Her throat's relaxing, allowing better access and swallowing him whole again.

I push my fingers in, three of them sluicing through with ease. Using my thumb, I circle her clit until she's mewling beneath me, her chest reddened with a sexual flush and her lips swollen from it.

"Does it still hurt, Lucky?"

She nods with her mouth full of a professor's cock.

"Where?" I tease, then flick her clit. "Here?"

She croons her confirmation, her mouth thickened and words unintelligible.

With my gaze solely focused on her, I reach into my back pocket and pull out a condom—a special trinket I've kept on me and saved for this very moment—and slip it on my hard, throbbing cock.

Clover's eyes roll back into her head as she bucks her hips and orgasms with a mere graze of my fingers past her clit and down.

Then I drive into her while she's still riding high.

I bury myself so deep, my ass cheeks ache with the pressure. Clover is as succulent as I dreamed. I'd sink my balls into her, too, if her pussy would allow it.

Clover's garbled scream reaches my ears at the time I realize she's much tighter than I imagined. I've stretched her to her limit. My fingers curl against the floor in surprise.

"Lucky, you're so much smaller than I thought you'd be."

Her soft mouth pops off Rossi's dick. "And you're both a lot bigger than you were in my fantasies."

"Then we all agree this is fucking phenomenal," I say.

She smiles. Rossi looks at the ceiling and makes a mournful sound but doesn't retreat.

I pull out, and it's torture, before returning home and finding the deepest part of her. I do it again, my return more forceful with each slow drag from her slick warmth. Clover's muscles flutter around my cock, the beginnings of acceptance, and I become harsher with my movements—I will be buried, she will be my grave, and I will go into my coffin with a smile.

She shudders beneath me. I catch her orgasm as it explodes through her body, lapping it up like I did her blood, her pussy, her life.

I wait until she's sated—requiring the type of patience of a saint—before Rossi growls, "Come inside her."

He doesn't say the words that should follow: *Come inside her because I cannot.*

"Yes," she breathes in agreement. "Both of you, come at the same time."

She grabs Rossi again, head bobbing and making loud sucking noises. Rossi groans, then pulls out of her mouth, jerking off erratically as he loses control.

My pounding courses through her body, so powerful and rigorous that I send her shoulders crashing into the wall. Clover takes it, her sensitive nub rubbing along my shaft with a swelling second orgasm.

The release explodes from me like a gunshot, so vigorous and thick that she'll be coated by cum, and it'll be dripping out of her cunt.

Rossi shouts his release, angling himself to spill all over Clover's chest. It drips off her skin, onto my diamond, and across the floor.

It's with that vision that I buck into her one last time, my head dropping into the nape of her neck when my body tries to recover.

"Oh ... my god..." she says.

I rise, wanting to carve her satiated expression into my mind.

A vibration comes between us, and she looks down in surprise.

Fuck. My phone.

With great reluctance, I lift off her and pull my phone from my back pocket. Rossi collects himself, shoulders heaving as he does up his pants.

I don't adjust myself or my pants as I read the message. From the corner of my eye, I notice Clover enjoying the view.

Tempest: Rossi's office. Now.

"Everything okay?" Clover asks.

Sex with her must have messed with my ability to control the mask. I work to put it back in place when I respond, "Yes. We're needed elsewhere."

I look at Rossi in silent communication. His chin jerks with a nod. "Help her dress, Rio."

I would have, anyway.

I assist Clover into a stand, taking time to delicately trace my marks. And with a gentleness that I don't reserve for anyone else, I help her into her jacket, smoothing it from her wrists onto her shoulders and covering her breasts with her bra and shirt.

Then I go to my knees, pulling up her leggings and thong with great consideration for the bruises I've caused. I kiss the one closest to her apex before gliding my hands along her stomach and smoothing the hem of her pants.

Pushing to my feet, I give her one last once-over. "Are you okay?"

She smiles softly. "Never better. The ache is gone. Sated."

"Good." I caress her cheek before turning for the stairs. "You're ours now. You've soaked my lips, my cock, and my soul. I'll be back for you."

To prove my point, I pull her to me and seal my lips on hers, but not as a kiss.

As a devouring.

She responds in kind, and my lucky clover even exposes her teeth and gnashes my lower lip, drawing blood and dragging it between our lips with her tongue.

The taste of her pussy mixes with the blood and it takes all self-control, all training, all thoughts of *anything* but the girl clawing at my shirt to roughly pull away from her and say hoarsely, "Go."

Gasping for breath and clutching at her throat like she has no idea who she is, Cover nods, looking around the area before her brows crash down with confusion.

"Wait ... where's Rossi? And where's the grimoire?"

But I've taken that moment to vanish from view because if I waited any longer, I'd claim her again.

And I'd chain her here.

CHAPTER 35

CLOVER

I burst into my dorm room, relieved to find Ardyn sitting on her bed reading with Hermione curled up on her lap instead of out with Tempest.

"We have a problem," I say.

Ardyn sets down her book. "What's wrong?"

"The grim—wait. Weren't you supposed to come get me after an hour if I didn't surface from the basement?"

"I was standing outside with Tempest when Professor Rossi came out. He gave us a curt nod and moved on."

I take a beat. Her saying that name makes me remember his dick in my mouth and his salty, warm, musky cum.

Schooling my features, I say, "Well, good. Because it was all very professional and he gave me the all clear."

"I can see that." She smiles, but it's forced. "You look like you've sobered up."

More like I was roughed up.

I stare at my friend, ashamed. "I shouldn't have lied to you about the coffee."

Then I make the mistake of moving. Sprinting from the TFU

library to the dorms was rough. My neck throbs. My jaw hurts. My chest joined in during the run. And my vagina ... well, let's say Rio began his own percussion on my body, and it hasn't stopped playing since he left.

"You okay?" Ardyn asks.

I rub my thighs together, making it worse for my body but triggers an excellent memory of Rio between my legs.

So much better than reality.

"The grimoire's gone," I say.

Ardyn leans forward with interest.

Aggravated, Hermione leaps off her lap and finds a less mobile spot under my bed.

I move to sit across from Ardyn, wincing slightly when my butt hits the edge of my bed.

"It was gone when I went to leave..." I shake my head, dumbfounded.

"Was there a moment you took your eye off it?"

Yes. Many.

I feel so stupid that I forgot about the grimoire, open and vulnerable, nearby. First with Rossi, then with Rio. But I was so sure it was safe while we were ... busy. Did Rio take it before he left? Did Rossi? Or is there another voyeur I need to become concerned about?

"Clover."

My unfocused gaze comes back to Ardyn.

"What's going on?" she asks. "You're not telling me something."

I rub my face, tired, frustrated, and bamboozled all at once.

"Wait—what's that on your neck?"

I freeze, staring out between my fingers.

"Right there." Ardyn points at the side of my neck. "Is that a ... hickey?"

Damn. I thought my hair was dark and thick enough to cover

Rio's markings if I pulled my hair forward and popped the collar of my leather jacket. In my fidgeting, I must have shifted my disguise and put his bite marks on full display. One of them, anyway.

"Ummm..." So much of me wants to keep lying to her. But the other, panicky investigator part needs her help figuring out whether I've been betrayed *and where the fuck Sarah's book went.* "Yes?"

Ardyn's back goes rigid, and she gasps. "Who?"

"Well, it's complicated."

"I'm an expert at complicated." Ardyn presses forward on her thighs. "Tell me."

"The hickey's from Rio."

There is *no way* I'm telling her about Rossi yet. Or the group sex. I might make her head fall off.

Ardyn's mouth parts. "Excuse me?"

"Yeah. We've been circling each other for a while, and it finally happened." I squirm in happy remembrance.

"But I thought I left you down there with Professor Rossi."

"You did. But he left." *Lie.* "After..."

"After *what?*"

I waste a few seconds debating what to tell her and what to keep. Ardyn's been nothing but loyal. When she first started dating my brother, I worried that loyalty would be skewed. So far, Ardyn's proved me wrong.

Frankly, if anyone can stand up to him besides me, it's her.

"I lied. Rossi was there too." I inhale, then blurt, "After he pulled down my shirt and looked at my breasts, Rio showed up."

Ardyn's jaw drops.

Might as well wild out. "And I've also slept with Xavier Altese."

Her mouth forms a bigger *O*.

"And Professor Morgan."

Ardyn's jaw unhinges.

I lean back, grimacing. Waiting for the lecture to befall me.

Ardyn blinks, collecting herself. "I'm—I'm not sure—there's —you?"

She holds up her hand in a *let me process* motion.

"Oh no, I broke your brain."

I predict what's going on in her mind, explaining, "I'm a big girl, and I'm handling it."

"Are you?" Ardyn bites her lower lip. "Clover, we were here discussing how dangerous these men are just a few hours ago."

"Not all of them," I say in a last-ditch defense. "Unless you're including Xavier in the mess my brother's in, too."

Ardyn works her jaw, neither confirming nor denying. "But you're hooking up with Rio, and I'm happy you got to realize your childhood crush. Really, I am. But Clover ... he's Tempest's best friend. And he's involved in some shady activities."

"That hasn't stopped you from falling in love with my brother."

Ardyn pales. She clutches her knees and presses back. "Are you saying you're in love with Rio? What about Xavier? Morgan? Rossi?"

"I told you it was complicated." I billow out an exhale. "I feel a connection with all of them."

Ardyn eyes me cautiously. "Even the professors?"

"All. Of. Them."

Ardyn holds her hands to her face and whispers, "This is terrible."

"Please don't judge me. I didn't plan to want more than one relationship."

Ardyn shakes her head. "I'm not judging you for having more than one hookup or crush—I'd never do that. I'm worried about something else."

I cock my head. "You really don't care?"

"I couldn't be happier for you about that. I just wish you'd chosen other guys on campus. *Anyone* else."

I reply sagely, "The heart wants what it wants."

"But Clover ... oh, my god. These men..." Her eyes move back and forth frantically like she's reaching for a valid argument. "You can't sleep with the professors. You could be expelled. Their careers could be ruined."

I frown. For some reason, I didn't think that would be the reasoning she'd reach for. The worry lines on her face were pointing to something deeper. More insidious.

"Please don't tell my brother."

"*Hell* no." Ardyn's hands drop from her face. "You can do that."

I snort. "I'm never doing that."

"Okay. I need to think." Ardyn slaps her legs and breathes deep. "Besides dropping that bomb on top of my head, you've also lost the grimoire?"

I nod sagely. "And I'm pretty sure Rossi took it since Rio gave it to me. It doesn't make sense that he'd want it back. Does it?"

Ardyn frowns. "What would Rossi want with it?"

"That's the thing—nothing. Rossi practically laughed me out of the library after I told him about the missing jewels—"

Ardyn looks at me sharply. "You told him?"

"It sort of burst out of me," I admit. "While I was horny, hurting, and arguing with him."

Ardyn's lips flutter with an exhale. "Of course you were."

"I'm not lying when I say I feel a connection with him. That wasn't the elixir. I trust him. It doesn't make sense, and it's kind of weird since he's so much older, but that's where my heart's taken me. And if he took the grimoire, then..." I lift my hands, then let them fall. "Then I won't know myself anymore."

"Don't be so sure," Ardyn mutters.

"What do you mean?"

"You think you know someone, and they could turn out to be totally different." Ardyn rubs at her upper arms. "The more I think about it, Clover, the more I'm sure finding Sarah's jewels is far too dangerous."

"Oh, come on." I laugh. "I'm chasing a 200-year-old jewelry stash for a school essay that everybody's forgotten about or decided doesn't exist. What can possibly be so dangerous about that?"

"If you've gained Professor Rossi's interest, then there's something about that treasure we don't know about."

Ardyn sounds so certain. But that would mean Rossi used me. Tricked me. Seduced me for something other than caring about me.

I narrow my gaze at her. Her reaction to my confession of wanting these men wasn't just concern.

It was *fear.*

"Is there anyone else you've told?" Ardyn asks, her brows pulling in. "Xavier?"

"I haven't told him."

Ardyn's shoulders sag with relief. The back of my mind *pings* with suspicion at her reaction.

"But I did talk to Professor Morgan about it."

In response, Ardyn's head falls back like she's asking the ceiling for a good prayer for my survival.

"He's the one who assigned the paper, Ardyn," I argue. "You can't blame me for discussing my research with him."

"Yes, but you know what money brings out in people, especially lots of it. Greed. Self-preservation. Violence."

"I can keep going without the book—though I *will* find it. Remember the message written in invisible ink? I memorized it, and we destroyed it. I can continue my research."

Ardyn worries her lips. "What if Rossi took the book because he wants you to stop?"

"Then he can suck it because I'm far too deep into finding answers to ever want to stop, stinky grimoire or not."

"Okay, so what are you going to do next?"

I cross my legs and focus solely on Ardyn. "Go to Anderton Cottage."

Ardyn rubs at her lips, her gaze sliding away.

"And I'm not stopping there," I continue. "That cottage is Sarah's last location before being arrested. The message about flowers and stones and summer has to be around or in that house. I'm sure of it. She wouldn't have wanted her daughter close in a time where they were being investigated."

"You're not planning on going there tonight, are you?"

I want to. I'd planned to when we revealed the secret message and solutions began stacking in my mind. But then Professor Rossi feasted on my breasts with his eyes and left me tingling and aching. Rio fixed that with mind-blowing sex. Then I took Rossi's dick in my mouth. And the grimoire went missing.

I'm sore and pissed off and need a shower. I'm in no condition to go on an incognito hunt where I'm allegedly violating Tempest's privacy again.

"No," I say. "Not tonight."

"Good." Ardyn pushes to her feet. "I have to go. Tempest had an errand to run, but he should be finished by now, and I'm staying the night with him."

I ask her wryly, "I don't suppose you want to search the cottage for me?"

"Sure."

My chin snaps up. "Really?"

"Yeah. I can't promise I'll find anything relating to flowers, but I'll definitely take a look around."

"Thank you." I'm breathless with sincerity. "That would mean a lot."

Ardyn smiles in response, the corners trembling, and her eyes hooded with an unreadable emotion. "I'll do my best."

I eye her curiously as she grabs her things and reaches under my bed to coo at Hermione before leaving.

Ardyn doesn't look back before she shuts the door.

CHAPTER 36

RIO

The grimoire. *My gift to Clover.*

Rossi swiped it from under Clover by seducing her and taking advantage of her vulnerable position.

And I went along with it.

Anger sweeps over my reluctance to face Tempest like a tidal wave.

Rossi better have a good excuse for messing with Lucky that way. Truly, is he interested in this so-called treasure hunt, so much so that he was willing to have us fuck, then trick Clover?

I do not appreciate being used that way. If that's the case, I'm not above the careful planning of Rossi's missing person status.

Why did he take the book?

This question clouds my thoughts as I knock, then twist the knob to enter Rossi's office.

The interior is much like Rossi—dark wood, buttery leather chairs, full bookshelves ordered in neat lines. His desk lamp is on when I step in, but the overhead light is off.

I've learned this is how Rossi prefers it, to be laced in blackness while barking orders from his desk.

It's hard to reconcile the imposing boss, his dark hair and olive skin complimented only slightly by the arc of light, but fully received by the environment the light can't reach, when we just had group sex together.

"Rio," Rossi says from his desk. His tone gives no indication of our time in the library's archives. "Take a seat."

A skilled study of the room shows Tempest in one chair across from Rossi's desk and Xavier Altese standing uncomfortably behind him.

I've schooled my features enough times not to emote the eyebrow twitch that wants to occur upon noticing Xavier and sit in the chair next to Tempest.

Rossi regards the three of us, taking his time to meet our eyes before moving on to the next.

"I'm afraid I have a confession to make," he says with a grim twist to his lips. "I can't keep it to myself any longer."

I move an infinitesimal amount away from the back of the chair, braced for a fight. Tempest will go for me, first.

"The three of you are aware of the history of Titan Falls," Rossi continues, "and the skeletons it's built on."

I nod, even though I'm now confused. If he's not confessing our moments with Clover, what is he doing?

"You're well aware of the fate of the Anderton witches, then, but you may not be aware of the legend behind them."

Fuck. This is about the jewels.

"With all due respect." Tempest cuts in. "Are you referring to what my sister's obsessing over? What does that have to do with us?"

"Allow me to continue without interruption, and I'll tell you." Rossi's tongue is coated in acid. "For it has quite a lot to do with the Vultures and is crucial to our livelihood."

I sense Xavier's gaze above me, bouncing between me and

Tempest, hoping for clarification. He's smart enough to keep his confusion silent.

"Professor," I say. Without moving my head, I gesture with my eyes to Xavier. "Should we be discussing this in present company?"

Rossi's black eyes capture mine, slick with impatience. "Yes, because I need him."

Tempest frowns, angling in his seat so he can observe both Xavier and Rossi.

I do the same. This is getting more riveting by the second.

"Before she died, Sarah Anderton stashed away her fortune so no one could find them. It was her last revenge against the men who executed her, so they couldn't get rich off her death." Rossi splays his hands on his desk. "I've been trying to locate it."

Tempest rubs his mouth and jaw. I rest my elbows on my knees, staring at Rossi in a new light.

He was Bianchi's lead assassin, until he disgraced the outfit and tried to escape the life with his wife and child. Rossi's punishment for that was swift and brutal, and he was exiled to Titan Falls, where he took charge of other younger men who defied or insulted Bianchi but were too valuable to die. I've come to know Rossi as detached, unforgiving, and exacting. A man like that would never entertain a search for hidden treasure.

"This is serious," Tempest says to Rossi. "You're serious."

Rossi responds with a sharp nod. "I'll admit it was in the back of my mind as an interesting fable until recently, when Sarah's grimoire was discovered. In it, there is evidence that the jewels indeed did exist, and she left a message for her daughter to retrieve them from her hiding place."

"But her daughter died, too."

Rossi, Tempest, and I swing our heads to Xavier, the three of us surprised to hear him talk.

"Yes," Rossi says carefully. "She disappeared soon after

Sarah's death. It was assumed she died, too, though her body's never been found. Thus, the jewels were never recovered."

"And you know where they are?" I ask.

Rossi shakes his head in the negative. He reaches under his desk, revealing the thick, unsavory grimoire before setting it in front of him. "But I have this."

"That's—didn't you give that to Clover?" Tempest asks me.

I nod, careful not to remove my focus from Rossi. I'm all too interested in how he will navigate this phase of his confession.

"I took it from her," Rossi says to Tempest without an ounce of remorse. "It should concern you that Clover is getting much too close to the Anderton jewels. She found another clue tonight by revealing a secret message in one of these pages. That she ultimately destroyed," he grumbles.

Rossi gestures to the grimoire. "If I hadn't taken it from her tonight, she would expose the existence of priceless gems hidden somewhere on campus, setting the university into chaos as everybody and their mother tries to search for it. And that, my Vultures, would be *very* bad for us on many levels."

I'm forced to agree. The less the TFU campus is noticed, the better for us to complete our delicate work.

"Do you know for a fact it's real?" Tempest asks. He's the only one of the three of us comfortable enough with Rossi to be so candid. "Clover's doing what she normally does—getting annoyingly involved in solving a sordid mystery so she can be at the top of her class."

"She was trying to solve the secret of the Anderton daughter's name, which was harmless, until I realized it could be involved with locating the lost jewels," Rossi answers.

"How does that make sense?" Xavier asks.

I send him a warning look. *Shut. Up. Imbecile.*

"If I left the grimoire with Clover," Rossi says, ignoring Xavier's question, "She could discover more and perhaps the answer to the centuries-old question on where it all went. That cannot happen because *I* want the jewels."

I'm a silent man, but at this moment, I'm struck dumb.

"You ... what?" Tempest says.

Rossi's expression remains stern, focused, and with no room for argument. And that this is *definitely* not a joke.

"Suffice it to say, if the Vultures find the jewels first, it will put us in an incredibly valuable position." He levels a long look at Tempest, then me. "A negotiable one, if you understand me."

The answer comes to me in a cold dose of clarity. Rossi wants to find the jewels, sell them on the black market, and give us enough money to escape Bianchi's clutches. That kind of currency could easily provide us with false identities and get us out of the country. Rossi has long given up his fight for freedom, instead giving in to his inner monster instead. He'd rather run a secret crime syndicate at a university than be a free man without his family.

After the emotions I saw him experience with Clover, I can finally understand the motivations behind the man.

Tempest and I stare at each other. His eyes reflect the same torrent of emotions behind mine—disbelief, adrenaline, *hope.*

Could we actually locate these jewels?

"Tempest, Rio, your job is to discover what else Clover knows and to alert me if she has anything else," Rossi continues.

"Is she in danger?"

The question comes out of me before I can stop it.

Tempest glances over sharply. I keep my features relaxed and unconcerned, even though inside I'm overflowing with the urge to protect her.

"Not as yet," Rossi says. "Believe me when I say that I am invested in her safety as well, Tempest. We all are. She's not a member of the Vultures, but she's blood. Nothing will happen to her on our watch. You have my word."

After what I witnessed in the library basement and Rossi's utter benediction and worship of Clover, his fear of touching her before he gave in, I believe him.

Jealousy doesn't grow out of that belief. In my mind, the more powerful people willing to stand in front of Clover and defend her, love her, the better. I'm even gratified that Rossi sees Clover in the same way I do.

Rossi says, "Xavier, I bet you're wondering why you're here."

Xavier gives a slow, wary nod.

Rossi continues, "I'm sure you've all noticed who is absent from this meeting."

That much is obvious: Morgan.

"Hunter Morgan isn't here because he can't be trusted." Rossi folds his arms over the grimoire. He doesn't react to its smell. None of us do. We've been around a lot worse. "Unfortunately, he is a wealth of information on the topic of witch trials and the occult."

Tempest grumbles his reluctant agreement.

"So Xavier," Rossi says, "Since you're under his tutelage, I'd like you to remain close with him and glean any information relating to the Andertons. Whatever you do, do not clue him into why or what you're doing. This is a chance to show your worth." Rossi lowers his tone. "Don't blow it."

Xavier responds with a pensive nod. "Honestly? It'd be nice to do something other than maiming and killing people."

I ask Xavier calmly, "You don't mind possibly betraying him?"

Xavier gives an empty laugh. "That guy is not my mentor, my idol, or my friend. I don't give a fuck what you want to do with him. And if this treasure trove of jewels can help you help me leave this life of captivity, then I'm happy to do it."

Rossi's gaze shutters as soon as Xavier says *leave this life*. But he doesn't argue the point or warn Xavier that he's not part of the escape plan. He's waiting for Xavier to prove himself.

We all have to, at some point.

"Tempest? Rio?" Rossi prompts. "Do you understand your orders?"

"Yes, sir," we reply at the same time.

"Good. As my trusted seconds, I have full confidence you will not mention this to Bianchi. Xavier, since you're new, I don't have the same level of trust. What I can tell you to earn your trust in return is that yes, I will help you escape the Bianchis if you assist us in discovering the Anderton jewels."

"Really?"

The poor boy's face lights up at Rossi's words.

I know a lie when I see one.

While Rossi has an impeccable mask in place, I sense the untruth in his words and his willingness to sacrifice Xavier to get what he wants.

I've gone through too much betrayal and death to warn him, so I lean back with an emotionless expression while Xavier says, "Then yes. Absolutely, yes. I'll do whatever is needed."

Rossi lowers his head in thanks. "I'm aware how fantastical this sounds. With this grimoire—which you found, Rio, and I am forever grateful, though I wish you'd given it to me—we're closer than anyone else in history."

I dismiss Rossi's casual disapproval over my choice of recipient. I'd peel my skin off my bones for Clover, never mind surprise her with an ancient spell book that she jumped for joy over. "What was the secret message Clover uncovered?"

I feign ignorance, like I didn't hear the same thing he did. Rossi's lips turn down. He won't reprimand me. Rossi won't take any chances in revealing his reverence over Clover or the proximity of his cock to Tempest.

"It said, '*we are at war, my flower, may you find spiritual peace where our stone is circled by summer.*'"

"A poem?" Xavier asks.

Rossi says, "I'll do my work to decipher it, but I'd like the three of you to test your skills as well. Fair warning: Clover is also working on this. I wasn't able to get the grimoire away from her before she revealed the clue."

It's because of her the clue was revealed.

I keep that fact to myself. I may not use it often, but I value my tongue. Especially now that I get to use it on Clover.

Tempest pulls his lips in, scowling. I can relate. I don't want Clover coming any closer to our circle of Vultures than she already has, yet this treasure hunt of hers is bringing her on our doorstep no matter how much we try otherwise. It didn't occur to me that giving her the grimoire would cause this mess—I had no idea any treasure existed.

I wish I could tell him I'll die before anything happens to her.

"Meeting adjourned," Rossi bites out, waving his hand for us to leave.

We comply, none of us ones for small talk, and head for the door.

Until a sharp knock comes from the other side.

The three of us stop moving.

Tempest turns his head to Rossi. "Expecting anyone?"

Rossi growls, "Not unless Morgan was tipped off somehow."

Xavier throws up his hands. "Don't blame me. I'd rather not talk to any of you."

I'm the first to break the tension, turning the knob and throwing the door open. I want to remind them we're at a university in a professor's office and it's probably a student desperate for an extension on Rossi's impossible assignments, but I like to reserve my words for more important matters.

Ardyn stands on the threshold, pale and with a conflicted

twist to her lips.

Ardyn stands on the threshold, pale and with a conflicted twist to her lips.

"Ardyn?" Tempest barrels past me and cups her shoulders. "What's wrong?"

Ardyn's blond curtain of hair obscures her expression as Tempest leads her inside. Xavier and I part like two rivers to let her through.

Rossi glowers while hunched over his desk, his hands splayed like two tarantulas spotting a delicious birdie nearby.

"How can we help you, Ardyn?" he asks.

There's no attempt to hide his annoyance.

Ardyn pulls out of Tempest's protective grip. "I have to tell her."

Uh-oh.

I swivel my head to look at Tempest.

He asks his girlfriend softly, "Tell Clover what?"

Ardyn takes a deep breath. "It's all happened so fast and I can't keep lying to her—"

I cut in, "What's happened so fast?"

Ardyn locks her gaze with mine, her eyes burning with bright intensity and seeing directly into my soul.

Shit. She knows.

Well, why shouldn't she. I'd thoroughly marked my lucky clover, it's no wonder she confessed to her only trusted friend.

I'm not ready for *my* only trusted friend to hear it, though.

Ardyn hesitates, holding my gaze, then blinks and addresses the room. "She's asking questions, detailed ones, about all of you. And she's started to notice things that I can't explain away."

"Not possible," Tempest bites out. "I've kept Clover far from us and what we do. Lied to her, betrayed her, sacrificed for her. I've put up walls around my sister no one without my permission can climb."

"You've spent years protecting her," Ardyn says to him gently, "and it's worked, but she's becoming a different person. Growing confidence. She's finding herself here, which I think we can all appreciate. But it's making her notice situations that aren't right and question those around her. Us. *Me.*"

As if they're the only two in the room, Ardyn walks to Tempest and grips his hands in her own. "She knows I'm lying to her and she's starting not to trust me. That's going to trickle down to you, and then what do we do? What will we do if she cuts herself off from us?"

"All the better." But Tempest's features war with his words. "She'll lead a happier life without this around her."

Ardyn appeals to Tempest through her lashes. "I remember you saying the same to me." She lifts her chin and releases his hands. "Except that you gave me a choice."

"Your concerns are noted," Rossi says. "But our oath stands. No one is to discover us."

"Um." Xavier makes a face and points at Ardyn. "Then what's with her?"

Rossi scrapes a hand down his face. "A temporary weakness. Ardyn's proven she can keep her silence and will *continue* to do so. Otherwise, she understands that any betrayal on her part will come back to her lover tenfold."

Ardyn's color turns gray at those words. She fumbles for Tempest's hand and squeezes until her knuckles turn white. "That's why I'm here. But *you* have to understand that she'll come to the answers herself. Our interventions aren't working. There will come a point—"

"Enough." Rossi lifts a hand in her direction. "Clover is bright, but she's distracted. She wants to find the jewels more than she wants to find out what her brother's involved in. We can use that to our advantage, giving us time to initiate our plans, so by the time she figures us out, it'll be too late."

"Do you know why Clover wants to find the jewels?" Ardyn blurts out. She steps forward, centering herself in front of Rossi. "She wants to give them to Tempest and to anyone else in this room who needs it so you can escape the criminal servitude you're all in. That's right," Ardyn says when Rossi's eyes widen. "She's at that level of knowledge and she wants to use it to *help* you. That's the girl you're dealing with and who you're icing out."

"Clover wants to do *what*?" Tempest croaks.

Ardyn turns, the lines of her shoulders softening. "You've worked so hard to keep the worst from her. Didn't you ever think there'd come a time where she'd want to keep it from you?"

"She doesn't owe me anything," he grits out.

"It doesn't matter. She knows you're in danger and wants to help, with or without you cluing her in."

"Fuck." Tempest paces the room.

I can commiserate. I had the vague notion that I could care for Clover while keeping the Vultures separate from her. I don't want her discovering what I do—how I kidnap men and women. Her brother commits murder. We're all killers in this room. The one exception is Ardyn, but even she's faced down her enemies with Tempest's help.

"Clover may believe she can accept the darker part of humanity," I say, "but it's another thing for her to comprehend what Tempest and I have done to bring ourselves to this point."

"And me," Xavier mutters.

I glance at him. Ardyn regards him without surprise.

"Her morals are strong," I continue. Everyone's eyes return to me. "But they can't compete with our black hearts. I agree with Rossi. Clover can't get to the truth."

Ardyn releases a sound of frustration, then appeals to Tempest. "The only way to do that is to physically restrain her, and even for you, that's going to far."

Tempest closes his eyes, then nods. "We have to get her to leave campus. For good."

"This isn't the way!" Ardyn cries at the same time my heart plummets.

I can't have that. Clover can't leave my sight. Ever.

"That won't stop her mind from churning," I argue. "She'll continue to investigate."

"Then what do you propose?" Tempest asks with a spurt of anger. "Suggestion box is open."

"*Tell* her," Ardyn says stubbornly. "She may surprise you like I did."

"Refocus her efforts," I say, talking over Ardyn. "Use her to locate the jewels. For all we know, it's a fruitless effort, but it'll be enough to draw a line between us and her determination to discover more about the Anderton witches."

"It is not a wasted effort." Rossi's soulless gaze snags mine into a strangling hold. "If we don't find it, you're trapped here, and I will not accept that."

"We had a plan," I say to him calmly. "One without the need for missing eighteenth-century jewelry."

"This expedites it." Rossi rounds his desk, his imposing form eclipsing us all. "The longer I'm imprisoned here, the more young idiots are sent my way." He whips his arm in Xavier's direction, who scowls at him. "The more innocent souls I'm forced to corrupt. I am *done*, Riordan. I don't care who hears it anymore. If I get my hands on that jewelry, I can finally win against a man who has taken *everything* from me. So no, I refuse to accept our mission as fruitless. And I certainly won't allow a young girl, no matter how beguiling, foil an escape from decades of suffering.

"We are to do *nothing* to draw Bianchis attention. Do you hear me?" Rossi roars the question.

Ardyn is the only one that flinches.

At our acquiescent silence, Rossi adds, his shoulders heaving, "That includes explaining the reality of our lives to Clover Callahan. *We* get to the treasure first. Before her. Before anyone. Is that understood?"

"Understood," I murmur. Tempest and Xavier follow suit.

Rossi turns his back to us while waving his hand dismissively. "Tell her we rescue ducklings for all the fucks I give. Now get out. All of you."

It's rare that Rossi allows his temper to flare so brilliantly. I'm not the only one who sees that, as we all quietly head to the door without argument.

Xavier exits first and Ardyn and Tempest step in front of me. I prefer being at the back so I can assess all threats before leaving a safe room.

It also gives me the advantage of hearing the lowered conversations of those ahead.

"I can't do it," Ardyn whispers brokenly to Tempest. "It's not fair to her that I know, and she doesn't. If you all keep refusing..."

"I know." Tempest squeezes her shoulder.

"I'll have to tell her myself," Ardyn finishes.

I lower my head in a sigh. That's the last thing I want to hear. It puts both Tempest and Clover in harm's way.

And it risks Clover hating me forever.

"Give me some time," Tempest says to her. "I will only ask this of you once. Rossi may have a way out for us without having to burden Clover. And it's a life sentence you'd be giving her, Ardyn. You know this."

Her shoulders sag. She nods.

I release my bated breath.

For now, Clover is safe.

For a time, she can be mine without disgust marring her bewitching face.

CHAPTER 37

CLOVER

I t doesn't take much time to decide to do what I promised Ardyn I wouldn't.

After cleaning my "wounds," in the bathroom with some alcohol, I grab my moto jacket, charcoal cashmere scarf, boots, and bag, and exit the dorms without running into anyone.

In the mood I'm in, I kind of hoped Minnie would step into my path. I'd have no problems punching her in the throat. Who needs a curse when you're getting ninja lessons from the handsome, cut, well-endowed Riordan Hughes?

My neck warms at the remembrance, triggering a gentle throb of his bite mark there, and it makes starting the trek through the dirt footpath into the cold, dark woods more bearable.

I use my phone's flashlight to help me wander through the areas the moonlight can't reach. Leafless, brittle branches stroke my face and body like skeletal hands clawing up from the ground. I'm not afraid. More perturbed that they can't set their desperation aside and allow me through.

The winding path to Anderton Cottage is a difficult but a familiar one, especially at night. Ardyn let slip that she was meeting Tempest for dinner, and I don't mind if I run into Rio again. It would distract me, though, and without the grimoire for reference, I can't let that happen.

I have two goals once I reach the cottage: Search for the grimoire on the small chance it ended up there and see if there are any objects or clues pointing at the message written in invisible ink.

This was Sarah and her daughter's home. If there are any more clues to be found, it's there. I'm sure of it.

... may you find spiritual peace where our stone is circled by summer ...

It's not a lot to go on but it's all I have.

And it's enough to pass the time before I land on the cottage's porch, the windows dark and the house silent.

None of the boys must be home. Good, but I've thought that before and been wrong.

And this time, I don't have a copied key.

They are much too cautious to leave windows and doors unlocked.

I hop off the porch, the curious, icy fingers of the wind picking up where the branches left off. Covering the bottom half of my face with the scarf and circling the wood-paneled architecture, I wonder if Sarah ever thought to build a hidden entrance into her home. It makes sense, given her efforts in letterlocking and invisible ink. I doubt the noblewomen wanted to knock on her door to acquire her services.

It's a search that needs more than a flashlight at night. With more time, I'd pull blueprints and read as much on seventeenth century homes that I could. From what I've been able to glean so far, people from centuries past *loved* secret passageways as well as their invisible ink and booby-trapped letters. During the

Protestant Reformation, there were "priest holes," panic rooms that housed those who didn't practice what was preached. In war, militaries developed classified technologies in hidden rooms. Escape staircases were placed between castle walls.

If I were Sarah, I'd damn well do it, too.

Huffing out of my nose, I survey the backside of the cottage, gliding my light across the stone and looking for subtle seams indicating a trapdoor. I'm careful not to light up the windows in case someone *is* home.

My shoes crunch against loose stones and the frozen forest ground. I can't do this forever—it's really cold. I turn, squinting at the circle of woods enclosing the cottage from TFU view.

Would Sarah have a tunnel? It would be perfect—both a secret entrance for her clients and an escape hatch when needed.

With a new burst of energy, I head toward the tree line, Rio's marks on my body acting like candlelight on my skin and heating me all the way through. All I have to do is remember what we did together, and I find warmth.

It might be the placebo kind, but it'll do for now.

Fifteen minutes go by and I'm no closer to finding an underground tunnel than I was a hidden trapdoor. I start to think maybe revealing Sarah's hidden message in her grimoire gave me too much confidence. My lingering suspicions over Ardyn provided me with enough energy to get here, but the pleasant aches in my body from Rio are turning into whines.

With great reluctance, I turn back. I *hate* returning home with empty hands.

An exposed tree branch writhes out of the ground in front of me and I register it too late. With a loud *oompf!* I fall to the ground, my hands scraping against small rocks and sending them scattering.

My left ankle sings with pain. Groaning, I roll onto my back and sit up to inspect the damage. I prod at my ankle gently. It's yelling at me, but I don't think anything's broken. The true test is to put weight on it.

My head snaps up. "Wait."

A rock that I'd shifted during my fall *cracks* against something hard multiple times before fading into a soft echo.

I was so busy making sure I didn't maim myself that I failed to register the unnatural sound until now.

Pebbles press into my knees as I move into a crouch. I search the ground to find my phone and angle my app's flashlight to where the sound came from.

In a slow, rising arc of awe, I move the light over an intimidating pile of rocks stacked on top of one another like there's been an avalanche and they'd fallen off the side of a mountain.

Is this what Sarah meant when she wrote about a stone circled by summer? It's winter season, but...

My flashlight freezes on the small opening in the middle, an opaque black hole about the span of my hips if I wriggled and dragged myself through on my stomach.

"Nope," I vow, telling myself not to do it.

But we all know how that tends to turn out.

I crawl toward the opening with trepidation. Once I reach it, I crouch down, squinting with one eye as I angle the light inside, as if that'll make my vision 20/20.

As a test, I palm another rock and toss it in.

And just like the first, it tracks downward with the sound of a skipping rock, falling, falling ... then silence.

I sit back on my haunches. "Shit. I'm gonna do it."

I settle onto my stomach with my flashlight arm outstretched. I also move my pained ankle in a cautious circle, ensuring that wherever I end up, it won't be as a limping idiot. It throbs in response, then fades.

Enough to explore, I'd say.

Wriggling forward, I stick my hand clutching my phone in first. It illuminates like a small cave with a black bottom.

Black bottom?

With a gasp, I bend the light until it faces down.

Revealing stairs.

With ... skulls lining them in a circle.

Wriggling with more fervor, I get the top half of my body in. With just my legs hanging out of the hole, I'm able to twist until I'm face up and pull them in, too. There's enough room on the ground and above to stay in a seated position. With heavy breaths, I take stock of my limited surroundings.

The air is mustier here, thick with soil and the sharp scent of stone. Smooth, gray rock closes in on me in a tight square with a rounded ceiling. My flashlight bobs with my adrenaline and nerves, then skids to a halt when I notice a fracture in the smoothness.

No, not a break. A *drawing*.

A single flower is carved directly above the stairs leading down.

I work to swallow. "Guess I'm going on an adventure."

I reach the first stair by shimmying forward on my butt. My legs drop down with no issue—no traps, no swords coming out of the wall, no avalanche of stone on my head. I look up and check just to be sure I've entered something stable.

Of course I haven't.

With halted breath through clenched teeth, I butt-walk some more, until the floor disappears, and I'm immersed in a rimming of skulls.

My breaths are louder in here. I keep my flashlight angled down as I move, away from the former faces that instinct tells me are Sarah's kills—thankful my phone's fully charged. I tell myself if the bottom leads to a dead end, I can always work my way back up. It's not like I've traveled into a maze. Just a straight line down that spirals a little the deeper I get. It's okay if sightless, dead eyes watch me. No problem.

Twenty minutes in, I'm wondering if there is an end. My heart thuds against my ribs the same way my butt hits each stone stair. My bag reluctantly drags behind me, strapped to my shoulder.

Finally, my boots hit a different surface than another stair I've become familiar with. The texture is rough and there's no sharp edge. Raising the flashlight, I illuminate a tunnel that's the approximate height of a person before humans grew past 5'4".

Luckily, I'm 5'5". Rising, I duck my head to enter and keep it bent as I follow the tunnel. If my sense of direction hasn't failed me after navigating a tight spiral staircase, I'm headed toward Anderton Cottage.

My heart starts to race. Is this the same path the nobles took to make a deal with their contract killer? Did Sarah's daughter try to use this to escape when their home was invaded? Did Sarah?

I picture smaller, delicate footprints beneath my foot, spaced out in a panicked run.

But in mere minutes, I reach a dead end.

Or ... not so dead, because there's a ladder made of rope directly in front of me.

It doesn't swing or have the color of normal rope. It's so old and frayed, there's simply no color, not even when I glide my light across the closest step. And it leads up.

Centering myself, I hold the light above my head. It flashes dully on something and I return to it, studying it until I believe it's the lever to a hatch.

I come back to the rope ladder, my lips twisting. *Am I really going to try to climb it?*

Yes. Yes, I am. I haven't come this far for nothing.

Shoving the phone in the middle of my bra with the lens facing out (it's an extra pocket), I grip the side of the rope, testing its ability to hold me by pressing one foot down, then the other.

"Not so bad," I say to myself. "If I fall it's only ... ten feet. Totally fine."

With those assurances circling my head like frantic, tweeting birds, I begin my climb, the rope moaning with aggravation the higher I go.

"Yes, I know," I say to it, "I wish you were a spiral staircase, too."

I slip once during my ascent, my palms burning as they clutch the rope for dear life. But I make it and free one hand to push at the hatch. It doesn't budge.

I figured the lever would be too rusted with age to be of use, but I twist and push at it, and to my surprise, it gives with a lonely groan.

The hatch is heavy, like stone and wood had a baby, and I moan with effort as my muscles scream to maintain balance on the rope and push the door away from my head.

My body jerks down and I nearly lose my hold.

Shit. The rope's stretching. Before long, it'll snap, and I really don't want to go with it.

With a jolt of determination and a heart now living between my ears, I give one last heave. The hatch sways on its hinges then slams down on the other side.

I don't have time to be thankful. I hang onto the new floor I've found, my fingers sliding against the dust, and do a standing push-up, hearing the soft *plop* of the broken rope hitting the bottom of the tunnel below.

My knees come next, and I manage to shove myself out of the hole and land in a tangle of limbs on the ground, breathing heavily. My flashlight glows between my breasts, creating a circle of light on a ceiling, but it's one I'm unfamiliar with at Anderton Cottage.

I rear up. *Oh no, did I end up in the wrong house?*

A distinct smell wafts into my nostrils. Coppery with decay overlaid with the sharp chemical scent of bleach. I wrinkle my nose.

Pulling the phone from my cleavage, I swing it around, stalling on what appears to be an apothecary chest. Ornate flowers and leaves are carved into the cherrywood, a beautiful addition to an otherwise plain room with an uneasy smell. There are no windows. Two scratched and dented wooden chairs are centered, back-to-back. A shiver runs through me at the cold feeling of multiple presences, getting icier the closer I travel to those empty seats.

It's with relief that my flashlight glides over a staircase to the left—leading *up*. I scramble toward it, taking the stairs with ease now that they can fit a modern person, and come up against another dead end.

I throw my hands on my hips, inspecting the doorless wall. What kind of stairs lead to nothing? Have I followed an underground tunnel into a dungeon?

I think of those lonely chairs below with long scratch-marks on the seats.

God, I hope not.

I never thought I'd get tired of puzzles, but tonight, I've reached my limit. I kick at the wall with frustration, refusing, absolutely *refusing,* to turn back. Without the rope ladder, I'll have to jump, and I've already twisted my ankle once.

As I'm figuring out what to do, the wall suddenly opens outward. It causes the type of jump-scare that makes me rear back and teeter at the edge of the staircase.

Then the opening fills with a tall, lithe figure with deep frown lines on his face and folded, heavily tattooed arms.

"Well," Professor Morgan says. "This is a problem."

CHAPTER 38

CLOVER

Morgan pulls me out of the stairwell by the arm.

"How the *hell* did you get in there?" he asks, but it's with a strangely calm manner that belies my sudden appearance in a doorless, windowless part of his home.

He closes the section of wall behind me. My jaw drops once I see the other side. It's a wall of books. There was a hidden door in Anderton Cottage this whole freaking time.

I point at the bookshelf. "You knew about this?"

Morgan splays his hand against his chest. "Heavens, no. I'm just as shocked as you are. My goodness—there's a secret basement in my home? How could that be!"

My vision grows small as I glare at him.

Smiling wryly, Morgan drops the act. "Had to try. More to the point, how do *you* know about it?"

"I didn't. I sort of stumbled across it."

Morgan squints at me. "That's not good."

"Why? It doesn't look like any of you are doing much down there. If it weren't for that wooden chest, it'd be as bare as a prison cell."

"How right you are," Morgan says softly. He's not looking at me, but at the portion of the floor-to-ceiling bookshelf we walked through.

He returns my stare. "Show me."

I stiffen, then retreat a step. "I don't think I want to go back down there."

Morgan appears genuinely contrite when he says, "Sorry, sweetheart, but you don't have a choice."

That's why I don't register his arm clamping around my bicep until it's too late.

When someone puts their hands on me without permission, my instinct is to fight, even if it's a man I've dreamed about naked.

"Hey—ow! You're hurting me."

I try to wrench out of his grip.

"I have the sense you're not about to come willingly." Morgan drags me the few feet it takes to get to the bookshelf.

His strength is surprising for a man so lean. I'd thought Morgan would be the last to win a fight if faced off with Rio or Tempest. Clearly, I'm wrong. His bicep pops and writhes under the white button-down he's rolled up his forearm, which has distinct lines of muscle running through it, protected by snaking veins and tattoos.

Keeping his hand clamped on my arm while I glower at him, he pulls aside a framed picture on the wall to the right of the bookshelf. I stop struggling when I notice the color of the picture beneath the protective glass—a browned cream, wrinkled and torn in small sections, with reddish ink detailing the cartography of mountains, forests and the small houses peppered within.

... It's a map of Titan Falls in the 1700s.

I've usually been caught before I've snuck this deep into the cottage, so this is the first I've seen of it. It's enough to stare hard at the image, searching for houses I've never recorded in my own research and buildings where bare forest nooks now stand.

And I specifically note the lack of a tunnel running through the underground beneath Anderton Cottage.

My eyes trail across the 16x20 frame before they snag on something in the bottom corner. At first, it looks like a flaw, and if I hadn't endured what I'd just been through, I would've considered it that and moved on. But I can't unsee the flower above the stone staircase in the cave.

Just as I can't look away from the same symbol drawn in the corner of this map.

I'm so busy staring at the symbol I don't notice the code Morgan pounds into the keypad he exposed by swinging aside the map.

The hidden seam of the bookcase clicks open, refocusing my attention.

"Wait—" I point my free arm in the direction of the map. Morgan doesn't heed my pleas and pulls me back into the dark.

"You *must* show me how you got into the basement, Clover, before the rest of the boys return."

Morgan takes the stairs at a fast clip despite the lack of light. Because I'm attached to him, I stumble behind, careful not to twist my ankle even though the fates seem to *want* me to break a leg tonight.

"Why? I thought you guys knew everything there was to know about the cottage, hence why you're constantly kicking me out of it."

We reach the bottom of the stairs. After a *snick* of sound, a flame flickers between us, casting Morgan's face in a mixture of gold and black. Save for his eyes, which are smoldering bright green through the fire.

"You above all else should know Sarah enjoyed keeping her

secrets, Clover." Morgan smiles a deathly smile above the flame before swinging it around to light a rusted wall sconce.

My stomach does a funny dance at his grin, dread and anticipation swirling into a dangerous concoction.

Morgan releases my arm to light other sconces within the room. My legs itch to make a run for it—

"If you try to run up the stairs, you'll find yourself up against a dead end a second time," Morgan says while lowering his arm from the third sconce. "But if you're a good girl, I'll show you the trick to getting out."

I cast a wishful gaze up the staircase flickering with shadow and light. It's the easier one, for sure. "Good thing I know of a second exit—one you're desperate to figure out."

After the last sconce is lit, Morgan prowls over. "This isn't the time to play games with me."

"Isn't it?" The wall sconces create a frame of fire around our bodies. "You think my search for the Anderton daughter's name is nothing *but* a game. You've had no faith in me this entire semester, yet the minute my hard work leads me to something you don't know, you manhandle me to get me down here and show you. Like you deserve it."

Morgan fights for composure, his lips curling and his eyes turning hotter than the fire he's bathed us in. "You have no idea what you're tramping through, little leaf. All I'm trying to do is keep you blissful in your ignorance."

"Great." I lift my hands and slap them back against my sides. "Another male defender I don't need. How often do I have to tell my brother and his minions that I'm an adult who can decide when she doesn't want to pretend anymore?"

A rough cackle leaks from Morgan's mouth. "Minion? You think I'm Storm Cloud's *minion*? Far from it. I'm happy to see him dead—sorry, but I am. There's no love lost between us. And what I'm doing now, with you, isn't for him." Morgan takes a step closer.

Determined to show him I'm not afraid, I maintain my ground, though my heart skitters in its cage like a poor, shaking mouse.

I stare up at him, the tips of his shoes contacting mine.

Morgan is no less handsome close-up. His pore-less, smooth face is totally at odds with the black ink he buries into his skin everywhere else.

"This is for me," Morgan murmurs near my lips. "And possibly you."

"Me?" My voice betrays the hardness I'm forcing into my gaze as I regard him.

"You say you want truth and honesty. I'm afraid it'll be enough to break you. That's why you must tell me, Clover, where the second entrance is in this basement, so I don't have to make another sacrifice. I don't want to bring you to him."

I feel the weight of my brows before the realization hits, and my forehead clears. "You don't have to follow Tempest's orders. He's told all of you to stay away from me, but he barely knows me anymore."

I think of my moments with Rio and the way we fatefully came together, no matter what my brother tried to do to keep us apart. It could be the same with Morgan.

"I want my own life, Morgan. You can tell Tempest the same."

Morgan's lips curve in another smile, this one more sorrowful than the last. "Little leaf, you truly believe that your brother is the villain in your story, don't you?"

He lifts his hand, trailing an inked finger down my cheek. I've memorized his tattoos to the point that I'm aware of the rune that paints this finger. From my perspective, wealth and abundance. From his, failure and greed.

"Oh, you have no idea," he says, leaning forward to brush his nose against my cheekbone, following the trail. "And you are so beautiful in your innocence."

I've been alone with Morgan plenty of times before, but never in a locked basement hidden to the average TFU resident. There's a new danger at play, one that could burn or have an afterglow, I can't be sure.

All I'm aware of is, I don't move away.

"I can see why there's so much desperation to preserve you," Morgan whispers into my ear.

Shivering, I close my eyes.

"Because I'm powerless to do anything but the same."

His mouth comes down, his lips brushing the spot underneath my ear. Butterfly touches, not a kiss but not a tease. It's a fight, a battle for both of us, not to succumb.

"Tell me," he says, whispering across my neck and collarbone.

I've never felt such a compulsion to confess. I've entered another world, an older one, the walls surrounding us stained with the blood of so many innocents, invisible to the naked eye, but I know what splattered across the stone hundreds of years before, ruby red and violent.

I'm sorry for the daughter and the way she was plucked from existence. I can't feel the same for Sarah, a mistress of murder and familial destruction, though her execution was horrendous. It all happened here. Someone could've died in the spot where I stand, fruitlessly defending against Morgan's seduction.

A cold dread falls on my shoulders like a blanket over a coffin, divisive against Morgan's hot breaths playing across my exposed skin. It carries the anger of spirits and a heathen scent.

I clutch at Morgan's shoulders. "There are recent deaths here."

Morgan's muscles tense under my grip.

He pauses, his lips hovering inches from my clavicle. "Little leaf, are you thinking of death while I try not to ravish you?"

He shifts, his thighs knocking against mine and a third, solid length joining in.

Lust rockets through me with the speed of a single firework, throwing me off balance and skewing my thoughts toward him and not *it*.

But it won't let me go.

"I can smell it," I say. "The bloodshed, the tears. I didn't connect the dots before, but ... it's too strong to be ancient. I'm not that strongly connected to Sarah to be able to *scent* death in the air, but I do here. It doesn't make sense—"

"Clover." Morgan pulls back and cups my face. "It's best not to think about what these walls have seen. One tends to go down a rabbit hole of fear and torturous curiosity."

"Do you believe me?" I search his eyes.

Morgan's lashes lower. "There's a reason this room isn't on the local campus tours."

"I've found out about you," I say, refusing to let it go. "That you, my brother, Rio, are all involved in criminal activity. This is a convenient room to have removed from all TFU blueprints."

His gaze zeroes in. "I'll be the first to compliment you on your connection with death. In fact, I'm impressed. I thought I was the only one who appreciated the history buried here, the bodies that ran rivulets of blood across this floor. But even you can understand you can only step so far into this world and come out clean. Don't play with fire, Clover. You know what happens in the end."

I wrap my hands around his wrists as he continues to hold my face in his hands. "That's where you're wrong. I'm not afraid of it. I'm ... I'm..."

Morgan's fingers tremble against my temples. *Strength, weakness, movement, instability, clarity, conflict, joy, sorrow...*

With a piercing gaze, he prompts, "Say it, little leaf."

"I'm..."

"Say it so I can kiss you." Morgan's eyes brighten to a super-natural degree, a sheen of manic shattering the green into multiple, fragmented layers.

But ever so beautiful.

"I'm drawn...

"*Say it* so I can swallow you whole," he rasps.

"I can't resist the darkness," I cry out. "I've tried—I'm trying. Being here with you is wrong. And you distracting me with a soft touch when I *know* what you are isn't fair. You aren't a professor. You're not my friend. You're—you should be my enemy."

"Yet?" Morgan bares his teeth, but I'm not afraid.

"Yet I can't resist *you*," I breathe, and it's like I've disengaged my soul, allowing it to seep through my exhale and into his mouth, so willingly, so sudden and brutal that I blink rapidly against it.

He pulls my face toward him, the tips of his teeth running along my lips. "Tell me where the entrance is, and I'll continue to fight against making you mine and let you go."

It'd be so easy. And the right thing to do.

But his hardness presses against my core, the heat of his impossibly strong body warming through the cold spirits of this basement wanting to engulf and make me theirs. It could be Sarah—it could be her victims, but it's a warning nonetheless.

A warning not to speak of the way out to Morgan.

"I can't..." I whimper, truly conflicted on what to do and how much I should keep to myself.

The tunnel doesn't lead to a treasure. The jewels aren't down there. It's merely another entry into a room full of sorrow and torture, and I've broken the rope that secures it.

Why *can't* I tell him? Morgan loves what I love. The fact that neither he nor I are repulsed by our current behavior in this ghostly chamber... he would help me. Morgan would understand more than anyone why I can't stay away.

"Don't make me seduce it out of you," Morgan warns. "Because I will. Consequences be damned, I *fucking will.*"

I attempt to escape from his hold. Morgan holds me firm.

I stifle the sob wanting to rip out of my throat. It's not from fear. I've fantasized about Morgan after he took me from behind so often that the thought of at last knowing where all his tattoos lead would be exhilarating. To taste him would be to discover the true flavor of forbidden nectar. And not because he's a professor —he didn't deny my accusation that he's far from a tenured teacher.

No, it's because Morgan represents a concealed danger I've thus far ignored. If I unearth it, I'd have to accept the truth of my family, the viciousness of my brother, and the obliteration of the morals I built around myself in defense.

If Morgan drags me into the throws of another orgasm, God knows what I'd give to him in return.

Bad things happen in threes.

"Don't do this," I plead.

"I wish I could stop myself, but then you showed up in a place where you shouldn't. A forbidden fruit for me to pluck, with no one around to save you."

Morgan tangles one hand into my hair until he wraps it around the back of my neck. The other hand, he uses to cup one of my ass cheeks, squeezing painfully before he presses me into him.

The entire length of Professor Morgan fights for space between my thighs. He presses against my folds as if our clothes don't exist.

I clench my teeth, trembling in his grip.

"Tell me," he grits out.

Does Morgan honestly think he'd force me? Reading his face

for the answer gives me nothing. He's tense with determination, shaking with effort and crumbling willpower. Yet in his eyes, I can get to the truth, like skipping a rock over a lake flattened like glass. Ripples of desire that continues well below the surface and reflecting well above. Morgan sees it in me, too.

He knows I'll gladly submit to him.

Maybe that's what scares us both.

It's tempting to see how far I can push him. To make Morgan break first since I'm the one who broke last time.

But the symbol floats inside the blackness of my head, a carved, mysterious flower demanding attention.

... **we are at war, my flower** ...

I am at war.

And I want Hunter Morgan.

My hands push between us, coming up against the hard ridges of Morgan's torso through his shirt. Instead of finding purchase there, I drift to the button of his pants.

"*Clover,*" he warns, his body going rigid.

Though he doesn't shift. He doesn't turn away.

With the flick of my thumb, I pop the button and ease the zipper down. My breathing's haphazard, my blood tingling with shredded nerves. It's as if this were my first time, and in a way, it is.

I hook the hem of his pants and push. They fall to his feet with a soft *hush* of fabric. My fingers immediately brush against hot skin. I waste a precious few seconds being shocked at his lack of underwear.

A deep rumble emits from his chest. He asks with a pained voice, "Are you surprised, little leaf?"

CHAPTER 39

CLOVER

I'm too mesmerized by the long spear of his cock to meet his eyes. It juts between us, released from his confines and pointing at me with intention.

And also tattooed.

I lower to my knees, fascinated with the length and power of him the entire way. I didn't get to see him last time. He'd turned me away and fucked me from behind.

Five thick, black ribbons circle his dick, starting at the base and ending a few inches from the folded skin of his tip.

Using my middle finger, I tentatively brush against the middle circle. "Did these hurt?"

His dick jumps against my touch. Tendons jut out from Morgan's neck when he responds, "Like you wouldn't believe."

"And you did it four more times?"

"Yes. I like pain. Pain looks for me always."

I turn my head sideways when I notice an abnormality under one of the tattoos, a ridge that shouldn't be there. Like scar tissue.

His hand snaps down and he grabs my wrist, stopping any further exploration.

"Clover," he tries one more time. "I've been a good boy. Do the same for me and walk away. Do the right thing. Tell me where the passage is, and we can then go on as normal."

I shake my head. "I was never normal, Professor Morgan."

"Then allow us to be as we were. Straight-A student and gifted professor who had one quickie in a classroom. That's all"

I stare up at him with wide eyes lined with false innocence. "Is that truly what you want?"

"Fuck, no," he hisses. "It's what must be. If you do this, if we fall into each other, then I can't avoid my purpose any longer. I have to do as he asks—"

Morgan cuts himself off, sucking in a breath through his teeth and releasing my wrist with a sudden drop.

I'd stuck my tongue out and licked the underside of his tip, preventing Morgan from saying anything else.

There's no blame in that. The last thing I want is to have Morgan mention my brother as I'm on my knees in front of my professor.

I reach for Morgan, wrapping my fingers around his shaft and squeezing. He arches into my grip with a groan, cursing under his breath and muttering Latin, as if appealing to whatever he worships will save him from me.

I smile before opening my mouth to take him in. No one's ever seen me as a devil. I'm always the angel, the princess, the one with clean hands. It feels *good* to get dirty, to blow my hot professor in a hidden basement and make him beg me to give him what he wants.

For too long, I was doing the begging.

It never occurred to me that I never had to ask.

I could just take.

My tongue glides under his shaft as I widen my mouth to

suck him down. After he looses one last groan into the air, Morgan grabs the top of my head by my hair's roots and shoves himself the rest of the way in.

I gag, choking on him and pushing against the front of his thighs. His muscles are so sturdy, my fingers don't make any indents.

"Be careful what you wish for," he says, pulling out until only trails of saliva keep us connected, then ramming back in.

My gag reflex threatens to take me over with a vengeance. I keep it at bay by focusing on the tattoos crowding his stomach and engraved over the deep V of his pelvis.

Morgan wants me to be scared. He wants the tears in my eyes to be real and not from the pressure of fighting my gag reflex. He probably wants me to use my teeth and bite him in defense.

Too bad for him, experience has taught me that biting is fun.

When he pulls out and shoves back inside, I allow my teeth to skim across his sensitive skin. With both hands buried in my hair, he stalls with a surprised groan.

Morgan's balls smack against my chin. It's a wonder I could deep throat a man so long and hard that I can feel his pulse on my tongue.

After taking heavy breaths, he swears, then releases my head. He pulls out and steps away, his dick bobbing, with a painful grimace on his face.

"I underestimated you," he says hoarsely, tossing his pants and shoes into a pile.

I continue admiring him on my knees and how the bottom half of his white shirt spreads to showcase the thick Celtic curls I noticed on his stomach. Thick, black ink travels down, over his thighs, shins, and calves. Even his knees haven't escaped the needle that's buzzed over his entire body.

It makes me wonder, if I shaved his head, would there be tattoos there, too?

Morgan rounds to the apothecary chest, pulling drawers open and rummaging around.

I rest on my legs, unbothered by the view of his pert, tattooed ass when the tail of his shirt flutters as he moves with furious precision.

Fear doesn't make its way into my body until he swings around with metal glinting in his hands.

I was so consumed by winning this war between us that I hadn't considered Morgan might escalate it.

"I noticed the bite mark on your chest," he says as he stalks closer. The sconces highlight him like a wild animal approaching his prey during a forest fire.

Even a desperate predator has to eat.

Unconsciously, I cover that part of my chest. "And?"

"And if another man gets to mark you, then so do I."

My nails twitch against Rio's mark, inadvertently pulling off a scab. "What makes you think it was another guy?"

"Oh, little leaf," Morgan chuckles. "I can recognize an attempt to lay claim on you a mile away. I can fucking *smell* it."

I use the shadows to hide my grin. "You're jealous."

"Far from it. You are a woman who allows a branding and refuses to have one forced upon her. You wanted those marks."

I blush, but I don't give him the satisfaction of an answer.

"It stands to reason you wouldn't mind another marking."

He lifts the blade between us, twisting it idly. The firelight turns the edges molten. I'm both repulsed and intrigued at the sight, a contradiction of senses invading my chest, making me heavy and light, unsure and tempted.

My adventures over to the dark side were baby steps up until this point. First, sex with a stranger in the forest—Xavier. Then submitting to Rio's strokes, sucks, and teeth in the archives, tasting the forbidden nature of our relationship—my brother's best friend. And during that, I took my professor in my mouth, one who fought against touching me until the last minute, when he couldn't take it anymore.

Now, my favorite professor might use this knife to carve into my skin, and I'm hypnotized.

I'm also hating myself for enjoying the dark so much. It's like my tastes belong in secret undergrounds.

"Second guessing, are we?" Morgan asks with amusement. "You can always end this stand-off of ours and tell me where you popped up from."

I lick my lips, tilting my face so the sconce nearest to us highlights my profile. Morgan watches the play of reflected flames on my skin. His dick twitches. This must be as painful for him as it is for me not to feel him between my legs.

I ask myself again: *How far can I push this man?*

Morgan's teeth gleam as bright as his polished blade. "You daring girl. This doesn't scare you, does it?" He turns the knife sideways. "I'd always thought my fetishes would be terrifying to a pure soul like you."

"There's nothing to be afraid of, yet." I shift on my haunches. "You haven't told me what you're going to do to me if I don't tell you my secret."

I work to keep my expression contained. I can't *believe* that just came out of my mouth. And, goddesses forgive me, I love how it tastes.

Morgan's eyes slant. The blade stills. "Crawl to me and I'll show you."

My middle curls and thrashes with pleasure. Hindered by the stiffness of my jacket, I slide it off. A low sound of approval reaches my ears, Morgan remaining where he is, observing me from the other side of the room.

I move to all fours, my underwear feeling sticky and wet between my thighs. Hair falls over both shoulders. The V of my shirt gapes open. I'm aware of his view of the tops of my breasts, curved and full from my push-up bra as I quietly pad toward him. More of Rio's bite marks score the tender skin there and as I hold Morgan's eyes, I try to read what he might think of that.

Morgan lowers his chin, exuding his iniquitous desires through his stare alone. If another man's feverish release of desire bothers Morgan, I can't discern it.

I push forward in slow arcs, allowing his gaze to travel down the curve of my back and up the arch of my ass, my shirt riding up and likely revealing the two small dimples at the small of my back.

Morgan's lips part. His chest moves in faster spans, his cock spearing out from between the folds of his shirt, the veins pulsing under the ring of tattoos.

I stop at his feet, lifting my face and nuzzling his hot dick before wetting my lips and—

Morgan has the tip of the blade on the underside of my chin before I can blink.

"Did I give you permission to do that, little leaf?"

I don't dare shake my head with the nasty prick I feel under my chin.

"You're so eager to get me off, aren't you?" Morgan swipes his tongue across his top teeth. "Youngbloods, these days. You don't understand the ecstasy of waiting. The tension, the *ache* of denying oneself until you're at the brink of insanity and can't take it anymore. Now that, sweet Clover, is true rapture."

I inadvertently swallow the buildup of saliva in my mouth which pushes the knife harder into my skin. Heat singes the spot, and I know he's broken skin.

Morgan's stare trails down my face to the knife. He pauses at the small amount of blood collecting there.

"See? This is precisely what I mean. If you want a man like me, you have to be patient. Along with a strong stomach, of course, because with the proclivities I have, I do enjoy blood."

My heart beats out of my chest. I don't dare move. It's not clear whether Morgan wants to fuck me with the knife or kill me, and this dance with death isn't as terrifying to me as it probably should be.

"I'm going to cut you now."

Morgan says it casually. He pulls the knife from my chin, circling it in his hand, metal flashing, before he *snicks* my skin under my collarbone—exactly where Rio bit me.

I swallow a cry but can't stop my body from jerking away after he cut me. Glancing down, trickles of blood immediately pool at the collar of my shirt. More blood follows. Morgan cut me deeper than I considered he would.

"Why did you do that?" Hissing with pain, I raise my head to meet his eye, then consider my mistake.

All casualness is gone from his face. Feverish intention replaces the patience he preached.

He whispers, "Take your blood in your hands, little leaf. Cover your palms."

I stare at him.

Morgan takes the time to flick his gaze up to mine before returning to the horizontal slash on my chest. "Was that not clear? Paint your hands, then jerk me off with your blood."

My brows jump, but it's mild surprise compared to the simmering eagerness in my belly and wanting to know what comes next.

I'm a novice at this, so it's with hesitation that I brush my fingers through the small rivulets of blood. I decide to take my shirt off, though it's well past salvageable no matter how much I bleach it.

Morgan grunts with pleasure.

Mesmerized, I watch lines of blood seep into the hem of my bra, scarlet red blooming over the baby pink lace.

Using both hands, I collect the blood on my chest as it slows to a weep from the cut. I hold them in front of me, my fingertips a blackish red in the flickering firelight. Then with shaking hands, I reach for him.

Morgan's head falls back as my wet hands encase him, slick with still-warm blood. It's more slippery than any lube I've used, the tip of him slinking out from my palm before I move to squeeze at the base, then cup his balls.

"Gods, girl, you are such wicked, pure addiction," he groans to the ceiling.

His balls are rock-hard in my grip. Morgan's been holding himself back for too long that the ache must be close to unendurable. Yet, he grinds into my hands with practiced ease, the metallic scent of my blood reaching my nose as I stain his dick with it.

It's an unexpected branding—one *I* get to do. My blood is on him, my life essence sinking through his ink and coating his untarnished skin. My tongue pokes out from my lips and I lean forward.

"Yes, little leaf," he croons. "Do it."

I dare to flick my tongue against his tip, collecting drops of pre-cum, my blood, his scent, my ichor, in a single swipe.

"Swallow the darkness, Clover." Morgan's voice is like sandpaper. "Give in to me."

Relaxing my jaw, I cover his tip with my lips, then glide all the way down.

Copper and salt hit my tastebuds. Morgan is completely shaved and my nose bumps against the smooth, taut skin of his stomach as I open my throat and give him complete access.

Morgan moans in Latin, appealing to unknown gods or the devil as he thrusts against my face, collecting my hair and tangling his fingers in it.

"Touch yourself," he grits. "Because I can't."

I'm so swollen and desperate for release, I do exactly as he says, diving into my pants and swirling my bloody finger over my clit. With Morgan invading my mouth, I bounce on my fingers while sucking and swallowing everything we are to each other.

"You're so naughty," Morgan says above my head. "That pretty mouth is getting so dirty for me. Yes, little leaf, get filthy for me. Kneel in my circle, become mine..."

Morgan's words are like a chant, surrounding me in pleasure and smoke. My thighs tighten. Tension builds at my clit. Morgan's balls harden into solid rock. I hold off on flicking my clit until I can feel him ready to explode.

When his cum bursts inside my mouth, I bring myself over the edge, his salt gushing down my throat as my eyes roll back into my head and I fly high while kneeling before him.

Morgan holds my head, refusing to remove his cock until I've swallowed all of him. I moan in response, the sound muffled and garbled, my eyes hot with pressure and tears from gagging streaming down my face.

When he pulls out, I expel a gut-wrenching breath, inhaling desperately and uncaring of the drips of saliva and cum trailing down my chin.

Morgan's tone is barely above a rasp. "Fuck, I had no idea..."

Swiping my chin, I stand topless before him, letting him see the mixture of fluids on my heaving chest, my nipples hard and pert.

"You are a beauty," he marvels, his bloodshot eyes wide. "A rare creature, indeed. Here."

With the quiet, careful movements of a wildcat, Morgan approaches the apothecary chest and pulls open one of the higher drawers. He takes out gauze, antiseptic, and bandages. He turns, and glancing through errant strands of his hair, he crooks a finger. "Let me take care of you now."

With my brows pulling together, I tentatively walk over,

unused to being so amazingly abused then so gently thought of after.

A deep, vertical line of concentration forms between Morgan's brows as he taps an alcohol swap on the cut he made. My lips stretch with the sting of pain that follows.

"Shh," he soothes, his thumb stroking the sting away.

Using the steady fingers of a surgeon, he folds gauze, presses it over the wound, and places a flesh-colored bandage over it. He meets my gaze as his fingers smooth the edges, and I find myself falling into his soft sea of green.

After catching my breath, I say, "I'll tell you where the hatch is."

Morgan cocks a brow, surprise evident on his face. "Oh?"

"If you let me study the map upstairs."

Morgan purses his lips. "The one the keypad is hidden under? It's an old map of the Titan Falls area, nothing special. Why would you want to look at it?"

Morgan had me in the throes of pleasure. I'll never deny that. But during his brutal play, I realized Morgan enjoys a game, a give and take. If he wants something from me, then I must ask something of him.

And I want a closer look at the symbol written on the map.

Morgan gives me an assessing stare, searching for holes in my logic. He'll find none since a drawing of a flower means nothing to him.

"Does it have anything to do with the missing jewels?" he asks idly.

The intensity of his gaze contradicts the ease of his question.

"I think there might be something there relating to the daughter's name."

Not entirely a lie, but not the entire truth, either.

"Getting closer to the answer, are you?" Morgan passes me, dragging a finger along my jaw as he does. "I'm not surprised."

A flicker of emotion crosses his face, but he gives me his profile before I can read it.

Morgan collects his pants and pulls them on. I do the same with my shirt, my blood cold and thick.

"Show me," he says, his eyes glittering with excitement.

I stride to the corner of the room and bend at the knees. Tracing my fingers across the gritty floor, I find a small hook indicating a seam and pull, two square sections of floor pulling up like an accordion to reveal the black depths below.

Morgan's sharp intake of breath behind me exposes his shock.

I turn my head toward him. "I accidentally broke the rope climbing up. You'll have to jump down, but there's an exit on the other side, under a pile of large fallen rocks in the woods."

For the first time, Morgan hesitates before approaching. He can't take his eyes off the rectangular hole. "Was there anything in there?"

I shake my head. "Dust, stone, bug carcasses. That's it."

"It can't be." That strange madness slithers behind his irises again. "No one's traversed this in hundreds of years. This has to be where she hid the jewels. You didn't look hard enough, little leaf."

Maybe not, but...

"I had my flashlight on my phone. All I saw was cave walls and a staircase leading above ground."

"Sarah wouldn't have built this if it didn't *mean* something," Morgan hisses.

"I think it was meant as an escape route for her and her daughter if they were ever discovered, or a place where the nobles could come and contract with her—"

But Morgan's beyond reason. He slides to the edge of the hole, his legs dangling down as he stares feverishly into the black. "This could be the answer. I may not have to..."

He blinks as if shaking himself out of a stupor, then regards me.

"Thank you, Clover. Enjoy the map upstairs. There's an outline of a square at the top of the stairs near your foot. Press the tip of your boot on it and the door will open. I'll be down here, exploring."

With a heedless leap, Morgan disappears from view.

CHAPTER 40

MORGAN

I land with two feet on the ground, my weight sending a restless cloud of dust around me.

Coughing, I pull out my phone and engage the flashlight while spinning in a cautious circle.

The cone of light calls attention to small footsteps through the layers of neglected filth on the ground—Clover's.

Clever girl. She's discovered so much more than anyone's given her credit for. I don't believe any of us saw this coming. Not Storm Cloud, Tongueless, me, or my uncle. The jewels were a fantasy in my mind, especially when my uncle spouted off about them. There was no way he'd get his hands on relics hidden for hundreds of years and discovered by no one.

Even his threats against Clover seemed inconsequential, so out of reach was his greedy desire.

But now.

Oh, now...

My little leaf has gotten herself into trouble.

I shouldn't have gone as far with her as I did. I was convinced my antics would send her screaming into her brother's arms, not crawling and kneeling at my feet, topless and bleeding with my blood-soaked cock in her mouth.

I groan at the reimagining. I'm tempted to go find her and bring her down here to have more fun. No woman has accepted me so completely before, not unless I pay them handsomely. It's as if Clover is meant for me instead of this legend my uncle chases.

Devilish gods help me, I want to save her.

After a cursory check for stability, I follow Clover's footsteps into the tunnel, noting and testing crevices and small holes.

Nothing jumps out at me as one of Sarah's infamous hiding spots. At least, not yet.

An idea comes to light the deeper I travel into the cobwebbed tunnel. Perhaps if I took credit for this find and told my uncle to excavate for the treasure here, Clover could be spared.

There's no need to involve her if my uncle's focused his attention on Sarah's underground entrance. Where else could she have put her valuable treasure, anyway? *Another* secret tunnel? A *second* concealed torture chamber in this damn cottage? Anderton Cottage is rumored to have all kinds of rooms deliberately left off county records, but other than her basement for disposing of her victims, that's all it is: rumors.

She wasn't a fucking genius engineer, after all. There has to be an end to all this.

The jewels must be somewhere nearby. I just haven't pulled out the right rock or keyed the correct pattern on the craggy walls. Sarah's diabolical, but even she had to think of a conclusion to this hunt.

A thick slab of stone halts my forward momentum. I swing my light, and it bounces up a set of spiral stairs, which I take while crouched low. It's much easier for a slip of a girl to traverse than a man of above-average height.

My muscles strain as I'm forced into more of a crouch the

higher I go. At last, I find flat, wide ground. Unable to sit up, I slide onto my belly and wiggle out of the minuscule opening Clover promised would be there.

I get stuck twice. Once at the shoulders and again at the hips, but after shifting and a bit of weightlifting, I move the rocks enough to shimmy out.

My efforts backfire when, right as I pull my feet from under, the entire rock formation groans with warning before crashing down and filling the opening in a puff of white sand.

I stare at the mess I made, dusting off my hands, then scraping back my hair.

Smiling, I unlock my phone and type a message.

I've found something I think you should see. Bring tools.

CHAPTER 41

CLOVER

I'm relieved to find the simple cut-out in the stone wall when I reach the top of the stairs. With thighs still trembling from my orgasm, I push the square with the top of my boot. It gives an inch before an audible click, at which point the wall in front of me loosens on its hinges and swings open.

I blow out a breath. Being locked under Anderton Cottage with Morgan wasn't as horrifying a thought as it should be. But being locked under here by myself when no one but a man touring unstable tunnels for a treasure knows?

Kind of shitty.

Tentatively, I push open the concealed side of the bookcase. I haven't heard footsteps or low, male voices, though something tells me I wouldn't. Morgan's and my voices didn't carry as they should in a vacant room. We were muffled from within—soundproofed.

Ardyn's words return: my brother and his friends are involved in something dangerous.

Would Tempest call my snooping around his cottage for missing jewels as dangerous as his job? Probably. He's careful not to expose the worst parts of himself, but I'd be blind not to see the cold blood flowing in his veins and battling with the morals our father worked so hard to leech out of him.

Me, I'm hot-blooded and brimming with morals, or at least I thought until these past few months.

Morgan caused me to see more holes growing inside me than I thought. He's making me see gray where there should be black and white. I shouldn't want blood and sex to mix, yet ... I'm interested to learn what else Morgan likes to use to get off.

I push those thoughts aside once I confirm the cottage remains deserted and step all the way in, shutting the door softly. I turn straight for the map, delicately lifting it from the hooks attaching it to the wall and resting it at an angle on the floor.

I sit in front of it, crossing my legs and resting my chin in my hands, focused on the tiny symbol drawn in the lower right corner.

What could it mean? Is there something within this map that matches it? I study the inked trees, a headache growing when I peer to hard between the leaves in search of a twin symbol. I was a master at finding Waldo, but with such faded ink written on a large piece of paper that looks to have been crinkled and smoothed out again, I can't spot any black flowers hidden anywhere else.

Tracing the road leading from Anderton Cottage to the town, I follow along through the previous versions of Titan Falls University, which were stone manors and other status symbol structures created on the backs of slaves and lived in by dukes, earls, marquises, and whomever else bowed to royalty. Titan Falls was primarily an English settlement, and through Sarah's trial transcripts, I learned she was on one of the first boats gaining passage to the new land. In England, she was like any other townsfolk, living modestly and moving about unnoticed.

I'm sure her practice didn't start here—she must've tested and improved upon her poisons when she was a young girl, considering how good she was and how many people she killed before getting caught.

Her life isn't in this map. It appears as any other old cartographer drawings I can look up at the library. The one thing it has going for it is that it hides an electronic keypad allowing entry into Sarah's kill room.

I sit back on a huff, angry with myself that I gave up my secret tunnel lair for ... this.

It's with a rush of frustrated energy that I turn it to its backside, moving the metal sliders keeping the backing in place and lifting the thick cardboard to access the fragile paper below.

I'm past needing gloves. I've lost the grimoire and gave up my one piece of leverage to get it back during a period of blood-lust, softening when Morgan touched me so tenderly after spilling my blood. It was if he didn't just want me; he cared about me.

I don't fall into complete disrespect. Lifting the map gently, I flip it and inspect it in its purest form, without glass or frames. When I tilt it, a corner flaps forward. I glance at the movement, then back to the middle of the map.

Then return to the dog-eared corner.

Lamplight shines through pin-prick holes, so tiny they're microscopic.

But they form a pattern.

With a quiet, stunned exhale, I push to my feet, the map raised high. I twist until the lamplight shines through the entire map.

Pinpricks light up all over the page, a map within a map. Pathways un-inked on paper glitter in my shaking hold, one leading into the middle of the woods where a triangle of stone,

Rio's favorite perch, sits within the tall trees. It's a perfect view of campus and the mountains framing the town.

Another lighted path leads to Anderton Cottage, a trail discovered long ago. It's the one I take and the route the boys prefer since most students don't like to walk within its shadowed, unprotected depths.

What interests me most is the cluster of stone blocks, unseen to the naked eye and only visible when lit up. It's the same clump I'd crawled through to get here, their heavy bodies hiding the entrance to the spiral staircase. But on this map, they're stacked with precision, not haphazardly angled and eroded like they are now. Their construction can't be seen behind a thick copse of inked trees unless you knew it was there or stumbled upon it in the dark like I did.

A symbol of the flower flashes above it, the third one I've seen. I'm not surprised it's revealed at that location—that same symbol was carved above the staircase. It's a sign, an arrow of sorts, pointing those who are aware of it in the direction they need to go.

Strangely, another flower comes to light, cast directly above the cottage's chimney.

Frowning, I lower the map to study the chimney in the middle of the room, preserved in its original state while other parts of the cottage were renovated over the years.

Before making my way over to get a good look at the fireplace, I put the map back in its frame, clip it in, and hang it in the same spot I found it. There's no telling when anyone will get home—I didn't think to ask Morgan, he was a bit of a distraction—so I have to work quickly and be careful not to leave evidence of my snooping behind.

The last thing I want is for Tempest to unhinge his jaw and breathe fire on me.

Morgan hasn't surfaced by the time I clean up in front of the bookcase and go to the fireplace, walking a full circle around it and dragging my hand along the rough brick.

I don't feel any irregularities besides erosion and age.

Crouching in front of the fireplace, I peer inside, noting the gray ash and black scorch marks on the bricks.

It's a working fireplace. I've seen the guys light it a number of times, making it impossible for the upper sections of the chimney to hide anything worth saving. Heat, smoke damage, rodent animals escaping from winter that chew and claw at things—something up there would fall victim regardless of what century it was hidden in.

Would gold and gemstones? Maybe not, but the amount would be so heavy, it would've fallen through and given the guys a shock by now.

I push my lips to the side, staring hard inside the fireplace and searching for a flower symbol.

Nothing appears, even when I brush aside ash, coating my hands in charred wood.

The alcove appears completely innocent and built to do what it was supposed to—make fire and create heat. Yet something holds me back, feeling ... *wrong*.

Then I see it.

The bricks lining the bottom are different from the fireplace and chimney itself. Lines through the ash from my fingers show their small rectangular sides facing me, instead of the long side like everywhere else.

Spurred by my observation, I stick my head in and feel along the edges. It doesn't take long to find a gap between the bottom and the side, enough to hook my fingers to the second knuckle.

Prying it open turns out to be an effort in patience. My grip slips in the dirt, my palms sweaty with adrenaline. I break one nail and almost pop another one completely off, but I don't relent. I swear I feel it give on my fifth attempt.

Gritting my teeth, I give one last push, my heart thick in my throat and prickles of sweat at my temples. The layer of brick finally gives, tilting up with my strength and scattering ash and bits of wood all over the floor.

With the new trapdoor I've discovered leaning against the other side of the fireplace, I fumble for my phone to light up the hole I've uncovered.

Did I find it? My brain beats at me relentlessly. *Is this where she hid the jewels? Was it really so close by for this long?*

Holding my breath, I lean forward and light up the interior.

The space is *tiny*. If I swing my feet over and jumped in, I'd still be exposed from the elbows up and there would just be enough room to lie down, if my knees were bent.

As I shine my light in, I think, *priest hole*, the small, hidden rooms famously built in Roman Catholic homes to hide their priests from raids. They were constructed in fireplaces like this or behind false walls and pantries. They were used in the late 16th century and into the early 1700s. Sarah Anderton could've easily learned about them and wanted one for herself.

Clutching the edge with one hand, I sink my flashlight in farther, no small part of me hoping to discover a literal treasure chest. I have to fight through cobwebs and stale air, sneezing and sniffling as I upset what was undisturbed for hundreds of years.

When my light glides over a lump in the corner different from the other piles of dust and ash, I return to it.

And scream when a skull stares back at me.

CHAPTER 42

CLOVER

My butt bones bang hard against the floorboards when I fall off the rim of the fireplace and land on my ass.

Skeletons and gore don't bother me. It's when they surprisingly gape out from unexplored holes that gives me pause.

Collecting myself, I return to the fireplace. As if to prove to myself that I'm not a chicken, I perch on the edge of the priest hole and slide in.

It's like I predicted—my shoulders and head poke out and I duck down, crouching at the knees, to get a better view of the skull.

Holding my flashlight steady, I slide it over a former person, the skeleton brown with age. Clothing scraps drape over the ribs, brownish red in color. Lace once adorned the collar, though it resembles more of a dank spiderweb now. A broken lantern lays beside the body, the glass long shattered.

Raising my phone, I scan the wall behind the sagging skeleton. The jewels aren't here, but maybe another flower is. I glide the circle of light sideways, my subconscious registering an abnormality before my body. I backtrack, resting the light on not a symbol, but a word.

LILLIUM.

Crunch.

The toe of my boot hits something and I scuttle backward, draping the word in shadow as my light dives over the culprit.

A skeletal hand, its finger bones intact, splays out in front of me, its wrist capped with decaying lace and a long-rotted sleeve pieces of the radius, ulna, and humerus bones, but it's what is under the hand that makes me peer closer.

A leather-bound book, covered in dust and ash like the rest of the hole.

Tentatively, I nudge it from under the skeleton. My preservation instinct kicks in—this could be the latest find of Titan Falls history, one that could be published in brochures to attract more rich kids from the world's most powerful people because everybody loves a morbid tale.

She's old, this skeleton. From the drapery of the remaining clothing, it appears it was a dress, so I'm calling her she.

When the hand drops from the book, I crack the front cover open. Hovering the light over the page, I read the inscription, faded, damaged, and barely legible.

Lillium Anderton.

My mouth falls open. "Oh..."

I raise my eyes to the skull, the black pits of its eyes staring aimlessly above ground.

"Did I find you?" I whisper.

It's been assumed the Anderton daughter was tortured and executed with her mother. That's what the trial transcripts said, anyway. But ... anything can be doctored for the right price.

"Did Sarah pay to have you written into the transcript and your name stricken from the records?" I ask the empty skull.

It makes sense. Sarah never gave up the names of the nobles

who contracted with her—they made sure of that and executed her swiftly once it was discovered she was underneath the church being interrogated. She could have made a deal with them in exchange for her silence. She could have asked for her daughter to be protected.

And most importantly, her jewels, meant for her daughter.

It never made sense to me why Sarah would leave a fortune for a girl scheduled to die with her.

I lean closer to inspect the skull, needing to be sure. Sarah's daughter was disfigured. A hermit that Sarah spent time tutoring and indoctrinating so her daughter could flourish under her legacy. The daughter didn't have to become what a woman was expected to be during that time—uneducated, mannerly, tending to the home and bearing children. She got to be as educated and murderous as Sarah.

"Lillium," I breathe out, inches away from the hanging jaw. "Pretty name."

From this vantage point, the asymmetry of her face becomes obvious. The skull is slightly angled toward the wall, one side in shadow, but my phone highlights how one side is noticeably larger than the other, half her forehead bulging and one eye socket considerably smaller than its twin.

"I really did find you," I say to her, then glance upward. "But what are you doing in here?"

I frog-walk back to the book, heedful of pages that could disintegrate with one turn, and aim for the last written entry. Everything that comes sooner, I can read later since I'm pocketing this book as soon as I leave.

The writing is so faded, I have to squint to read.

Dearest Mother,

If you are reading this, I have expired. I am running out of light and have lost all sense of time as I wait for you to return to me. You created this space for me to hide in if we were ever discovered, and here

I sit, my last true vision other than stone walls was your worried face as you slid the lid in place. You constructed it so it cannot be opened by a person without the knowledge that it exists.

Did you mean for me to die in here, Mother? Was all your practice on me a poison?

There is no food left. I have no water. I am sitting in my own filth, waiting for you.

If this is my grave, I am trying my hardest not to believe you put me in it knowingly.

I love you. So dearly. But I cannot hang on any longer.

Your daughter,

Lily

I hold my hand to my mouth, breathing through the space of my fingers.

Lillium ... Lily ... my flower...

"The *fuck*? What the hell is this mess?"

A loud voice jolts me out of my stupor.

I mutter, "Shit," before clambering to my feet and poking my head out of the hole.

Tempest's furious blue eyes greet me as I rise. "What the *fuck* are you doing in my fireplace, Clo?"

CHAPTER 43

CLOVER

Most people wilt under my brother's ice and fire.

I'm not most people.

"I've become your new chimney sweep," I quip, then hold out my hand. "Help me out, would you?"

Unamused, Tempest grabs me by the elbow and pulls me out, but not before peering in. "What is this?"

I find my balance and brush at my pants and shirt futilely. Ash and grit fall from my head as I move. Movement at the door catches my eye, and I realize Tempest didn't come alone.

Rio stands nearby, his expression pinched with concern. Xavier is beside him—*Xavier's here?*—his brows raised as his focus pings between me and the fireplace I just crawled out of.

And Ardyn comes out from behind Tempest, helping me brush the filth off and leaning close to my ear. "I kept them away as long as I could. Didn't you get my text?"

No, I was busy communing with a skeleton.

"I asked you a question, Clo," Tempest says.

I answer my brother, "It's a priest hole."

"A what?"

I motion in the direction of the fireplace. "Tiny, hidden rooms created in the sixteenth and seventeenth centuries to hide priests that practiced outlawed religion during raids."

Tempest nods like this is supposed to make sense. "Why is one in my living room, and what were you doing in it?"

"Sarah Anderton used the same method to hide her daughter when she was arrested." I point at the fireplace again. "It's true. Her daughter's body is down there."

Tempest's eyes widen. Ardyn gasps. Both head toward the opening and scrutinize the hole.

"Are you all right?"

I turn to Rio's quiet voice. In the coming storm of my brother's temper, Rio exudes calm, though his eyes fill with concern.

I resist the urge to curve into his arms and hear the steady beat of his heart. I finger his mark on my chest instead, his stare catching fire when it follows my hand.

Then it turns into twin daggers.

"You're hurt," he says.

My pointer finger nudges against the bandage I forgot Morgan placed there. In a panic, I try to figure out the best excuse as to how I cut, then bandaged myself, then opened a priest hole in their fireplace after I was saved by Morgan stepping through the bookshelf.

Tempest's head snaps up.

"*Morgan*," he hisses. "Clover's here. Did your phone not alert you?"

Morgan takes in the scene in front of him and waves Tempest away. "Oh, we're past all that. Clover's fully aware of the basement because she found a second secret entrance to it earlier this evening."

Silence.

Tempest blinks. "Is this house fucking *Encanto* now?"

"You've seen that movie?" Morgan asks. "Huh. Didn't think it'd be your cup of tea."

My brother literally vibrates with rage. I tell myself to brace for it when he whirls on me.

"How many times have I told you to leave this house alone? *How* many fucking times? Why do you refuse to listen to me when all I'm trying to do is *keep you safe!*"

Tempest roars the end of the sentence, his face so white with rage, even Ardyn has a tough time holding him back.

It's so tangible that Rio steps in front of me to take the brunt of it.

I place a hand on the small of his back in warning. "Rio. It's okay. I can handle it."

"The fuck are you doing?" Tempest asks him.

He searches the space between Rio and me, and you don't have to be as sly and cunning as Tempest to see the electricity sparking between our bodies.

Tempest cocks his head, his eyelids lowering with deadly precision. "Tell me what the hell you think you're doing."

"She doesn't deserve this from you," Rio responds quietly. Unhurried. "You've just come from a meeting where it was determined Clover knows how to find the jewels more than the four of us combined."

"Meeting?" Morgan asks, coming up to our group. He curls his lip at Xavier still hovering in the doorway. "Sports Balls was invited but not me?"

Then Morgan sends me a wink like he doesn't regret missing any meeting while he got to play with me in the basement.

Heat splits between my core and my cheeks, and I don't mind it at all.

Morgan's inclusion of him seems to wake Xavier up. He pushes off the doorframe and comes to a stand beside Rio, folding his impressively tanned arms and assuming a defensive stance.

"I'm with Rio," he says, facing my brother. "While we were all chitchatting, Clover discovered another clue, which was in front of you this entire time. In the middle of your fucking sitting room! I reckon we should be asking her what she found, not lecturing her on breaking and entering, which she does anyway."

"Oh, you reckon?" Tempest's eyes become maniacally bright. "You *reckon*, do you? You, of all the people in this room, should understand the base fear I experience when someone I love is threatened. It's why I don't have many of them. But I will protect the two of them I *do* have until I die. I don't care if you find the balls to stand up to me. I will still get to my sister."

The muscles in Xavier's back bunch under Tempest's threats. I raise my other hand and stroke the vertical line between them, communicating a soothing force.

These two men's shadows might swallow me, but Tempest notices the movement.

He licks his lips the way a pit bull does before charging. "Someone explain to me why my sister is stroking you right fucking now."

"Tempest." Ardyn wraps her arms around his waist. "How about we focus on the two areas Clover found? If we all put our heads together, we could end this."

Fury billows out of his sails. "That's the thing. There is no end."

She tips her head up to him. "There could be."

"What needs to end?" I step through Xavier and Rio, who reluctantly part for me.

Morgan appears relieved to have me in his sights again, his hand twitching at his side like he wants to drag me back to the basement and have more fun with me rather than deal with family drama.

"Have you found the jewels?" Ardyn asks instead.

My focus flits between her and Tempest. "Tempest knows about this?"

"We all do," Rio says behind me.

He finds my hand and squeezes. Tempest snarls, and he drops it.

"Enough," Tempest snaps. "Clover, you need to leave."

"The hell I do."

The last vestiges of Tempest's patience leave his body. "*Leave.*"

"No!" I match his fury.

"Why can't we just explain everything to her?" Xavier asks.

"Because I refuse to allow it!" Tempest reels on him, his fists clenched and shaking. "She is the last of us. Do you understand? Clover is the only soul providing any sort of happiness in this hell we call home, and I will not allow any of you to destroy it." He includes every man in the room in his unrelenting stare. "I am in charge here, and I'm telling you to back the fuck off my sister. Clover, either you listen to me, too, or I will put you on the first flight home."

I choke on my indignation. "You can't—"

"*Yes, I fucking can!*"

He rounds on me. Instinctively, I retreat, my back slamming up against a hard wall of muscle. Morgan's hands come down on my shoulders. He says to Tempest in that light, maniacal tone he has, "I'd ask you not to scream at her anymore."

"Do all of you want her to die?" Tempest asks incredulously. "Is that it?"

"On the contrary," Morgan says. "I very much prefer her alive."

"Ardyn?" Tempest includes my best friend. "What's your opinion on this?"

Ardyn rubs her lips together. I plead with her through my

eyes for her to take my side. I *am* the one finding the clues. If they're all so interested in the jewels, they need me.

"I want you safe, too," Ardyn says to me. "But I want you to make your own decisions."

"I choose to be included," I say before Tempest can interject. But history should've proved to me that it's pointless.

"Too bad I outvote all of you," Tempest seethes. "Clover, you're going home. Morgan can fill me in on what's downstairs, and we'll search this priest hole for clues. Xavier, since you're the least of the assholes, you can escort her home."

Xavier jolts, his expression conflicted.

"Don't you want to know what I know?" I ask in a rush. "I have experience with this, I've read the grimoire, and I've found clues you won't be able to connect without me—"

"I'll do just fine," Tempest cuts in. "Considering I've survived the worst without you for most of my life."

I rear back, scalded with hurt.

"I'm determined to keep it that way." Tempest's expression is hard and impenetrable. "If a freshman playing amateur detective can break open a centuries-old mystery, then with our experience, so the fuck can we."

Morgan squeezes my shoulders, then backs away. "Sorry, little leaf. Our undertaker has spoken."

Rio gives me a long look, so loaded with guilt and pity that I glare at him and glance away, blinking back tears.

Ardyn moves toward me, but I hold up a hand.

I thought Rio, Morgan, Xavier, and Ardyn cared about me.

Turns out, Tempest's rule of law means more to them than my heart.

At my expression, a piece of Tempest's rage seems to fracture.

"Xavier," he says hoarsely, flapping a weary hand. "Take her. Please."

With a sigh, Xavier turns and gently holds my arm. "Come on. Maybe we can get through to him when he's not so riled up."

I'm stubborn enough to hold my ground and keep sparring with my brother, but I also know that I've mined that priest hole for all it had to give—and I took the journal. So however confident Tempest may be that he's smarter than me, he's not better or faster.

I allow Xavier to lead me out, listening to Tempest bark, "Morgan, get in there and see what you can find. Rio, with me. We're going into this tunnel. And Ardyn? Meet me in my room, I'm not about to put you in any more danger, either..."

"Ex*cuse* me?" she says.

My lips press together wryly as I exit Anderton Cottage.

At least I'm not the only one annoyed by my brother this evening.

CHAPTER 44

XAVIER

Any chance when I can get Clover alone is a good one. Her brother is a terrifying breed, to be sure, but I only seem to sense that when he's nearby. When Tempest is at a distance, the reality of him doesn't appear so bad. With Clover on my arm, I can imagine an above-average life where I really am an exchange student enrolled at Titan Falls, meeting the love of his life, and taking her on a stroll through the forest before I ravish her on a nearby rock.

"We do enjoy the woods, don't we?" I say with a smile.

I'm too immersed in the fantasy of us to realize my timing might be off.

"Yeah," she responds softly, her eyes on the ground.

Her tone snaps me out of it. This isn't the Clover I've come to know. I place my hand on her shoulder, guiding her into a stop. "It's unfair how he treats you."

"The worst part is, it's not."

Clover lifts her head, her eyes shining obsidian. "Tempest doesn't want me to end up like him. I can't hate him for that. But it's so frustrating. Even when I think I'm staying away from his criminal stuff, I end up in the center of it. How was I supposed to know he wanted Sarah's jewels, too?"

I stuff my hands in my pockets and toe the loose dirt between us. "It's ... more complicated than that."

"And you know what's funny?" she continues as if I haven't spoken. "At first, I just wanted to find it to get an A on my paper. Maybe achieve a bit of scholarly fame in the academic world. But by the end, all I wanted to do was find this fortune so I could give it to him."

I draw my head up, staring at her. "What?"

"Yeah." She laughs. "Hilarious, isn't it? The very person I'm trying to save is trying to save *me*, so we've effectively cancelled each other out."

"I see it now." One side of my mouth pulls up in a grin. "The infamous Callahan stubbornness."

"Tell me about it. What shocks me is that I had no idea you were involved, too."

I blow out a breath. "Consider it indentured servitude."

Clover's eyes grow small as she thinks. It occurs to me she can parse more out of my one sentences than most people, but I'm past caring. Tempest snarling orders, Morgan covering me in bloody gore, Rio creeping around ensuring I don't try to escape... I'm so tired of it.

"Where did you get your scars?" she asks quietly.

Her attention drifts down my chest, pausing on my stomach where, under my peacoat and shirt, a lumpy slash of scar tissue mars my body.

She continues to drift down, pausing on my right knee.

"I was an idiot." I mean to leave it at that, but her inquisitive expression, coupled with her genuine concern—something I've so lacked—forges me on. "An idiot who was excessively proud of myself. I dated a girl, thinking she was just another football groupie I could have fun with and discard. She wasn't. Meghan was the daughter of a Clan Chief. The Mafia. The O'Malleys. When I ghosted her, her father exacted retribution for her broken heart. Put me up for sale and gave me to a group that mutilated me."

Clover retreats. Infinitesimally, but I still feel it.

"I'm not that man anymore," I urge, then laugh hollowly. "I am so far from that moronic boy who thought he was greater than God. I promise you, Clover. If you think I'm using you the same—"

"I don't think that," she cuts in. "I'm stepping back because I'm *horrified*."

Tears prick in her eyes, glimmering dewdrops in the forest. "How could they do that do you? And for you to come out of it like this, so charming with that smile, so caring and wanting to meet my needs when you've lost everything."

I step forward and cup her under the jaw, tilting her up so I can see her beautiful, open face clearly. "I've been forced to endure things. Do things I don't want. Bad things. Things I don't want to do. But each time I'm convinced I wouldn't survive, I think of you."

Clover's eyes soften. She folds her hands on top of my own. "I'm not that special. But I'm glad I can give you what you need."

My grip tightens. Not out of anger, but disbelief. "You are my moonlight maiden. I will cling to her whenever the chance arises. That makes you exceptional. To *me*, you are incredible, Clover."

Tears track down her cheeks. My chest wrenches at the sight.

I smooth the pensive line between her brows. "You are gloriously intelligent, you know that? Finding an underground tunnel and a false door under the mantel, and right under your brother's nose, no less. Be proud of yourself, not sad. I hate seeing you sad."

Clover pulls at my hand until it frames her cheek, and she

nuzzles into it. Tingles spread from her touch and into my bones. Frankly, I don't think I'll ever stop thrumming whenever I'm around her.

"You mean so much to me," she says, her warm lips brushing against my palm. "I've been afraid to say it. What if I popped the bubble? You and I, we shouldn't work, yet we do. So well."

"If it weren't for you and the moments I can steal with you, where I can be who I want and not who I am," I admit in a rare moment of vulnerability, "I would have given up months ago."

Rather than my words bolstering her, Clover deflates. "Sometimes I think my discoveries are useless, that whatever Tempest and the rest of you are enduring, I'll never be able to help."

"That's where you're wrong," I whisper, leaning in. "You help me every day."

She shifts, and I catch her lips with mine, pulling her against me and tenderly pulling her lower lip into my mouth, sucking and stroking with her tongue.

My moonlight goddess is roughed up, cut, bleeding, dirty and exhausted. A soft touch is needed for both of us. Since meeting her, I've discovered it's not just me who craves a gentle hand. It's my new goal to prove to her that I can be that man.

At the same time, Clover squeezes my thigh. Tingly pleasure bolts through me, charging through my balls and making them slam together at the ready.

I can't help sucking in air.

Clover pulls away, her expression curiously searching mine.

I take the opportunity to smooth my hands under her trousers and cup her bare ass, yanking her against my body.

Then I change my mind.

This isn't a time to be dirty with her. I'd like to show her the tenderness I can't truly put into words.

I drag my fingers across her hips in the lightest touch. Her lashes flutter. Her body sags, relaxing. Then I dip into her front, finding her swollen, slick lips so soft to the touch, and slide two fingers in.

Her head falls into my chest, her hands clutching my shirt and tangling the fabric. Clover moans softly, her exhale hot against my skin. I tease my thumb across her clit, stroking with gentle, determined movements.

My mouth dips to her ear. "You deserve so much more than me. Yet I can't let you go. Won't. This, right here, is what's right."

Her silky walls spasm around my fingers. Clover lifts onto her toes as if she could climb me, riding my fingers and making sweet, soft croons against my shirt.

I smile at the soft, angelic sounds.

"Come," I urge gently.

She jerks against my body, and after one last, long exhale, she quakes until her limbs loosen, and I have to hold her to keep her steady.

Clover's head falls back, her eyes glazed over, and a cute, tilty smile spreads on her lips.

I pull my fingers out of her and suck on them, making sure my face is as close as possible to hers. "Mm. Perfection."

She bats my hand out of the way so she can pull my lips to hers.

The kiss is long, sweet, and personal. We're not simply holding each other; we're in an embrace.

Jesus.

All at once it hits me.

She's it for me.

A twig snaps nearby, drawing our heads apart. I keep my hands clenched on her arms as I glance around. Clover does the same, her nails digging into my waist.

"What's that?" she asks.

"Could be Rio," I suggest.

She gives a sharp jerk of her head. "Rio would never announce his presence if he were following us."

I stare down at her. "You sound so sure."

"I would know."

I don't have time to ponder her statement. A shadow moves off trail, too swift to be a tree branch, too unnatural to be a creature.

"Stay behind me." I push Clover until I'm in front of her, one hand keeping her there while I pull out my phone to dial Temp—

Clover screams as she's ripped away from me.

"No!" I leap into the bushes where she's disappeared, pushing aside wild brush that scrapes my face and tangles my legs.

Clover cries out again, galvanizing me to hack out of the forest's hold and get to her.

I stop just short of another clearing, crouching into the shadows and not giving away my location as Clover is dragged through, the moonlight bright on her face as her hooded abductor yanks her backward by the collar of her jacket.

I have enough time to text Tempest: **Trouble. Come.**

Then I brace.

Clover digs her heels in and spins to face the man, using one of her arms to catch him under his armpit, steps one of her legs between his, then pulls until he trips sideways and falls to the ground.

Where did she learn to do that?

My lips pull into an impressed line.

I take advantage and plunge out of my cover, yelling, "Clover, run!"

She doesn't look back as she sprints back into the woods.

Grabbing the biggest rock I can find, I rush the hooded man before he can right himself, slamming the rock onto his head.

He grunts, flopping to his stomach.

I slam it again.

And I'm actually thankful to Morgan for giving me the fortitude to hold the bloody rock with both hands and arc my arms down for a final blow.

One of my arms abruptly stops its descent, held back by a surprise guest.

My shoes leave gouges in the forest floor as I fight against this new person's restraint, but I'm too late.

The rock is snatched from my grip and used on my head instead.

My last thought is, *Clover...*

before everything goes dark.

The professor.
The stalker.
The disgraced athlete.
The psychopath.

Who *stole* her?

Order your copy of Loyal Vows,
The gripping conclusion.

ALSO BY KETLEY ALLISON

all in kindle unlimited

If you want more bullies and secret societies, read:

Rival

Virtue

Fiend

Reign

The Thorne of Winthorpe:

Thorne

Crush

Liar

Titan Falls:

Cruel Promise

also writing as S.K. Allison,

contemporary romance:

If you like your bad boys and bullies as standalones (no series, one book, a happy ending), read:

Rebel

Crave

If you like a grump turned into a protector for his woman, read:

Rock

Lover

If you like your playboys with tormented hearts and scars, read:

Trust

Dare

Play

If you like small-town, angsty vibes:

Home for Always

Made in the USA
Monee, IL
05 November 2024

69447435R00233